MW01153458

WHEN SHIPS SALUTE

WHEN SHIPS SALUTE

Susan K. Flach

ACKNOWLEDGEMENTS

I want to thank God for the multitude of blessings in my life. For the wherewithal to write—every thought translated to words on a page brings me such joy.

A shout-out goes to my husband, Steve, who often gets to hear these thoughts as I discuss with him the current endeavors I'm working on, always listening in with apparent interest.

To all my rough draft readers: Nancy Root, Haley Dziobak, Aaron Dziobak, Katelyn Mater, Denise Majdan, Ellie Tribbett, and Alyssa Anderson—thank you for offering up your insightful critiques.

Thanks to Bernie Arbic who took the time to discuss my project and offer information about the Soo. His books— City of Rapids: Sault Ste. Marie's Heritage

&

Upbound Downbound: The Story of the Soo Locks
(Along with Nancy Steinhaus)
—were very helpful, informative, and interesting to read.

Also, Meredith Sommers at Bayliss Public Library for sending the Polk City Directory—thank you.

Credit given to information derived from National Geographic's— Pearl Harbor and the War in the Pacific.

And finally, to all those who continue to enthusiastically read and share with others about my books. I appreciate you so much!

Thank you!!!

~Susan K. Flach

PROLOGUE

My, how she had always loved the placidity of the tin room that housed the high school pool. Taking long-reaching sweeps through silk sheets of liquid. The echo of whistles pulsating in the background while bursts of staccato strokes forged out a rhythm amidst the sloshing chorine.

But that day held a different sort of milieu.

Shards of ice split across her skin as she dove into the water. Arms and legs propelling in an efficient fashion, she maneuvered her body through the deep end. Swooping down to the bottom, she entered a province of stripes. (Ribbons of red stretching on for miles.) Years later, she'd remember the stripes—in dominance. *And the cold.* Not that the temperature was, in truth, frigid. But all-the-same—it felt that way. During previous swims, garbed in her suit and cap, there'd been no sensation of bone-chilling cold. And yet that day, with the minimal material of her underthings covering her body, she felt naked. *And cold.* Flesh peppered in goosebumps. In a liquid swirl above, the muted sound of splashes filled her ears—a reminder that she wasn't alone.

A flitter of relief.

Safety in numbers, right?

One splash, two splash, three splash, four.

No, she wasn't alone.

Exhilaration shot through her veins. For a split second she felt her blood begin to warm. She was doing this. *Really doing this.* Being part of the group. The one who showed minimal fear in any situation. Who liked to live life on the edge. The idolization ran deep and wide—dominated the school. If being honest, wasn't this what she craved? Maybe even longed for? And yet she'd always been held at bay. Pushed aside.

The cold returned. A memento of reality. Why today anyway? What was this going to accomplish—this swim? Would she fit in better now? Somehow be cooler? This sudden inclusion from *the group* offering new meaning to life?

A voice shouting from above interrupted the barrage of questions that were zipping through portals in her brain. Her body stilled in cold alert. "Someone's coming...hurry—"

hurry

Time unfolded in a blur of splashes. Arms and legs fighting against the pressure of liquid. Dripping wet bodies lifting from the high school pool—dashing toward the locker room. One, two, three, four, five—all accounted for, breathing heavy in a frantic rush. Slick hands on metal, pulling against the door handle. Jiggling. Yanking. The panicky feeling of the no-give latch. Trying over and over again in slow motion repeat.

Slippery skin huddled together, pressing, darting glances over shoulders. Urgency. Frustration.

"Hey...over here...this way—"

...this way

Snippets of words and phrases echoed across the natatorium, ricocheting through ripples of the abandoned pool. Whizzing through water-logged eardrums, they drowned out the heavy beat of her pulse as she began to run. A rolling heartbeat born in equal parts from risk-induced stress and the hasty ascent into chlorine filled air.

Go...go...go! The lights...out in...gym...sneak through! ... to the lockers...back way...

The rush of cohesive movement. Groupthink in forward motion. Panic driving the quickness—sheer desperation forcing her body into the lead. The sounds of one, two, three, four following closely behind.

Pushing against heavy swinging doors.

Plunging into darkness.

The smell of old sweat mixed with the putridity of industrialized cleanser.

Air filling the throat. Thick. Warmer than it should be.

A lack of echo

The rush of trepidation.

Sound of a switch—loud and reverberating.

The blinding glow of gymnasium lighting flickering to life.

Wooden bleachers—filled with faces. *Students!*

(Who were all there for what...some sort of assembly?)

(It *was* homecoming week after all.)

Ricochets of gasps.

Followed by laughter.

The realization that you are all alone in your nakedness, water sliding off your skin, see-through undergarments clinging, dripping, hiding nothing. A split-second search for the others—one, two three, four. Where are they? Nowhere—to be found.

The blur of the lights, screams of laughter, swaying free-throw line below your feet, in-bounds stripes isolating—separating you from the crowd—elongating. (Ribbons of red stretching on for miles.)

An instant to focus.

A pair of eyes burning into yours from across the gymnasium. A gleam of satisfaction, mouth forming into a smirk.

And the bitter taste of humiliation.

CHAPTER 1

December 1941

"Patient is arriving," a booming voice echoed into the hallway. "Going into ward-two, bed-four. It's been a long trip for him and now a decline in condition. He isn't currently stable. Patsy, we'll need two bottles of fluids from the cabinet. Ella, thanks for lending a hand, coming over from your customary unit. Can you assist with this one coming in?"

The swish of metal doors coming ajar, letting in a blast of cold air stopped Ella Hurley in her tracks. It had been a busy morning at War Memorial Hospital, and she was feeling the fatigue. Climbing up her neck, it seeped into her bones threatening to take residence. Refusing to give credence to the pain, she unlocked her shoulders and rolled her neck. Taking a long breath, she let it out slowly. An injury at the Carbide, auto accident on Easterday, and three admits back-to-back with the flu—all before 10:00 a.m. No time for respite. Not a quick sip of coffee with the girls in the break room. No gossip about the latest happenings around town, or updates on the newest battalion arriving at the fort. She hadn't even peed since leaving her house in the wee hours of the morning.

But this most recent patient's arrival was different—part of the war effort. It was a soldier coming home. And with the shock of the bombing at Pearl Harbor still so fresh, it seemed a little inconvenience was peanuts compared to all that was going on throughout the world.

Ella straightened her white nursing pinafore. It was a little disheveled and marginally soiled. But there were no smudges of blood discoloring the front—at least not as of yet that day. "I'm here, Dr. Northcott." Her answer was shouted into the blur of movement that was coming to life around her. Falling into alert attention, she watched as a gurney rushed into the hallway, leaving a trail of cold air in its wake. Racing beside the moving wheels, Ella was first to reach the ward. Adjusting pillows and throwing back covers, she helped to make ready the transfer of patient to bed. In no-time-flat, several others had gathered on all sides making the slide an effortless endeavor.

Effortless indeed. And yet there he was, the injured soldier, by all counts probably a strapping young man. Days before, fit, in the best condition of his life. How easily he floated from gurney to white metal hospital bed. As if he didn't weigh a thing. In one fell swoop. Ella's eyes took a brief sweep across the newly arrived patient. A swollen, bruised face, with eyes closed, reflected back at her, unrecognizable as a U.S. soldier by any shape of the imagination.

"We need a blood pressure," Dr. Northcott called out as Ella peeled back the sheet in search of a good spot to poke the skin for an IV insertion. Preparing the tourniquet, she made the stab, found blood, and hooked up tubing, allowing fluids to begin pouring into the veins.

"Pressure is 65 over 40," someone shouted above the din of movement.

Ella held the container that was wedged between the grasp of her fingers a little higher, encouraging a faster flow. "More fluids," Dr. Northcott asserted in an urgent tone. "Retrieve two bags of blood from the cooler. He may be losing blood. And take another pressure."

"60 over 35." A voice lifted into the air.

Fastening the container she was holding on a hook, Ella jumped into action. Teaming up with an orderly, they lowered the patient's head and lifted his legs into an elevated position in attempt to increase blood flow to the heart, at the same time upping the needed pressure. The patient's skin, coated in a sheen of sweat, was growing paler by the minute in-spite-of the array of bruises peppering like tattoos.

Ella swallowed down a bout of an unexpected wave of sadness as a cart filled with bags of blood and an array of medical instruments was rushed into the ward. She had a bad feeling. *He wasn't going to make it.* This soldier, so young, who had been sent away—stationed halfway across the world—was going to give his life for his country on this very day, right there, locally, on the home front.

War was everywhere.

Even right there—in Sault Ste. Marie, Michigan. But Ella knew that already, with all the soldiers arriving to Fort Brady as of recent, setting up shop, taking over the town. But this soldier—dying in front of her—he'd been there—*really there*—suffering a direct attack at the hands of the enemy. All the bombs. All the boats. Planes flying. Soldiers being buried alive in the bowels of sunken ships.

"Our patient, that's due to be arriving soon, was stationed in Pearl Harbor," Lillian Cloutier had told her earlier in the shift. Ella had just finished administering morphine to the occupant of ward-four, bed-three. The auto accident on Easterday had resulted in a broken right arm, a dislocated left shoulder, and a cluster of minor injuries. Lillian, a registered nurse that she often shared shifts with, had an armful of supplies for dressing the wounds and scrapes to the lower legs. "He is in the Navy. Stationed in Hawaii of all things." Lillian shook her head. "Probably had been enjoying the weather, poor kid. He was one of the unlucky injured during the surprise attack."

Ella placed the needle and syringe that she was using on a tray to be sterilized later and bit her lip. *Kid?* She and Lillian were all of twenty-years-old. How much different in age could the soldier coming into their care be? "His injuries must have been bad enough to be sent back then?" Her brow lifted in question.

Lillian began wrapping the leg suspended in front of her in a hurried motion—talking more than paying attention to what she was doing. The patient flinched, grimacing, in-spite-of the recently administered pain medication. "Yeah…apparently. Bad enough that he could be of no further use to Uncle Sam…at least for the time being."

Ella grabbed the soiled supplies Lillian was using as they fell to the floor. Scooping them up, she deposited them in a waste can. Lillian kept talking—going on about the multitude of injuries there had been in Hawaii—how many soldiers were being sent home. The longer she talked, the more layers of bandaging that went around the leg. Tale after tale of the soldiers. Swipe after swipe of the encircling gauze. Ella knew that supplies were at a premium right then. War rationings were everywhere. Besides, the patient's calf—it was starting to look bigger than his thigh. "Lil," she interjected, nodding toward the leg. "The dressing?"

Lillian glanced down. "Oh." She let out a chuckle. With a slight shrug, she began the process of unwrapping, all the while continuing to carry on in a chatty tone.

Ella took a chance. Listening for a pause in the inflection of Lillian's voice, she dove in. "I don't understand then," she lifted her brow, steering the conversation back to the patient in transit. "Why are they sending him though, if he isn't stable enough for the ride?"

Lillian grabbed a pair of scissors, began snipping away at the extra wrapping. "I guess he was… stable. But there's been a change while in route…a sudden decline. It was unexpected."

"He's bleeding internally," Dr. Northcott called out, gaze focused on the newly arrived soldier. "Where's my other bag of blood?" Ward-four was a flurry of action. They had already dumped in three units and his pressures were barely staying above water. Ella checked the drip of the fluids that flowed into her patient's pale arm, making sure the needle in the skin was still in place. All was intact. But tensions were high. It seemed the medical team knew what Ella was beginning to feel deep inside. All their efforts, all the interventions, they weren't proving effective.

It just wasn't going to be enough!

They were going to lose him if they didn't act fast.

The whole morning had been unfolding in a frenzied whir. Ella could feel it from the minute she stepped foot onto her floor at War Memorial. There was a buzz in the air. An unsettled energy. An injury getting rushed in from the Carbide was never a good thing. She'd barely a moment to deposit her bag in the locker room, when her first assignment had been handed over. But Ella was always up for a challenge. She liked to keep her mind well occupied. It helped her to stay focused on moving in a forward direction through life. A busy day was a good day.

But there was a difference between busy and crazy! To put in every effort and then lose a life—it didn't seem acceptable. Ella didn't *want* to accept it. *Wouldn't.* And yet what choice did she have? Here it was, another war effort failure, on the heels of Pearl Harbor! And it seemed this one belonged to her! All the scurrying around, the efficiency of movement, astute intervention, precision in execution—none of it was paying off. *They were losing him.*

Her new patient was dying.

"Prepare for transfer to the operating room."

Ella could hear Dr. Northcott's voice as if ringing through a tunnel. Shaking her head to clear the unwanted clatter, she snapped back to the present. Yes—of course, surgery, in-order-to stop the internal bleeding. The efforts *were* still on then.

"Blood pressure is 58 over 30."

A group of orderlies rushed into the room.

Seconds later, a squadron of clinical uniforms surrounded the hospital bed and the transfer back to gurney was complete. Ella helped to guide the fluids that were still dripping into the sunken veins of her patient as he was jiggled onto the mobile cart. A sense of urgency was filling up the atmosphere, growing stronger by the minute. Workers were scurrying. Directives being shouted.

Caught into the whirl of movement, Ella couldn't help but draw a parallel connection between the current situation and what had gone on at Pearl Harbor earlier that month. What had it been like during the surprise attack? The overwhelming amounts of catastrophe. The living caring for the injured. Chaos ensuing at the scene of the bombing. Soldiers being carted to the infirmaries. The exigency to preserve life. The inability to carry out the task. Large blasts shaking the walls even as the effort was made.

She'd seen the film released by the United States Navy. The motion picture of how it had all gone down. The destruction. The sunken ships. Smoldering fires. Destroyed supplies.

Lives, taken too soon.

The sense of urgency!

Urgency to save the soldiers' lives.

Urgency to save this soldier's life!

The gurney was prepared and ready. In a moment, it would be wheeled into a stark white hallway headed in the direction of surgery.

Ella eyed the military crop of brown hair that rested against the pillow atop the cart, slightly overgrown due to time spent in the infirmary. No longer was there a sheen of sweat covering the skin of the patient, but the coloring, so pale, amidst a covering of swelling and discolorations, practically glowed under the bright glare of the hospital lights. The even rise and fall of the chest belied the struggle to take air into the lungs. The inability to sustain a steady pulse. The battle to keep a vascular pressure high enough to pump blood.

Ella bit her lip. Whispered a prayer. *Don't go yet. Get stronger. Stay with us.* Her words floated into the circulating air that hovered above the patient.

Pivoting to leave as the cart began rolling away with a team of medical personnel flanking its sides, something in Ella's peripheral vision caught her attention, causing her to turn back. For a moment, she paused, motionless. Eyes, blue, flickering open, searching for something—a promise of life(?)—locked onto hers and stayed there. Ella's breath caught in her throat. Her mouth went dry. All she could do was stare. One second, two seconds, three. The connection was intense, holding her tightly in its grip. Moments in time—standing still, suspended, as if in another time and place. And then the lashes fluttered shut, resting once again on bruised cheeks and a ghostly countenance, while the stretcher was rushed toward another section of the hospital, Dr. Northcott taking the lead.

Dear Thomas,

This house is an empty shell. The people indoors are not well.
Inside their barren minds they yell. Come back our boy...

Farewell.

~E.

CHAPTER 2

~Three weeks earlier~

"Damn soldiers," Melvin Hurley grunted as he settled into his easy chair. Lifting a clear liquid drink to his lips, ice jiggling in the glass, he took a swig. The substance, though clear, smelled strong, ruling out the possibility of water. Ella watched him with a frown from across the room. *Better clear than amber,* she thought to herself. Amber being the color of whiskey. Those days—with amber liquid in the glass—turned out to be the worst. *The whiskey days.* "There's so damn many of them," Melvin continued while wiping his mouth. "Blocking the sidewalks. Blocking the streets. Can't even get down Ashmun anymore. Don't know why they think we need so many around here anyway?"

"You know…Melvin…the Locks," Grace Hurley started to interject. But her voice, too mousy, was swallowed up by a vibrating cough coming from across the room. She looked away and pulled her stringy brown hair into a ponytail as her husband finished hacking. Or just flat out ignored her—which was happening more and more often these days.

"Yeah, yeah…the Locks," Melvin scowled. *"It's all about the Locks,"* he added in an irritated sing-song tone. Wiping a hand across the reddened skin of his face where more than a few days of stubble resided, his bloodshot, gray eyes swept over his wife in disdain. *He had heard her after all.* But that didn't make Grace feel better.

Didn't make Ella feel any better, either.

She thought about bringing up the importance of the Locks to her dad and the role they played in the war. Even though the U.S. wasn't officially involved in the war at that point, the country was still on alert, participating in a peripheral manner. And ninety percent of all iron ore—a much needed entity for supplies—was shipped through the Locks. But Melvin knew that already. *Of course, he did*. Which then, in fact, proved positive that Sault Ste. Marie *did* need the protection of the soldiers.

But the topic of the Locks and the water that surrounded it was a temperamental one. Ella knew that. And even understood. *Of course, she did!*

But that didn't change what was happening outside the Hurley family. Elsewhere, the rest of the world was at war. And just because the U.S. hadn't entered officially, didn't mean their resources couldn't become a target for the Axis forces—Germany, Japan, Italy. The Soo Locks could very well be a prime spot for bombing, in turn stopping the chief system of iron shipping in the country. The threat loomed large. And Fort Brady, sitting atop Easterday Hill, was filling up weekly with soldiers being transported into town to help ease the risk of peril.

Melvin set down his glass and took a drag on a cigarette, blowing puffs of black smoke into the air. The smog it created swirled toward the floral curtains that hung on the far wall of the living room. Ella's mom, Grace, had tried to make the house pleasant for the Hurley family. Using what monies they could afford from her dad's job at the electric company and her parttime job at Woolworth's, downtown, she'd put up wall paper, hung hand-sewn curtains with tie-backs to cover the windows, and placed a smattering of decorations, making sure their house was a cheery place. Or so it *was*. For the first several years of Ella's life.

Until they lost Thomas.

Then everything changed.

But life goes on, they say. You learn to adapt—in some ways. *Or you don't*. But either way, time keeps ticking away.

"When is supper," an enthusiastic voice called out as the form of a nine-year-old came bounding into the room. All heads turned, tensions lifting in simultaneous motion. The relief was palpable and shared by all three adults in the room. The boy, Charles, was adorned in bib overalls and a striped shirt. Taupe eyes regarded the people gathered—*his family*—as he did a quick flip of his head, clearing brown-colored bangs out of his eyes. The same brown hair, Ella realized, that used to be hers for most of her growing up years, before she lightened it to a honey gold, deciding on a change as she entered adulthood. Even the eyes were hers—though her own were a shade darker, qualifying them brown.

Charles crinkled his nose. "A fella gets hungry. What time did you say, Mom?"

Grace, wiping hands across her apron, offered a smile. "Soon, Chance," she replied. "I have a casserole in the oven."

"Good...then do I have time to play some catch outside with Kip beforehand?" Walking over to the davenport, Charles stooped to the floor and picked up his mitt. His eyes were questioning, laced with bountiful energy.

"You do...but stay close by and listen for my call."

Charles barely heard the words that were offered from his mom as he fairly flew through the front door. Exiting onto Maple Street, he headed to play ball with others from the neighborhood, including his pal Kip, under a fast-growing evening sky.

For a moment, those left inside the gray shingled house, sat in paused reverence to the youngest family member that had just claimed their full attention as he whisked his way through the living room.

Charles Hurly.

Darling Charles. Or Chance rather, as they mostly referred to him. *Darling Chance.* Never spoken was the real reason Charles's name had been transitioned to Chance. What they were really implying when they involved him in friendly banter—calling him Chance instead of his given name, Charles.

He *was* in-fact, *their* chance—indeed, their second chance at life.

Arriving as an oops—as was the behind-the-scenes word throughout their home—he was a means to salvation as well. More-or-less. On some level at least. He was their second chance at conducting life on a day-to-day basis. Some days their sole reason for waking, and walking, and eating and talking. Especially where Melvin and Grace were concerned. They needed the spark and life Charles offered around the house to keep them going. If only sometimes at half-mast.

He wasn't Thomas.

Their beloved Thomas, who could never be replaced.

But he was young, and boy, and full of spark and zest for activity. And he offered some type of proxy for another life they would never get to watch play out. Simply put, he filled a void. Or at least partially filled it.

Melvin still drank—too much.

Grace still laid around—too much.

Ella still worked to stay busy—too much.

"Careful. Don't run into any soldiers out there," Melvin barked over his shoulder as the screen door shook with the left-over movement of Chance's exit. "Might not be any placed for you to play ball, with them taking up all the room on the streets." He wagged his head and took another swig from his glass. "Why they think we need so many—"

But his words drifted without end into the smokey living room air, falling onto deaf ears. Grace had withdrawn to the kitchen and Ella to her bedroom. Who knew how long and loud the rant would go on tonight? Better to not give credence by being an engaged audience.

Ella wondered what Siobhan would think about her father's carrying on about the soldiers all the time. Having escaped the living room, she sat on her bed folding her freshly laundered nursing pinafores and skirts, still crisp from the drying rack. In-spite-of the dismal mood occupying the home, a smile found her lips as she imagined Siobhan's reaction when it came to the topic of the soldiers in town.

Siobhan's ideas on the influx of military enforcements in town were in such stark contrast to that of her dad's. The two of them were practically polar opposites on the initiative.

"It's like heaven on earth," Siobhan told Ella one day as they were perusing the sidewalks in town, stopping to eye an outfit displayed in the Penney's window. A floral long-sleeve A-line dress with a matching belt was peering back at them. "Ooh, I like this by-the-way," she interjected.

Ella nodded. "I suppose. But I think I like these better." She pointed to the next window over which displayed a female manikin in slacks. "They just look so comfortable."

"Maybe. I suppose…in the winter. In the winter they'd be warmer for sure. But anyway…what was I just saying?" Siobhan gave a head nod to a cluster of soldiers who were walking on the other side of the street. "This is heaven I tell you. If there is anything good to come out of these times of war, it's having all these soldiers being shipped into town. I mean, don't get me wrong, things are bad alright, but having these uniforms walking around everywhere…this is simply grand."

Ella laughed. "If you say so." If there was ever something to laugh about during times as these, it would come in the form of Siobhan's famously funny comments.

Siobhan Alby.

Her Siobhan.

Best friend extraordinaire.

Siobhan—wild and free! Much like her rumored heritage from the Chippewa Tribe.

Siobhan's mom, Katherine, a little too unbridled in her younger years, had been a teen when she'd run away, returning only to be united in matrimony to bachelor, Jack Alby, who had been pining away for a wife. A baby girl named Siobhan was born within their first year of marriage. Dinner discussions all-across town were spent trying to figure out just how many months it had been since the nuptials between Jack and Katherine had taken place, and the child's arrival at the local hospital. It could never quite be proven that the timing of the baby didn't match the marital arrangement.

But Siobhan sure looked a lot different than Jack.

And not much like her mother either.

But a strong resemblance did exist to that of the Chippewa tribe on the outskirts of town.

As far as Ella was concerned, Siobhan's ancestry line had the ingredients for true beauty, all high cheekbones, brown eyes, and long flowing dark hair.

And never a better friend to be found.

Loyal and not afraid to speak her mind. She wasn't one to conform to society's norms and expectations. It's like her rumored beginnings had lent itself to unbridled behavior. Not born in corral, she was free to be like the wind.

"Plus, besides having all the handsome fellas milling around," Siobhan continued as they eased away from the Penney's display, "isn't it nice knowing that the Locks are getting so much protection now with the soldiers and all? I heard that there is worry over the threat the Germans could have on the Locks."

Ella's eyes widened marginally. "Really...how so?" To her, Germany seemed like a world away.

"Well, they say...the Germans...could send ships into Hudson Bay...and attack that way. With ships. *Or* with submarines really. Submarines are sly you know. Sneaking through water unseen...until it's too late. Then...out come the torpedoes.

"Yeah that'd be—"

"It...for the Locks, you might say."

Ella grimaced.

Everyone knew that the Locks were indispensable. Connecting Lake Superior and Lake Huron, they were part of the St. Mary's River, and one of the busiest shipping channels in the world. The Locks' mechanisms were in place to even out the depths between the two great lakes, Lake Superior, being the deeper of the two. After a freighter entered a lock, the gates would close around it, allowing the levels of water to either rise twenty-one feet, if the vessel was going from Huron to Superior, working its way up to Minnesota. Or vice versa, drop twenty-one feet, if the ship was in route, going the other way, heading toward Ohio or eventually out into the Atlantic.

Ella eyed Siobhan's long brown hair blowing in the wind as she talked. It was nippy outside, making their jaunt on the downtown sidewalks chilly. Winter would be arriving full bore all too soon. The stuff she was telling her—it seemed there had been some type of inside information going on. For a moment Ella contemplated whether or not her friend had been spending more time with the soldiers then she even knew. It was possible, she supposed. But then again, the threat of being bombed—that was no secret. All too often, they'd experienced the bomb raid drills in school around town.

Ella pulled her coat more tightly around her shoulders. By then, they were in front of Barish Brothers. "Better safe than sorry," she told Siobhan.

Better safe than sorry.

Words to live by. *Or to wish you had!*

The phrase echoed through Ella's mind, and she brushed it away.

Right then, Siobhan grabbed her hand, helping to interrupt her thoughts. Bringing her into focus.

"Hey…would you look at those fellas," she said, focusing on a pair of soldiers headed their direction, less than a block away. Uniforms crisp, their eyes were smiling. Clearly, the girls had captured their attention. They were in range.

Siobhan let go of Ella's hand and gave her a little jab in the ribs. "There's a couple of fine dames," one of the soldiers spoke into the air, loud enough that the girls over-heard. Ella could feel Siobhan perking up beside her. Sure enough, there was soon to be an encounter.

"Hello there, ladies." Olive-green caps were tipped in greeting as they approached.

Siobhan's smile was flirtatious. "Hello there, Soldiers," she answered back. Beside her, Ella's nod of the head was a little more reserved, but still qualified as cordial.

"Private Smith and Private Johnston here." The one that had first spoken held out a hand. "But you can call us Ted and Chet."

"Ted and Chet," the girls repeated.

"Siobhan and Ella," Siobhan offered as handshakes were exchanged. Smiles were landing everywhere. Not too bad looking either, Ella noted. Clean shaven and snappy with their army cuts, bangs pushed sideways over the brow.

"Ella and Siobhan, nice names," Chet said. "You hometown girls?"

As if that wasn't obvious, thought Ella. But she nodded anyway. "We are," she concurred.

"And you, fellas…are you staying up at Fort Brady then? *As if that wasn't obvious as well,* thought Ella once more. But Siobhan asked the question anyway, knowing that it would lead into the fact that she lived closed by, in a neighborhood off Easterday. *There had to be some sort of points given for easy access to the fort.*

The conversation between the foursome continued, the soldiers indeed becoming impressed with Siobhan's proximity to their barracks. One subject led to the next, mixed in with plenty of flirtatious banter. But the cold air eventually got the best of them, and it was decided—or mostly presented as a fantastic idea by Ted and Chet—that they should take their fun elsewhere, somewhere in doors.

Siobhan was all in. "Yes, I think we should," she concurred, nudging Ella in the arm. "You fellas crack me up." The soldiers looked pleased with her statement, happy that they'd made a good impression with their wit.

Ella brushed a strand of her honey-colored hair from her eyes, the wind making a mess of the do she'd created with rollers prior to their jaunt downtown. The soldiers were handsome and plenty of fun. But thoughts of the hospital found their way into her mind. "Sorry to ruin plans," she said. "But I have to work early in the morning. Duty calls."

The guys could relate, being all-too-use to *duty calling*. But that didn't stop their efforts. *"Let's hang out for at least for a little while,"* they said. They'd have her back, safe and sound—on to slumberland—in no time flat.

"Oh, come on, Ella, please," Siobhan coerced in a lighthearted fashion.

But Ella just shook her head.

After arriving back at home on Maple Street, she thought of Siobhan. Hoped like anything that she was using some sort of good judgement hanging out with the soldiers, even if they were good-humored in nature. But the questioning thoughts regarding her friend didn't last long, fading easily as she drifted into a night's sleep. Work really would come early—and truly, always did.

It was only a few weeks later after Siobhan and Ella's excursion on downtown Ashmun Street, that the City of Sault Ste. Marie was indeed reminded of the reason for having the soldiers stationed by the Locks in an all-too-real way. On December 7th in the early morning hours, the naval base at Pearl Harbor on the Hawaiian Islands was ferociously attacked by a fleet of Japanese warplanes. It was a ravaging surprise! Thousands were killed and thousands were wounded. Many of the U.S. ships were either sunk or simply destroyed. America was left reeling in the wake, the idea of being an untouchable entity quickly erased.

War had come to the homeland.

The next day, President Roosevelt made an announcement, listened to by citizens everywhere, either by radio or through the wooly picture of a black and white television set. It was official—the United States of America would be joining the war.

CHAPTER 3

The next few shifts at the hospital, Ella thought often about the soldier-patient that had gotten whisked away to surgery, while clinging to his last thread of life. Had he even made it? Word was-yes. But he wasn't out of the woods yet. They had stopped the internal bleeding and stabilized his pressure. But he was currently comatose, his condition being watched closely for any type of deterioration.

"I heard it's still touch and go," Lillian said, a brown bottle of medication in her hands. Headed into ward-two, she was passing by Ella in the hallway and overheard her asking. "Are you talking about Benjamin?"

"I don't know, am I?" Ella picked up a thermometer from a metal cart. She was headed to ward-two as well. She and Lillian shared assignment rooms that day—as it seemed was often the case.

"If you are talking about our injured soldier from Hawaii, then yes, that is his name."

"Oh, okay, well I didn't know. But you've heard something then?"

Lillian kept walking, with Ella following closely behind. Often much of the conversation shared between workers at the hospital was exchanged in route or between tasks. This day was no exception. "I've only heard that he is stable, but it's marginal. I don't think there is too high of hope right now. He hasn't woken up yet." Their steps slowed as they reached the doorway of the ward, and Lillian offered Ella a parting glance. "The next couple days might just tell the tale…but I'm not sure that I'd place any wagers just yet."

Ella paused momentarily. "Yeah, I suppose…maybe not," she answered, words spoken mostly under her breath. Separating, they both headed toward their side of the room, Ella sighing as she walked. For some reason Lillian's report was settling hard on her intellect. It left her feeling sad and she wasn't sure why. There had been many patients in her care over the last couple years, not all of them making it through to tell the tale of their hospitalization.

It was noontime before Ella realized that the feeling of melancholy was still lingering, shadowing her nursing duties as she went about her day. "Dr. Northcott," she said in passing, having run into him in the hallway after lunch. "I've been meaning to ask…how is the soldier we cared for earlier in the week? Benjamin, I believe is his name." Not that she didn't trust what Lillian's information, but it'd be nice have another opinion. Possibly a more hopeful one?

"Yes, Benjamin, of course," Dr. Northcott answered. He shook his head. "He's still in the critical observation ward. He hasn't woken up yet. I can't say that he's doing poorly exactly…but I can't say that he's progressing like we'd hoped either."

Ella nodded. So, Lillian was correct.

"But say, listen," Dr. Northcott continued as if an idea was occurring to him. "Why don't you pay him a visit? I know he's still in the critical ward, but now that he's not requiring hourly medical attention, he probably isn't getting the human interaction that might do him some good. Especially right now. The next while may be crucial. Who knows what it is that might cause him to pull through? Just that little needed extra something."

Ella mulled over the idea the rest of the day and found herself at war in her mind, unsure of the logic of why. For some reason the suggestion of paying the soldier a visit had her on edge, making her feel off kilter. *Why not pay him a visit—see how he is doing,* she thought one moment. Then, *no I don't think I will after all,* the next. But when it was time for her shift to be over, she found herself heading to the other side of the hospital in-spite-of her misgivings. Arriving at the critical observation desk, she asked for his ward and room number. The only information she had on him was "Benjamin" and "Soldier." But that was enough. They pointed her to room five.

Ella walked halfway down the hall and turned a corner, while counting the numbers above the doorframes, finally coming to room five. Hesitating for a brief moment, she peered through the doorway, surprised to find only a single hospital bed occupying the space. She was so used to dealing in oversized wards with long rows of cots and beds. What did it mean that he was so isolated? Eyes adjusting to the lack of lighting in the room, she noticed two containers of fluids hanging on a pole. A conglomeration of tubing tethered the patient to the medication. The drips created a rhythmic motion in the quietness of the room. Everywhere there were instruments and doctoring utensils sitting in waiting—should they need to be called into action. The atmosphere felt sterile. Serious. Grave.

Ella proceeded forward in a cautious motion. As if being careful to what—not wake the patient? And yet isn't that what the medical staff would like to have happen? Letting out a slow breath, she continued her advance, arriving at bedside in a somewhat less guarded manner. Taking in the resting figure, with head, latent, on the pillow, covers pulled to the chin, she right away noticed some variances from the rushed scenario that was his arrival at the hospital. Sure, he was still fragile in appearance, face swollen from injuries, but his coloring had transitioned to a healthier hue. The chalk white boy from days prior was gone. He looked like he was resting—comfortably.

And yet the prognosis was still undecided.

Peering down at the soldier's body, Ella found herself at an impasse. What to do? Talk to the fella? But what to say? Continue staring at him? That felt awkward. She folded her hands together, for what reason—to prevent them from reaching out? Possibly laying cool fingers against his cheek? Gently swiping the brow? It all felt undecided and gauche. Why had she even come?

Because she was a nurse.

And she cared.

In the dim lighting of the room, she found a chair and pulled it to the bedside. For a few minutes she sat, staring at the rise and fall of the soldier's chest. Benjamin. For a wistful moment she wished she was brave enough to sing a tune. Would that help? What would some of his favorites be? How about a selection that had been popular in Hawaii—before all the bombing? Then all at once it hit her—*singing? What No!* She almost laughed aloud. What was she even thinking? In retrospect she felt stupid. Her line of thinking was digressing. Maybe it was time to go. Head out—go home. It had been a long day at work and now that she was more relaxed, taking a load off her feet, the tiredness was beginning to set in.

She made motion to stand. Then went still, as a flicker of movement on the pillow caught her attention. Something was happening! He was stirring. The patient's lashes fluttered for a few seconds, then opened completely. And she found herself staring into a pair of blue eyes. The same as earlier in the week, though that time from a gurney being rolled toward the operating room. Ella held her breath. Was it just a moment captured in time? Or was he awakening? Was his condition changing for the better?

Unlike the previous time in the hallway, his eyes did not close again. For a few moments he seemed disoriented. Ella readied to call for a nurse. Maybe this was some type of episode, and he would begin to deteriorate quickly. But shortly-thereafter, the eyes seemed to focus, locking on her face. His mouth opened and then shut again, lips, so dry, they were sticking together. Ella paused, holding her breath. Dare she lift a spoon filled with liquid in their direction? She decided *yes* and watched as he eventually took a sip. Afterward, he tried to speak again.

"Where," he began. His voice was raspy and barely audible. "Where...am...I?".

Joy circulated inside of Ella's chest. As well as a teaspoonful of caution. She was so happy about the turn of events and yet at the same time, didn't want the newly wakened patient to be frightened. "You are in a hospital," she said in soothing voice. "You've been injured, but you're getting good care." The way he was staring into her eyes, as if holding onto her every word, she found herself adding, "You...you are on your way to getting better, though." Inside, she hoped she was speaking the truth.

"I...I am...was I—"

Leaning in, Ella strained as if to listen. Clearly, there was something the soldier was trying to say. But being so weak and exhausted, he couldn't quite get it all out. Finally, his eyes fluttered shut again and her heart took a dive. But then, seconds later, they reopened. Looking right at her, he offered a feeble smile.

Cautiously, Ella found his hand and gave it a squeeze. "It's okay, Benjamin," she said. "You don't have to talk right now. But...you...but you will...soon." Again—it was a hope she had no right to offer.

"Thanks," he seemed to mouth. Then eyes closing once more, his chest fell into a rhythmic pattern of sleep.

And Ella ran to the front desk.

Two days later Ella arrived at the hospital ready for work, having fought off the blustery elements of an icy winter morning. Some days it seemed the dark cold seeped into one's bones, holding them hostage for hours at a time. Until, after scurrying around between patients, layers were shed, and with them the idea that you were ever cold to begin with, emerging, the idea that somehow the four walls of the hospital were in-fact housing an enormous amount of heat. That day in particular, Ella found she was looking forward to the warmth that would hopefully find her later in the shift.

Removing her double-breasted rayon coat, she shook the snow from her scarf and began to apply her nursing cap, tucking the honey-colored strands of her hair into place. Checking into the nursing desk on her hallway, she found ward-four was her assignment for the day. And word around the hospital was—the beds were full. Lillian wasn't on the schedule, so she'd be sharing the space with another nurse. Probably Helen.

Gathering her things, Ella made her way down the hallway, remembering to grab some extra bottles of antiseptic out of the central cabinet in passing. It seemed they always ran short on busy days like these.

After visiting the soldier earlier in the week on the critical observation unit, Ella had found herself returning to the scenario several times in her head. She couldn't help wondering how he was doing. *Benjamin.* Had he continued to improve? The encounter they shared—him waking and speaking—had it been a fluke? A chance happening? Had he returned to his state of comatose? And yet still another thought found its way into her mind—had there been a reversal in condition and he'd since declined? Or worse? They were thoughts she couldn't seem to shake.

While making the early morning trek through the snow in route to the hospital, Ella vowed that later on in the day, once things settled into a manageable routine, she'd check in on the soldier and see how he was doing. Get an update on the state of his condition. Or at the very least enlist Dr. Northcott's knowledge—see what updates he had the skinny on.

Walking through the doorway of ward-four, Ella let all thoughts of the soldier go, focusing on the patients she'd be attending to throughout the day. A child who'd had their appendix removed. Another who'd had a sledding injury, resulting in broken bones. An elderly person with frostbite. And that was just to begin with. She eyed the long row of metal beds that awaited her attention. It was the early morning hour, and most were fast asleep. Ella drew in a silent breath, enjoying the moments of pre-dawn quiet. By all accounts, quiet was a good thing. A sign that those in her charge were, for-the-present, comfortable and stable. She could begin her day by taking care of their needs in an orderly fashion.

Walking to the far side of the room, Ella took note of the sleeping forms that were eclipsed by the silhouette of her nursing pinafore as she made her way by. The soft padding sound of her white shoes was the only thing that stood between her trained ear and the rhythmic vibration of unlabored breathing, telling her, all was for-the-moment, okay.

On the opposite side of the ward, in the dim light of the room, she could see her fellow nursing companion, Helen—just as she'd expected—attending to those she'd been assigned to for the day. Ella lifted a hand in greeting, and Helen waved back while leaning over an elderly gentleman, whose head was propped on pillows preparing to receive some sort of liquid medication from a spoon. The plan was, she would begin her care there at the end, and work her way back down the line.

Pockets loaded with supplies, Ella prepared to approach the bedside of her first patient. A sleeping form bundled under a pile of blankets.

After taking a prolonged peek, she'd gather the remainder of supplies needed to begin care. While allowing time for her eyes to adjust to the dim lighting left over from the night shift, Ella went still in her tracks.

Caught unaware by what she was deciphering in the darkened space, a peculiar awareness reached out to squeeze her chest. A strong feeling of familiarity landed directly thereafter. A sensation of deja'vu. Unwittingly, Ella took a step back. And didn't know why. Except that if the feeling she was experiencing was in line with of what she strongly suspected to be true—the patient lying in the in bed-one, was none other than the soldier who'd sustained injuries in Hawaii.

How could it be?

It was so unexpected.

And yet—it could—*be.*

Really—why couldn't it?

With baited-breath Ella drew near to the metal rails of the bed. "Benjamin," she whispered in a barely audible voice. And yet the lashes that fluttered opened upon her approach seemed to take note of the salutation in-spite-of the lack of volume. The blueness of the eyes that stared up at her, shining under the soft, background lighting was all the confirmation she needed.

It was Benjamin indeed.

Somehow, someway, the soldier she had been so concerned about had found his way into her care!

The relief she experienced was enormous. Mixed in with other emotions that were unexplainable.

He was alive! The soldier that the staff at the hospital had come to favor, that they had fought to save, that they had worried over and prayed for—he was alive. And obviously well enough to be released from critical observation.

The soldier-patient, too, appeared a little taken back, his eyes opening wider as he shook away the fuzzy grip of sleep. "It's you," he offered in a marginally surprised tone.

Ella froze in place. "Me," she questioned, her brow forming in a perplexed line. "It *is* me...but how do you mean?"

Benjamin licked his lips. They seemed to be stuck together. Ella's eyes drifted to the container of liquid that was hanging beside his bed, thinking that it was good he was still undergoing IV therapy. "You," he cleared his throat. His voice was still scratchy. "I've seen you before. When I was on the other side of the hospital." He shook his head. "I don't know…maybe another time too."

Ella smiled then. He was right. She *had* been there. Twice at his bedside. And at key moments. Once when he'd been rolled away to surgery in a fight for his life. And then again when he'd awoken from a comatose state. Both times he'd looked directly at her, but she hadn't been sure he'd actually *seen* her in those particular moments. Clearly, he had. At least once. Her heart swelled a little. One never knew how your presence was going to affect another. Hopefully, in this case, maybe it had been a positive encounter.

Either way, here he was, appearing to be doing better than the trajectory of his condition on previous days. "You're right, we have crossed paths before." Ella smiled. "Benjamin, correct?"

He nodded.

"You've been under the care of War Memorial for several days now. I'm so glad to see you doing better."

At this, Benjamin gave a nod and looked away. Shifting in bed, the blankets fell away from his shoulders, Ella taking in the state of his condition. He was officially her patient for the day, and he'd need an inspection at her hand. For the first time since his arrival to the hospital, she took note of a cast on his left arm. Bones, broken from the Pearl Harbor tragedy. And the healing bruises on his face. The swelling was still there too and maybe would be for a while. "May I," she asked, while reaching out a hand. With a soft touch, Ella felt for the rows of stitches that littered both sides of his cheeks.

Benjamin flinched only slightly. "These, look like they've been in for a while," she said. "They'll need to come out soon. Maybe today. I'll speak with Dr. Northcott." Benjamin nodded and looked up. Their eyes met and for some reason the space between them seemed unexpectedly close. Ella backed away and stood up, thankful for the lack of lighting in the room. She couldn't tell for sure, but her face felt warm. Inside, she chided herself. She was acting unprofessional, letting herself feel awkward in front of a patient. "Anyway," she began tidying up the area beside the bed, "either way, I'll be back later to cleanse them with some antiseptic. Breakfast should be here soon. Do you need help…I mean, have you been able to eat?"

She could feel Benjamin's eyes studying her as she busied herself. A patient—a soldier—who had been though a great deal and was now trying to sort out the situation. She was only part of the progression—the next step in the whole traumatizing event start to finish. He'd obviously been though a lot. "Yeah, I can eat," he said, holding up the arm that was free of a cast. Ella stopped what she was doing and looked in his direction. "I'm right-handed," he explained.

Nodding, Ella offered a smile in acknowledgement. Smoothing her nursing pinafore, she explained that she'd be back to check in on him after tending to the other patients in her care. Her voice came across as therapeutic, yet professional, and she walked away, thankful that she had regained her composure after the initial shock of seeing him in one of her beds.

Though, throughout the rest of her shift, she found herself having to reign in an attitude of excitement at having discovered him doing well medically and having been place under her care, to boot. After all the recent tragedy of war—in particular the Pearl Harbor bombing—it felt like something was going right for a change. By helping to care for a wounded soldier and nursing him back to life, it seemed that she was somehow doing her small part for the war effort. Really making a difference.

It was midway through the day before Dr. Northcott had time to removed Benjamin's stitches. Ella, having cleansed the area prior to him beginning the task, had been careful to avoid pressing into the bruises. Only once had he glanced up at her while she was wiping, with a look that spoke of discomfort, but when asked about it, reassured her to keep going. With a brief pause, she continued to dab, using gentler strokes. Then Dr. Northcott took over and soon all that remained were little pieces of wire on a tray and leftover marks on the patient's skin that would take a while longer to heal, along with the swelling and the contusions.

"Dr. Northcott," Ella called into the hallway after they had finished up. He was off to see others that needed his attention. Exiting ward-four, the door shut behind him as Ella caught up. "There is something I've been meaning to ask about Benjamin," she said. "I've been caring for him all day and noticed there aren't any broken bones on his legs. And yet he hasn't been able to move them to get around. Is there a reason?"

Dr. Northcott looked thoughtful. "Not particularly," he reached for his chin in contemplation. "But you do realize all of this is still very fresh. A few days ago, he was bleeding internally, then comatose. Give him time. He's in a weakened condition. That's most likely it."

"Of course," Ella replied. It made sense. She was glad for the opinion.

The next time Ella came into work, she made a pointed effort of looking over the names on her list of patients, instead of walking into the assignment blind. Arriving at the nursing station, she picked up the paper and found the roster. Ward-four was written at the top of the page. Unwittingly her heart picked up in tempo and she tried to calm it down. *She was being stupid*. Everyone deserved a chance at taking care of the soldier—not just her. But against all control, heart thumping, her eyes scrolled down the list in fast motion.

Benjamin M. – Ward #4/Bed #1

The words jumped out at her. So, he was still there. And he was going be her patient again that day. *Okay then—good. Better her to be his nurse, really*, she rationalized. She had taken care of him on the shift prior and had started to build a level of trust. Ultimately, wouldn't that lend toward healing? And wasn't that what was what was important after all?

After checking on her other patients down the row, Ella finally arrived at his bedside. She had told herself not to hurry. *There was no hurry*. Approaching under the dim lights of the room, she sensed he was still sleeping. For a minute, she watched the rise and fall of his chest. Finding it to be in regular rhythm, she prepared to leave and come back.

Better to let him sleep. But just as she was walking away, a crinkling sound on the pillow let her know he was turning his head.

"Good morning," she said in a soft, early morning tone.

"You're back," a voice said in return. Ella focused her gaze in the darkness of the room. Even though she could hear the words being directed her way, she could swear the eyes facing toward her were still shut. *Odd.* She leaned in for a better look and her suspicions were confirmed. The soldier's eyes were in fact closed.

"Yes, I am," she answered, wondering how he indeed knew that it was her if he wasn't *actually* looking. Though maybe he had looked at some point, and she'd missed it she realized. Releasing the question from her mind, Ella continued on in conversation, making small talk, breaking the ice so-to-speak, as she often did with her patients before digging into the current state of their condition. She found it helped to soften things up before getting down to the nitty gritty of their care for the day. She figured sooner or later Benjamin would open his eyes while she was chatting on. He was probably still tired and taking a while to wake up. But after a few minutes of conversing, they remained closed.

Finally, she couldn't stand it any longer. "Are you—" she started, then stopped. She didn't quite know how to phrase what she had on her mind. "I've noticed you are not opening your eyes today…right now. What is going on?"

There was a pause. Then a sigh. "Yes…I know." Another pause. "It's because I can't see."

Ella sucked in a breath, shock filling her veins. This was such a turn of events.

"I mean when I open my eyes, all I see are bright flashing lights. So, it's better to keep them closed."

"Oh." Ella's brain raced. She didn't quite know what to think. "Have you told this to a doctor?

"I Have. They've done an exam. No clear answers yet."

"Okay…okay well, they'll figure something out, I'm sure. We'll see what they come up with. Meanwhile, maybe you just need more rest."

Benjamin nodded and looked away. Discouragement was evident on his brow. Still, he didn't open his eyes.

Ella's heart lurched in her chest. "So," she said forcing a cheery sound to her voice. "How about breakfast?" Have you been able to navigate eating, without being able to see, I mean?"

Benjamin shrugged. "I'm doing okay. Getting by."

"I'll tell you what I'll do," she said. "I'll deliver your breakfast tray personally. Make sure you have things set up where you need them."

This time Benjamin didn't reply. But Ella kept her word. After checking on the rest of her patients, she returned with a spread of oatmeal, toast, canned peaches, and milk. Taking a bedside tray table, she pulled it over his lap. And though not the optimal situation, arranged things in an order where he could at least find what was needed. She paused before walking away, wondering how in all actuality he'd navigate the situation satisfactorily.

But she didn't have time to find out. That day's workload was particularly heavy, the sick flooding into the hospital, with—if not the flu—some other type of respiratory virus. As always, winter proved to be the season for these types of things. And normally, Ella didn't mind the busyness. But for some reason, with the soldier included in her assignment, she found herself wanting to designate an increased share of attention his way. *As part of the war effort.*

Still, when lunchtime rolled around and she saw Benjamin's struggling with his soup, Ella hurried to finish the task she was involved in and made her way to his bedside. "Can I help with that," she asked, gentle on approach.

Benjamin stopped what he was doing, spoon pausing in route, little if any liquid left on the utensil. He looked frustrated. His eyes were still shut. "Suite yourself," he sighed. "Though I don't know how anything's going to help at this point."

Once again, Ella's heart filled with compassion. Some things seemed so unfair. From what she'd seen of her patient so far, it was clear that he'd been at one time a strapping young man. Now she was sure he felt like nothing more than an invalid. She pulled up a chair. "Here...let me," she said, taking the spoon from his hand.

It was clear that he felt uncomfortable. And for a moment Ella questioned her course. Still, she proceeded forward and began scooping the vegetable beef soup from bowl to mouth. The first two spoonfuls felt awkward. But she steeled her resolve. "Nutrition is key to getting on the mend, you know." Ella ignored the idea that she and the patient were so close in age. She couldn't be intimidated if she was going to be of help. And that was what her profession was all about, after all—helping. "We've got to do our best to get you on the track to feeling better. So, if this is the way we have to do things for a while...so be it, Benji."

The second Ella said the word, she realized her mistake. On her off times from the hospital, she had begun to think of the soldier-patient as *Benji* in her mind. It was a pet nickname of sorts. But to refer to him by that familiarity in person, it felt like crossing some sort of professional line. "I mean, Ben—" she started to correct. But out of nowhere her patient began to laugh.

"Benji" he chortled, merriment coming up from his throat. "Haven't heard that one much." Ella felt horrified, her cheeks rapidly heating up. "But, no...I actually like it," he continued, sensing her reserve. "It kind of works." Another bout of laughter, then, "Benji," he reiterated again, as if to see how the word sounded coming out of his mouth.

"How about we keep eating," Ella interjected, trying to cover her embarrassment. She brought up another spoonful and Benjamin took it down easily, still half smiling through leftover laughter. The moment though—it had helped to ease the tension surrounding the meal. Soon, Ella, too, lightened up and soon they began joking back and forth. Things felt good between them. As good as things could feel under the present circumstances. After the soup, she set the rest of his lunch up in a way that he could reach for things on his own. But instead of leaving to let him eat in solitude, she stayed, keeping him company by striking up blithe conversation, taking the load off all that he was having to endure. And spending far more time with him than she ever planned.

Dear Thomas,

Few were the moments. Far reaching are the memories. Forever are the markings of regret.

~E.

CHAPTER 4

Ella was busying herself around the house on Maple Street. Her parents were due to be home soon from work; her mom from Woolworth and her dad from the electric company on Ashmun. When they arrived, there were certain expectations—like dinner would be started. And the mess around her father's easy chair would be cleaned from the night prior: empty glasses that stank of stale liquor, cigarette butts, newspapers, all magically whisked away, only to resurrect themselves over the next several hours of the evening.

Peeling potatoes in the kitchen, she heard the first of the voices materialize, doors—entry, then porch—slamming in echo. "Grace, where are my ga-damn slippers?"

Ella knew her mom wasn't there yet to answer the demand, it was still a few minutes too early. Setting down the potato peeler, Ella set out toward the living room. "*Sitting directly beside your chair,*" she was about to tell her father, when her mom, right on que, walked through the door, letting in a waft of cold air.

"Grace...my slippers, I said," Melvin repeated.

With a face void of emotion, Grace pointed to the magazine rack that sat next to his favorite lounger. As more often than not was the case, his slippers were peeking out from the bottom. Of course, Grace hadn't heard Melvin the first time he'd made the demand, because she hadn't even made it inside the house yet. But what was the point of arguing. In silence, she set down her things and made her way into the kitchen.

"Potatoes are almost peeled," Ella called over her shoulder. "And I've started on the salmon loaf."

Her mom nodded, sadness emanating from her eyes. So much unhappiness—surrounding all of them. Would they ever stop being downtrodden?

In the other room, Ella could hear her dad grumbling, the newspaper crinkling between his fingers. Odds were, there was already a glass of something sitting on the end table beside his chair. One of several more that would appear over the next few hours. "Yeah, yeah, yeah…Coast Guard patrolling the Locks," he mumbled. "As if we don't know that already. Between them and the Army setting up in town, sending all their damn soldiers, can't get around anywhere these days."

Ella braced herself. The tirade was starting up again. Hopefully it wouldn't escalate. There was always a possibility that the rant would reverse itself and peter out. Holding her breath, she glanced over at her mom. But as usual, Grace's face offered up no expression.

Ella disliked the continual complaining—always on the same topic. She understood the aversion toward the Locks. And yet now that they were officially at war, wasn't it time to set certain feelings aside for the good of all? Sure, there were more soldiers in town. Yes, the Locks were being closely guarded. But it was no secret that with the war going on, the call for steel had increased and Locks were an intricate part of the demand. The Soo was on the main route for shipping. After the depression, much cargo had already been going through the Locks. But now, the need had increased and would continue to do so while the nation was in its current state.

The following day was the weekend and though Ella had the shift off, she found her thoughts drifting—vacillating between thankfulness that her father hadn't gotten out of control on the night prior, and switching gears toward the hospital, wondering how her soldier-patient was doing. How were his eyes? Was he getting any stronger? Was he eating okay?

Christmas was only a few days away, and though things would be simpler this year with all the rations going on, Ella had decided to do a little decorating around the house—for Chance's sake. Having run the idea by her parents and getting little more than a grunt in response, she had taken their reaction as an approval and proceeded forward. Eliciting Chance's assistance, they began digging out boxes from years prior, Ella trying to concentrate on the interaction with her brother and not what might be going on at the hospital. Though in-spite-of her efforts, at times, she would find herself digressing—thoughts wandering back to ward-four.

"Look at the red bells I found," Chance said, dangling two glittering ornaments in the air. They had just dug into the second box, and Ella was untangling a string of lights.

"So, you did." Ella smiled. She knew most of the bells they owned were silver, only a few, red. She could tell it made him happy to have unearthed the coveted pair. It was like winning a prize. Secured in each fist, Chance began zooming the bells through the air as if they were planes, zipping, soaring, swooping.

Ella tried not to laugh. "Easy does it there, Ace. We don't want to break those, or we'll have no red ones at all. Only the silver left."

Chance landed the planes on the coffee table runway. "Well, we don't want *only* silver. That would be boring." He pulled the planes up at the last second as they ran into a pile of newspapers.

Ella held her breath in hopes the bells were still in one piece. But Chance was gathering them up again, safely in his grasp, away from the collateral damage. It seemed they were still intact. She picked up a piece of shimmering garland from the box perched at her feet. It was one of the few pieces of garland they owned. The rest had gone thread bare. "How about we attach your red bells to this and hang them on the wall," she said. "The silver ones we can put on the tree."

"Okay," Chance answered, bounding off the floor. He ran over to the coal stove in the far corner of the room. "How about here?" He held the bells up next to the smokestack.

Ella followed his movement with her eyes, nose crinkling as she watched. "Sorry, Ace…your planes would overheat and burn up if we hung them there."

"But…but that is where Santa will be…when he comes down. In the chimney? I want the bells to be close to him when he comes inside the house."

Disappointment fluttered across Chance's face. Clearly, he'd acquired an instant liking for the red bells. How quickly attachments could form with nine-year-old boys. Ella lifted her brow, a solution coming to her. "You know…I think that's a great idea…wanting them next to the chimney for Santa's arrival. But how about we change it up a bit…move them over somewhat…for safety's sake. I'll tell you what I'll do. I'll cut the garland in half and then we'll have a piece to string each bell on. You can hang a bell on either side. Then they'll flank the stove."

"Flank?" Chance lifted his eyes in question. It was as if that was the only word he had heard. A short explanation later, he seemed mostly appeased and they went about making the necessary adjustments to hang the ornaments safely in place.

After that, they strung together popcorn and cranberries to hang on the new synthetic tree that their mom had purchased at Woolworth. This year there'd be no smells of pine or spruce filling up the living area. Due to lack of manpower for cutting and shipping, fresh trees were in short supply around the country. But artificial ones were going at a good price, so they were doable, and though lacking for the holiday in the homey traditional aromas, they were the next best thing.

Chance and Ella had just finished putting the last silver bell on the tree when their parents padded into the room, awake for the day. For a quick moment, Ella found herself wishing that they would experience some type of sentimental emotion as they noticed all the decorations in place. Some type of peace and hope of the season. A nostalgic reckoning. But nothing of the sort was reflected in their eyes, save a flicker of interest at seeing Chance bounding with excitement.

It was too much to ask, she supposed.

Later in the afternoon, after Chance had been out sledding with his pal, Kip, for the better part of an hour, he came inside, chunks of snow falling from his outer-layerings, an accumulation from the make-shift snow-mound they'd been using at the end of the block. "Back out to the front porch," Ella heard her father say.

"But…but—" Chance began backing up, wedging himself between the open door which led to the porch. Cold wafts of air poured into the room while he stood only partially blocking the artic chill that was steadily creeping between his legs. The temperature felt like sub-zero. It made Ella think of the soldiers that were being sent into the area for the sole purpose of training in these types of frigid temperatures. In-order-to be better geared for extreme weather conditions when transferring post to Northern Europe—another place the magnitude of the war was being fought—they were first sent to Soo, Michigan, to prepare. *The current cold snap would certainly be accommodating for what was needed,* she thought.

Chance began fumbling with the thickness of his mittens and lost his hold on the doorknob. It started to swing further open, and another burst of cold air found its way in. With quick reflexes, he pulled it back. "I wanted to ask," he continued, voice aloft, while working to keep a tight grip on the door. "Kip wants to…I want to go fishing. Ice fishing."

"No!"

The entirety of the room turned toward Melvin.

His voice was adamant, echoing loudly across the walls. There'd be no discussion. Ella could see him eying the liquor cabinet even as he gave the one-word answer.

"Why? Please? We'd be careful. Kip knows a good place to go. It's not *that* cold."

Not that cold, Ella coughed in question.

"My answer is final." Melvin continued to look the other way.

Chance's voice rose in decibel. "I just don't see why though. Kip is allowed to go." A foot stomp followed. Right then, Grace walked in from the kitchen, she was shaking her head, alarm mixed with sadness glistening in her eyes.

"Listen to your father, Chance," she said, looking pointedly at her son.

But Chance wasn't giving up. He was used to getting his own way. Why would this time be any different? On a sudden change of strategy, he trained his gaze on Ella. "How about you, El? You could take us. That way we wouldn't be going alone and—"

Ella's heart picked up in tempo. *Don't look at me,* she thought. A panicky feeling swept through her veins. Immediately her thoughts went to Thomas. Just a year her junior, everything they did—they did together. As playmates. As siblings. For the first eight years of her life. But having Chance around was a different sort of relationship. More often than not, it seemed she played a parental role with him. But not that day. She wasn't going to have this put on her. The idea of it all made her want to run a million miles away. How she wished she would have picked up an extra weekend shift at the hospital after all. Escaping to work would have been the easy choice here.

But that wouldn't solve anything, really. And she knew it. Ella waited for her parents to make the next move in the conversation. Take the heat off her back. But the seconds were ticking away in silence. Chance was looking hopeful in her direction. And Melvin and Grace, it seemed, were receding into themselves—her dad shifting his position in the easy chair. No doubt headed to the bureau next, in search of a new glass to house his liquor for the day.

Ella stiffened her shoulders. "I'm not going out in this frigid weather," she eventually declared, even as she watched Chance's face begin to fall. "But,"she continued, an idea coming to her. "How about I take you and Kip to Pullar Stadium later for open skating?"

Chance seemed to stir this idea around in his head while Ella held her breath. "Okay…yeah, okay," he eventually said, his face brightening somewhat. "I'll go ask Kip." And with that, he turned to make his way back through the porch and out the front door, leaving the leftover iciness of the winter to swirl in in his wake.

Turning to look in her parent's direction, Ella sighed in relief, but found both were averting their gaze.

CHAPTER 5

Ella had a spring in her step the next time she made her way into War Memorial Hospital, the snow falling powder soft around her shoulders, bits of white catching on the strands of her hair, as she sifted through the accumulation on the sidewalk that led to the front entryway door. It was Christmas day. And although under most circumstances she'd rather spend the holiday at home on Maple Street, somehow it felt like the right thing to do, going to work—being at the hospital, caring for the sick, those that were unfortunate enough to have to spend time away from family. And besides, if she were being honest, the idea of seeing the soldier, Benjamin, on such a special day, was adding to her excitement. She could only assume, considering the state of his condition on her last shift, that he'd still be registered as a patient again that day.

The hospital seemed a little more alive as Ella made her way down the corridors, in search of her assignment for the day. A little merrier. A little more festive. Strings of garland were adorning the walls, dug out of storage from years past. And there was a good-sized artificial tree set up in the cafeteria. Lillian breezed past her in route to the nursing desk, which was central to their hallway. "Merry Christmas," she called while lifting off her scarf.

"Merry Christmas to you," Ella said in return.

After discarding winter coverings and fastening their nursing caps in place, the pair met back up at the nursing desk in front of ward-four. "Was Santa good to you this year," Lillian asked as they browsed through their perspective list of patients. "Or have you been more naughty than nice?"

Ella chuckled. "Well, that depends on how you look at things… wouldn't you say?" She thought of her stocking that hung at home on a hook beside the coal stove. With all the rations that were in place this year, she couldn't imagine it would be filled with too many delectables. But that was okay. Doing without. It was all part of the war effort. It was the least she could do. Besides, before leaving the house for work, she had noticed a scented bar of soap peeking from the top—and that seemed exciting enough. She'd take a look at what else the stocking contained later, after her shift. She turned to Lillian. "What about you? Did you receive anything special?"

"A pair of gloves. Of course, you could call those more of a necessity. My old ones were thread bare." Lillian leaned over to look at the paper in Ella's hand "Let's see…if I'm right in my assumptions after looking at my assignment, I do believe you got another Christmas present today as well."

Ella shot Lillian a questioning look. "Is that right? How so?"

"Well, he's not on my list…so I assume he's on yours."

Ella's heart unwittingly picked up in tempo. "I don't know what you are referring to but—"

"Oh, but I think you do…the soldier, he's assigned into your care today…and if I'm right, I assume that makes you plenty happy. Merry Christmas."

Ella opened her mouth to argue and then shut it as Lillian began speaking again. She could feel a flush forming across her cheekbones.

"Besides, want to know a little secret from a nosey elf? He's been asking about you. *When does nurse Ella work again?* says he. So there. You are welcome."

Ella tried to contain her excitement. *He'd been asking about her?* But that meant nothing really. He most likely appreciated the care she had given him during her past shifts. But Lillian was right about one thing—he *was* listed on her assignment that day. So that was nice. She had taken the time to make token gifts for those that would be in her care. Twigs of holly bound with twine so that they could hang as ornaments. It was the least she could do for the sick stuck in the hospital on Christmas. She'd be more than happy to give one to Benjamin, hopefully brightening his day, if only a tiny bit.

Although if he couldn't see—

Ella began the care of her patients at the opposite end of the ward from Benjamin's bed, starting with those that had pain and needed immediate attention. Or simply those who were awake. She could see that Benjamin was still fast asleep. *Merry Christmas*, she thought, watching his chest rise and fall beneath a crisp white sheet, while making her initial walk-through. Take all the rest you need.

By the time she got back to him, he was sitting up in bed eating breakfast seemingly with very little trouble. Upon her approach, he looked up from his plate. Immediately his blue eyes came to light. It took a few seconds of gathering composure for the significance of what was playing out in front of her to register. "You can see," she exclaimed as it finally hit her.

He chuckled. "That I can…and truly, right now, for that I am very happy."

Ella experienced a bout of goosebumps. Was Benjamin trying to flirt? Surely not. Wiping the notion away, she took his statement as face value. *Of course, he would be happy to see again.* Who *wouldn't*? Still, she found herself reaching for her hair, tucking back a strand in self-conscious effort. "Well, I'm so happy for you too. When did this come about? Have the flashes gone away then?" A rush of questions swept through her mind. Frankly, his condition was a bit boggling.

Benjamin tried to hide the flicker of disappointment that crossed over his face by offering a smile. "Not completely. I mean…today, right now…yes. But then I've had other times over the past few days where the symptoms have gone away…and then come back, afterwards."

"Well, they're gone now…so that's good." Ella was careful to keep the concern from her voice. "Let's focus on that." She held up the holly knitted in twine. "Merry Christmas," she said.

Benjamin's face came alite in such a way, that her stomach caught in her throat. In that moment, despite the fading bruises and lacerations, it became evident to her just how handsome he was. Never before had the realization of it hit her in such a way. The way his bangs swept to the side, hanging over his brow, the military cut having grown out over the past weeks of his injury. His chin square, mouth perfectly shaped. And of course, his eyes.

Ella felt caught in a spell and knew she had to snap out of it. Biting her lip, she shook her head, if only slightly. But it was just enough.

Benjamin took the holly from her hand. "Merry Christmas to you. And thank you for this. It was thoughtful. You sure know how to cheer a fella up." *And there it was—the truth between them—she was just a nurse trying to cheer her patient up.*

"Certainly. And it's nice to see you doing well with your breakfast."

"You mean… and not spilling it all over the place because I can't see what I'm doing one damn bit?"

Ella paused. She knew the subject matter was sensitive. How could it *not* be? And yet, it seemed she'd heard an element of jest in Benjamin's voice just then. "Yes…just that," she answered, taking a chance in being playful back, hoping to lighten the mood for a wounded soldier stuck in the hospital on Christmas day. Yet a part of her was guarded—she didn't want to add insult to injury. But the smile Benjamin gave back made her relax fully. She had made the right call.

"It's not only your sight, though. You look stronger too. Like you are doing better…all around." She was switching back to nurse mode. Making an assessment. Even his coloring was improving, the pinkness of the cheeks giving off a brighter hue.

Benjamin looked away. Though only for a second. It was apparent to Ella in that flicker of time there was some thought he was concealing—a memory he wished to bury. *Was he okay then—really?* Her thoughts went to Pearl Harbor. Surely that event wasn't something easily erased from the mind.

When he looked back up though, a grin was forming on his lips and Ella was set at ease. "Maybe I owe it to Christmas then. The sudden improvement. A fella can't stay down on Christmas, can he?" He pointed to his eyes. "Even these peepers…they have decided to cooperate for the moment. Apparently, they are determined to appreciate all-the-day is going to bring."

Ella laughed, an idea coming to her. If it was the Christmas ambience that was working in helping to lift the spirit and heal, then she would go with the plan that was formulating in her mind. "You know…speaking of Christmas, this afternoon there will be caroling around the tree in the cafeteria. How would you like to go? It's going to be very festive. And on Christmas day, we could all use a little festiveness."

Within seconds, Benjamin's face became solemn. Pale even. "No, I don't think—"

But Ella wouldn't have it. "Have you been out of this bed yet?"

"No, I—"

"Well, you should have…you should be…getting up…it's time."

"But I can't even—"

"We don't know for sure what you can and can't do, really. But staying in this bed…you're never going to find out. Besides, I wasn't talking about walking into the cafeteria. We can gather some orderlies… help you slide into a chair. Wheel you in. It would be a start."

But Benjamin wasn't prepared to commit. "We'll see," he said as he looked away.

When it was time for caroling later in the day, Ella stopped into the cafeteria after checking on a patient who'd had an emergency appendectomy the night before. A child of ten, who, though still drowsy from the operation, had moments of lucidity, and knew they were missing out on Christmas at home. Ella had spent much of her time at bedside, tending to not only physical needs, but emotional as well. A lonely young lad who only wanted to have the comfort of the familiar. His family. His home. It made her think of Chance, her brother who was close to the same age.

And then, of course, Thomas.

The first thing Ella noticed when she rounded the corner to the cafeteria, was the sizable group that had gathered to take part in the Christmas festivities. That, along with the tree, central to the room, decorated in shimmering gold bulbs and clusters of red berries, a feathery angel adorning the top. The picture it presented was both welcoming and festive. And though this year's tree wasn't as large as the previous fresh cut pines, situated on a stool, it filled sightlines from every part of the room. And that felt merry enough.

But as Ella began to peruse the crowd congregated in the room, she had to give credence to the foray of nerves that were flickering through her veins. All due to one, Benjamin, her soldier-patient. In the back of her mind, she had the feeling that he wouldn't show up for the occasion.

Although he had seemed willing enough to participate in the joviality of the holiday as she interacted with him throughout the shift, she could sense the resistance that was reflected in his eyes when it came to the idea of getting out of his hospital bed later in the day. He just wasn't there yet. He wasn't ready to get tossed and shuffled around by a pair of burley men, when only weeks before he-himself had been the one filled with strength and vitality.

If only he could realize that in order to gain this part of himself back, he was going to have to start somewhere and participate.

That's why Ella had instructed the orderlies to show up at his bedside no later than 3 p.m.

But then she felt guilt—was she pushing too far? *Who knew if walking again was even a possibility?*

Staving away jitters while glancing around, Ella was in the process of mentally preparing herself to go back and give one more pep-talk, when she spied a handsome young man sitting erect in a wooden wheelchair, half-way across the room. For a split second, she almost didn't recognize the face that was staring up at the tree, seemingly studying the lights as they reflected from the golden bulbs. Nor the broadness of the shoulders. The strength of the chest.

He'd come.

Her patient, Benjamin, had gotten out of that stupid hospital bed and came to the Christmas festivities after all!

Ella couldn't help the joyous feeling that zipped through her heart. Nor the smile that lit up her face. She wanted to run across the room— *and what*—hug him? She took a calming breath in order to settle herself.

Just then, Benjamin turned, and their eyes met. *You came*, she told him with her smile. *So proud of you.* Benjamin, too, seemed happy to be there—or at the very least contented, possibly relieved. Although it took a second or two for a certain glimpse of sadness—or something else unreadable—to disappear from his expression. The same one that had been, moments before, staring at the reflection of the bulbs.

Their gaze held for a moment longer but was soon interrupted by the sounds of music filling the room.

Hark the Harold Angels Sing.

Patients and workers alike, along with some family members, began to lift their voices in chorus. The sound, though not particularly grand, spoke of sentimental feelings from Christmas past. Of holiday nostalgia. It was a sweeping moment in time when the spirit of the song made one forget about all else. And to the unfortunate stuck in the hospital, that alone was a blessing.

Other selections followed: *Silent Night. Deck the Halls.*

Ella sang from her heart while taking in all who had gathered to participate in the make-do festivities, her eyes finally landing on the tree in the center of the room. She kept willing herself to not seek out Benjamin, where he was perched next to a group of mobile patients from ward-two. But a couple of times—or maybe more than a couple times—she couldn't stop herself from looking his way. And though not visually moving his lips in song, he seemed engaged in the moment. At ease in being there. It made her happy she had pushed the issue after all.

It was while *God Rest Ye Merry Gentlemen* was being sung that she took opportunity to sneak another glance. This time, as if feeling eyes on his face, Benjamin turned her way and their stare met. Suddenly, she felt exposed. First instinct was to avert her gaze. Act like she was just perusing the crowd. But something was stopping her from breaking eye-contact. Was it in the way he was looking at her? *How was he looking at her exactly?* Like there was something there between them? Maybe it was just the sentiment shared amid the setting of patient and caregiver. But why then, Ella wondered, was her skin heating up? Why did it feel like she was having a hard time catching her breath? Like the words of the song were getting stuck in her throat. Finally, Benjamin turned away, focusing on the tree instead.

Ella felt relieved.

And yet flustered. Like she had somehow lost control.

So, when her patient from bed-six asked to be wheeled back to the ward, she was all-too happy to oblige. By then, the carols were starting to dwindle down, soon the festivities would be over, though if she remembered correctly, there had been talk of punch and cookies following the singing. Still—for some reason, the escape felt welcome. She needed time to reset.

And reset, she did.

By the time she got around to checking on her patient in bed-one again later in the shift, he was already transferred over and tucked in by the orderlies, the mood surrounding the encounter of their prolonged stare fading into the past. Professionally, she could almost talk herself into that it never really happened. And yet the idea that he had gotten out of bed and sat up in a wheelchair, leaving the confines of the ward—that was nothing to be ignored.

For some reason the recent memory of it made Ella want to jump for joy.

"Benji!" Her voice was filled with animation as she approached the foot of his bed. She realized the verbal faux pas the second his name left her lips. But on her own time, in the back of her mind, that is how she had been continuing to refer to him—*as Benji*. It was an endearing term, and she knew it. Though somehow, she was unable to stop herself—if only in the privacy of her thoughts. But the slip ups—they were so embarrassing. It spoke of an intimacy that she hadn't wanted to advertise. Certainly not directly to her patient. "I mean—" Her voice stammered a little.

But the way Benjamin was looking at her—a little surprised and yet completely pleased at her choice of greeting—the words of explanation in getting his name wrong again evaporated into thin air. She could feel her cheeks heating up.

"You are so cute when you blush. Has anyone told you that?"

Benjamin was not going to let the moment go. Clearly, he was feeling the joviality of his recent accomplishment too. His eyes were all lit up. He was on top of his game. It was a side of him she hadn't opportunity to witness before. In her mind, Ella knew she needed to reel back the conversation—bring it back to a professional stance. But he was catching her off guard with this new persona. And besides, *she* was the one who had slipped up with the familiarity.

"Anyway…as I told you before, I like it when you call me Benji."

Ella lifted her brow—in question or cringe, she wasn't sure, as she continued to will the skin on her face to cool.

"In fact," Benjamin continued, "I'm going to ask that you refer to me as just that from now on. Deal?"

Ella didn't know what to say. On some level she was happy that this affection was something they could share between them, that they meant enough to each other to entrust a nick name when conversing. And yet, why did it feel like it was crossing some sort of line? Her first responsibility belonged to the professional demeanor she'd been called to. It wasn't as if she was dealing with a young child. Of course, then a pet name would fit in appropriately. But in-spite-of any misgivings on the matter, Ella found herself nodding her head in response to his request.

"Okay...Benji," she said in a tentative voice, trying out the sound of the name they'd agreed upon.

Benji—*as he had somehow just become*—was beaming.

"Well, anyway," Ella said shaking her head as if to bypass the moment, skipping ahead to the original intent of the conversation. "You...you did it! I'm so happy you got up...out of this bed. It had to feel...didn't it feel good?"

"Hated the thought of it. But you are right...it was good to get out of this damn bed. Must have been the spirit of Christmas past that got me to do it. Or who knows... the present or future." He chuckled, then paused, looking right at Ella, his voice taking on a soft tone. "Or possibly, you."

Ella swallowed. Attempted to clear her throat. "Well, it was the perfect day for it to happen," she said. Her head felt like it was spinning. Again, she fought the warmth that was trying to return to her cheeks. "It was nice to be gathered around the tree...singing. And it was leaps and bounds for you. I'd like to think it will be something to build on... that you'll keep getting stronger. That it will only get better from here."

At this, Benji looked away, the light in his eyes disappearing marginally. Ella felt the alarm. Possibly, she'd opened her mouth too far. Said too much. She should have taken residence in the celebratory posture they were sharing. Not pushed toward future occurrences. It was enough that he had done what he'd done that afternoon. Maybe it was too much for him to look toward the future. He might be someone who only faced one day at a time.

"But that's nothing to worry about for now," she clarified. "You did what you did, and it was swell seeing you out there. Did you get any of the cookies and punch they were offering by the way?"

Benji looked up, the hint of a grin forming on his lips. "Yeah...the cookies and punch. I had some. You missed it. I went on a real bender after you left."

Ella chuckled at the sarcasm in his tone, happy that the mood was shifting away from the spiraling descent of the moment before. But in the back of her mind, she was filing away something else that he'd said. *After you left.* So, he'd noticed her leaving the cafeteria, then. For some reason that made her feel warm inside. Made her want to stay. Pull up a chair and talk for the remainder of her shift. But there were other patient's needs. Tasks that needed completing before she punched the clock in the up-coming hour. Still, it was hard to pull herself away. She found herself lingering at his bedside making small talk, reveling in the smile that eventually made its return full bore.

Too soon though, she felt a sense of responsibility tug at her. Glancing at her wristwatch, Ella jumped out of the relaxed position she was holding against the tray table next to his bed. After explaining the need to see the others in her care, they said their goodbyes and wished each other *Merry Christmas* for the second time during the space of her shift. All seemed perfect. Considering the circumstances, it had been a splendid day. It was while she was preparing to leave though, that Ella felt an intense gaze coming at her. Something in the air had shifted. Benji's demeanor had changed. It was in the way he was studying her. It wasn't the sort of look that had made her blush in the oh-so-recent past. The I've-captured-your-eye, there-is-something-between-us type of stare that got her right down to the roots on her scalp. This was something else. A new awareness.

A premonition.

Benji shook his head slightly. "I don't know what it is," he said slowly, as if he was giving an idea much thought. "But just now...just then, while you were standing there...there was something about you... something that looked so familiar."

Dear Thomas,

The culpability of your absence rests in everything I see,
resides inside of me.

~E.

CHAPTER 6

Siobhan lived in a little brown shingled house north of Easterday hill, right next to Fort Brady—as was so happily reported to the soldiers she encountered on the streets. And though the house, itself, was rather tiny, the garage with an efficiency apartment above, was the source of the family's pride. Too hear the Alby's talk, they owned their own village. And it was true that the parcel the dwellings sat on was almost double the typical lot size around town. But as far as aesthetics went, it didn't come close to comparing with the fancier homes south of the hill. In fact, some might describe their property as borderline gauche, if not shabby.

That didn't stop Ella from enjoying visits to her friend's house, though. In fact, it was something she looked forward to very much. Time spent with Siobhan, was considered some of her better moments in life. Not to mention the atmosphere around the Alby home made up for what Ella's lacked—lively conversation, a tidy back porch free of liquor bottles piled up around the trashcan, a certain joyfulness in embracing day-to-day life minus the underlying sentiment of gloom.

Shortly after lunchtime, Ella had taken a local bus to visit her friend who had the weekend off from her job at Michigan Bell. Holed up in Siobhan's room—which consisted of barely enough space to fit a single mattress and a chest of drawers—they were sorting through some of the poems Siobhan had written in school. Silly as they tended to be, quite proud of her efforts, Siobhan had compiled them into a journal. And yet her tone was self-depreciating as she read each one aloud.

"Listen to this one." She held the page at an angle, as if to decipher the writing. "It is off the cob. It's called the Dead Hooper. *If you want to jive with me, it's copasetic. But if you don't move those pegs, it's going to*

48

be pathetic. If you can cut a rug, its killer diller. But if you're not knocking it out, you'll be worse than Mr. Miller."

Ella broke into laughter. "Oh Mr. Miller! That time he tried to show us how to dance in homeroom. What was it…the foxtrot?"

"Not sure…think it was more like the jive. But will we ever know?"

Both girls were laughing now, the journal hanging precariously in Siobhan's lap. She caught the spine just before it slipped off and fell to the floor.

"No," Ella answered, swallowing back more laughter. "We won't."

A few more poems were read. A few more chuckles shared between friends. Then, deciding on a change of scenery, they made plans to take their show on the road and head downtown to Portage Street, Siobhan promising to quote a few of her wittier works from memory while in route. Pulling on extra layers of outer wrappings to stave away the January cold, they stepped into the brisk air, making their way down a shoveled path that led past the garage on the corner of the Alby's lot.

They were almost to the garage, when Siobhan pointed to the window that faced out above the tan wooden roll-up door. The opening was barely wide enough to wedge a car and a half through its entry. "Did I tell you we might be getting a soldier?" She was looking at Ella with eyes that betrayed a certain excitement the lines of her mouth were hiding.

Ella crinkled her nose, momentarily confused. "Get a soldier," she reiterated in question.

"Yes," Siobhan answered, her voice growing in enthusiasm. "I'm not supposed to share the news yet because it isn't certain. But there is a good chance it will happen. You know with the large influx of soldiers… they are short on housing. They can't fit them all in the barracks at Fort Brady. Right now, they are putting them up in the Christopher Columbus Hall, the Union Carbide, the American Legion…even some gyms around town."

"Yes…I've heard." How could Ella have missed it, with her dad heatedly reporting the updates on a nightly basis?

"Well…we have the garage apartment. So why wouldn't we want to help out? Share the space for a soldier in need. It's the least we could do…offer a soldier a little comfort after all they are doing."

Ella thought of her soldier at the hospital, *Benji,* and tried not to chuckle, questioning whether she had been offering him the "comforts" a soldier deserves, or quite the opposite—by persisting to push him *out* of his comfort zone.

"Anyway," Siobhan continued. "Lots of people are stepping up around town to house a soldier. Give them a room of some sort. So why not us? We have the perfect spot, with our apartment and all."

Ella glanced at the window where Siobhan had been pointing earlier. "True…it does seem it would fit the bill. And besides, you are so close to the fort. It wouldn't take long for a soldier to walk back and forth. Would you get one or two?"

"Not sure." Siobhan's expression was growing more animated by the minute. She reached for Ella's coat sleeve and squeezed. "Oh El… it's so exciting. I can hardly stand it. Whoever it is…one or two, I hope at least one of them is a real dreamboat! How did I get so lucky getting this sort of chance?"

Ella laughed. "I hope luck turns out to be on your side then. But don't get ahead of yourself. Promise me you'll be careful…whatever happens. Whoever it turns out to be."

Siobhan turned away from the garage as they continued walking down the narrow snow-shoveled path that led to the street. "I'll be fine. I'll be careful. I always am," she said.

Navigating their way onto the streets that led to town, the girls told themselves they'd call for a cab or catch a bus if they found the winter air eventually too unbearable. In the mean-time, they kept walking, keeping themselves warm with jovial conversation. Making their way down Easterday hill, they passed by a house that had a pile of sandbags peeking out from the rear. *Anti-aircraft nests.* They were being set up around town. Some, as evidenced by this one, in civilian's backyards. Housed with artillery, they were used by soldiers, who, hunkering in the protective barricades, would watch for warplanes flying overhead, hoping to shoot one down before any real damage was done.

"We might get one of those too," Siobhan pointed into the backyard as they went by. "We've got the perfect place for it. Up on the hill."

Ella nodded, trying to peer through the tiny gaps in the layers of sandbags to see if this one was occupied. From her distance, she thought she saw what appeared to be an army green helmet moving around inside but wasn't sure. She'd heard that the nests could house five or six soldiers at one time. If this was the case, they were well hidden from obvious view, because she wasn't certain she could see any from her angle.

The girls kept walking, heading down Ashmun Street, visiting the store windows of the downtown sidewalks before they crossed over to Portage, where more shops and local businesses lined the narrow motorway. The Hotel Ojibway, sitting on the east corner with its tall brick exterior, blocked the northerly windchill for a few minutes, offering them a reprieve before they rounded the building toward the Locks. As they turned the corner, icy air coming off the waterway hit full force, bringing back their fight against the cold.

Pulling scarves up around pink cheekbones, they shivered while keeping a steady but slowing pace. At this rate, they'd be calling for a cab soon. Or possibly make for the nearest bus stop. They'd already covered a considerable distance on foot. Up ahead, was Locks Park. No longer accessible to pedestrians, it had been fenced off and guarded since the looming threat of war, voiding it from being the unrestricted the tourist attraction it once was.

But the nearer they got to the water, they could still see the layout of the St. Mary's River, along with certain activities being conducted, in-spite of the impeded view. Soldiers walking. Men working. Steam being used to remove ice from the sides of a lock.

They edged a little closer, and the profile of the international railroad crossing just above the shipping canal came into view, offering a frame to the Locks setting. Siobhan's eyes lifted toward the skyline.

"Ever think about just getting on train," she asked. "Head somewhere. Anywhere. See what's out there?"

Ella frowned in concentration as she followed Siobhan's line of vision to the framework of metal scaffolding. She could see the train cars moving in the distance as they lumbered across the bridge. Little rectangular cubes shuffling across the sky. Had she—thought of what Siobhan was proposing? Certainly, she'd contemplated what her life would look like had things been different for her family. If circumstances had played out more advantageously. Somedays—often, if she was honest—she thought of escaping. But that was what work was for, she supposed. And what she did for an occupation—helping people—it was rewarding, if not at times wearying. But getting worn out in and of itself was a form of escape. The more exhausted the mind—the less time for dwelling on anything, the past in particular. But had she thought of physically leaving town?

"No…not really," she said.

Looking over at Ella, Siobhan dropped her eyes from the horizon. "Really." The expression on her face, her tone of voice—it was as if she was surprised.

"Well don't looked so shocked." Ella started to smile in-spite-of the heavy thoughts she'd been sorting through moments before. "I just haven't that's all. And anyway…what about you? You…talking about wanting to leave…when not an hour before, all you could think about was how your new soldier is going to look…the one that might move into your garage apartment."

Siobhan let out a hardy chuckle. "You are right…I guess I'm not cooking with gas." She turned away from the ice-laden strip of water that trailed beneath the international railroad crossing. "I can hardly hop a train anytime soon…not when I might have a dream boat moving into the apartment…which, by the way, is a clear view from my bedroom window. Did you know that? Did you even realize that? Have I ever told you …oh yeah, do you remember the time—?

Ell nodded. "Yes…I remember," she said, a look passing between friends. More laughter followed.

"Well anyhow," Siobhan cleared her throat. Her eyes began to sparkle. I hope we get our soldier…or two…soon. I mean, really, it could happen any day now. Or any time, in fact. Come to think of it…there could be one waiting for me when we get back home from our walk."

Ella lifted her brow, her mouth forming into an *O* of surprise. But she supposed Siobhan was right. *Anything was possible.* The changes around them seemed to be occurring quick as a flash anymore.

"I say." Siobhan looped her arm through Ella's coat sleeve. "Let's call for a cab and head there now."

CHAPTER 7

The next shift at the hospital, Ella strolled in with a cheery cadence to her step, excitement coursing through her veins at the thought of seeing the soldier-patient. *Benji*-as he insisted on being called. Of course, she had been the one who had started the exchange of familiarity, so on all accounts the blame rested with her. Not that she wore any blame. If anything, the idea that they shared a pet name between them brought a blush to her cheeks. Made her heart flutter in weird ways. Made her feel like they shared some type of special bond. And if being fully honest, she knew it was more than a nurse-to-patient connection. There was something she was feeling toward him that could be catalogued in the romantic category. *There-she had admitted it!* This thought prompted her to check her professional stance as a nurse. And at the same time. made her feel very alive. Often the latter winning out in her daydreams as well as in her actions. *Was that it then*, she wondered—the idea of forbidden fruit with professionalism gone awry that stirred all these new feelings inside of her?

But as she made her way down the hallways in route to her nursing station, another thought hit her full bore. Confirming the idea that this was something more. *What if—maybe Benji wouldn't be there at all that day*! The last time she had interacted with him—on Christmas—he had made so much progress. It was such a milestone, him getting out of bed. Maybe he had embraced the advancement whole heartedly, realizing that the possibility of getting back to his old self lingered at his fingertips. Maybe he had progressed by leaps and bounds over the course of days that followed.

And had since been released from the hospital and sent home.

The idea caused Ella to go still in her tracks. Heart sinking, she raised a hand to her throat, then took in a large breath. She was being ridiculous. This is how things played out at the hospital. Patients got better—they went home. Stirring back into motion, she proceeded forward again, though at a more sluggish gate. Then, nearing the nursing station, she regained her earlier momentum and fairly flew in to take a look at her assignment.

As her eyes scanned through the list of names, the print nearly jumped off the page. Ward-four, bed-one, Benjamin M.

He was still there!

Ella worked to contain the happy feeling that danced around in her chest as she began preparing for her day of work on the floor. Several patients had been assigned into her care—an infected wound, two pneumonias, a kidney infection, among others. But as she walked through the doors of the ward, she could feel herself being pulled to the bed at the far end of the room. *Was he asleep? Awake for the day?* She forced her thoughts away—back into nurse mode—and began checking, one by one on the others, making sure they were all in good stead.

Time passed, and with initial assessments complete, she began making her way between the long rows of metal beds, heading toward the patient that had secured a place at the back of her mind. She couldn't *wait* to see what progress he had made since she had last seen him. It had given her such a sense of satisfaction to see him up out of his bed, participating more fully with life. She knew it had lifted his spirits as well. She had witnessed the transformation in his eyes. She was so happy for him.

"Hello there…Benji," She approached his bed. The *Benji* part was added with incertitude. She could see that he was awake and sitting upright. Not meaning to, her words had come out in a soft tone—loaded with too much meaning.

But not before Benji's head shot in her direction. "Ella," he said. "It's you."

She chuckled a little. "Yep…it's me." She waited for a return of laughter to reach her ears. But it never came. Maybe, then a smile—some form of happiness at her arrival. Or at life in general. But the eyes she saw looking up at her appeared dull, lips downturned. And the movements of his head—they seemed—it appeared as if he were searching for something.

The exact location of her face!

He wasn't able to see!

Ella sucked in a breath. How could this be? The last time she had been with him—?

"It's a mighty fine after party isn't it doll?" Benji's voice was loaded with cynicism. And something else too. Pain, Ella decided. Although she was sure it was something he was attempting to mask.

"Meaning?"

Benji huffed. "Meaning? Meaning I can't see a damn thing… once again. These peepers are useless. I might as well stay blind on a permanent basis. At least that way a fella doesn't build up hope."

"When?" Ella took a hesitant step forward, inching her way closer, like a pedestrian toward a wounded animal. "When did this happen?"

Benji turned away. "Yesterday."

"I'm sorry…I don't understand either. Have you…have you spoken with anyone yet…the doctors? Do they know?

Benji nodded his head one time. "A Doc came by earlier this morning. I said something." His voice faded away.

The air was thick with discomfort, leaving Ella ill at ease. A fast turnabout from the shift prior where she and Benji had experienced so much positive interaction together. She fought to keep her spirits from taking a fast dive. In knee-jerk reaction, she did the one thing that would hopefully save the moment.

Switched into nurse mode.

It would solve nothing to sink into melancholy with Benji. Wouldn't help the situation. She was taking it all to heart, making it personal. *It was time to stop.* She needed to think of him as a patient—nothing more.

"Do they have any answers yet?"

Benji shook his head.

"Well, they'll be looking for solutions…exploring all options, I'm sure. Don't…don't give up hope." She began cleaning off the bedside tray, at the same time putting herself in closer proximity. Anything to keep herself busy—yet let him know she was nearby. "Meanwhile," she said picking up a water pitcher, shuffling it to the side of the table with the intention of filling it when she left. "Let's get some breakfast for you. What will hit the spot this morning? Porridge? Eggs? Dry Cereal? You name it...I'll have it here in a jiffy,"

Benji scrunched his nose and for a few moments Ella thought that was all the response she was going to get. "Honestly," he eventually muttered, still not looking her way. "That all sounds crummy. Not that hungry this morning, I guess. In fact—" Sliding down in the bed, he pulled the covers up to his chin. "I think I'll get some more shut eye. I doubt if it's even light outside yet."

Ella felt a sadness well up in her chest. This was not the Benji she had hopes of seeing that morning. "Okay," she breathed. "Yeah...okay." There was no point in trying to interact with him further. Let him sleep. Or lay there. Or whatever it was he wanted to do. He obviously needed time to regroup. If regrouping was even possible. Ella felt his discouragement. Slowly, she began her retreat from the bedside—he silent under the covers, listening for the sound of her footfalls as she walked away.

An hour and a half later, she ordered two slices of toast to be brought to his bed-tray along with a dollop of his favorite jam. A gift from a local during times of rationing. It would be hard, but she couldn't let him slip away from participating with the routines of the day that easily, it had been decided in her mind.

Ella was busy tending to patients when Benji's tray was delivered, but she couldn't help but peek over in hopes of catching his response. Did she realize she had been the one who had ordered it for him? He had raved about the jam on more than one occasion, knowing full-well it was a rare treat. Would he assume that it had been her sending it to him?

She glanced one time, then two. Three. But the mound of covers remained unmoving. Staving away disappointment, she fought with herself over the idea of marching across the room and giving him a little shake. Or a big one. Instead, swallowing down ire, she continued on with the needs of those in her care. By the time she thought to peruse the ward again, she was pleasantly surprised to find him awake, sitting upright, putting bites of toast toward his mouth. A flicker of hope found its way into her veins. It was something at least. A start.

But hope waivered, when mid-morning, Ella sent orderlies to help him get out-of-bed, just as he had done on Christmas. She was counting on the idea that he wouldn't object to the plan, wouldn't let lack of eyesight hold him back from the task of getting up and getting stronger.

The refusal, though, was adamant—with no room for discussion. Ella could hear the contention coming from several beds away.

She considered going over to see what might be done to help but realized at that point there was no use. Simply put, he was having a bad day. A falling-off from Christmas day. Better to not push too far. But why the decline in condition? Why the regression? It was a perplexing, troublesome notion. And obviously, with good reason, one that was bothering Benji too. Fighting melancholy over the situation, Ella continued about her day, completing tasks, taking the sentiment with her into the lunch hour.

After swallowing the last few bites of her bologna sandwich, she stood up from the table in the breakroom and washed her hands over the basin in the corner. Drying them with a towel, she smoothed out her nursing pinafore. In an attempt to put off discouragements of what might unfold over the remaining hours of the afternoon, she made her way into the hallway that led back to her floor.

She had just passed the elevator bay and was in fast route to the corridor which led to the nursing desk in front of her ward, when she heard Dr. Northcott's voice coming from an approaching inlet. An idea coming to her, she thought to hurry her steps so she might catch him and ask more about the patient in bed-one's condition. Would the blindness reverse itself? Or was he on a downward decline? And why the back and forth? She had been so hopeful for him.

Nearing the inlet, the seriousness in Dr. Northcott's tone made Ella take pause. Clearly, he was in the middle of a discussion. What was more—with Dr. Farr. A specialist in dealing with neurological conditions, who sometimes travelled to the hospital. Something about the phrases they were using, certain terminology, caused her to wonder who it was they were discussing? *Could it be Benji?*

Something inside made her say *yes.*

The sensible side of her brain told her should just keep going and make it a point to catch up with Dr. Northcott at a different time in the near future. Clearly, this symposium was meant to be a private venture. And yet she had so much invested in their soldier-patient—as a caregiver, and now as a comrade of sorts. She wanted to know what was going on. *Had* to know.

"Since Pearl Harbor—" she heard Dr. Northcott say.

Ella took in a breath. Held it tightly in her lungs. She was right. She knew it. They *were* discussing Benji.

"That is my assessment," Dr. Farr answered. "After examining him, talking with him on more than two appointments, the discrepancy between the physical exams have a slim margin. His reaction times are very consistent. Along with the tests that have been conducted. There are very few variances."

"And yet the outcomes can vary significantly on a day-to-day basis." Dr. Northcott's voice was thoughtful as he spoke.

Yes, significantly, thought Ella."

"Some days he can see with 20/20 vision. And the next, he can't see at all. Or if he can see minutely, it is only in a series of bright flashes. This being the case, due to the bothersomeness of the situation, he won't open his eyes at all...of course."

"Of course...it would be hard to blame him on that account."

Ella cringed, recalling Benji's description of the flashes.

"And then the weakness of the legs...I haven't quite determined, but I'm mostly certain it is following the same course. Only a few days ago he was making great strides in strength, coordination, and sensation. Standing, even."

Standing? Ella's eyes widened ever-so-slightly.

"In an upright position, feet firmly planted at bedside and with very little assistance. And yet now, once again on examination there is virtually no response from his lower limbs." Dr. Farr paused. Ella imagined him shaking his head in a discouraging manner.

"And your conclusion?" Dr. Northcott's voice was serious, low, muted. Ella found herself leaning forward, straining her ears toward the sound.

"My conclusion is that he is suffering some sort of strain from his experience at Pearl Harbor. More than physical though, it's some sort of mental strain. And even though the symptoms are manifesting as physical, they are really due to the experiential trauma that has a grip on his brain. Trauma from the attack while stationed in Hawaii. Somehow the mental disturbance he has suffered is causing him to be unable to move forward with his physical progress in healing. Or even if he does make some sort of progress, it is soon stifled by the mental strain of the memories and the regression manifests itself once more."

Dr. Northcott sighed. "I suppose...what you are saying it makes sense. As much sense as anything is making with the young soldier's condition. Although not typical to anything I have myself witnessed up to this date. And yet if this is the case...what are the recommendations then? How do you move forward with something like this?"

"Time."

Ella could hear the shuffling sound of papers being rearranged. As if they were being straightened and tucked away. As if treating Benji's situation strictly as a clinical concern—cut and dried with no room for hope in healing. *Folder sealed. Case closed.* She felt a swirl of nausea passing through her stomach. *This couldn't be it—end of story for the patient in bed-one.*

But Dr. Farr wasn't done. "Time...or possibly psychoanalysis. Revisiting the situation to work though the mental blocks that are preventing the physical healing needed to move forward. If that is even something that the patient is willing to participate in. Some aren't. They don't care to revisit the past and in in the process again suffer the pain of the trauma. It can be difficult to convince them that this is indeed the problem at hand. That they need to fix the mental in order to resolve the physical symptoms. And then there is the other possibility."

Another possibility?

"The possibility of brute determination. The sheer will of getting better. Focusing all the mental effort on pushing past the pain of it all and *just doing it, dammit!* There are those that beat the ailment with this type of psychological attitude. But it takes a lot of encouragement and internal fortitude…and it of course, it doesn't always work. But I don't want to say it can't happen. It does happen…for some."

Returning back to the ward, Ella shuffled around thoughts regarding Dr. Farr's assessment and recommendations about Benji for the rest of the afternoon. So much to process. But although far-fetched from anything she had ever heard, it made sense in a way. How Benji seemed to make progress and then digress for no apparent reason. It seemed he was stuck and needed help moving forward. Had he received the news? Did he even know the doctors' thoughts on the matter? As of earlier that day at breakfast time—she had to believe, no. How would he react when he heard the report? Would he follow the counsel given for help in healing? Or would he resist all that was said to him and fall deeper into a depressed state? Which, in the end, would do nothing to help his condition—if what Dr. Farr was saying was correct in assumption.

Ella was still sorting through all she had overheard in the alcove when she approached Benji's bed later in the day. It was time to cleanse his wounds, still healing from the Pearl Harbor attack, in-order-to make sure infection didn't set in. Wheeling a cart of supplies and a metal basin of warm, soapy water, she announced her presence.

As she made her way to his side, he looked toward her, but not *at* her, and she felt her heart drop. Secretly, she had been hoping his eyesight would have returned by then. *That what Dr. Farr was saying wasn't true after all.*

But it was time to face reality square on from a medical perspective.

"Good afternoon, Benji," she said in a cheery voice. "I'm here to cleanse the wounds where your sutures were taken out." She eyed the more obvious markings that covered his face. The bruising around them was fading. The swelling receding as well. So much so, that sometimes she had to do a double take when she looked in his direction. It was almost as if his appearance was metamorphosing—changing him into another person completely.

Out of nowhere, a feeling of deja'vu settled over her psyche, rendering her speechless. For a few moments, quietness settled over the space between them.

"Hey…you there?" Benji's voice held a joking tenor to it, breaking the silence.

Ella shook her head. "Yeah…yeah, I'm here," she said.

"Okay swell…for a moment there I thought one of my wounds were scaring you. Like they had taken a turn for the worse. Gone hideous. Gangrene or something."

"No…no, not at all." Her words came out through forced cheer. "In fact, they seem to be healing rather nicely." *Now if only, you could heal as nicely on the inside,* she wanted to add. Instead, she picked up a cloth and dipped it into the basin of water. Benji heard the sound and settled into his bed, resting his head on the pillow.

Ella came closer and sat on the edge of his bed. "This shouldn't hurt," she reassured before reaching for the cheekbone under his left eye.

"No," Benji said in muted tones as the cloth touched his face. "No… it doesn't hurt."

Ella swallowed and forced away the fluttery feeling that was circulating through her stomach. Why did it feel like she was anything but a nurse at the moment? *How easily she transitioned from medical professional to floozy,* she thought. She couldn't even concentrate. At this rate, she was sure to make a mistake. Truth was—she was being a disgrace to her profession. The last thing she wanted to do was cause harm to any of her patients. And yet if she couldn't put her head in the right place—something along those line was bound to happen.

Focusing on these thoughts, Ella kept wiping with the soapy water she had prepared, all-the-while ignoring the shakiness in her hand. Afterward, she reached for a receptacle of antiseptic. Allowing time for his skin to dry, she began pouring liquid from the bottle onto a conglomeration of cotton balls. Benji laid there, still, while she made her preparations. *What was he thinking?* She continued maneuvering about. What would he think after hearing the news on his condition? *The assessment of Dr. Farr.* At that thought, a protective pang zipped through her insides. She felt it fiercely—the need to protect him from what was yet to come. A sudden yearning passed through her veins, and she fought the urge to glance over at him, knowing that he couldn't see the direction her eyes were landing. At the moment though, with all that was going on in her mind—the mix of strong emotions scattering around in her brain—it wouldn't be wise. To look.

And yet she couldn't seem to stop herself.

With him lying there—appearing so—so what? Vulnerable? Peaceful? *Handsome?*

A stray thought fluttered through her mind. Was that the bottom line? Was she attracted to her patient?

Did she find him handsome?

Ella sucked in a breath.

Benji stirred in bed. "What's going on," he asked, his voice quiet again.

She had paused for too long. Surely, he had detected the lack of movement at bedside. For what length of time had she been staring at him exactly?

"Nothing...I—" Gathering her thoughts, Ella cleared her throat. "I was just giving time for the area to dry...where I cleansed, I mean."

Benji narrowed his brow. "Okay...okay if you say so." This time there was no humor in his voice. Only inquisitiveness. Possibly a mix of confusion and concern. "Because you are starting to make me wonder if there really *is* something horrendous going on with my face."

Ella let out a smattering of laughter. Clearly, he had felt her looking then. She was being so dumb. She needed to watch herself. Draw on her professionalism. "No, really," she said, "you are healing nicely. There's nothing horrendous about it...about your face...at all."

Inside Ella cringed. She knew her thoughts were not being conveyed as intended. The more she talked, the worse things were starting to sound. She grabbed a cotton ball "Here we go," she said while beginning to dab. This time Benji did flinch. But that was okay. It was expected. And nurse to patient—it was more typical of a reaction.

Ella almost sighed audibly in relief.

When the procedure of cleaning Benji's wounds was finished, Ella tidied up and grabbed a flask filled with eye wash along with a bottle of drops prescribed for aiding in healing. Although in healing of what—she wasn't sure. If the symptoms Benji was experiencing was the result of psychological trauma, what good were the drops actually doing then?

"I ah…have these drops for your eyes," she said, watching him lying there, head propped by pillows, body reclined in what could be considered more of a sitting position. She stared a few seconds longer than was necessary. Probably longer than she should have. But it was sad to her, all that he had been through, the ordeal he had suffered in the war. Physically. And now mentally. He looked so vulnerable. The whole situation that he was having to endure—part of which he didn't even know existed yet. She wished she could change everything. Make it all better.

"Yeah, okay," he said back.

Ella leaned close, first applying the eyewash. Giving it time to take effect, she cradled the bottle of drops in her hand, waiting. Finally, enough time had elapsed. The ticking of the wall clock fell in line with the pulse in her veins. *His pulse too,* she wondered? Even the breaths between them were starting to feel in sync, somehow. *What was going on?* She felt herself getting sucked into a moment. "Now the next set." Her voice came out quiet. Too quiet. She unscrewed the lid. He nodded and a modicum of left-over liquid escaped onto his cheek. Ella reached out as if in slow motion to dab it away. The simple act caused a sprinkling of goosebumps to cover her arms, making her want to shiver. Benji's eyelash fluttered in return.

An unexplained fragment of stillness settled on the room, holding the juncture securely in place.

Out of nowhere, it occurred to her just how close their proximity. And yet this was just a medical task—the nearness couldn't be helped. Ella took a breath and opened his eye lid with her forefinger and thumb. Applied the drop. And then proceeded to lift the other.

There—done, she thought. But before she had a chance to back away, leaning over him as she had been, to deliver the drops, Benji opened his eyes. Ella swallowed hard. In those seconds, his irises seemed so blue. More so than she had ever noticed before. And somehow, they seemed to be looking right at her. Almost as if going through her. Seeing every vulnerable part. Every secret thought.

But she knew better—it couldn't be.

And yet, the feeling continued—so strong. "It seems," she began in a raspy voice, then stopped, her own eyes not blinking. For the first time ever, she became conscious of his lips, millimeters from her own. "Right now…I could swear, Benji…it almost seems as if…as if you can see."

This time Benji's lids didn't flutter an iota. The stare between them seemed tangible. Fixed. As if they were glued to one another's faces in real time. As if it wasn't just an illusion in Ella's mind. It was as if they were actually staring into each other's eyes. *Like two young lovers.* "I can," he finally offered in return. His voice was just a whisper. "Right now…I *can* see. I *can* see…*you.* Somehow, I am actually able to see again!"

CHAPTER 8

No longer were there any doubts in Ella's mind. There was no more denying the attraction that had been brewing in her thoughts since the wounded soldier had arrived at War Memorial Hospital. She had feelings for her patient, Benji. She knew it. He knew it. They both shared the sentiment. Although not discussed aloud, it was made evident in the looks that passed between them. In the one long look that officially started it all—the one that told them all they needed to know. She no longer needed to pretend she was only his nurse—only his assigned caregiver at bedside. It was obvious that they wanted to be together, any chance they could. That they wanted to share in each other's company and convey what was in their hearts through articulated action.

It was such a relief to finally be so open with the flirtations, the physical contact—accidental and not so accidental touches—the prolonged glances. All of it adding up to a budding relationship between nurse and patient.

"I'm so glad that you can see. That your eyesight is still with you," she said one day. It had been a busy morning on ward-four, and she was just then getting a chance to spend time with Benji, other than having checked in earlier to perform brief tasks.

"I'm telling you it's the magic eye drops," he laughed. "I don't care what anyone says, you put some type of magic potion in that bottle. I know you did. One minute I couldn't see and then the drops and then bam...clear as day my eyesight returned."

Ella was grinning from ear to ear. "Okay...you got me. I did do it. I have a secret potion that I've been experimenting with at home. I don't know, somehow it seemed...it just seemed the perfect time to try it out. Glad that it actually worked." She followed up her statement with a wink.

Benji raised his brows. He was sitting on the edge of the bed. Getting ready to transfer into the wooden chair Ella had wheeled to his bedside. It seemed his legs were getting a little stronger as of late along with his blindness reversal. "Me too," he said. "Your potion is killer diller. I'm glad you decided to try it out." He braced his arms on the mattress while preparing to maneuver his lower body. "Glad you tried it out…on me, that is."

Ella couldn't help it, she blushed.

A warm flush swept through her veins as she began wheeling him through the ward in route toward the doorway. She was so happy that Benji's mood had improved. And that he seemed to be healing, now more willing to participate with the end objective of his care. She only hoped the progress he was making wouldn't somehow reverse itself, getting interrupted by some lurid memory surfacing from the attack in Hawaii.

Most of the time, she held back these thoughts, and kept them at bay. For the time being, she was just so happy about the sudden turnabout of his condition—and that is where she would hang her hat.

Pushing Benji through the hallway, Ella paused to talk to fellow staff members who seemed to share in the joy of his improvement. He had been in their care for so long—weeks— that many had grown attached on some level. In a way, he was their very own poster child. A representation of the war in which they were all so concerned. He provided tangible evidence of what they sought to learn about through the delivery of weekly newspapers, or via the earnest voice of reporters, emitted through radio soundwaves.

After a few minutes of light banter, Ella began moving again, the wheels of Benji's chair rotating over the white linoleum tiles of the corridors. A few turns into the ride, and she spied a familiar face coming their way. Lillian Cloutier. Her fellow nurse and work companion. She had been off work as of late after an ankle sprain. Ella missed her.

"Lillian…Lil," she called out. Lillian was dressed in an A-line skirt and a sweater, with a brooch at the neck. It was odd seeing her out of her nursing pinafore. "When are you coming back to the hospital for work? We can really use you around here. It's been busy."

"I imagine," she answered. "With all the snow and ice out there, there's been lots of injuries to tend to I would think." She pointed to her leg where an ace wrap peeked above her boot, her lips twisting into a sheepish look.

"Speaking of...how is your ankle?"

"Better...I'll be back to this old hospital shortly. Next week, possibly sooner. Although I admit, fear of slipping on ice again has me in its grip. Even today, getting out was nerve-wracking, somewhat. But enough about me," she said, turning her attention toward Benji who was sitting stoically in his mobile chair, watching the conversation flutter back and forth between the two nurses. "Would you look at our patient...up and at em. It's a transformation."

Benji smiled, boasting of pride in progress. "Nurse Ella has magic potions," he said, glancing over his shoulder.

"What?" Lillian looked confused.

"Long story," Ella chuckled. "But true that he's doing better. Isn't it amazing?"

"Yes, it is." Lillian seemed to study Benji's face. "You've changed so much since coming here. And even more since I've been gone. I hardly recognize you." She examined him some more. "Yeah...changed a lot. In fact...it's bugging me...you almost seem rather famil—"

Benji looked up expectantly.

Lillian shook her head. "Oh, never mind. I've probably just been gone from this place too long. Anyway, glad to see that you're doing better. Making progress. And whatever the case...I have to agree, Ella does have magic potions. She's on the beam."

At that, all three laughed.

"I had some time between rounds, so I thought I'd take him to the big windows. Let him see the outside world." Ella pointed in the direction the wheelchair was positioned.

"Snow and more snow." Lillian gestured with a nod of her chin. "That's all there is out there. But it's better than staring at the white walls of the hospital I suppose." She glanced at her watch. "Anyway...I must be on my way, and I know you are on a short leash. Soon enough, the patients of ward-four will be calling you back. Enjoy your time."

Commencing into motion, Ella and Benji continued on down the hall until they reached the chamber adjacent to the cafeteria. A small floor-space with elongated walls and big windows. Perfect for viewing the outdoors. The stark white of the winter filled the room boldly. Benji took it in with contemplative eyes. Ella watched him for a minute.

"What are you thinking," she finally asked.

It took him a few moments to answer. "Not much. A lot." He turned to look at Ella. "Don't' get me wrong, I'm glad for where I'm at…how much progress I've made lately. I just wonder when I'll actually get back out there." He pointed at the window. "And what back out there actually means anymore."

Ella frowned. She was happy that he was confiding his feelings. It was better that than keeping them bottled up inside. And yet she worried that things could easily take a turn. He'd been doing so good as-of-late. Too much introspective thought, and regression in the wrong direction could set in. Still, talking it out might be a good thing, she supposed.

"What are the things you worry about?" Her voice was soft as she posed the question. They'd never really talked about the future. It was one step at a time.

"I don't know." He lifted a hand toward his head. "It is hard sometimes. There's stuff up here. Demons chasing me I guess." Taking a deep breath, he turned toward her with a sheepish grin. "Anyway… enough about that. We've come out here to have a good time. Get away from sick bay. It feels good to see the sky, the light of day, the earth, snow-filled as it is."

Ella eyed the brightness of winter as it swept into the room, thankful for the lanky expanse of windowpanes that allowed for the broad influx of light. "How about a game," she suggested. "I could bring in table big enough for a checkerboard."

Benji's face brightened. "Not a bad way to pass the time. You get the game and it's a contest. Although I'd hate to embarrass you."

"Let's just see who embarrasses who." Ella was laughing as she left to collect the board and checkers.

They were laughing *together* by the time she brought back the table and worked to scoot it in place. Afterward, he set up the board and arranged the pieces, so they were all set to play. Clearly, the mood had been lightened with the new ambience of a little friendly competition. They proceeded to take their turns at play, moving checkers about, all in earnest, and yet giving grace to themselves and one another with each out-maneuver.

It was all in fun. And a *lot* of fun.

Just what the doctor ordered.

They were having the best time in each other's presence, accompanied by a lot of looks passing between them. And plenty of blushes on Ella's part. She had to admit, her heart was being stolen away. By the time she was rolling him back to ward-four, she could think of nothing else but how it was their destination to be together. Clearly, he was meant to be her patient. This was how the start of journey together was intended to be.

Having finished pushing him back down passageways travelled less than an hour before, too soon they arrived back at bedside. Ella stood by to watch as a motivated Benji slid himself from chair to mattress. Afterward, he settled in, and she made sure everything he needed for the remainder of the afternoon was at his reach, promising she'd be back in a jiffy with a fresh pitcher of water.

Flitting happily out the exit, Ella entered the hallway in route to retrieve the water, all-the -while passing by the nursing desk as she had done myriads of times before. But this time something was catching her attention. A folder containing large print. A patient's chart. With the name *Marek* written across the front. **Benjamin Marek** to be exact. The initials (BJ) were in scripted alongside.

Ella went still in her tracks.

Her thoughts began to churn.

How familiar that name was to her. *Too familiar.* Her brain took a trip back in time, stumbling over the sound of the syllables echoing in her mind. *It couldn't be!* And yet there it was—in writing. Mocking her. Pieces of a puzzle she didn't even know her synapses had been assembling, began falling into place. Not wanting to read further, denial bargained with her intellect over the discovery of new truth. And yet she couldn't stop her eyes from wandering down the page.

To the room assignment that accompanied the name.

But there it was. Bold lettering jumping from the folio. Smacking her in the face.

Ward-four/Bed-one

For a moment or two Ella couldn't breathe. (Benjamin M. Ward-4/ Bed-1) Benji—*her Benji*, wounded soldier, war hero, who had been on her daily assignment for weeks, was really Benjamin Marek from primary/secondary school. BJ—*BJ* Marek to be precise.

How she loathed the sound of the name on her lips.

She could feel her eyes narrowing into two slits, her brow furrowing, nose scrunching. She felt duped. Totally and utterly duped. How stupid she had been not to see his chart—to not have read the full name of her patient. She never knew his last name. And yet it wasn't uncommon to bypass the official document of a chart—leaving the contents in the hands of the physician for review. But still—to miss something this big?

Her soldier-patient had looked so different than the BJ she knew from childhood. But with the newly-handed knowledge, looking back over the trajectory of things—that had probably been in large part due to the injuries covering his face. The past few shifts, though—there had been something about him. A feeling of familiarity when certain looks crossed over his features. And all-at once, it was there—hitting her like a ton a bricks. *He really **was** BJ Marek!*

How could she ever have missed it?

And to think she had assumed he was a soldier from an outlying area who had been transported to War Memorial Hospital as a nearest option for treatment. Not a hometown boy from Sault Ste. Marie itself. Never that.

Never once that.

Ella hardly knew what to do. She couldn't think straight. This changed everything. The patient in the other room, lying in bed-one was no longer Benji, injured soldier from the war. He was BJ Marek. She felt stymied. Unable to move. Glancing down at her hands, she saw that they were shaking.

Water. She was en route to fill the water pitcher.

But the water was for Benji. *Or now, BJ, rather.*

She was in a tailspin.

Ugh!

"El…you okay?" she heard a voice calling to her from behind the nursing desk.

"What? Yeah…yeah," she answered, shaking her head. Once again, she broke into movement.

A few minutes later, she had the pitcher in hand, trying to control the uneven sloshing of water that was making its way to the rim. *Proceed forward*, she kept telling herself. One step at a time. One foot in front of the other. But her mind was in a whirl. It was hard to concentrate. Finally, she reached the entrance to ward-four.

Walking through the doorway, she proceeded down the long row of beds that were her assignment for the day. Not once seeing a single patient. *Just keep going*, she thought. All-the-while, she fought the urge to run. Really, she could have sent someone else back with the water. Why hadn't she? The lines in the linoleum that sectioned off the beds were turning into stripes in front of her. Elongating. Stretching—taking her back to another point in her life. Ella's eyes fought to ignore them, to not get sucked in.

Forcing her vision in an upward direction, she could faintly see the outline of the figure occupying the bed she was heading for. She was almost there. It was too late to turn around. Or was it? *Yes, truly, it was.* Drawing from her professionalism as a nurse, she finished the last bit of the journey to the far side of the room.

Taming the shakiness of her fingers on approach, Ella fumbled to set down the water pitcher, before looking up to face what she already knew in her heart to be true. To confront the recently-discovered truth, head on.

With quiet resolution, she lifted her eyes.

"Ella…what is it?" A deep voice projected at her from bed-one, breaking through the fog in her mind.

"You look like you've seen a ghost."

Indeed, she had. She had just seen a ghost, indeed!

CHAPTER 9

~1929~

Eleanor Hurley pulled on her wool coat and began making her way down the dimly lit halls of the school. It was time for recess, and she was in-line, being herded, along with the other students toward the playground. Walking single file, she reached in her pocket and pulled out a knitted hat, fitting it on her head. Wisps of cropped, brown hair poked out spiritedly from underneath. Though it was still fall and first snow hadn't yet made its presence known, the air could still be nippy outside. Especially first recess of the day.

Feet trotting forward in progression, keeping with the other children heading for the large, double doors at the end of the hall, she peered here and there, hoping to spot her best friend, Siobhan, so they could play together—with any luck, on the swings. That is, if they weren't taken by the time they got to the gravel mound where the A-line poles and rope-threaded rubber seats were perched, atop. Trip trap trip trap. The convoy of students passed by the other third-grade classroom and Eleanor strained her neck around for a look. All appeared quiet, save a pupil or two still fiddling around-getting ready. No Siobhan. Eleanor figured she must already be outside. *Hopefully she had thought to save a swing.* And a high-reaching one too.

Eleanor hated that Siobhan had gotten placed in another classroom that year. She was her best friend. It was not the same without her sitting at a desk nearby. There was no one in particular that Eleanor had cliqued with in class, so at times she felt alone and awkward. Recess was no exception—until she and Siobhan relocated each other.

Finagling her way down the steps that led to the entryway at the rear of the school, Eleanor pushed through the double doors, feeling the first splash of cold on her cheeks. Outside, she took pause. At first glance, Siobhan was nowhere in sight—but up ahead there *was* a group of fifth graders, pushing and shoving, laughing, joking. Looking like they owned the place. With BJ Marek in the lead—*of course.*

Making herself as inconspicuous as possible, she veered from the sidewalk to escape any possible jeers. Or in any way take the chance of getting noticed at all, really. She knew all-too-well how it could go with that group. *Harmless fun*, one recess monitor had said. *But always at the expense of others*, Eleanor thought. And as-of-late, it seemed she was becoming more of a target. *That BJ Marek.* He was atrocious He thought he was such hot stuff. He could give some awful looks. Could make someone feel so small. Why did it seem he suddenly felt the need to pick Eleanor out of a crowd? In years prior, she had found ways to fly beneath the radar, successfully shrouding herself from the group of older students, who, as always, flaunted the great, BJ Marek, at the helm of the ensemble.

It seemed she had made the right move. There was a clear path toward the playground equipment with just enough space to avoid walking through the congestion of fifth graders. Marching at a fast clip, she couldn't help but feel a bit of freedom with each step that took her farther away. Though the burst of laughter she heard in echo over her shoulder, left her a little unsure about things. *Had they spotted her after all?*

Picking up speed, she began heading for the swings. But upon arriving, it was clear Siobhan was nowhere to be found. It was possible that she was just a little late getting outside to recess. After all, she could be known to dawdle. Maybe, somehow, Eleanor had missed her when they passed by the third-grade classroom. She would still show up in a minute or so. Eleanor decided to grab a swing, in the meantime, while she waited. Even though there weren't two open, they'd figure that part out later.

After swinging for a few minutes and still no Siobhan, Eleanor let her gaze begin to wander. The higher she swung, the further out onto the school grounds she could see. Across the way, she noticed a group of students gathering by the baseball field on the far side of the playground. It looked like they could be starting up a game. Another glide into the sky and she could see a ball, big and red, in someone's hands. It was probably going to be kickball.

Eleanor's lips began to turn in an upward direction. She loved kickball. But then swinging some more, further honing her gaze, she noticed that the group congregating on the field contained some fifth graders as well, along with ones she recognized from third and fourth. Instantly, her smile collapsed. She wished the fifth graders weren't there. She really wanted to join in on the game. And with Siobhan not showing, there really wasn't much else to do that recess.

Two more pumps with the legs, two more breezy passes through the sky, Eleanor made a decision. Fifth graders or not, she'd not let that stop her. Last game, she had gotten in some pretty good kicks. Besides, she knew she was fast. Confidence bolstering, she jumped off the swing with a flying leap through the air.

Landing with a thud, she began making her way toward the baseball field, hastening her stride with each step, should she decide to change her mind. The closer Eleanor got, she could see that students were lining up against the fence. Soon, they'd be picking teams, so she moved a little faster.

Arriving to the field, she made for the fence to get in line with the others and tucked herself in beside a third grader. There it felt safe. Taking pause, she performed a quick perusal of the other pupils gathered, getting a close-up inspection of those involved in the would-be game. Her face fell when she noticed Jimmy Adamik as one of the team captains. She should have known. Beside him, was BJ Marek, his best buddy and fellow fifth grader, helping him make the picks.

The selection of teams continued and with each new spot filled, Eleanor felt herself sink further into the fence. The options were getting slim and still she wasn't getting chosen. It was making her second guess the decision to leave the swings. Even less athletic third graders than herself were getting their names called out. She kept waiting for the words *Eleanor Hurley* to vibrate though the air, landing on her waiting eardrums. But pick after pick and it wasn't happening. It seemed a shame. Did they even know her hidden talents? She'd make a great addition to either team. If only they'd let her prove herself by showing her speed and skills.

Finally, it was down to three students. Two third graders and one fourth grader who had a clubbed foot. Eleanor held her breath. She could see Jimmy Adamik eying her. Although she didn't particularly want to be on his team, she *did* want to feel included. At that point—*anywhere* on either side would be nice. She was sticking out like a sore thumb. It was embarrassing. The confidence that should be radiating from her face over contributions she could make toward winning the game was instead hidden behind feelings of shame. She wished she could snap out of it. Fake self-assuredness.

But she could see BJ Marek leering at her.

Eleanor shrank further back. The metal spokes of the fence poked at her spine.

Jimmy Adamik leaned toward his fellow fifth grade pals. "I think it's down to Hurley in the hat," he said. There were a couple nods. A few snickers. Eleanor held her breath. *What about her hat?* She half considered reaching up to see if it was on funny or something. But any notion of that was soon interrupted.

"No. Not her," came the voice from directly behind Jimmy. "Don't pick her…We don't want that one. She's worthless." The directive was given with volume and clarity. There was no mistake on the intent. Everyone at the fence could hear it, plain as day.

Eleanor as well as anyone.

Eleanor *more* so—than anyone.

Once again BJ Marek had succeeded at making her feel perfectly awful. Useless.

As if she needed any help with that.

Dear Thomas,

Where is the sound of your laughter? Desperately, I try to find it. But it keeps disappearing into the whispers of the wind, the ticking of the clock, the mundane tones of echoing chatter.

~E.

CHAPTER 10

The smell of eggs frying in bacon grease filled Ella's senses as she made her way down the stairs at her home on Maple Street. It was a good sign that food was being cooked so early in the morning. Her mom must have the day off from Woolworth. The idea that she was up and at em was a positive thing. So many days Grace hibernated in her bedroom, interacting very little with the rest of the family. And who could blame her really? Except, inside, there was a part of Ella that did. *Blame*—it was something that should be shared as a family.

Ella just wished she'd come around more—if not for Melvin and herself, then at least for Chance. "Morning, Mom," she said, walking into the kitchen. Olive and pastel green two-tone cabinetry filled the room with color, reminding Ella of better days when her mom cared to decorate their home with feminine touches.

"Morning." Her mom's reply was more of a muttering, barely audible over sizzling sounds coming from the frypan.

Ella began mixing some powdered milk while her mom finished her preparations at the stove. "Things are staying busy at the hospital." She lifted her eyes hopefully, giving an attempt at small talk. But Grace's back stayed turned. A nod of the head was her only reply. Taking in the greasy hair, fastened haphazardly at the nape of the neck, and the dirty apron that hung loosely on the hips, Ella let out a sigh. It was evident that self-care was slipping. And the unlaundered clothing wasn't due to rationing either. The box of soap in the basement was still full.

Grace scooped up some eggs and handed over a plate. "Thanks. Looks tasty." Ella tried to meet her mom's eyes, but she looked away, walking over to the percolator instead. Pouring a cup of coffee, she set it on the table in front of Ella's plate.

Steam rose into the air, filling Ella's nostrils with the robust flavoring. "Ah…coffee So wonderful." She took a sip. "It's a coffee day then?" A commodity truly affected by rations; it wasn't always a coffee day. Again, a barely-there nod was offered by Grace. Clearly, there would be no conversations around the table that morning. But then there rarely was. The breakfast, though, that was something at least. An act of service. Ella supposed it would have to be enough.

Her mom dished up her own plate and sat down, and they ate in silence.

Minutes dragged on, the quiet giving room for noisy conversations to be conducted inside the mind. *Hurt and sadness and pain.* Not a dialogue Ella wanted to partake in. She clanged her fork louder, set her cup down a little harder in distraction, trying to make it go away.

Her mom kept eating—looking sad, eyes shadowed underneath by years of grief. Ella studied Grace's face for a few moments, realizing how much she resembled someone who'd given themselves over to alcohol. But this Ella knew couldn't be farther from the truth. Not after spending most of her adult years cleaning up Melvin's empty liquor bottles on the back porch. Mopping up the verbal messes he made with his mouth.

Ella finished eating and washed the dishes in the sink, letting them airdry in the rack. The dismal mood was eating her alive. She could hear the radio playing in the sitting room and a thought came to her. Exiting the kitchen, she made her way over to the receiver.

The Glenn Miller Orchestra was performing one of their latest hits. She gave a hefty turn of the dial. In an instant, big band swing music filled the air. It wasn't long before her mom entered the doorway.

"What on earth on you doing," she yelled into the room.

Ella laughed. The echo of it sounded a bit insane. What *was* she doing? So much had been going on as-of-late. The U.S. officially entering the war, the continuing somberness around the Hurley household, and now the discovery of BJ Marek as the soldier in her care. It was all weighing her down—a bit too much. She needed some sort of relief. An escape.

In the past, her work had been just that—an escape. *Well, no more.* Or at least for the time being—as-long-as BJ resided as a patient there. But even when he was well enough to no longer have need of a medical facility, there was *still* the matter of the heart—

Ugh!

Ella reached for the dial and cranked the music a little louder.

"Eleanor…I said—"

"Playing music, Mom," she called back. "I'm playing some good ole music. Don't you like Glenn Miller?"

"I'm not…I mean—"

But Ella wasn't listening. Swaying to the melody, she began jiving around furniture, moving in sync to the big brass sound. After a few minutes, she held out a hand toward her mom. "Oh, come on…nothing like a little music. How about a dance?"

Grace looked horrified. All-the-while, Ella kept moving in her direction, shifting her hips this way and that. As Ella's fingertips remained extended, palm up, in a motioning manner, Grace's eyes widened, head shaking in adamant refusal. But by the time Ella was directly in front of her, it seemed there was nothing she could do but join in. Though be it a little less enthusiastically.

Still, it was something, if not fun. Ella swung her body back and forth, dipping low, her mom in-due-course attempting to imitate in return, eventually picking up her own momentum. After one particularly robust movement, a burst of laughter left Ella's lips. In answer, a tiny smile formed on Grace's face. The first one Ella remembered seeing in a long time.

They continued on until the song ended and the music was replaced by talk coming over the soundwaves. Afterward, Grace went wordlessly back into the kitchen to finish her household tasks in solitude and Ella continued about her day. Later, she checked in on her mom, as she did periodically, only to find she had retreated once more to her bedroom. There she'd most likely stay for the remainder of the day. Or at least until Melvin returned home and expected dinner. And, of course, the never-ending supply of drinks.

As anticipated, Grace Hurley was still there when Chance arrived home from school that afternoon. "El...Mom," he called, entering the front door. "Who's here...I'm hungry."

Ella listened for movement from her parent's side of the hall, but there was none. "I'm upstairs, Chance," she yelled, not sure how well he could hear the reply. "I'll be right down." Ella passed by her parent's bedroom in route to the stairs. The door was cracked, and she could see her mom laying there, face toward the wall, not stirring in the least. She shook her head. Wiping the frown from her brow, Ella forced a cheery smile onto her face and went to greet Chance.

"There you are." Chance was pulling off his rubber boots. His eyes lifted when he saw Ella. "This fella is hungry. What's to eat?"

Ella tried to remember what was in the kitchen cupboards and then an idea came to her. "Don't take off your coat," she offered with a smile.

"What?"

"And put your boots back on. We're going to Kresge's"

Chance's face lit up. "Really? Kresge's? That's a swell idea. I love that place."

Ella smiled. "Yes, really. How does a strawberry sundae sound?"

"Or a banana split?"

Ella reached over to ruffle the top of Chance's head. "Or a banana split." *Darling Chance.* My, he was a bargainer though. Why was he so hard to resist? Ella joined him in putting on winter layerings, then they headed out into the cold. A note was left on the table for Grace, should she make it downstairs to read it before they returned.

Chance fairly skipped through the streets as they made their way into the main parts of town, while chattering animatedly about his day at school. Ella worked hard to keep up, careful not to slip on the ice as her fellow nursing companion, Lillian, had. The last thing she wanted was a trip to her own hospital. *Oh, the hospital.* Without warning her thoughts transition to Benji. *Or BJ, rather.* With purposeful effort, she willed the image in her mind away, glad for Chance's stories as a distraction. Shaking her head, Ella focused on listening a little more carefully to what he way saying.

"So, then, Miss Atterton put Bobby in the corner at the back of the classroom. And then Kip started laughing, so then he got in trouble too. And I was trying so hard not to laugh too because Kip was making faces at me. But I did it."

Ella lifted her brow. They had turned in a northerly direction, and the wind was beginning to whip at her face. "You did what?"

"I kept a straight face. I didn't start laughing. I didn't end up in trouble. That Kip—"

"Yes, that Kip," Ella echoed. Inside, she wondered how much learning was taking place within the walls of the elementary, with all that her brother was sharing. Closing in on town, Chance's tales of classroom antics ended in abrupt fashion as they crossed over one more block and found themselves enveloped in the hustle and bustle of Ashmun Street.

Eyes wide, Chance took in their surroundings. Downtown—it never got old. Especially from a child's point of view.

Tall brick buildings, sidewalks covered with awnings, storefront windows filled with delectable's. Pedestrians on foot, soldiers in uniform, automobiles lining the streets. The city bus's stopping and starting, yellow taxicabs, neon signs strategically hung—powered by electricity coming from the canal.

They made their way up one block, then two, until reaching Kresge's dime store. Ella noticed a spring in Chance's step as they entered through the glass doors. She smiled to herself. Wasting little time eyeing the goods for sale, he made straight for the expansive countertop that was the soda fountain. A long row of high-post swivel chairs filled its length. Chance hopped on one, and Ella took the seat next to him.

Facing a tiled backdrop with round mirrors and a display of sundae fixings, Chance began reading the ribbony signs that littered the walls. "Fresh strawberry sundae fifteen cents. Hot coffee five cents. Please pay when served. Thank you. No tipping." With earnest endeavor, his eyes scanned down the length of the counter, until they landed on a banner to the far edge of where they were seated. "There it is...Banana split fifteen cents. Yes...I'd like one of those."

Ella nodded her head. She had been forewarned. A pleasant smell wafted pass her nose as she eyed an advertisement for a baked ham sandwich. It sounded like just the thing. And oh, the aroma of it. But it might spoil her dinner, that late in the afternoon. In the end, she stuck with an ice cream topped with fudge, and of course for Chance, the coveted banana split.

They had been served and were busy enjoying the contents of their bowls when a dark head of hair caught Ella's attention from the corner of her eye. Jet black waves, with a broad neck and bulky arms, perched at the end of the soda fountain counter, several seats away. Within seconds, her heart began an anxious staccato. She'd know that thick head of hair, that stalky build anywhere.

Even though it had been years.

It was Jimmy Adamik from back in school.

BJ Marek's best buddy and comrade in mean behavior. *Ugh!* He was second only to BJ's cruel persona throughout the growing up years. But a close second, none-the-less. Ella felt her stomach begin to churn. Inside, she wanted to hurry up with the ice cream and get the heck out of dodge. But that wouldn't be fair to Chance. She eyed her brother scooping morsels of banana in his mouth, talking animatedly between bites.

No, it wouldn't be fair at all.

This was her problem, not Chance's.

She gave a quick glance over her shoulder and saw Jimmy looking her way. Though by the look of confusion on his brow, she had to guess he hadn't quite placed her. *Yet.* How long before he pieced it together? Reaching up to smooth her blond hair, she remembered how it used to be short and dark throughout her youth. Funny how much *she* recognized *him*, when BJ had looked so different than she had remembered. But this guy sitting at the countertop—it was Jimmy Adamik alright, appearing as though he hadn't done much productive with himself since high school.

Why was she so affected by him, anyway? Why was his presence getting to her? But inside, she knew the truth—a month ago, he *wouldn't* have mattered to her. His stupid sneers could take a long walk off a short dock for all she cared. But the soldier she had been taking care of, who she'd been falling for, who in all actuality happened to be BJ Marek, was Jimmy Adamik's best friend back in the day—*Ugh*!

It was all getting so tangled in Ella's mind.

"How come you are not eating?" Chance's voice broke into her thoughts. He was more than halfway done with his banana split.

"What?" Ella looked at the spoon in her hand, that was suspended in mid-air. "Oh…no reason." She laughed a little. "Just…I'd better get going, hadn't I? Or you're going to beat me."

Chance kept scooping up bites at a steady clip. "Yep…and mine's bigger too."

"Sure is…your stomach must be a bottomless pit."

Ella forced herself to keep eating, training her attention on Chance, trying to enjoy the soda fountain ambience, all bright lights and fun foods—happy times to be had by all. She was thankful that the place was starting to pick up in business, getting close to the dinner hour. Hopefully the seats at the counter would begin to fill in too, blocking her view of Jimmy. More importantly, obstructing his view of her.

And it worked—focusing intently on her little brother—for the better part of a half-hour, the time that it took for her and Chance to finish their ice cream, all-the-while carrying on important conversations about school and interactions that included stories about his best pal, Kip. Finally, they finished up.

Grabbing a napkin from the dispenser, Ella wiped her hands. Chance started putting on his coat, while setting aside his gloves and hat to add later. They were going to browse the store before starting the walk back. Ella put on her coat too, trying to tell herself not to look over her shoulder, toward the far end of the counter. But somehow, seemingly of its own accord, her neck twisted around.

Jimmy Adamik was still there. Joined by a couple others she couldn't place. *Forget about him*, she told herself. *Forget about Benji too*. At least for the time being—at least until she went in for her next shift at work. But forget as she may, right then it was too late, as Jimmy swiveled in his seat and looked directly at her. Ella watched in dismay as a fragment of recollection set in, followed by a sense of complete recognition. The look that he sent her way was compiled of absolute disdain. Like she was no greater than dirt.

Turning away, she swallowed twice. Waves of memories washed over her, filled with all the reasons she couldn't stand Jimmy Adamik, But, more importantly, why she hated BJ Marek, as well. Shutting her eyes for a moment, Ella paused, and opened them again. Letting out a breath, she reached for Chance's coat sleeve. "Let's go. It's time to head back."

"But you said—"

"I know what I said, but it's getting late and—"

"We were going to shop though. You said we'd look around."

Chance's eyes were littered with disappointment, his mouth puckered into a frown. Ella shook her head. He was definitely hard to resist. She fought to not look back over her shoulder, to keep focusing on Chance's face. "Okay," she sighed. "I did promise. But only for a little while."

When they arrived back at the family home on Maple Street, Ella wanted to breathe a sigh of relief, though she wasn't one hundred percent sure why. What had she expected from Jimmy Adamik back there at Kresge's? Several years had passed since high school. She shouldn't have let him get to her so much. One look at her mom though, and the relief she was momentarily reveling in dissipated.

Something felt off.

"What is going on?" Ella did a perusal of the living room. The easy chair was empty. "Where is Dad?"

"He's not here," came the mousey answer as it lifted to her ears.

"Not here?" Ella knew there was more to the story. By this time of the day, Melvin was always in his spot, glass of liquor in hand.

"I had a banana split, Mom," Chance's voice broke through the strain as he peeled off his jacket. He was all smiles in-spite of the tension pervading the room. "We went to Kresge's"

"Did you see the note?" Ella re-directed. Her mom was pale, transforming her to levels that went beyond her usual depressed state. Surely her grim demeanor wasn't about their outing to town. She'd done the very same thing on several occasions before. Notes were left all the time. It was a frequent form of communication around their place.

Before Grace had an opportunity to answer, a cold waft of air filled the room. A burst of commotion followed, and all eyes were drawn to the front doorway. "What are you looking at?" The jumble of words toppled over themselves as Melvin Hurley fumbled his way into the living room. Snow-laden boots landed where they landed. He could barely keep himself upright, let alone walk a straight line. Void-of-all-refinement, he made his way to the easy chair and landed with a plop.

"Grace," he bellowed. "Come get this damn coat off me. I'm hot." His face was beet red. A sheen of perspiration was covering his forehead.

Don't move, Grace, Ella wanted to say. But she stood there and watched as her mom helped to awkwardly remove the jacket that her dad seemed incapable of doing. Ella turned toward Chance. "Better go tidy up your room a bit. We'll call you for supper." The smile that had been lighting up his face on the walk back from Kresge's was now all but gone. With wide eyes, he left to go upstairs.

"Whachyou juss standing there for," Melvin slurred. His eyes were on Ella, while her mom carried the coat away. "I'm celebrating t'day… Get your father a drink."

A chill climbed up Ella's spine. "What…exactly…are we celebrating?"

"Weeeer celebratin that…Melvin Albert Hurley is no longer employed!"

"What?" Ella looked over at her mom. *How could this be?* But Grace was staring at the floor, dejected as ever—more-so than usual.

"Yep…had enufffff of that place…and all they kept shoving down my throat. Think they know so much…well they don't know nothing. Not anymore…not w'out me there. I quit. Damn electricity anyways… who needs it? Not me…not us. Back in the good days they didn't even have electricity…and they were jusss fine. That place can shove it up… shove it their ass I say."

Ella stood still as a mouse. She didn't know what to do, what to say. How could he do this? At a time when the work force was increasing tenfold, when work hours were longer than ever, all in contribution to the war effort—he was just going to up and quit? And for what reason—so that there would be more hours in the day to tip the bottle?

Where would his irresponsible actions leave them as a family?

She could see her mom wringing her hands, still staring at the floor. A faint tremor had taken over her body. Ella narrowed her eyes. She knew exactly where that left them—she and her mom at least. They would have to step up the contributions—work more than ever to make ends meet.

Through a narrowed brow, she watched her father, cockeyed as he was in the easy chair, a complete louse. Her blood began to boil as the ramifications of everything began to weigh down the entirety of the room. Seeking Ella out, it closed in around her, swallowing her whole.

Melvin snapped out of his momentary stupor. Saw Ella eyeballing him. "Watchoo looking at girl…never laid eyes on a free man before? Free from the duty of the labor force? Well…nowya have. I said getcher father a drink."

In a stupor of her own, Ella stood there unable to move, while the clock on the wall counted off the seconds. Finally, coming to life, she turned on her heels, and made for the stairway, not caring that the glass door slammed hardily behind her, vibrating with a strong force.

As far as she was concerned, Melvin Hurley could get his own damn drink.

CHAPTER 11

Dreading what the day would bring at the hospital, Ella made her way through the doors of War Memorial with a sluggish gait. Trying to calm her mind, she thought back to shifts over the past few weeks when her mind was void of the information that was currently circulating through the synapses of her brain, poking at her as it did with a vengeance. Back when she didn't know that Benjamin in bed-one was really BJ Marek. *Ignorance truly was bliss.*

Just put one foot in front of the other, she kept telling herself.

When in actuality, every part of her wanted to turn around and run the other way.

With all that was going on at home though, she needed this job more than ever.

"Hello, Ella," a lady sitting at the front desk just inside the main doors, smiled at her as she passed by.

"Oh…hi," Ella answered, trying to snap out of the daze she had entered. Offering a cursory wave, she kept to her slow-moving pace. Leaving the main corridor behind, she entered a series of hallways. One step. Then another. *Just keep going.* Without warning, her eyes were drawn to the arrows painted on the walls. Her focus honed in and the arrows lengthened beside her as she went, turning into stripes.

Long, red stripes.

Elongating and stretching, the stripes pointed in all directions: the cafeteria, waiting rooms, the surgical unit. With a palpating heart, Ella fought the site of them as she went, concentrating on finding the hallway that led to the central nursing station. By the time she reached the desk, she was feeling short of breath and jumpy. It took a few moments to center herself.

"Looking for this," Florence, the ward clerk, asked, holding up a clipboard with the list of assignments.

Ella nodded her head in a jerky motion. But instead of grabbing the clipboard, at the last second, she took a step back. *She already knew full well who would be on the list.* "You know…I think I'll just…go take care of my things first."

Florence lifted her eyebrows and set the list back down. "Suit yourself."

Ella dawdled as long as she could, taking off her winter outerwear, pausing intermittently to take in deep breaths. The minutes ticked off, and she knew that there was no other choice. She had to get to work. Rolling her neck from side to side, she smoothed her nursing pinafore and straightened her cap, before heading back out to the nursing station.

With a shaky hand, she eventually lifted the clipboard and began compiling information on her list of patients: an infected dog bite, two with pneumonia, a child with tonsillitis, a kidney infection, a cholecystectomy. *And of course, Benji.*

But this she already knew. She just *knew* he'd be on her assignment list for the day. What she didn't know was how she was going to deal with the idea, now that the realization was there of who he really was. *BJ Marek.* The person she'd least likely want to interact with in a professional manner. Let alone a personal one.

Be still the heart.

Walking through the doors of ward-four, Ella gave a sweeping glance down the long rows of white metal beds that were hers for the day. Where to start? Her concentration was off, and she knew it. So much to attend to. A multitude of needs to focus on—and not just the patient at the far end of the room. But Benji was everywhere. Staring back at her with every cover she lifted, with every introduction made to freshly-awakened patients, with every table-lamp she switched on to begin implementing care.

Every inch of her skin was conscious of his presence in the room.

She couldn't escape him.

And yet, when Ella finally made her way to the far wall, hands shaky, holding on to the sides of her nursing apron, she found he wasn't looking her way in the least. Curled into a ball, he was sound asleep under the covers. She breathed a silent sigh of relief. Taking a few seconds to collect herself, she watched his sleeping form, measuring the rise and fall of the blankets. The rhythm was easy and steady. It was all the assessment she needed for the time being. Clearly, he was in good stead. With stealth of a special service soldier, she began backing away, leaving him to sleep the morning away.

But just as her feet had eased into a reverse pattern, the mound of covers shifted. Ella's heart began to pound, and she froze in place, holding her breath. If she didn't move a muscle, maybe the stirring would stop. A quiet escape would still be possible. Counting the seconds off in her head, she'd only gotten to three, when the movement started again.

"Hey—" A sleepy Benji rolled over and looked up at her, a soft smile forming on his lips.

"Hey yourself—" was her every instinct to say back, in an equally subdued, early morning voice, reserved for someone you had a special connection with—a blossoming romantic one. In-spite-of all that she had discovered about who he was and who he had been in her life. In-spite-of all she had been warring with herself since discovering the chart at the nursing station—this was the very reaction she found flowing up from depths of her heart. It wrapped around the essence of her soul. Made her want to sob.

Instead, she sucked in a breath.

"Hello…good morning," came the reply from her lips, pitched in a professional nursing voice, if not a tone that was a little curt.

Benji' went very still. His face filled with confusion. Dark pupils mixed in with the blue of his eyes as they looked up at Ella in a studying sort of way—as if there was something more he was expecting. *Because, surely, he'd missed something.* A viable thing that would soon be coming his way—an explanation of sorts, a jab in the arm, *ha ha funny,* a burst of laughter maybe. *Just kidding—good morning, Benji—I've missed you.*

A swirl of confusion wrapped itself around Ella. It was obvious to her in the moment that Benji, *or BJ rather,* had no idea who *she* was. Disconcertingly, that revelation brought with it a sense of relief. And yet she knew it would only be a matter a time before he figured it all out. Besides—she knew who *he* was. That was enough.

Now to separate the two—the soldier named Benji who she'd come to care for—*too much*—from BJ Marek back in the day.

"I'm just making my morning rounds, checking on patients. So, I'll be back later," she told him. Ella could hear the coldness in her own voice, and it made her want to cringe. But more than that, she could see the bewildered expression catching hold of Benji's brow, and it made her want to run a thousand miles away. Clear her mind.

She had to sort things out. Remind herself of what was at play here—what was really going on. Steel herself in-order-to deliver the type of professionalism that was needed in this sort of situation.

"Okay…okay, yeah," Benji shook his head as if to free it. He appeared a little in shock. Caught off guard. He didn't know what to say, how to react. And it was still early morning, he was just waking up. Overall, things seemed a bit fuzzy. Maybe this was all a part of that. Slowly, he eased himself to a semi-upright position in bed. All-of-a-sudden, he seemed tongue tied. Like, now that he had offered his heart-felt greeting and it was rejected, he didn't know what else there was to say. He needed to gather his own thoughts.

Ella didn't know what else to say either. She had said what she needed to say as a nurse, and it was time to leave. Preparing to exit the vicinity, she eyed a few items of garbage strewn about and busied herself for a few moments picking them up. All-the-while, her heart pounded like a snare drum in her chest. Surely loud enough to be heard by Benji in the early morning quiet of the room.

She could feel him looking at her.

But she wouldn't return the stare.

Finally, he reached for a glass of water on his bed-side table and took a slow drink. The discomfort of the moment was broken—enough at least. Ella took the opportunity to snatch up one more piece of trash and scooted herself quickly away. Behind her, there was a two-second pause and then the sound of covers being resituated and the plop of a body turning over in bed.

She sucked in a gulp of air. Why was it that she wanted to run a million miles away? Her body felt completely overwhelmed. She had an incredible need to scream and cry. And cry. It felt like loss and anger and confusion all rolled into one. She hardly knew what to do with it all.

But she did know—she couldn't focus on her other patients in the current condition. Leaving the ward, Ella discreetly made her way to the lavatory and took the time she needed to recompose before further attempts at the day, while fighting the flow of tears that wanted to come. Realizing, as she stood there, leaning on the sink, inhaling in, exhaling out, through controlled breaths, that this was the very reason relationships between caregiver and patient were discouraged.

Whoever had initiated that rule—how wise they had been.

The morning passed by surprisingly quickly as Ella set about to deal with her other patients. There was much to be done: IV treatments, antibiotics for the two pneumonia patients and the kidney infection, wound care for the cholecystectomy and the dog bite, surgical preparations for the child with tonsillitis. Not to mention, careful monitoring of one of the pneumonias and the patient with the kidney infection who were hovering on the verge of getting sicker. Thankfully, it made for little time to concern herself with Benji.

But eventually the time came when she knew her patient in bed-one ought to be tended to as well. He had needs too—albeit not as acute as the others. Still, he was assigned into her care after all. Though, to be fair—by-all-rights, he should probably be transferred to another nurse, she realized. It was something she would look into in the near future.

For the moment though, Ella focused on gathering the needed medical supplies before heading to his side of the room. Before arriving at bedside, she steeled herself, by inwardly willing away all emotion and focusing on the list of tasks at hand. "You've had breakfast, I see." She eyed the meal tray that was pushed to the side. No greeting. No intimate, small talk. She was cutting right to the chase. Nursing interests only—nutrition *was* important after all.

Benji looked up from the book he was reading. This time he didn't look as surprised by the coolness in her tone, but there was a still an element of confusion written across his face. A subdued acquiescence.

Though it was clear he didn't know the how or the why of what was going on. "I did," he answered. He was still looking at her, questioning.

Ella began laying out supplies. "I have a list of a few things I need to do for you right now, but I'll do the best I can to get all done in good order."

"No rush on my account. I have all day."

Ella gave a curt nod. "Of course." For a moment, she paused, then continued with the preparations. Out of the corner of her vision, she could see the frown that was forming on Benji's lips. Her astute professionalism was playing havoc with his mind. But she had no choice in her actions. "Anyway," she paused. "I have to tend to your wounds, check your blood pressure and temperature, and then I do have an update on one of your vaccinations."

"Whoa," his eyes widened. "Are we talking shots here?"

"We are."

"Well, that's just crummy."

Ella couldn't help it, her face registered surprise. "Don't tell me, a strong soldier like you is afraid of a little poke," she said.

Benji crinkled his nose. "Well, I don't love them, if that is what you are wondering."

For a quick second, Ella wanted to smile, even laugh, but she reigned herself in. "We'll save that for last then. Or maybe we should do it first…get it over with."

Benji looked resigned as he let out a sigh, his face conveying the pout of a young kid. "Last is fine," he grimaced.

Ella began her tasks by assessing the wounds on his face. It seemed they were mostly healed, but she performed a quick rinse and applied some antiseptic for good measure, making sure they stayed that way. While performing each task, she was careful to avoid direct body contact. There would be no prolonged acts of cleansing across the cheekbones—as close as she was to his personal space. Wipe wipe. Dab dab. Pat pat. All done. Wipe wipe. Dab dab. Pat pat. All done.

"There's that," Ella said, stepping away from his bedside, feeling good that she had managed to dodge any close-encounter *looks* as she worked. "Now I'm just going to check your temperature, take a blood pressure, measure your pulse."

Benji still wasn't saying much except muttering a few *okays* and *yeah sures.*

Ella moved in with the thermometer. "Here's this," she said, offering the probe. She wasn't about to stand there holding it the whole time—that could get uncomfortable. "It goes—" But skin-to-skin contact interrupted her train-of-thought as the handoff transpired, making her want to shiver. She shook it off.

"Yeah...I know where it goes." Benji stuck it in his mouth.

Ella began cleaning up supplies from the wound-care she had performed, while waiting for the mercury on the thermometer to rise. When enough time had elapsed, she took back the probe, with careful avoidance of any touch. The application of blood pressure cuff wasn't so easy, though. There would be no way to elude him this time. So, she held her breath while inflating the sleeve, concentrating on the discomfort the lack of oxygen was bringing to her lungs. Then, focusing on the calibrated dial on the cart at bedside, thankful for the avoidance of eye contact, she listened for the tones to start and stop.

But when she went to remove the cuff, it seemed luck wasn't on her side, and Benji caught her eye. The look that passed between them was only a few seconds, and yet it was enough time to deliver damage. Ella couldn't think straight. Her hands fumbled awkwardly as she shed the wrapping and peeled it away. "Lastly...Pulse," she breathed, and Benji held out a wrist.

Pressing her fingers against his skin, she tried to ignore the burning sensation that was lighting up her nerve endings from the direct, skin-to-skin contact. As well as the thud of her own pulse. It was a long minute to count, and she had to start over several times, sure that she was getting her own heartbeat mixed up with his. The silence between them felt deadly.

For so many reasons.

When Ella pulled out the shot, thankfully the sight of the needle offered a breakthrough, dispelling the thickness in the air. Benji was clearly not a fan. So much so, that Ella almost laughed while administering the poke. She had never been so grateful to deliver a vaccination in all her years as a nurse. By the time she was leaving the bedside, the distraction was so great from Benji nursing his own wounds, she was able to make an exit with little ado. "Oh, you'll be alright in a day or so," she called back to him while walking away, a twinkle forming in her eyes.

For the next several hours, Ella stayed busy enough to not let the idea of Benji get to her. Besides a few check-ins, making sure he was in stable condition, she managed to keep him at bay in her interactions and in her thoughts. But when she was on an errand, sent by Dr. Northcott to pick up some medications from the pharmacy and happened to be passing by the cafeteria, she noticed that he was up in a wheelchair, being wheeled about by an orderly.

Her first reaction was visceral at just sight of him, followed by relief that he was up and about. But something caused her to go still in her tracks. Benji was in the midst of having a conversation with the orderly, and there was something about the look on his face—or could you say that it was a sneer really—that brought back a plethora of familiarity.

BJ Marek in the flesh.

In that moment, he looked so much like the boy she had known throughout her childhood, that there could no longer be any doubt. The resemblance was dead-on. Uncanny that she hadn't put it together sooner. Preparing to continue on her way, it was the look on the orderly's face that made Ella take pause. There was something about the deflated expression on his face—the manifestation of having been recently chastised—that made Ella want to investigate further. When the orderly spoke again—the realization hit her that she was within hearing distance.

"If you would like me to, I can," he articulated, body language in an open posture, set in backdrop against his crisp, white uniform.

"Isn't that what I just said two seconds ago?" The question was thrown into the air as more of a lashing.

Ella froze. The voice. The coldness in the tone. The air of superiority. It was like hearing BJ talk instead of Benji—yet really a combo of the two. The cynicism in the expression taking dominance over what she had come to know in most recent times. An attack of goosebumps covered her skin.

"Yes…and I am happy to accommodate… if you are ready then—"

"I already said I was ready. What I don't understand is why it is so hard to get what you need around here…when you need it."

"Okay then…let us—"

The orderly's words were cut off prematurely. "Okay then?" Benji's voice rose in agitation. "No…let *us* be clear who is working for who around here."

Ella felt like screaming. Or shaking. She wasn't sure which. Flashbacks to her schooldays were coming in rapid succession. A thousand thoughts began circulating in her head. One of which was to run into the cafeteria and ream Benji out for speaking to the staff at the hospital in that way. But before she could will her feet into action, the orderly had already set the wheels of the chair into motion, exiting on the far side of the room.

Having a hard time concentrating on the task at hand, Ella continued on to the pharmacy, redirecting herself on a couple of occasions when she absentmindedly took a wrong turn. Indeed, the BJ who she knew and remembered, had once again emerged. And just in time too. She had needed a good healthy reminder.

Ella got held up in the pharmacy. Taking longer than she would have liked to make it back to the ward—in-turn hurrying up her pace— when she passed by an alcove south of the cafeteria and noticed a wooden wheelchair perched in front of the narrow window that occupied the far wall. She was all but past the inlet, when a certain something about the occupant brought a flash of recognition to her brain.

Without warning her heartbeat sped up in tempo.

It was BJ.

Ella knew she should just continue on.

But something stopped the movement in her feet. The abruptness of it all was like a crash landing. Narrowing her brow, she did a double take, studying, making sure it was indeed Benji. Sure enough it was. Ella shook her head, blood still boiling from the earlier treatment she had witnessed of the orderly. There was so much she would like to say to him. But as her patient—the moment was not right. Who knew what might fly out of her mouth? The notion of professionalism made her re-think her steps and keep moving after all.

It was a second too late, though.

Benji pivoted around in his chair, eyes widening as he turned. "Ella," he said.

Ella's breath caught in her throat. The encounter hadn't been planned and now she didn't know what she wanted to say. "Out and about, I see," she began a little too tensely, then stopped. Words began to swirl in her brain, welling up inside, wanting to reveal themselves in swift, consecutive order. Before she could stop herself, she blurted. "It does make me wonder though…running into you…seeing you out and about. Has it become clear to you yet? Who is working for who around here?"

Benji looked taken aback. His mouth dropped slightly. Seconds later, a sheepish look found its way onto his face as he studied Ella's eyes. *What was she getting at?* Finally, he bit his lip. "You…have you," he gestured toward the cafeteria. "Are you referring to—"

"Yep." Her answer was firm. "I sure am."

Benji rubbed his jaw. "That was—"

"Not well handled." Her eyes narrowed. *To put it lightly.*

"Yeah…suppose not." He looked away. She couldn't read his expression. For a few moments there was silence in the alcove. She debated about reviewing the entirety of the scenario that she had stumbled upon with the orderly in the cafeteria, chastising him a little more, but then thought better of it. Enough had been said on the matter. There was no sense prolonging the discussion. He seemed to have gotten the point—loud and clear. Might as well get moving on— back to the ward. She opened her mouth to indicate her intention, when Benji turned back to face where she was standing. "So…Ella, you've had a busy morning. An entire busy day, really. I haven't seen much of you… at all, today." His eyes were wide, inquisitive.

"It *has* been…busy."

Benji stared at her. Clearly, he wanted more of an explanation. Their relationship up until then warranted one. Obviously, there was more between them than how her behavior was presenting itself that day.

"Do you want to tell me what's going on?"

It would have been easy to say *Nothing, nothing is going on*. Play dumb. Play off their whole connection as if it had been of no significance after all. But obviously that wouldn't work. Not where she was concerned. That just wasn't her MO. Too much had passed between them. Ella opened her mouth to speak, then closed it again. "Nothing I have time to go over at the moment," she sighed.

Benji's jaw twitched. It was evident that he was trying to hide the dejection that was emanating through his eyes.

Ella took a step to leave, but instead found herself drawing closer to his chair. As if to what? Reassure a patient out on a stroll that all would be okay? "It's good...to see you up and moving about like you are, though. It's good that you are building your strength."

"Don't," he said. "What's changed today? The last time you were on shift, I felt something from you...and have been for a while. Don't pretend that you are suddenly just my nurse and that's it. That there's not more between us." He lowered his head.

Ella didn't know what to say. She wasn't prepared to tell him the truth, that she knew who he really was. "It's not that I—" She pivoted to leave. The air was quickly growing thick. The alcove too small. She pointed down the hall. "But I really better—"

Benji glanced up and reached for her arm. She was still close enough. Still within his grasp. Ella turned back. Although not meaning too, she met his gaze and went still. His fingers were burning into her skin, causing reactions she hadn't anticipated. Her heart began to beat fast. The way that he was looking at her—with so much tenderness and affection, mixed with genuine confusion, it was getting to her, taking over. In that moment he was Benji from ward-four, her patient, that she'd grown fond of in so many ways. No past, only future, only present.

Benji narrowed his gaze, tilted his head slightly as if in thought, sorting through questions. "Is that it then?" He kept staring, thinking.

"Wha...what?" Ella's mouth went dry. The way he was studying her. Her heart picked up in tempo—but this time for different reasons. What was he getting at? Had he figured it out?

Benji bit his lip. "It is because you are my nurse? You have decided that you can't get close to me in any sort of personal way because you are my nurse, and it would cross lines...wouldn't be the right thing to do?"

Ella felt a modicum of relief. He'd only been referring to their professional relationship—nothing more. But the respite lasted only seconds. *No, no that's not it at all,* she wanted to say. *Don't you realize who I am? Don't you see that I know who you are? I'm Eleanor Hurley from back in school.*

And you—you are BJ Marek!

CHAPTER 12

"Yes...yes that's it. It's because I'm your nurse." *That's why I'm acting aloof and businesslike where it's concerning you.*

That's all Ella had to say on the matter. It was the perfect way out. Benji had offered her the escape, bringing up the possibility. And she would go with it. After all, it made sense. But for some reason, in the light of all that had passed between them during his hospital stay, it hardly seemed enough.

Yet it would have to do.

Benji nodded his head one time, eyes narrowed, mouth set firmly. *Okay, if you say so.* Resolution was setting in. Clearly, there would be no argument on his part. No begging. But of course, she wouldn't have wanted that. Anyway, there was nowhere for the discussion to go. No tete-a-tete about all the reasons they should keep things going between them—if only in secret. That would only lead to other things—truths of who they actually were to each other.

But the look on his face—quickly forming into stone-cold hardness. *It screamed BJ Marek.*

Once again, Ella chastised herself for not seeing it before. Looking away, she began smoothing her white pinafore. She needed to reset her mind—get back into nursing mode. Stop thinking about her patients as the people they were *back when*, who they had been before stepping foot into the hospital. All that mattered was that they were human beings who needed her care—there could be no other thought on the subject.

She cleared her throat. "Well...well, I suppose...I need to be getting back. Check on the others. Are you...are you okay staying here? Do you want to go back too?" A groan was stifled at the back of her throat. It sounded like she was fumbling her words. It was obvious, she disliked the idea of walking with Benji down long hallways after the uncomfortable, pseudo-conversation they had just partaken in. But as a caregiver, she had to ask.

"No…thanks for the offer…but I'm copacetic." His expression had settled into a stoic reserve. He wheeled a little closer to the window. "Think I'll just enjoy the view some more. Clouds are getting dark… looks like it could snow."

Ella nodded. For a split second, she considered whether he had enjoyed his assignment on the Hawaiian Islands for the length of time he was there—getting away from all the cold, northern weather and all. Certainly, any positive memories had been erased with the trauma of the Pearl Harbor bombing. Rest-assuredly, nothing was left but the distress of all he had experienced first-hand. She was sure if she asked him, he'd tell her—*who cares about balmy temperatures and fair skies*. All that remained in his mind was an army of oversized birds toting Japanese symbols, swooping through the air. Blue skies painted fiery red and black.

In silence, Ella left the alcove. It was good to think of Benji in that way. As a soldier. Of who he was in his experiences serving the country. About the soldier he had become and still was. Who, consequently, had become her patient at War Memorial. Nothing more—nothing less.

The rest of the afternoon progressed with little fanfare. Ella made a few sweeps past Benji's bed after he arrived back to the ward, checking to see that he was in good condition. With relief, each time, she found that he needed little of her assistance, so time was spent focusing on the others in her care.

She had just finished up administering wound care to her patient with the dog bite and was heading for the medicine cabinet to retrieve antibiotics for bed-five when Dr. Northcott flagged her down. There was a new medication he wanted to implement on bed-one.

Ella could feel her face falling. She had hoped to make a graceful escape at the end of her shift. No more confrontations. No more encounters. She'd decide how to handle future situations at a later date. But for the time being—*just to get through that day's assignment*. In quick repair, she pasted on a smile. She couldn't let Dr. Northcott see how she was being affected. Simply put—it was unprofessional.

"Of course," she said. "A medication?" What were they trying on Benji now? What had they come up with to help in his healing?

"Yes…an elixir. It's something new we're implementing. It consists of a variety of things…some of which are vitamins."

"Oh…okay," Ella answered. This, she hadn't thought of. Vitamins huh? Well, if Dr. Northcott said so. What she really wanted to know—was how long until they started working? How long before he could be released from the hospital, and she could have back her peace of mind?

After administering the antibiotic, Ella returned to the medicine cabinet to get what she needed and headed to the other end of the room. Drawing closer to bed-one, she noticed the patient in question was eating dinner, sitting up, propped by pillows. Her steps slowed. She hated to interrupt. A quick glance brought her eyes to the round clock on the wall. Her shift would soon be ending. There really wasn't time to put this off. True, there was the possibility of passing on the duty to her replacement. But that lacked credibility. How many times would she be able to get away with pulling stunts like that?

Her thoughts were still in a quandary, feet slowing, forward motion practically pended, when Benji looked up from his plate. For a moment, his blue eyes locked onto hers and she felt her throat go dry. With very little acknowledgement, he returned to his food and proceeded to take another bite.

Ella's heart picked up in tempo. Everything felt wrong about her being there—attending to BJ Marek as a nurse. The awkwardness of the situation weighed heavy in the air. And yet there was a certain something in her brain that was going a little haywire as she watched his jaw working—even while he ate. A visceral feeling that had been set into motion. An innate attraction. It seemed there was no repair. *It was too late*, she realized. Even as she allowed herself this thought—she hated herself for giving in to it.

Ella cleared her throat and held up the bottle in her hands "Hello, Benji," she made herself say. *He wasn't BJ*—not for the moment. She just had to get through this task.

"Whatcha got?" He still didn't look up from his plate.

"It's something Dr. Northcott asked me to give. Did he mention it to you?"

Benji took another bite of mashed potatoes. Swallowed. "If he did…I can't remember…maybe——"

"Okay…well I have it here. It is an elixir of medications that will help in your overall healing…some vitamins too."

Benji kept his focus on his dinner tray. Kept taking bites in consecutive order. Ella was glad for the reprieve from eye contact. And yet—this felt all wrong. The spirit of strain floating through the air. "Sounds like a concoction to me," he said between swallows.

I have to agree, Ella wanted to say. "But if it works…then all the better." A pause. "In moving forward, I mean."

Benji's fork halted in route to his mouth. Turning, he looked directly at Ella. The consternation in his eyes, the setting of his jaw—it all but read *moving forward huh, so that's what's best here—between us?* "Doctor knows best," he eventually said.

Ella almost jumped. His choice of the word *best*—it was a duplicate of what had been contrived in her mind. She felt the heat of his gaze and wished for him to look back down. At his plate, at his bedcoverings— anywhere but directly in her eyes. There was something so strong there—pulling, pushing, tugging. She shook her head to break the spell. "Anyway," she motioned to the bottle. "I have it here…ready for you."

"Pour away."

Ella closed the distance between where she was standing and Benji's bedside table, needing to use the surface for pouring and measuring. How quickly the space around them transitioned from large to small. Closed in. She could sense his every movement. Even the rise and fall of his chest. Working hard to keep her hands from shaking, she filled the medicine cup to just the right level, eyed it under the light, and handed it over.

Benji took it, his fingers brushing hers ever-so-slightly. Ignoring the chill the simple touch brought to her skin, Ella watched him drink it down. *Hurry up already*, she kept thinking, glancing at the wall clock. She couldn't get out of there soon enough. Every nerve ending in her body was screaming out for a thousand different reasons. She just needed her shift to be over.

And yet in the midst of it all, there was a tiny part of her brain that kept remembering Benji's referral to her magic potions in the eye drops that day when his sight had been restored and she had to stifle a smile. *Concoctions—potions—oh boy.* She wondered if his thoughts were traveling along the same lines. *Here she was again, with another concoction.* Was his reflection on the interaction aligning itself with hers? Catching his quick glance in her direction as he set the cup down, Ella wondered if she had done a good enough job holding back the grin that was betraying the memory circulating through her brain. Otherwise, the betrayal of her thoughts would just be another piece of confusion to add to the mix. And neither one of them needed that.

It was a struggle to get out of bed the next morning. Another day. Another shift at work and Ella still hadn't decided how she was going to handle Benji being assigned as her patient. She could go to her nurse manager and ask that he no longer be allocated into her care. It's what she should to do—was *going* to do. She just needed to think up a good enough reason for the request. But her feet were dragging. Her thoughts weren't clear on the matter of how to carry it all out.

Down the hall, she could hear her father snoring. A series of loud, post-drunk snorts.

What *remained* clear in her mind, was that she needed to get moving. With Melvin no longer working, now drinking more than ever, the Hurley family needed her income. She wasn't about to lay this all on her mom. Mostly, she worried that her mom was getting close to giving up. Ella needed to show her support by doing what it took to help out.

The sounds of Chance scurrying around to get ready for school echoed up the staircase. "Mom, where's my hockey puck?" The words reverberated from somewhere below.

"Last seen—" The voice of her mom faded, and Ella couldn't quite hear the rest. But they were up at least—her mom was up—doing their part to face the day. Ella needed to do her part too.

Making her way to the lower floor, she stopped to turn up the wooden radio that sat on the bureau in the sitting room. No music to brighten the morning, but she could hear the crackling sound of a news report and that was always important.

Now more than ever, our efforts on the home front will count toward helping the young men and women who are deployed in this war. Japanese forces have begun to attack the Philippines. As we know, after Pearl Harbor, the United States is fully engaged in this war. They need equipment to fight the good fight. We can help at home—

Ella turned the dial back down and continued on to the kitchen for breakfast. *Enough said.* Music wouldn't be her inspiration this morning, but if the transmission she had just listened to didn't motivate a work ethic, nothing would. Subsequently, she needed to quit thinking about Benji in a romantic light. He was a wounded soldier who needed all the help War Memorial Hospital had to offer. He had given of himself to the war—who was she to worry over such trivial things as dealings of the heart? But also, it wasn't wrong for her to ask that he be transferred into another's care—should she so decide.

Onward and upward soldier.

After a bowl of cereal, Ella put the powdered milk back in the cupboard, and finished getting ready with a resolved attitude. It was a calling to be a nurse. Regardless of the places her mind wanted to take her—there were those that needed her. Right then, the whole world needed her. To give all that she had, one bit at a time, in-order-to make it a better place. They were all in this together.

A half an hour later, when she received her assignment for the day, her resolve wasn't quite so strong. There was Benji's name on her list once again, big as life. And was she doing anything about it? *No.* And would she be—doing anything about it? *Probably not.*

Or maybe.

She just didn't know.

Choosing to put her mind in neutral, Ella tried to focus on the others in her care. Benji would be getting the same professional treatment as the rest—nothing more. And maybe even fewer hours allocated at bedside than the others, as he did seem to be relatively stable. She sighed in relief while fastening her cap in place. It was a good plan. As good as any she had.

During first rounds, Benji was asleep, so she rested easy, free to move about the ward, caring for her other patients. And the next time Ella made her way to the far side of the room, she found his bed empty. *What do you know—up and at'em*, she thought. Somehow, she'd missed seeing him leave. *Well, good for him.* It was great that he was exhibiting this type of ambitious behavior. This sort of thing would buy him a ticket out of the hospital in no-time.

Good news!

But she did need to find him, she supposed, and check in, perform some nursing assessments. The cafeteria was her first thought on where he might be, so she made her way there and ran into Lillian along the way. Lillian's ankle was fully healed, and she'd be back to work on Monday. Another bit of good news.

When Ella arrived at the cafeteria, just as she suspected, Benji was there. But he wasn't where she'd imagined. Instead of occupying his wooden wheelchair situated at a table, it was discarded in the corner, and he was sitting on a cushioned chair off to the side of the room. Once again, she found herself surprised. Taking a moment to compose, she prepared to walk over and partake in some sort of nurse-patient interaction. Ignoring the idea, that the day prior they had parted on less than the best terms due to the strain between them, she steeled herself for a better alternative.

The new precedence she'd be the one to initiate.

But if she'd expected the same frown from him as she'd received the evening before, she was surprised for a third time that day. The smile that greeted her as she approached caught her off guard. Without wanting it to, her heart fluttered. She took a breath, to slow it down. "Hi Benji," she said, working hard to keep her voice professional. "I found you." She motioned to where he was seated. "You look...comfortable. It's good to see this...progress."

"Hi, yourself, Nurse Ella. It's true...as you can see, I'm having a good day."

Nurse Ella? That was a new title coming from him. Why did she believe it held less than a professional connotation? Like borderline flirtation. And—my, the change in attitude from the day prior. But that was a good thing though—right? Just because she was planning on cooling their relationship didn't mean that he had to enter the doldrums over it. That wouldn't be healthy in healing.

"I'm glad you are doing well. It's so nice to see you up and about. And not just up and about in the wheelchair, but in a regular seat to boot."

"On the beam, wouldn't you say?"

"Yes, I'd say." Ella eyed the chair where Benji was sitting, a grin lighting up his face. She turned to look at his wheelchair where it sat abandoned several feet away. "How did you…how was it that you got to the seat you're in by-the way?"

Benji chuckled, pride emanating through his eyes. His mouth formed into a smirk. "Wouldn't you like to know?"

Ella narrowed her brow. Why was he regarding her like that? The look he was giving could only be described as playful. She found herself fighting back a smile, in-spite-of the whole *I'm a professional nurse* intention. "Yes, actually, I would like to know," she stated.

"And I'd really like to tell you…but I'm not going to."

Ella cocked her head. "Really…you're not going to tell me?"

"No…I'm actually not…going to tell you. But," he quickly added, "should you like to stick around and observe…you can see for yourself."

Ella thought of all she had to do for the afternoon. Antibiotics, dressing changes, IV administrations. What was Benji's game plan? Was he talking a few minutes here or the better part of an hour? *Oh, screw it,* she thought. After all that he had been through, she owed him at least this. "Okay then, it looks like I'm sticking around."

Benji folded his arms across his chest. "Good."

Ella gave a sweeping glance around the room and then back to where he was sitting. "Okay, I'm ready…show me what you have to show me. I have to admit, you have me on edge."

Benji motioned to the seat across from him, then crinkled his nose. "I'm not quite ready. But if you have a seat for a few minutes…I'm sure I will be…possibly soon."

"Possibly longer," he added under his breath.

What was this, Ella wondered. He was really toying with her. She felt stuck between a rock and a hard place. It seemed she had no choice in the matter. "Okay, okay." She shook her head. "I'm taking a seat. Sitting down."

Benji eyed her for a few seconds and her heart rate shot up. "So, tell me about your day…since I haven't seen much of you."

"That's not true…that you haven't seen me," she exclaimed. "Or… maybe so, but I did check in on you during early morning rounds, and you were sleeping. And then later…well, you were already gone. And so here I am making sure—"

Benji laughed. "Gotcha didn't I…I know you're busy. Still, tell me about your day. The weather outside when you came in this morning. Anything…I'm all ears."

So, he was lonely, then. She couldn't blame him. He'd been in there too long. They began to converse. How many minutes slipped by, she wasn't sure, when movement out of the corner of her eye caught her attention. It was an orderly walking at a fast pace, coming in her direction, words escaping from his mouth in a breathless rush.

"Can you come back to the Ward? Bed-six is acting strange. Hard to arouse. Confused."

Her patient with a kidney infection. He had been stable on last observation. But obviously there had been a change in condition. Jumping to her feet, Ella looked at Benji with wide eyes. "I have to go."

The last thing she saw was his nod of acknowledgment. Then she flew from the room.

For the next while, Ella devoted all her attention to the patient who had taken a turn for the worse. X-rays, blood draws, IV fluids, and a series of medications to stabilize. Dr. Northcott quickly got involved, along with another physician, and the decision was made to transfer him to the critical care ward.

By the time she had come up for air, Ella felt exhausted. Taking a minute to perform a few calming breaths, she attempted to let go of the tightness in her muscles. It looked like her patient was going to be okay. Just needed some extra TLC. A sigh of relief escaped her lips. After a moment or two, her thoughts switched to Benji back in the cafeteria. He had been about to share something with her. Possibly something important—real progress. She glanced to the far wall of the ward. Much time had elapsed since her hasty exit from his side. Maybe he'd already come back to the ward. A quick perusal told her bed-one was still empty. Smoothing her pinafore, Ella began to make her way back down the halls to see if she might catch back up with him.

Arriving at the cafeteria, she found the seats in the far corner of the room vacant as well. No Benji. No wheelchair either. Her heart did a little dive. Somehow it felt as though she had let him down. Yet these things happen. It was a hospital after all. Surely, he knew that. Surely, he understood. It didn't diminish her thoughts on the progress he was making. Intuition told her to head toward the alcove beyond the elevator bay. Maybe she'd find him there.

She wasn't wrong.

There he sat, looking out the window, as she'd found him on times before. He turned on her approach. Pausing mid-step, she waited as he took her in. Gone was the playful spark in his eyes, that she had been privy to earlier. But there was no disappointment or accusation either. Only a subdued light emanating from the blue of his irises. "Everything okay, then," he asked.

Ella nodded. "It will be."

"Good...that's good."

"Sorry that I got called away...It's just that—"

"It's just that it's your job. It's why you're a great nurse. I'd like to think you'd run that fast for me...if needed."

And I have, she wanted to tell him. She thought back to the precarious condition he'd been in on arrival to the hospital. All the intervening on behalf of the medical staff, herself included. Instead, she smiled.

"Come sit down," he said patting a chair beside him.

What? She all but took a step back. *She hadn't better.* For some reason the light of the window pouring into the alcove was providing an intimacy that had been absent in the cafeteria. It would be one thing to attend to Benji in a big room filled with people. It would still be considered professional behavior. But there, tucked away in a remote corner—all bets were off. Everything *seemed* different, somehow.

For a moment, she paused.

And then somehow found herself moving forward.

Benji's eyes seemed to take in her every step.

Ella tried to ignore the fluttering in her chest as she sat down. *This was still an act of professionalism*, she tried to tell herself. Maybe he was going to explain about how he'd gotten to the chair in the cafeteria after all. Maybe he just needed to share the experience—talk it out. One could argue that it was part of the progress in moving forward. A healing of sorts. She was doing the right thing—*being there in the private alcove.*

But the topic of transferring from wheelchair to cushioned seat in the dining area never came up. Instead, the conversation that flowed between them was about the most ordinary things. And yet, somehow, the mundane seemed like the most important matters in the world as they sat there, sharing their thoughts on the snowy winters up north, the best vegetable served as a side dish, their favorite models of cars.

The talk that was interchanged stretched on—seeming effortless. Soon, the thought of being in nurse mode began to disappear from Ella's mind. It was like hanging out, talking with a friend. Her friend, Benji. *BJ Marek was nowhere to be found.*

Or was it more than friendship? The way they were conversing—tones becoming increasingly subdued the longer they lingered. The way Benji was leaning in, closer and closer to where she was seated beside him in the chair. The way she wasn't moving away. How their eyes kept locking periodically—if only for a few seconds. How the rush of blood felt as it poured through Ella's veins, growing louder and stronger by the minute.

"Your thoughts," Benji asked. They had been talking about which birds fly south and which ones stay. There was a smattering of them congregating outside the window, where they were seated.

Ella was feeling distracted. It seemed at that point, the words flowing between them were less about content and more about body language used to get an idea across. The formation of syllables coming from the mouth. There was an enchantment in the air. Closing in around them. Certainly, she had felt a connection to Benji before. But not like this. What was going on exactly? This was something new. Where were her scruples given the situation? Where had nursing mode gone?

It was getting harder to think straight.

All she was conscious of was him. And how her body was responding to the presence of him being so close. *And yet, why was she letting him get so close?* Lines were getting blurred—erasing themselves by the second.

"Well…I know for a fact Robins come in temperate weather," Ella said, taking a breath. She needed to look away. Anywhere but into Benji's eyes. They were fast becoming her undoing. "They," her throat cleared, "are…not a winter bird. Their arrival is a true sign of spring. But the ones out now… I don't' know…Finches maybe?"

"Yeah…maybe."

But Ella had the feeling, Benji didn't give a rat's ass about birds right then. She could sense him looking at her, so she kept her eyes trained on the window.

"Ella," he said.

Still, she kept looking away. Light snowflakes were beginning to fall outside, somehow adding to the spell of the moment, drawing her in, putting her in a trance.

"Ella," he repeated.

She couldn't face his stare. She knew if she turned back—it was going to be too late. Too late for what, she wasn't sure. *Just too late.* But throwing caution away, she fought the very threads of sensibility that were ingrained in her persona, and rotated slowly in her seat, realizing the very second all lines had been officially crossed.

This time neither looked away. By then they were so near in proximity. He in his mobile chair and she in the seat, nestled in close.

Only a few breaths away from each other. A fingertip's reach. No more words were exchanged. No more talk of birds. Only the sound of Benji breathing out Ella's name. *Or was he even saying anything at all?* Ella couldn't be sure. All she was conscious of was the feel of his warm lips on hers.

And how it felt so right.

Yet so very wrong at the same time.

And still—so incredibly right.

Dear Thomas,

The sound of ships saluting after dusk silences the betraying beat of my heart.

~E

CHAPTER 13

We're all in this together.

A flock of warplanes flew over the water, descending on a fleet of ships. In black and white, explosions filled the sky, water, and land, followed by billows of gray smoke, destroying everything in its path.

The United States is at war. The bombing of Pearl Harbor has put us in the midst of a large-scale battle.

A squadron of soldiers marching in orderly fashion, saluting the American flag. Running, fighting, hunkering down, flying away in bombers. A V-formation of planes, soaring grandiosely, in domination of the sky.

A switch of scenery to images in a factory setting: Women in jumpsuits and safety glasses working on machines, smiling, determined, proud.

With all the soldiers signing up to do their parts, now gone from the home-front, we need your help in local job market. Sign up to work. Sign up today! And work plenty of hours.

You are doing your part!

Another shift in imagery: A grocery store with people in line to buy food. *These foods rationed today* written in large print on a sign. A woman and a child, grinning, holding up fruit. Clearly, they were happy to do their part, honored to buy only the *right* things.

Conserving resources and limiting consumption is another way we as citizens of the United States can be of help. Eat only what is available. And when possible, grow your own gardens.

A profile view of a determined soldier in fatigues and hard hat, rifle in hand, then took over the screen, filling up the front of the theater. Flanking him, the phrases—**Let's All Fight** and **Buy War Bonds**.

Another thing you can do to invest in the lives of the young soldiers out in the fields serving our country is to buy war bonds. Invest in your country. Buy defense bonds to keep the soldiers flying. Help them win the war. Let's all win the war!

We're in this together!

"Could you please pass the popcorn," Siobhan whispered to Ella.

"I knew it…you should have gotten your own."

The girls were having an evening out. Seated inside the theater on Ashmun, they had just finished watching the informational film on the war, as was current practice shown as a prelude to main event. A small reminder of what was going on throughout the real world, before the movie-goers escaped into a sphere of pretend. A tribute to the soldiers. A prompting of how they could spend their time—helping—when they left the theater again, entering back into society after the premier motion picture.

Siobhan swept her long brown hair over her shoulder. "Just this last time."

"Ha," Ella snorted, while rolling her eyes, then chuckled, handing over the container. "Have what you like."

"Quiet in front," someone behind them called out in a whispery shout.

The girls both turned around, annoyed. The featured film hadn't even yet begun. Across the front of the auditorium, they were still showing the customary cartoon clips that followed up the rendering of world events. "Shush," Siobhan said back, putting a finger to her lips. Ella stifled a snicker. They had messed with the wrong person. But right then, music began playing and a new picture flashed up on the screen.

All Through the Night starring Humphrey Bogart.

Forgetting about the rude person to their rear, they began focusing on the movie. It was supposed to be a good one. The girls loved Humphrey

Bogart. Especially Ella. It was advertised as a comedy gangster-spy film. Sure to entertain. And a little diversion from real life once-in-a-while was nice.

Setting the popcorn aside, they settled in to watch the story as it would unfold. Alfred Donahue—Humphrey Bogart—arriving at his bakery to check on a cheesecake he ordered. A nightclub singer just leaving the scene. Him finding out that his favorite baker had been murdered and not wanting the crime to be erroneously pinned on him.

Becoming engrossed in the action and entertainment, Ella began to lose herself in the plot, watching as Donahue, or "Gloves" as they referred to him, intervened on his own behalf to prove he was not the suspected killer, indeed.

The movie was just what was needed. A perfect escape. The perfect amount of laughter. The perfect amount of intrigue. A swell outing with a great friend. In the end, it was the unexpected twist that had the girls on the edge of their seats. As it turned out, Nazi spies might have been involved in the baker's death.

And with that plot unfolding, once more Ella and Siobhan were reminded of the war that they are involved in. Of how Hitler and his Nazi's, with their evil schemes, were trying to take over Europe. How the United States, after an expanse of time staying at bay, had finally entered the great war-conflict to fight against it all.

"That was on the beam," Siobhan said as they filed out of the theater. Next stop was Woolworth's for a bite to eat. They had attended a matinee and it was still light in the sky. "Will your mom be working?"

"Not today." It was one of Grace's rare days off. With her dad deciding to quit his job, her mom had upped her hours. And so had Ella. They crossed the street, in front of a poster displaying a man in a blue suit, with stars and stripes hat that read *Uncle Sam Wants You*. Ella grabbed Siobhan grabbed coat sleeve. "Anyway…don't keep me waiting, you started to tell me about your new soldier."

Siobhan grinned from ear to ear. "So I did. Did I mention he is real dreamboat?"

"Once or twice."

"Let me just tell you again, he is. He's all moved into the apartment. And speaking of once or twice… I've brought him dinner once or twice. I think he liked it."

"Did you cook or did your mom?"

Having made their way down the length of the downtown sidewalk, they stepped beneath the striped awning that outlined the frontside of Woolworth, and Siobhan opened one of the entry doors. She lifted her eyebrows. "My mom cooked, of course. But he didn't need to know that."

Ella laughed. "Of course, he didn't. So, just dinner?"

"Maybe…or maybe I stayed around a bit to visit." Siobhan gave a wink.

"Yes…I'm certain you did." Ella laughed some more.

The girls migrated into the soda fountain and got settled in, ordering a hot bowl of soup along with a soft drink. They'd keep their options opened for ice cream later. A wooden receiver was playing from behind the counter, and they listened as the news broadcaster announced that the U.S. was now part of a force called the Allies in the South West Pacific, combining with the British, Dutch, and Australia. Ella hoped it would help the cause—countries with similar goals, working together to create a stronger power against their enemies. When their orders arrived, they dug in and shifted the conversation away from the particulars of the war—having been spurred on by the latest updates on the radio— back to more personal matters, like Siobhan's new soldier friend. Or apartment tenant, such as he was.

Siobhan crossed her fingers. "Well, it's too soon to know for sure, but I think he likes me. And I know I like him." Her eyes drifted off for a moment, lips forming into a dreamy grin.

Ella watched her with a curious inspection and shook her head. "What's his name?"

"His name?" Siobhan snapped back to the conversation. "James O'Malley. Did I mention he is a dream boat.?"

"Only once or twice…or a thousand times."

"He has a military cut of course, but his hair, I can tell if it grew out…he would remind you of the surfer sort. He just has that look. In my mind I sometimes refer to him as *Surf*."

Ella thought of her recent interactions at the hospital. The way she'd thought of Benjamin as *Benji* in her mind. And how that in-turn had transitioned into his official nick name. But in all actuality, it wasn't his name at all. It was BJ Marek, as *she would do well to remember*.

In-spite-of that nagging knowledge, Ella brought a hand to her lips as memories from the last episode of her shift at War Memorial washed over her, a blush highlighting her cheekbones. *The kiss.*

Siobhan paused what she was saying, noticing Ella's change in temperament. "What's up with you? What's that look for?"

Ella froze, quickly putting her hand back down. "Look?"

"Yeah…just then…you had a funny look on your face…kind of dreamy or something."

Her mind began to spin. There could be no telling her best friend Siobhan about Benji. *BJ Marek*. Just the thought of his true name, the real person he was, brought a chill to her torso, that began working its way up her spine. "I…ah…I was just thinking about something funny at work. Nothing worth repeating."

"Okay—" Siobhan drew out the word. "If you insist. Didn't appear like a funny…ha ha look to me though."

Ella opened her mouth to speak, then closed it again. "From how you described your soldier, I'd say Surf it is…should you chose to call him that," she eventually said. "Can't wait to meet him."

Turning the conversation back to her friend's love interest seemed like an effective approach. By all appearances, Siobhan forgot all about the *look* on as Ella's face, gladly taking up the torch in the discussion of James O'Malley. After finishing their soup, it was decided they indeed had room for ice cream, so orders were placed. Two hot fudge sundaes. As soon as the glass-footed tulip dishes were delivered, they began to dig in.

After a few bites, Siobhan wiped a dollop of chocolate from above her lip with a napkin. "I hope he'll stick around though," she said.

Surprise lit up Ella's face. "What do you mean, stick around? Didn't he just get to town?"

"I know…he did. But I've heard talk of soldiers getting called away at a moment's notice. With the uncertainty of the war and all, I guess you just never know. From what they say, it can all be so very tight-lipped. You're given an order to board a freight train on a mission without any knowledge of the end point. You discover your destination while en route."

"Well, I hope that doesn't happen. But I have to admit, the way you're describing it, it sounds kind of intriguing…mysterious. Though scary, I suppose, too."

Siobhan laughed. "Doesn't it though…so very covert…secretive. Just as long as it's not my James, though. Not my Surf."

"It's *your* James now, is it?"

"Maybe…we'll see." Siobhan scraped the bottom of her dish, scooping up the last of the fudge. "Although, I've heard that Bob Hope has been making appearances at some of the military camps around the country, entertaining the soldiers. Maybe if James was sent to the right place, he might get to see him perform. So, there's that."

The girls looked at each other. Ella lifted her brow, and Siobhan shook her head.

"Still, not worth it," she said.

After finishing the ice cream, they headed back out on Ashmun The weather was somewhat temperate that day, considering the typical harsh conditions of the north, so they decided to walk a little before heading home. Soon, their footfalls began taking them toward the Locks. They passed by a Chevy Coupe Pickup parked along the way and Siobhan whistled, causing a couple of soldiers to look their way.

"Sorry fellas, I was talking to the car," she said. "Isn't she a real humdinger?"

The soldiers agreed hardily and looked like they were about to head in the direction of the girls, in-spite-of the clarification on the whistle. But Siobhan waved them off. Apparently, James O'Malley was all that she needed for the time being. Though Ella wasn't sure where she, herself, stood in the romance department. *Or was she?*

"Can't wait for the Locks to open up for the season," Siobhan resumed talking as soon as the soldiers had taken the hint. She was still on the car theme. "Maybe we'll get to see some cool vehicles." Most of the cargo the freighters contained, was made up of iron ore and stone, but sometimes they transported automobiles too.

Ella nodded in agreement, half listening—half distracted. They were passing by a wire bin with a stack of newspapers from *The Evening News*, and she was trying to eyeball that day's headline. Too often, with the war going on, the news was only of severe report, speaking about fear of bombing attacks and such things as that. It affected everyone, even down to the youngest members of the family. Her brother, Chance, often came home from school talking about emergency air raid drills, having to take cover right during a mid-day lesson. Life in the Soo had certainly changed from all they'd known in the past.

But then again, for the Hurley family, life had become altered even long before even that.

The headlines from the paper didn't jump out as anything horrendous, and the girls kept walking, a shot of relief washing over Ella. Tiny bits of respite. They reached Portage Avenue, then Water Street. The frozen strip of the St. Mary's River was just ahead. In-spite-of the determination to enjoy a fun-filled afternoon, a measure of introspection found its way into Ella's thoughts, and she grew increasingly quiet as they walked.

By the time they reached the waterfront, Siobhan realized she had been carrying most of the conversation. For a few minutes, the pair stood staring out into the waterway, across to where the Canadian flag flew it's bold red and white vertical stripes. The wind, light and fresh, coming from the southwest, was like a temperate caress on their cheeks, reminding them of the promise of spring. Though it wouldn't be coming soon enough.

"What is it," Siobhan asked.

Ella startled. "Huh?"

"I'm losing you. Where have you gone? You've been quiet."

"No reason...and everything I suppose." Ella gave a cautious grin, thinking of all that might be weighing her down. The war, her dad quitting his job, her mom slipping further into depression, the melancholy memories of missing her beloved Thomas, and now having BJ Marek as her patient at work—*kissing him*. Tiny goosebumps found their way onto her arms as she reflected on this last thought. In-spite-of the unseasonably comfortable temperatures. Regardless of the warmth of her coat.

Siobhan nodded. She got it. Or at least she thought she did. The last part she had no knowledge of. Ella knew it would illicit a whole other conversation that she wasn't ready to partake in—delving into the BJ Marek discussion. They studied the icy channel some more, quiet falling between them once more.

"Is it hard for you?" Siobhan turned toward her.

"Hard?"

"To come down here by the Locks."

Ella thought for a moment. Hugging tensed arms to her chest, she squeezed. "Not really." She took in the components that made up the Locks. "Mostly it's the sound of the fog horns after shipping season starts up again." She gave a shake of her head and stifled a shiver. "Yeah…definitely the fog horns…they still get to me."

An empathetic expression found its way into her peripheral vision and Ella turned toward Siobhan, returning her look with a smile. *Enough about that.* More than ample amounts of melancholy had crossed her mind for one day. Ella dialed up her grin. "But on to better things," she told her friend. "It's a great day…let's enjoy. I'm going to enjoy it. Tell me more about James."

CHAPTER 14

~1930~

"Single file when you exit the bus."

Ella eyed her view of the water and parked ferryboats from where she sat in her window seat. Siobhan was seated next to her, leaning across her lap, trying to create her own sightlines. It was late spring, and the rapids of the St. Mary's were flowing freely. The Locks were up and running at full capacity. Miss Johnson, their fourth-grade teacher, had given the directive. It was time to get off the bus. Single file—*no goofing around.*

Such an exciting day! Fieldtrips were the best. A day to explore outside of the classroom. A true sign of the pending summer. A measure of exhilaration filtered through the air, touching all the school-aged children encompassed within its perimeter. Eleanor Hurley included.

That day they were going to take a tour through the Locks. And even though the students had grown up in the area and were used to ships coming and going, it would be exciting to learn about the process firsthand.

Plus, it was a day, free of chalkboards, pencils, and paper.

Ella left her lunchbox on the seat next to Siobhan's brown, paper sack and began to make her way to the head of the aisle. Miss Johnson had told them they would be eating lunch on a large, designated space on the lawn in front of the waterway, or if it was too cold, then back on the bus. She could see other buses pulling up too. The fieldtrip did not belong to fourth graders only, the entire upper elementary was included. For a split second, Ella felt a small weight of melancholy settle on her shoulders over this idea. But she brushed it off. It was going to be a great day.

Making her way down the steps to where they would begin the tour, Ella took her place in line along with Siobhan and the other fourth graders. One classroom of fifth graders was already there ahead of them, and the rest, along with the entirety of the sixth grade, were getting out of their perspective buses, heading over in bunches.

Ella felt the impending approach of the upperclassmen but kept her attention on the fourth graders in front and behind her, Siobhan being one of them. She was wiping a strand of her brown cropped hair out of her eyes, looking for the ship that one of her classmates had spotted coming up the river, when she sensed the close-by presence of students, older and bigger. Momentarily forgetting about the ship, Ella watched from her peripheral view as they closed in. From the boisterous sound of their voices, she knew they were sixth graders. But where were they headed? The back of the line was to her rear, snaking around the side of the Locks Park entryway.

In a moment Ella knew all too well what they were up to—they were planning on cutting. Setting her jaw, she faced forward, ignoring the commotion, ready to move forward at the beckoning of a school administrator. The arriving students just needed to go to the rearmost part of line. But in due time, an all-too-familiar voice caught her attention, thwarting her resolve. *BJ Marek.* She should have known he'd be at the head of the hullabaloo.

"Hey, fellow comrades," he called out to his group of friends, while coming up next to Ella. "Free spot right here. Empty space. Nobody's right here."

Ella couldn't help but turn away from her focused stare. *What was he talking about?* Of course, there was someone there. *She* was there, along with other fourth graders. The lines had long been formed. As she looked in BJ's direction, her eyes searching, connecting with the voice, she found him glaring—staring her down.

"Yep...no one is here as far as I can see." BJ looked right at her as he spoke each word, an arrogant sneer lighting up his face. The message was clear. *You are a nobody* he was telling her with his words, with his eyes, with his disdainful facial expressions.

"Wrong-o pal...we are now," said Jimmy Adamik, laughing, as they bunched their way into the line, causing Ella and other fourth graders to take a step backwards, in avoidance of getting shoved.

Ella felt her face heat up. Grabbing the sides of her dress, she balled the material into her fists, fingers curving around tightly as she squeezed. Siobhan's breath came in tiny puffs to her rear. She was pissed too. But what could they do? For a brief moment, Ella glanced around for Miss Johnson, her fourth-grade teacher. *Had she happened to notice the transaction?* Alas, she was nowhere to be found—probably somewhere at the very front, preparing to help guide the troops through the high points of the Locks.

Ella considered raising her hand or yelling out—*Hey, they cut*—but she knew it would be of no use. BJ Marek and his friends would only make her pay later. And the retribution, she realized, would be something far worse.

CHAPTER 15

Ella walked over to the nurse's station with her head in the clouds. She was feeling a bit featherbrained. The last time she had been at work, she had overstepped boundaries with Benji. *And how.* Kissing him was the last thing she had seen herself doing. Well, being honest, maybe she'd imagined it a time or two—but then had quickly pushed it out of her mind. It was a completely unthinkable act between patient and nurse. *Between Eleanor Hurley and BJ Marek.* And yet she had partaken—very willingly. With more abandon than she cared to admit.

Had enjoyed it a little too much.

What had she been thinking?

During a time when she had been working so hard to erect barriers between them, putting a reversal on any sort of budding relationship.

And now that it happened, she couldn't get the whole thing out of her mind.

It had been all she'd thought about over the last couple days away from the hospital. Well, not *all*—she had enjoyed her time out with Siobhan. And there was the matter of upheaval on the home front. That turmoil feasted on much of her brain activity. But too often, between everything—any pause in the action—her thoughts had returned to how everything had gone down between herself and the soldier-patient.

And it had gone down a little too good.

She would never be able to dispute her reaction, should he choose to confront her with it.

Anyway—*did she really want to deny it?*

She began tucking miscellaneous medical supplies into the apron pockets of her nursing pinafore, dropping a few items on the floor amidst the endeavor.

"You going to make it there, Ace," Florence, the ward clerk, asked, keeping an eye pinned to her activity.

Ella grinned sheepishly. She was in the process of making a mess. *And not just with the medical supplies she was dropping all over either.* Her life was following quickly behind. She needed to pull herself together. Clumsily letting go of another cotton ball, she hurriedly tried to scoop it back up, mid-fall. For the moment, the idea was not reconciling itself to her performance. Clearly, her brain and her heart were on two different pages. Her actions getting caught on a flustered page of their own, somewhere in between.

"I'm okay...I'll be okay," she finally answered back.

Florence lifted her brow. "If you say so. Let me know if you need any help." She went back to sorting files, keeping post out of the corner of her eye.

Stuffing the last of the wayward supplies into her pocket, Ella motioned toward the entrance of ward-four. "I'll be...I'll just be—" She could feel her cheeks growing pink. Then, bright red, as another thought occurred to her—had anyone seen the kiss?

Did anyone know?

Did *everyone* know?

When she met up with her fellow nursing employee, Lillian, a few minutes later, inside the walls of the ward, and there was no sort of obvious reaction on Lillian's part, Ella figured the indiscretion was fairly safe for the time being. Immediately a cumbersome weight fell away from her shoulders.

Five patients had been assigned into her care that day: A fireplace burn, a respiratory infection, gallbladder attack, broken femur, and of course—the famous, resident soldier. Ella was thankful for a lighter group. It was Lillian's first day back to the hospital, after her ankle injury, and it would be fun to catch up without the weight of a demanding workload.

After initial rounds, they had settled in to begin implementing care, Ella attending first to her patient with the respiratory illness and Lillian across the way, delivering care to an infirm of her own. Notably—Benji was two beds away.

Ella couldn't help but glance in his direction every so often as she went about doing her work, periodically exchanging small talk with Lillian across the aisle of beds. On initial early morning inspection, he had been sound asleep. But now she could see him stirring. Her body doing a stirring of its own. She felt giddy. Lightheaded.

"Sure hope we can take a lunch together," she called over to Lillian, using a little more animation than her usual style. "Catch up on things. So much we need to talk about, I'm sure." A half glance toward Benji escaped the corner of her eye.

Lillian was arranging some supplies on the cart parked next to the bed of her patient. She paused and looked up. "Yeah…that would be copasetic. As if that will ever happen." A chuckle and eyeroll followed.

Ella laughed too. "You're too right, Lil…chances are that won't happen. Fun to think about though."

"A grand idea. Say…do you have any bandage fasteners in those pockets of yours?" Lillian opened a bottled of antiseptic in preparation to begin working on an inflamed wound.

Ella thought about everything she had filled her apron with. Fasteners weren't on the list. "Nope…sorry," she answered with a measure of pizazz. "But I'll be happy to get you one." Why was she talking so stridently anyway? What was she trying to prove? Whose attention was she trying to enlist? Once again, she glanced in the direction of bed-one. This time Benji *was* looking her way.

Immediately, a blush found its way onto her cheeks, and she turned back to her work.

Her heart was beating fast. She was feeling a little crazy. With much concentration, she retrained her focus, and began pouring a cupful of elixir. Handing it to her patient, she watched him drink it down. Across the way, she could hear Lillian humming a Bing Crosby song. Why did she feel like joining in? This wasn't like her. She wasn't acting like herself.

For the next several minutes, with concentrated effort, she tuned everything out around her but the needs of her patient: counting respirations, assessing the workload of breathing by eyeing the degree of how labored the rise and fall of the chest, assisting with the breakfast tray in-order-to conserve energy for eating, encouraging boisterous coughs to loosen the phlegm—getting the crud up out of the lungs where it could fester and worsen the condition.

"Didn't know how much I'd miss this." Lillian had moved on to her next patient, still within conversing distance from Ella, though far enough away they couldn't speak in low tones.

"You never know what you have until its gone. Isn't that how it goes?" Ella was moving on to her next patient as well—one bed closer to Benji. When push came to shove, she had done a good job focusing on her last patient, taking care of what needed to be done without a constant barrage of distracting thoughts. Hopefully, this interaction would go as smoothly. She fought to keep her eyes from landing on Benji's bed as she walked around the white metal frames, but it was taking all of her will power.

On the opposite side of the aisle, Lillian was helping her patient sit up on the edge of the mattress. The patient looked a little woozy. "Doing okay over there," Ella called across.

Lillian stooped down to meet her patient's eyes. "I think we're okay. How are you feeling Mrs. Potts?"

Her patient nodded, lifting a hand to her head. "Just feeling weak."

"I agree." Lillian patted her on the back. "You are weak. It's a case of being laid up for too long. We'll take it slow and easy. We're going to sit here for a while, let your body adjust, before we try anymore movement."

Ella was preparing a pain shot for her patient with the broken femur. Was she imagining things, or could feel Benji's eyes on her as she moved toward the bed? Was he thinking what she was thinking—of how he had been laid up for a long time too, weakening the condition of his body? How it took a lot to get him moving again, up and out of bed, especially that first time. *Or was he thinking about the kiss?*

Goosebumps covered her arms. Ignoring them, she zoned in on her patient and administered the shot. Afterward, she laid aside the syringe and turned around. *She had not been wrong.* Benji seemed to be waiting for her—for some type of interaction with her. Their eyes locked and for a few moments she did not look away.

All of a sudden, she was back in that alcove with him on her previous shift—getting swept away. Experiencing sensations she never imagined experiencing with him. *Yes—definitely the kiss.* He'd been thinking about the kiss alright. It was written everywhere on his face. Just as surely as it was written on hers.

With deft movement, she turned away and sucked in a breath. Had she lost her mind? She was being so unprofessional. And here she was, administering care to another patient at the very same time. Acting like an imbecile.

Taking a moment to compose herself with a few carefully concealed gulps or air, Ella tuned out Benji once more, focusing her attention back on the patient-at-hand's broken leg: inspecting the cast for drainage, checking the affected limb's toes for good coloring and movement, and helping to assist with the setup of the breakfast tray afterwards.

A short time later, Ella decided it was time to visit bed-one and deliver care. There was no sense prolonging the interaction. He was assigned to her, after all. Grabbing a thermometer and a blood pressure cuff, she made her way down the remaining length of the aisle. She could see Benji sitting there, watching her approach. His breakfast tray was pushed to the side, alluding to the idea that he had just finished eating. The same energy that had been there with the exchanged look while she had been taking care of her last patient, remained active, filling up the space surrounding his metal bedframe.

She hardly knew what to do with it all.

For a two-second increment, she allowed herself to make direct eye contact, giving in to all the feelings and emotions that were evident between them. A remembrance of what they had shared on the shift prior. There was no denying all that had been.

"Good morning," she breathed. The voice that flitted from her lips hardly sounded like her own.

"Good morning," he answered back, followed by a pause. "And it is a good morning, indeed," he added.

Ella stirred into movement, setting her things down. *Dare she ask the reasoning behind that statement?* "Oh…yes? How so?"

"Well for starters, my favorite nurse is here." He winked.

Ella blushed. What to do with that inference? Once again, she realized there was no refuting all they shared. But how to move forward? How to proceed throughout the day—as nurse?

"And then there's the big bonus of being able to see."

Ella stilled. Her head tilted in question. "What do you mean? You've had clear vision for the last several days now, haven't you?"

"Not yesterday." The playfulness in Benji's expression faded. "Couldn't see a damn thing all day. Well, unless you count the bright flashing lights that keep coming."

Of all the things Ella had anticipated would come of the morning, this wasn't one of them. So many other issues to deal with—all along the nurse/patient scenario. So many things to sort out. But medically, she had assumed Benji was moving forward—getting better. Though in small increments, of course. But now with the revelation of this—it felt like a blow. Surely Benji was feeling the knock-back of it as well. Tenfold.

Like a lightning bolt striking her insides, she was jarred back into caregiver mode.

A little before lunch Dr. Northcott caught her in the hall. "We're having a meeting in-regards-to one of your patients. It will be held in the second meeting room. You are welcome to attend. In fact, we'd like you to attend."

Ella's first thoughts were of her indiscretions having to do with Benji. Surely that's who they were referring to as *the patient*. But then if so, she wouldn't be just *welcome* to attend. It would be a demand— prior to the administration kicking her out the door of the hospital. "Bed-one?"

"Yes Bed-one. And it's at 1p.m."

At 1p.m. when Ella walked into the second meeting room just past the central nursing station, she found Dr. Northcott, along with Dr. Farr, and Gladys Bukowski, the head nurse of her unit. For some reason, Ella's heart fluttered in her chest. She had the feeling this meeting was a big deal. And although the medical professionals gathered couldn't possibly know the lengths of her involvement with the patient who was the point of discussion, she still felt on edge. As if the feelings inside of her heart were written all over the expression on her face.

All eyes welcomed her into the room.

"Come on in," Dr. Northcott said. Ella took a seat at the table where they were circled. "We were just discussing the patient on ward-four, bed-one. Benjamin."

Ella gave a tip of the head. "Of course."

"We know you've been assigned to him on a regular basis, so we thought it best to include you in the discussion of his care. William?"

Dr. Farr nodded, having been handed the baton. "After reviewing the logs from my previous visits, and then from this current one, it is my professional opinion that the patient has plateaued. He is no longer making progress in his condition." He glanced around the table. "Do you concur?"

Dr. Northcott's face was solemn. "I concur," he said.

Gladys Burkowski cleared her throat. "Yes...this seems to be the case. Since transferring to our medical wing from intensive care, he had continued making progress from his injuries for a while but hasn't moved beyond the current state of his condition for a few weeks."

For a moment, the room was quiet. Ella felt like she was on stage. Clearly, they expected her to say something. She was up next. Only thing, she had more questions than answers. What would happen to Benji then if this was the decided conclusion? Was everyone just giving up on him? Would he live out his life decrepit—a wounded soldier confined to bed, a forgotten hero?

Had he given up on himself?

She thought back to what he had told her earlier in the shift, while she'd been implementing care at bedside. Just yesterday he hadn't been able to see. He had slipped backwards—*so easily.* For a moment she looked down. Then gave a slight nod of the head. "It does seem that way," Her voice was quiet, subdued. "Some days are better than others... and this seems to match his mood. I'm not...I'm not sure which seems to trigger which." *And hopefully she—herself—wasn't some type of trigger, to boot.* "Not that I blame him, I'm sure this whole thing is depressing.

But yes, I agree." She shook her head. "He hasn't seemed to move beyond his current state."

"Good to have input from all angles of care." Dr. Farr grabbed a pen and started scribbling. Then, stopping, he looked up from the clipboard in front of him. "Like I said, from all the tests I've conducted and comparing notes from visits, this is my conclusion. But it's always good to hear from those who care for him on a daily basis. See if something needs to be added or looked at from another perspective. There is always the chance I've missed something, since I don't' see him regularly."

"So, what's next for him?"

Ella's vision flitted over to Gladys. *That was her question exactly.*

Dr. Northcott sat up a little straighter in his chair. Directed his gaze toward Gladys and Ella. "After careful review, it's been decided that a convalescent home is the next stop. We have a division on the edge of town. We'll see to it that he gets transferred there."

Beside Dr. Northcott, Dr. Farr was nodding in agreement. "We would have expected Benjamin to start walking by now. At best, he can stand for a few short minutes. And even that isn't on a regular basis. Then of course, there are days he still can't see. The mental blocks seem to be securely in place. And until those are broken down, there won't be forward progression."

"We'll begin the transfer very shortly. Possibly even this afternoon."

Ella sucked in a breath, eyes widening, even as Dr. Northcott spoke the words. "So soon," she asked. Surely the move would come as a jolt to Benji. He needed time to prepare mentally.

She needed time to prepare mentally.

"There is a strong likelihood that it could be today, but we'll have to see how things play out."

"It's just that—" Ella stopped herself. She didn't want to sound desperate. Too attached. "Well, it's just that if he's had no forewarning, this may come as shock to him…I wouldn't wish him any setbacks, since it's agreed that he needs all the help he can get in moving forward."

"Help indeed," Dr. Farr broke in. "Yes, on some level he needs encouragement and help. Psychotherapy for sure. And if I'm right, he can get these sessions right at the convalescent home he'll be transferred to. But for the most part, moving forward is something Benjamin will need to do on his own. If it happens at all."

"But Ella has a point," Gladys interjected. "Give the poor boy some notice…if possible, that is."

Ella held her breath, looking up at Dr. Northcott.

Dr. Northcott appeared hesitant. "Well…okay for today. We won't make the transfer today then, but soon. Most likely tomorrow, and if not tomorrow, the day following. I'll go speak with him shortly, so he can begin to prepare himself."

Inwardly, Ella gave a sigh of relief. But the respite was short-lived. Who was she worried about being able to adjust to the relocation? Benji? Or herself?

By the time the next day rolled around, Ella had completed several sessions of self-talk in her mind, coming to the conclusion it *was* truly for the best—Benji moving to the convalescent home. For many reasons. The top one on her list—they could never be together anyway. It was only matter of time before he figured out who she was. At this point, he was going through caregiver crush. But eventually those feelings would come crashing down with reality. And in-spite-of her best efforts to put the kibosh to the relationship, somehow, she had managed backsliding, entering into a compromising position, even sealing the deal with a kiss.

Yes—it was best that he go.

And with that thought in mind, Ella transformed into nurse-only role for her next shift at the hospital, knowing full-well that it would be her last with the soldier-patient in bed-one. But it was harder than she thought when it came time to say goodbye.

With all of his possessions packed, Benji sat waiting in a chair beside his bed for the transport vehicle to take him away. Dressed in civilian clothes, hair slicked back at the sides, bangs falling to one side, periodically grazing an eye, it seemed official—this was it. He was moving on—and not in a good way. More like the end of the road. End of his career in the armed services. End of his stay at the hospital, eliminating any hope for further cure. Everything was over. Done. Finished.

But there was always hope.

Right?

Ella couldn't think about that. She refused to let herself contemplate anything more that the here and now, wishing a patient the best in a professional manner as they exited her facility.

Walking over to the portion of ward-four that had been Benji's for several weeks, her heart did a quick stutter. Somehow, he looked so vulnerable. Unlike the soldier she knew he had once been before all this had happened. So unlike the side of himself he had shown at various times while under her care; joking, flirting, exhibiting occasional stubbornness and self-preservation, earnestly trying to heal. *Very unlike BJ Marek from back during schooldays.*

"All set I see," she said on approach, keeping a lighthearted feel to her voice. She glanced around at his bed, at his bedside tray, looking for stray items that needed to be packed up, but everything seemed to be in order. She could sense Benji's eyes on her, watching. Finally, she ended her diversional tasks and looked back.

A lumped formed in her throat.

What had she expected from him? Whatever it was, certainly not the emotions that were transmitting from the expression on his face right then. Complete confusion and susceptibility as to why she was speaking to him in such a flippant tone.

Any yet, truly, she was acting every bit the professional nurse. No glibness intended. *This was best.*

"Yes…all set," he finally answered, a sigh escaping his lips. With a searching gaze, he opened his mouth to speak again. Ella imagined possibly to delve in deeper about how things stood between them— *after the kiss and all.* But much to her relief, right then a group of other medical staff members—Dr. Northcott included—began arriving to the bedside, along with the driver who would cart him away. She had timed her goodbye perfectly. And with the thwarted look in Benji's eyes, it seemed he knew it.

But Ella kept a pleasant smile pasted on her face, nodding her head in rhythm to the chorus of well wishes coming from all the employees and caregivers as they said their farewells.

Benji met their adieus with appreciation. Although it could be looked at as the end of progress, the realization was there that he had been given good care while under the patronage of the hospital institution, arriving as a soldier on his death bed. And truly most who had crossed his path had grown to care for him. He was leaving a tiny bit of himself in each one of their hearts.

For Ella, though, he reserved looks of perplexity and disquiet. A type of waiting. A questioning in his expression. Surely there would be something more coming from her lips in form of sendoff—a more personal goodbye. Possibly a longing stare from behind the crowd that had gathered. Even a discreet glance.

But Ella was nothing if not astute at remaining professional. And the crowd of medical comrades only helped to strengthen her resolve. She chuckled when funny vignettes were reminisced over. Nodded solemnly when heartfelt regards were spoken. Pursed her lips together over encouragements for future healing.

Inside she was dying.

She wanted to run a million miles away—and cry. She wanted to stay. Get rid of the others who had packed themselves around his bed. Rush into her patient's arms—hug him for the longest time. Tell him she would miss him more than he could know. Assure him that the kiss *had* meant something—made her feel lots of things.

All the things she wasn't allowed to feel.

He would realize this—in time.

The true chasm between them.

And then the real hurt would surface—for Ella.

It was best to end it there and then. It was the perfect timing for an ending.

"Goodbye, Benjamin," she said as the driver wheeled away his chair, her face a blank slate, save the congenial upturn of her lips.

The look on Benji's face though as his eyes sought to make contact with hers, while being propelled from ward-four was one that would haunt her for the days to come.

CHAPTER 16

Ella perused her list of patients. A bereft feeling settled into her bones as the name that was missing from her assignment dominated the empty space on the roster. *Benjamin M., bed-one.* For the past few weeks, it had been there day after day. A staple to the ward. And now it was simply gone. A ghost in her mind. Pressing her lips together, she looked up. She could feel Gladys, the head nurse, watching her, an empathetic glint in her eyes.

Ella nodded in return.

She didn't feel like talking.

She'd miss him. That was for sure. Maybe more people than she realized knew just how much. Or maybe not. Maybe Gladys' reaction was just an acknowledgement of a common sentiment. She'd miss him too. *They'd* miss him too. Most would, at least. He'd been well-received at the hospital. They were all in his corner. He'd given of himself to fight for the country. They were rooting for him—for all the soldiers. But he had been theirs.

With a sluggish gait, Ella gathered her things together and prepared to begin the day. Stuffing the pockets of her pinafore with medical paraphernalia, she headed to the doorway of ward-four. It was a room filled with patients to concern herself with, but her eyes were drawn to the empty metal frame at the edge of the long row. She had told herself not to go there. Not to linger on shifts past. But for some reason, she couldn't help herself.

Sadness welled up inside of her.

She missed him. What had been. What could have been. What could *never* have been.

If only she could remind herself of what truly *had* been.

She just needed a moment.

With slow steps, she walked among the long line of sleeping patients, making her way with the help of dim lighting that created a pathway through the room. Reaching the far wall, she paused to stare at an exposed, striped mattress flanked by a cement wall and a neighboring bunk. There were no comforts. No linens and a pillow to cozy up the stark-bare nook. No silhouette of a body to make the blankets breathe with the promising rhythm of life.

"Goodbye, Benji," she whispered into the dark. *Benji,* she said again in her head. *Not Benjamin. Not BJ. Just Benji.* With a discreet glance, she browsed the room, hoping no one had heard her. But there was nobody nearby. For once, Ella was thankful that she wasn't sharing a shift with Lillian. Although, the perfect distraction, she wasn't in the mood to fake it in front of Lillian during the shift—to chime in with her exuberance.

Solemness was on the agenda for the day.

And focusing like everything on her other patients.

"Nurse Ella, can I have a drink?"

Ella turned toward the raspy little voice that was submitting the request. "Why sure you can, Rosie." She reached for the glass on the bedside tray. Handing it over, she offered assistance in keeping it steady, while Rosie brought the water to her lips. The drink was a small sip.

Ella smiled down into a cherub face. Rosie was one of six patients on her roster for the day. And the smallest. At seven-years-old, she had come to the hospital after having a severe asthma attack. Having recently checked on her other five—a stroke patient, an intestinal bleed, a pneumonia, an infected wound, and a concussion—making sure their needs were tended to, that they were settled in and stable, Ella focused her attention on the youngest of the group.

Rosie's breaths came in wheezes between drinks and Ella cringed a little inside. It was definitely time for medications to be administered. Preparing what was prescribed, she offered it to Rosie. Then sat at bedside, talking and reading her a book, waiting for the remedies to take effect.

She was halfway through *Curious George* when she felt eyes resting on her. She lowered the book to her lap. "What is it, Rosie," Ella asked.

Rosie watched her some more. She looked so frail, huddled beneath the covers, skin pale, eyes round. "It's you, Nurse Ella," she said.

"Me?" Ella didn't have to feign her surprise. "What is it about me?"

Rosie coughed and Ella noticed that it was starting to loosen. That was a good thing. "It's just that you look sad today."

"I do?" Ella shifted in her chair. Of course, she did. She *was*—sad. And apparently, she wasn't doing a very thorough job hiding it.

"Are you? Sad?"

Ella thought for a moment. What to say? Seven-year-olds were nothing if not astute to emotions. If she said no, Rosie would know she was lying. And where would that leave the rapport she was building? Rosie's father was away serving in the war and her mother was at home tending to other children, younger in age than Rosie, impeding her visits to the hospital. So, Rosie needed to have trust in the staff, needed to feel safe and secure while in their care.

Ella tapped Rosie on the nose. "You know, you are a smart girl. There *is* someone that I miss. Someone that went away recently. I suppose that is making me sad. But being here with you is helping that sadness go away. Making it a little easier."

A grin formed on Rosie's lips. "Really? I'm glad I can help make you better. You make me feel better too." She paused for a moment, situating herself beneath the covers, the movement causing her to breathe a little heavier. "Did the person who made you sad go away to the war? My daddy went away to the war and that makes me sad. I miss him."

No, this person actually just came back from the war, thought Ella. But what a complicated concept. It was more information than her young patient needed to know. "Not exactly," Ella answered. "I bet you do miss your daddy, however. But you can be proud of him, for all he's doing for our country. You…young lady…need to rest though." She offered a smile and a pat on the head. "Let me finish reading this book, and then it's time for some shuteye before lunch.

"Okay," Rosie nodded, while Ella picked back up *Curious George*.

Afterwards, walking away, Ella sighed. It seemed she wasn't doing a very good job hiding the gloom over missing Benji. If her youngest patient had picked up on it, the others were noticing too. They just weren't saying anything. She needed to do a better job of keeping her feelings under wrap. Maybe she didn't feel like doing cartwheels that day, but neither should she be walking around in the doldrums. For the rest of her shift, Ella not only focused hard on the care of her parents, but on visibly reviving her own spirits too.

Her stroke patient, unable to lift her eating arm, Ella helped to feed, all-the-while asking questions about her family members. How many children did she have? How many grandchildren? All this, with a pleasant lilt to her voice. The longer the conversation, the more alert her patient became, leading to clearer pronunciations when speaking aloud. Ella checked her legs, exercising them with lifts and bicycling movements, all-the-while paying attention to their coloring and ability to move in comparison with one another. To Ella, it seemed the weak one was getting a little stronger. She'd make sure to let Dr. Northcott know.

Checking on her intestinal bleed throughout the day, Ella looked for the appearance of any new signs of bleeding, all-the-while keeping the conversation light. "Got anything left inside this body of yours? Any blood…say?"

Her patient nodded, a grin on his face. "I think so. There was hardly any bleeding this last time I used the stool."

"Well, that's a good sign. Let's hope the progress keeps up." The doctors were hopeful that it was due to hemorrhoids and not something worse. But they were keeping him at the hospital to make sure he didn't take a turn for the worse.

To the patient with pneumonia, Ella administered antibiotics, and checked her temperature and respirations, applying cool clothes to the forehead when a fever spiked. Then, offered drinks of liquid and spoonfuls of broth when it broke. In-between-times, she encouraged deep coughs to bring up the congestion and clear her chest. Throughout this, Ella kept a pleasant demeanor in place, speaking in soothing tones, interjecting carefree jokes when appropriate.

Breezing along the bedside of the patient who had suffered a concussion, Ella checked in often, making sure he was staying alert, observing for nausea and changes in vision or any signs of further neurological decline.

The patient with the infected wound, Ella spent longer periods of time, cleansing the laceration and the fragile skin surrounding the area. It was a work accident at the factory—and instead of getting better, it had become inflamed, festering and oozing with purulent secretions. With the affected arm propped on a pillow, Ella sat at bedside, generously dousing antiseptic solution to the site, afterward patting it clean, applying an outer wrapping. This was repeated two more times during the shift—all with upbeat dialogue as she worked.

By the end of the day, Ella was exhausted. But all the medical tasks and the work of pretending to be jubilant, had kept her mind occupied and at the same time, lightened the dispositions of her patients. She knew it was the right thing to do. Afterall, her patients didn't deserve to be brought into her despairing, bad mood.

Three weeks passed by.

And things got much better. The hurt of missing her soldier-patient eased. Ella continued concentrating on those in her care with a fierce passion, helping to lessen the burden of loss she was experiencing. Things were looking up.

Then one day, half-way through her shift, Gladys Bukowski, the head nurse, called her into the office. "Sit down, Ella," she said.

"Okay," Ella answered with caution. She took a seat across from Gladys. What was this about? Surely, a call to the office wasn't a good thing. But she couldn't imagine anything reproachful she'd done. *Aside from her fling with Benji.* Her heart picked up in tempo at that thought.

"I'll get right to the point. I know you're aware of our convalescent division." *Of course, she was aware. It's where Benji had been sent—to stagnate.* "Well, there have been a growing number of patients dispersed there…many of them soldiers from the war, injured and unable to continue on in their service. The sheer numbers of it all, is presenting a growing need…for nurses."

Ella nodded. It made sense. An expected fall-out from the war. But how did it involve her? She already *was* a nurse—doing her duty. Did they want her to recruit?

"That's where you come in. We think you would offer the kind of well-rounded experience that the convalescent home could use right now. And if you are agreeable…we would like to send you there. Reassign you."

Ella's brain immediately began to buzz. She couldn't think straight. "Oh," she breathed. It was the only word that came to her mind. Out of all she had anticipated coming from the conversation, this was the last thing she had expected. She lifted a hand to straighten her nursing cap. "I mean…what about my position here? What would happen to that?"

"It's not a permanent transfer. Unless of course, after going there, it's something you'd prefer to happen…to stay. We have considered the needs at the hospital and feel that this is the best move for the time being…transferring someone out. It's the appropriate move to make during these times…for the war effort. Hopefully soon, we'll be able to recruit more nurses."

"And everyone is on board then I assume? Has it already been discussed?"

"Yes…it's been discussed both here at the hospital and at the convalescent home. The proposal has been approved. Dr. Northcott has added his consent."

Dr. Northcott too? Well, it sure sounded official. How could she say no?

"You don't have to answer today. Give it some thought. But don't linger. We'll hope for an answer soon."

Ella could hardly think straight for the rest of her shift.

Nor when she went home afterward. Didn't pay a lick of attention to her dad's drunken rampages as he called out demands from his easy chair. Didn't go round and round in worry over her mom's deteriorating appearance as she slinked unobtrusively around the kitchen scrounging up something for dinner. Not even Chance's enthusiasm as he bounded in and out the front door, playing neighborhood ball with friends, proved to be a distraction from her menagerie of thoughts.

Ella could hardly believe it. They were asking her to leave War Memorial Hospital! It was such a shock to the system. And just when her life was starting to take on some semblance of order. True—maybe it wouldn't be forever, but there was always that possibility that it could turn out that way. The hospital had been her life over the past few years. Would she even like the convalescent home? Besides, it was farther away—the commute would prove to be more cumbersome, if not inconvenient.

But what was a little inconvenience when there was a major war going on?

What of the soldiers forfeiting their lives on the battlefield? What of the myriads around town, stepping up the hours on the assembly line? What of the school-aged children, spending time collecting metal, aluminum, and rubber, along with other materials that could be transformed into beneficial items for use in combat? There was sacrificing going on in all directions.

And then there was the biggest conundrum yet, overshadowing all thoughts of war—what of Benjamin Marek from bed-one?

Benjamin, the soldier-patient, who had been transferred to the Convalescent home.

Benji—*her Benji*—that she had been trying so hard to forget.

BJ Marek from back in school.

The situation was not black and white. There were complications going on in her mind. She knew what was best for the war effort, the hospital, the convalescent home, the soldiers' needs, and society in general, was also going to be worse for her personal well-being. Just when she had started to strengthen her resolve and ease up on the memories, she'd be forced to see Benji once more.

Was it wise to put herself on the front lines again?

For hours Ella laid in bed that night, thinking, deciding, perseverating, trying with futile resolve to find some semblance of sleep. There were so many reasons to say yes. So many reasons to answer no. *One big reason to say no.*

By the time morning dawned, brow heavy from lack of rest and layers of conflicting situations having ruminated through her mind, she knew the answer that would be given to Gladys Bukowski later that day at work.

Three days later Ella arrived at the convalescent home, having ridden the bus to the edge of town. It felt like the threshold of nowhere, compared to busyness of the hospital, which was located on Osborn Boulevard, closer to the hustle and bustle of the city.

Ella could feel the shakiness in her limbs taking over while eyeing the front entrance of the building, which resembled more of a sprawling old house. Even in the dim, early morning light, a large side yard could be spied wrapping around to the back. A place for the recovering wounded to get fresh air, she imagined. With benches situated next to oak trees, it would be nice in the summer, aiding in healing of body and soul. Especially soul.

Giving herself a hug while approaching an oversized, entry door, the realization hit that she, like the soldiers, could use some sort of healing. A restoration of her own. At the moment, it felt like she was falling apart. *Just why exactly had she agreed to come,* she wondered. The transfer *hadn't* been mandatory. And yet there she was, administering some type of self-torture to her psyche. To say she was nervous was an understatement. For a few fleeting moments, she considered turning around and running after the bus, asking to be delivered back to War Memorial. Surely Gladys would understand. Dr. Northcott as well.

Instead, she took a deep breath and proceeded up the steps of the porch. Half questioning what was expected at this type of facility—*was she just supposed to walk right in*—Ella reached for the knob and wiggled but found it to be locked. Soon after, she gave a few knocks on an upper, wooden panel, rapping lightly at first, then following it up with some hardy thumps.

It didn't take long for the sound of jiggling metal chains to reach her ears. And then the door swung open. Greeted by a girl who looked to be no older than a young teen, Ella was ushered in. "Hi…I'm Ella Hurley," she announced, holding out a hand. "Registered nurse reporting for duty."

"Welcome, Ella. I'm Sophia," said the girl in a soft voice. "I help out around here. I was told there'd be a new nurse arriving. They'll be happy for the help. There's been a recent influx of soldiers needing care."

And just like that—Ella was reminded why she came, her insecurities getting pushed to the back burner.

"Happy to help," she replied.

After a minute or two of small talk, Sophia proceeded to show Ella around, leading her past a front sitting room beside a staircase with dark wood railing, matching the rest of the ornate trim that garnished the floors and ceilings. A set of offices was tucked off to one side. From there a long hallway. Ella could see the place was much bigger than assumed at first glance and seemed to go on forever.

At one point, they reached a large dining area which could be considered more of a cafeteria, save the homey feel of the décor, flower-patterned wallpaper, large windows covered in drapery, and a grouping of davenports in the corner. Beyond that, was a recreation room. And then more hallways, which led to a series of bed chambers. Sophia told her there were more rooms that housed beds upstairs and that she'd be getting around to showing her those later.

For right then, she'd accompany her to the medication room and leave Ella to her occupation, after a quick introduction to Ms. Kijak the administrator. Ms. Kijak was all business. But she thanked Ella for coming, gave a brief a history on the facility and went through an itemization of responsibilities to be covered during each shift, while conducting a mini-tour of the medical supplies. Just the bare necessities. It was all that was needed, Ella supposed. There was only one thing missing.

A list of patients.

Ella had no sooner given credence to this thought, when Ms. Kijak handed her a piece a paper. The nervous feeling that Ella had upon arriving began to rekindle. It was a directory of names. Her patients for the day, and for the next several shifts—until further notice. *Would Benji be on the roster?* With a shaky hand, Ella held the thin material between her fingertips and began scanning through her assignments.

No Benji.

She read through it several times just to make sure.

He was not on the list.

Relief wrapped itself like a warm blanket around her shoulders. And yet there was an element of disappointment, digging at her, trying to rip holes in the silken material. She had begun to push the latter feeling away, when a sudden thought occurred to her. *Was Benji even at the facility any longer?* There was always the possibility that he had healed enough to leave and function satisfactorily on his own back at home.

The idea left Ella both reassured—and a little disappointed.

A few minutes later, she was inspecting the room, sorting through supplies, gathering provisions for the day, when she happened to notice an opened notebook, containing a stack of papers. A more extensive roster than her single-page list. She told herself not to look. But Ms. Kijak had already left the room, and her eyes couldn't seem to help themselves. *Just one quick browse.* There was nothing on the top sheet that caught her attention, and even while telling herself to walk away, she found her fingers lifting the page, peaking to see what was beneath.

And suddenly—*there it was*. Second column down. *Benjamin J. Marek.* The name practically jumped out at her, causing her to startle. Letting go of the papers in hand, Ella walked to the other side of the room, attempting to concentrate on the arrangement of medications in the glass cabinet against the wall. All-the-while trying to breath in and out.

So, he was still there at the convalescent home. So, what? She had expected as much. At least he wasn't on *her* list of patients. Surely, she could still do her best to avoid him. It couldn't be all that difficult. Tucking that thought away in her brain, she finished gathering her goods, and exited to explore the rest of the facility.

Ella was almost finished with her self-assisted tour. She had run into Sophia again by the front offices, who had given her an all-is-clear on exploring the second story. Travelling up the staircase, she delved into every hall that housed the bed chambers. Each passageway explored carried with it a tiny knot entering her stomach. Would Benji be around the next corner? Would she pass by one of the myriads of rooms that lodged the patients and spy him sleeping in bed? Or else, find him awake, sitting up, a shocked expression on his face as she peered inside? Yes—her body was in tense mode, no doubt about it. But after all was said and done, the exploration turned out to be a rather benign expedition. Ella hadn't run into him after all.

She was just circulating back to the medication supply room, contemplating how to begin administering treatment to those assigned into her care, when something about a worker she spied in the doorway of the rec room caught her attention. It was a young lady, similar to Ella in age—maybe a little older. Something about the way her blond hair was styled, too fancy for a day at work, the thick makeup above the eyes, long lashes—probably false. Her whole demeanor of owning the spot she was in, the reek of self-confidence. All-at-once, a premonition came over her. It was Jane Beckwith from back in school.

Sure, there were those changes that had come with age, but overall, Jane looked exactly the same. It would have been hard not to recognize her. Ella reached for her own blond hair—created from a bottle—pulled back at the nape of the neck. Would Jane recognize her? Jane, who was in BJ's Marek's inner circle. Who Ella had dreaded running into in the hallways at school, throughout the entirety of her growing up years, right along with BJ, Jimmy Adamik, and the rest of BJ's cohorts.

An uneasy feeling settled onto Ella's shoulders as she eyed Jane's white pinafore, similar in style to her own, although, somehow, Jane wore hers with a greater essence of fashion. *So, she was a nurse too then.* If only Ella had only known—would she had agreed to come to the convalescent home? She pushed the thought away. She had to make the best of the situation. Although just the sight of Jane's superior persona, the tilt of her head, the gleam of arrogance in her eyes, it was enough to throw Ella off guard. As if she needed those added feelings—with the knowledge that Benji was somewhere in the building as well. *BJ.* Just that quickly, Benji, the injured soldier from bed-one, had transformed into being BJ in her mind, given the sight of Jane.

Ella continued to stare at Jane Beckwith and saw Jane regarding her back. It felt like a standoff. All-at-once, an unsettling thought occurred to Ella. What if Jane *did* recognize her? What were the ramifications? Surely, none of them good. Heart beating fast, Ella fought the urge to turn around and walk back the way she had come. Or possibly even run.

"Why hello, Eleanor," she watched Jane's lipstick-covered lips say, even while contemplating her next move. Immediately, Ella froze, a sinking feeling settling into her chest.

CHAPTER 17

The buzz around the cafeteria was almost palpable. It was Friday and the students were hyped for the weekend. Just a few more hours to go and the ring of the freedom bell would resound throughout the hallways. It was like this every Friday. In turn, the teachers had a hard time keeping control the last few hours of the day. The cafeteria personnel as well. Customary practice was burgers and French fries, served on trays to students as they made their way through the line. End of the school-week grub delivered with a grimace by the lunchroom ladies. And although not burger-joint quality, it was considered a reprieve from the slop served into the partitioned plates Monday through Thursday.

Eleanor had just received her portion and was headed toward a table in the corner of the room, where she'd wait for Siobhan to join her. Junior high school was an adjustment, but she was falling into a routine, switching classes, learning to fly beneath the radar in the hallways in order to avoid attention from 8th graders. Mostly it wasn't too bad—being twelve and starting a new phase of life, beginning a new school—except the way her hair got greasy more often, or the emergence of pimples that had begun to find their way across her forehead and chin. She was no beauty queen, and she knew it. But what she lacked in attractiveness, she made up for in the classroom getting high marks.

And much to her relief, it was another year free of the class two years above hers—the one that housed BJ Marek. So that was always a reprieve, lessening her burden in a multitude of ways.

Eleanor set her tray down and was just about to take a seat when she noticed the typical Friday din in the lunchroom had gotten stepped up a notch. There was something about the noise level that seemed a little brassier, the voice qualities growing more gregarious. A certain change was sweeping through the air.

Eleanor looked toward the entrance of the cafeteria where the majority of the commotion appeared to be taking place and felt her heart drop to her stomach. *It seemed it would not be a BJ Marek free day after all.* But just what was he doing there? He and all his friends— hanging out in the junior high cafeteria of all things. Maybe being sent on errand to the office? Or visiting a coach from previous years? Who really knew? Who really cared? Not Eleanor, that was for sure. Taking a seat, she kept her eyes trained on her plate, hoping Siobhan wouldn't have a hard time locating the spot she had picked. Considering the circumstances, there was no way she'd be lifting her head, entering the warzone, looking around for her friend. No way she'd risk making eye contact with BJ Marek or any of his chums in the process.

But Ella didn't have to look up in-order-to realize the din she had detected moments before was shifting. Now moving, progressing from the doorway, migrating into the center of the room, where the tables were grouped together. Heart resounding loudly, she began to prepare her burger, every beat that pounded in her chest, willing the group to retreat instead of making their way closer to where she was sitting. *Oh, why hadn't she picked a table that was filled with more students?* It would have been the perfect place to hide, to just disappear. And what was taking Siobhan so long anyhow? *It wasn't too late.* There was still time to transfer seats and fade into the crowd. Eleanor kept her head low, waiting, counting the seconds until her friend would arrive.

Or until BJ Marek did.

"Oh, don't you just miss junior high, comrades?"

Eleanor stiffened. BJ's cluster was getting close enough that she could hear his voice. It scraped loudly against her eardrums.

"Yeah...would you look at all these cookies we're missing out on being at the high school," added Jimmy Adamik. That caused a burst of laughter to erupt from the group.

"BJ, you're such a gas. You too, Jimmy. I don't think there's one of us here that misses this joint. Not in the least." This time there was a feminine tone to the speaker. From under lowered lids, Eleanor caught a glimpse. It was Jane Beckwith, all done up with a bouffant hairdo. She should have known. Jane had always been part of the clique. A regular cheerleader for all the antics, if not a perpetuator herself.

"Says you," said Jimmy. "But just look at all these dames."

"Yeah…just look at them. Looks like they haven't washed their hair in weeks." More laughter lifted into the air, a few punches in the arm exchanged.

Self-consciously, Eleanor raised a hand to her own stringy strands. Were they referring to her? Without meaning to, she lifted her head. Now the entourage was only a table away, shifting randomly between the rows. In an unwelcomed instant, her eyes made contact with BJ's. She felt it—the second recognition set in, the elevated degree of awareness. A jolt of dread shot though her veins. She wanted to slink under the table—to just disappear.

"Well, isn't this just swell," BJ said, looking Eleanor right in the eye. "A table up for grabs."

Eleanor glanced around at the empty seats beside her, knowing it was too late. And just where was Siobhan exactly? Maybe she had gotten smart and run away. Far, far away.

At BJ's command, the group slid into the benches encircling where she sat, boisterously shoving and back slapping, acting up. They were a city unto themselves. Eleanor an alien in a foreign land. And yet, it should have been the other way around. It was *her* junior high now—not theirs. Never-the-less, when she saw BJ eyeing her burger, she felt helpless to respond. Why couldn't they just go back to the high school. Leave her alone.

"Hey…look…a burger," BJ said, grabbing the sandwich up off her plate. "And what do you know…I'm hungry." He took a bite and passed it to Jimmy, who flipped it over a few times before shoving a portion in his mouth. The others around the table laughed heartily.

"Hey…I'm hungry too," Jane whined. "What's left for me?"

Eleanor opened her mouth to protest, but BJ was already grabbing a handful of French fries off her plate and handing them over to Jane. Jane put one in her mouth and munched for a few seconds, before spitting it back out. "Ooh gross," she said, placing the pile back on Eleanor's tray, chewed one included. "Cafeteria cooking never changes. Think I'll stick to my packed lunch after all."

Eleanor swallowed down the bile that was coming up her throat, along with the anger that was circulating throughout the rest of her body. She eyed what was left of the rest of her food, regurgitated and mangled, and thought once again just how much she hated BJ Marek, Jane Beckwith, and the rest of their friends. Seconds later, from under lowered lashes, she watched as the entirety of the group simultaneously jumped up, and in the form of a circulating dust cloud, began circumnavigating the rest of the cafeteria looking for another victim to claim.

Although, for reasons she couldn't explain, it always felt like she'd been purposefully singled out—the personal recipient of BJ Marek's wrath.

CHAPTER 18

It had been a silly notion to think she could go a whole shift without seeing Benji. Ella realized this the moment she walked into the cafeteria. Just because he wasn't on her list of patients, didn't mean anything in a facility that size. Although the convalescent home was much bigger than assumed on first glance, it wasn't spread out like a hospital where you could seclude yourself in a ward for the entirety of the day.

But still, it was like her eyes were playing tricks on her when she saw Benji sitting, big as life, in the corner of the room. It stopped her in her tracks. Made her do a double take. It had been a busy morning, getting used to which patients were hers—and then the tricky task of locating each one when it was time to administer medications, identifying who was who, especially if they happened to be mobile and not in their assigned room. It had left her rather exhausted. And it was only half past noon.

Ella was in the process of rolling a wheelchair into the cafeteria, a little late on the draw, as lunchroom hours would soon be ending, but her patient had several needs that required attention before the trip. And then at the last minute needed to use the lavatory. Afterward, it was back to square one, getting him ready all over again.

It was the sound of Benji's voice that actually first drew her attention. She'd have known it anywhere. But though the familiar tone jumped out to her eardrums—the reverberation was confusing at first, because the voice she was hearing didn't belong to Benji, her patient from the hospital, at all. *But that of BJ Marek.*

And yet they were one person.

It took a minute to reconcile that notion in her brain. Left her feeling shaken. Caught off guard. Made her question whether the Benji that she had gotten to know at War Memorial even existed at all. The presence of the old BJ felt so strong in the room, washing over her with a torrent of memories.

In knee-jerk reaction, she took a step back, pulling the wheelchair with her. The patient she was pushing kangarooed against the wooden seatback.

"You are right, this food is slop," Benji was saying to the person beside him at the far end table. "But if you're not going to eat that… give it to me. On second thought…hand it over. I don't care if you were about to eat it or not." Roaring laughter around him followed.

Ella stared across the room, swallowing down a feeling of deja'vu.

Benji was surrounded by a group of patients, who sat, attuned to his every word, each joke at someone else's expense, all commands that left them subservient to his disposition. It was like he was some type of rajah. A king. A supreme ruler.

Or BJ Marek from back at school.

"Hey," the person sitting beside him attempted to retrieve his food. "That may be slop, but it's my slop."

"You're a day late and a dollar short," Benji said, shoving a piece of what looked like meat in his mouth. He chewed for a few seconds. "I have to say…that didn't taste too bad. Somehow, better than mine did."

"Wonder what they'll be serving tonight," another person sitting at the table interjected.

Benji swung his head around. "Are you looking my way?" He took a swig of water. "Because don't ask me. That's above my pay grade." Another round of laughter echoed throughout the group.

"Well…whatever it is," the patient's whose food he took broke in. "You owe me a portion. I was going to finish that."

Benji reached out to rub the guy's head. "I owe you nothing pal. You know you weren't taking another bite." The guy bowed his head, if only slightly, in defeat. And Benji beamed triumphantly, though it was really more of a smirk. A confirmation that he was still on top. That he still reigned supreme.

The group gathered around Benji consisted of young men close in age, mostly soldiers who had been injured on the warfront Ella assumed. But there were some others too, older, who for some reason or another resided at the home. They all sat chatting and joking, though the jests were mostly at each other's expense. And for some reason, the tone held a negative connotation, as if the humor was just a means of passing the time, a way to get by, considering the lot they had been handed having ended up in a place like the convalescent home.

"I don't know about you fellas…but could you please pass the sugar," the guy to Benji's left broke into the conversation, ending the topic of who owed who over the pilfered food. "Take a look over there… now there's a real dish if I ever saw one."

For a split second, Ella felt the contents of her mid-morning snack rise up to meet her throat, sure the comment had been in reference to her. After all, how many other females were in the room? But moments later, she watched as the cluster of men at the table turned in sync, focusing their gaze on the far edge of the cafeteria, opposite direction from where she resided. The lack of white attire on the girl they were gawking at told Ella she was from a different department than nursing. The way she was scraping food off the plates into the trash, most likely kitchen help. But all-feminine non-the-less. And considering the ratio of men to women, though not the most attractive in appearance, still a big hit among female-starved men. Nods of agreement were initiated all around. Followed up by *oohs* and *ahs*.

Benji lifted his hand, cutting into the chorus of ogling sounds. "Don't be a chucklehead," he said to the guy who had made the observation. "I've seen better…much better. Had better too."

"Hawaii?" It was the person sitting directly across the table throwing out the question.

Ella felt her stomach clench. While it should have bothered her that Benji was about to reveal how he felt about a multitude of women, possibly her not even making the top tier of the list, with the bombing of Pearl Harbor getting brought up, all other thoughts were super-ceded in her mind.

Benji *never* talked about Hawaii.

A two-second pause followed. "Maybe Hawaii…maybe other places," he finally said. A far-off look crossed over his features and Ella imagined him going there in his mind. Back to the bombings. But what-ever-the-case, it didn't take long for him to snap out of it. Pivoting in his seat, he turned back to where the girl was working on the stack of plates. "Anyway…if you ask me that dame is U-G-L-Y."

The guy sitting across from him shook his head in agreement while two others joined in, though moments before they had been taking an opposite stance. "Yeah man," one of them said. "U-G-L-Y." Ella cringed, hoping the girl couldn't hear what they were saying.

"Anyhow, who cares?" Benji's voice raised up a decibel. "Stupid dames," he appeared to mutter under his breath. "Who's up for cards later today in the rec hall?" All eyes around him widened in interest. A refrain of *yes's* and *I'm in's* ensued afterward, save the person sitting directly beside him.

"Don't think I'll make it. Can't sit up in this chair that long. My back starts to hurt."

Beni threw his head back, rolling his eyes. It was the guy whose food he had eaten earlier. "Don't be a drip, Shorty. Be a man." He slapped him between the shoulder blades. "I think your back will hold up. It's just a game of cards." A few chuckles were lifted into the air.

Shorty's eyes drifted downward. "Yeah…just a game of cards," someone else echoed. But Shorty's jaw was starting to set, exhibiting a form of resolve. Clearly the answer was no, but Benji wasn't about to let it go.

"What's the matter…is it nap time for you already? Or you got other things planned for yourself…alone in your bunk?" This brought on a new round of laughter.

Shortly was starting to look a little perturbed. "I said my back—"

"And *I* said…your back will be just fine. We'll be saving you a seat, Short. We'll expect you."

The sound of a fist being pounded against the table reverberated into the room, causing what plates that were left amongst the group to rattle. A glass tipped over, spilling its contents. The noise was startling. "And I said…I can't—" It was Shorty again, his face beat red. It looked like he was ready to blow a fuse. Ella wondered if it was time to step in. Deep inside, all she wanted to do was unobtrusively drop off her patient and disappear. *She just wasn't ready.*

She just wasn't ready to come face to face with Benji—or as it stood, *BJ*. Not there. Not yet.

"Whoa…whoa…whoa." Benji held up his hands "Take it easy, Short. You don't have to flip your wig. We'll excuse you this time. Go back to your room and take your nap or whatever it is you need to do."

Ella experienced a measure of relief as she watched Shorty push himself from the table, and begin wheeling hastily away, amidst subdued smirks and laughter. The biggest part of confrontation was over. Now for her to deliver the soldier she was pushing, to the nearest tabletop, and tip toe back out.

But some things, it seemed, happen a second too late.

She felt it—the instant everything changed in the room.

It was as if time stood still. Slow motion taking over afterwards. The exact moment Benji set his gaze in Ella's direction. The shocked expression that followed. The air of disbelief. All others surrounding him at the table faded away, the entirety of the cafeteria becoming fuzzy and unclear. All that was left was Benji. Sharp. In focus. Clear as a bell.

Ella wanted to disappear beneath the floorboards. Turn and run quickly away. Pretend she didn't see him, that she missed his eyes locked on hers. Instead, she froze.

The look he was giving her encompassed so many emotions: foremostly dumbfoundedness, followed by incredulity, anger, sadness, and then possibly a flicker of expectation. Ella hardly knew what to do, how to react. She couldn't even begin to imagine the sentiments that were reflected on her own face. *An overriding degree of professionalism?* She could only hope.

She grabbed hard onto the push-bars of the chair she was wheeling and squeezed. *What was to happen next*? She felt suspended in limbo. Surely, some sort of explanation on her part needed to be aired, of how she had been asked to transfer. How basically, she had no real choice in the matter. As she was contemplating the next move, something seemed to change in Benji's expression. A new type of awareness. A donning of sorts. Followed by a degree of bitter resolve. A shutdown.

That's when Ella knew.

He recognized her!

Maybe it had just taken the new setting. He could finally see her for who she really was. All had become clear in his mind. *Too clear.* Each one of the reasons he had ever hated Eleanor Hurley as a child were revealing themselves, popping into his head in consecutive order. Though she never understood any of them, really. All she knew, was that it hurt—it was hurting her right then. If Ella thought she wanted to escape before—right then, she could think of nothing else but getting out of the room. Simply disappearing.

But she was nothing if not professional. *Though at times that was debatable.*

With a flick of her eyelashes, she reset her thoughts, converting back into nurse mode, standing her ground, strengthening her steadfastness. Prior to the transformation, for a brief instant, she had allowed herself to see BJ for who *he* really was, understanding finally the reason he hadn't recognized her until that moment. He was truly a self-involved person. He saw only what he wanted to see. And for the past several weeks, during his time at War Memorial—what he had seen was only *himself.*

CHAPTER 19

Stunned back into reality, it took a few seconds for Ella to realize what was coming her way. A wheelchair at full speed. With Benji as the occupant. She lifted a shaky hand to straighten her nursing cap. When had that happened? She couldn't even recall the transfer from cafeteria seat into the mobile device. But it was possible she had missed the transaction. Her mind had been ultra-focused on one thing. Getting out of the dining room. And yet at the very least, she knew she needed to deposit her patient at a table. She couldn't just take off without getting him settled in.

But after that task was complete, a quick wave would suffice—wouldn't it? And then a pivot and an exit.

"Ella." Her name sifted through the air, reaching her ears with a certain urgency. Spoken as if time were of the essence. Did it look as if she were about to bolt after all—with no thoughts given to the patient in tow? Just an all-out sprint in-order-to take her leave from the room.

The chair wheeled closer. "Hello, Benji." Ella reached for her throat. The voice coming from her lips hardly sounded like her own, containing none of the angst she was currently experiencing.

Benji's eyes were wide with inquisitiveness. Truly, he looked stunned and a little breathless from the jaunt across the room. "What...you have on...you are here. Are you here? What are you *doing* here?"

Ella couldn't help the nervous laughter that escaped as she imagined the surprise picture she presented. Or was it in reaction to the way Benji was forming his sentences—hiding back none of the shock he felt at having discovered her inserted into his new life.

The way he was regarding her though. She was getting the old vibes. The ones that had been created at War Memorial. None of the attitude leftover from childhood. She felt herself sighing inwardly in relief. He didn't recognize her after all.

"The administration at the hospital asked me to help out here at the convalescent home for the time being. This is one of their divisions. Apparently, there is a shortage. Of help. Of nurses."

Benji was studying her through narrowed eyes as she talked. Was he remembering the impersonal way she had sent him on his way as he was being transferred from the hospital, cutting off any possibility of future relationships? Well good—hopefully the precedence would continue during the remainder of her stay. And all could remain on the up and up, making things easier between them.

He shook his head once, then rubbed his chin. "Well…this is definitely unexpected." Looking up at her, he paused. "But in a good way…right?"

Ella opened her mouth to speak. What did he mean by that she wondered? That their romantic-like relationship would get a chance to rekindle here at the new place? Or that this would be the chance to start again—in a more professional way? Clear the slate. She could only hope for the latter. Feeling tongue tied, she caught the stirrings from the patient of whose chair she was pushing. "Am I going to make it to lunch or what," he called over his shoulder.

"Of course." She startled into motion. A weight of relief escaped off her shoulders at being able to shelf the current conversation. She glanced back at Benji. "Not used to timing of things around this place yet. Think I'm getting a little behind."

Benji nodded in answer, letting her get back to her task. What else could he do? Obviously, work came first.

It was two more shifts until she encountered Benji again. This surprised Ella—the seeing him, then not seeing him, then seeing him all over again. Considering how quickly she had run into him on her first day of the transfer, she thought it would continue happening on a repeat basis. So when she spied him in the physical therapy room working on his exercises while going down the hallway on a medication pass, it caused her to do a double take.

There were others at the facility with the same haircut, similar in build. With the way his head was bent in concentration, nothing shouldn't have flagged that it was him. There were no clear sightlines. And yet there was something about his disposition that was sending signals of recognition to her brain. She meant to take only a glance and keep going, but for some reason she remained, hands chucked full of supplies.

"Damn these legs," she heard him say. "They are not working today. Can't make them do a damn. stupid thing. They are stupid. This is stupid."

The therapist beside him looked on with a supportive expression. "How about a rest," he suggested. "We'll take a five-minute break. Just sit for a while."

"That's all I do with my life is sit. What's five more minutes of sitting?"

Ella could feel the frustration in the air. It was practically palpable. Not only Benji's but the therapist's as well. She fought back a flash of melancholy on Benji's behalf. It seemed his progress continued to be stifled. Most likely from the mental blocks that still occupied his mind. She shifted the load of medical provisions in tow. It was time to continue down the hall. True, the battle remained. And true, she wished she could fight it for him. Win even. But after spending weeks with him as her patient at War Memorial, she knew there was nothing left to contribute on her part.

Her thoughts on walking away from the doorway were met by Benji lifting his head. Ella froze in place. Once again, it seemed she was a few seconds too late on things. The look on his face registered surprise mixed with the current vexation he was working through over his lack of improvement. "So…I see you are working today then," was all he said, but the expression on his face gave an open invitation for further conversation.

It would be rude to acknowledge the observation and move on. Ella nodded toward her full arms. "I am." She motioned to where he was seated. "And this…I haven't really checked out this room before. It's where you complete your physical therapy exercises, I take it."

Benji let out a sound of frustration. "If that's what you want to call it."

Ella peered further into the room. "It's on the beam if you ask me. Plenty of equipment. More than I would have expected actually."

"This place has to have something to try and get all of us beat up soldiers back to par. Not that it's working in the least."

Ella fought to keep her expression stoic, if not somewhat pleasant. "Well...it's a start anyway." She gestured with her raised brow, taking in the circumference of the room. By then she had taken a few steps inside. "At least it's here and available. The other part will come in time."

Hopefully.

It felt like she had said too much, her pat answers too cliché. The look on Benji's face was telling her as much. She wished she could turn around and leave the way she came, never having entered the conversation. Clearly, Benji was having one of his bad days. But she had been there, easily detected in the doorway—and now the words had already left her lips. Across the way, she could see the physical therapist eavesdropping. It would be hard not to in a room that size. And with what he had invested in the patient, it would be expected.

"Don't be so sure about that," Benji muttered under his breath.

"What?" Ella was sorry the moment she spoke the word. She should have just let it go. Ignored his statement. She knew it was born from irritation.

"I said...nothing appears to be *coming* in time. This is the new me. Like it or lump it. Navy Seaman Benjamin Marek reporting for duty. Oh wait...I can't do jack shit anymore ...so I guess there won't be much to the duty part. Sorry, Uncle Sam, I'm all washed up."

"Well, I—"

"Well, you're what...an eager beaver I'd say. Wanting me to work hard so I can fix myself. Fix all that is wrong here. Make me all better. Normal. Maybe you should just sprinkle some fairy dust over me. You know...with all your magic potions and all."

The physical therapist got up from where he was sitting, making his way between equipment pieces. Ella could feel her face heating up. What did the physical therapist think? That she needed his help? Oh no, she didn't—not in the least. She'd been down this road before. Experienced all she needed to experience in-regards-to BJ Marek. Navy *Seaman Benjamin Marek—Hmph!* That was a parody. All he'd *ever* be is BJ Marek from back in school.

She looked Benji right in the eye. "I was *about* to say…*well* I need to get going, I have medications to pass. Have a good rest of your day, Sir." Giving a quick nod of the head to the therapist, she turned and walked out the door.

When Ella left the room, she was shaking. She shook for the rest of the day—off and on. *That BJ Marek—he just made her livid.* Why did she let him get to her? Always had, always would, it seemed. If there was some small consolation—at least he wasn't her patient on that particular shift. That was *something* she supposed.

But all that changed the next day.

She could hardly believe it when she received the list from Ms. Kijak. It was a completely different roster of names than on her prior shift. Trying to hide the shock, Ella lifted her eyes from the typed column, half expecting a *got-you* smirk from Ms. Kijak. But she wasn't even looking. Ella cleared her throat. But that didn't get a response either. "Excuse me," she said. The paper made a crinkling sound as she lifted it into the air.

Ms. Kijak finally turned. "Yes?" She peered above her glasses.

"This…my assignment. It's not the same as yesterdays'. I just figured—"

"That you'd have opportunity to spend two days with the occupants of your assignment? Oh no…we can't afford that luxury. We are very short handed. We need to speed things along in your orientation to the facility. Today you'll be getting familiar with an entirely different group of patients. And the next day, another one. And so forth and so on."

Ella hoped she didn't appear as dumbfounded as she felt. What could she say in response to the answer she'd been given? It would be unprofessional to argue her point. Spoiled and immature actually. And hardly patriotic when there was a war going on.

Gathering her supplies, she began making her way through the convalescent home in search of those on her roster. Some were still in their beds, some roaming the halls, and some had already made their way to the cafeteria for an early morning repast. As in days prior, she found it quite a chore to locate each patient. Not having a face to match the name, she had to rely heavily on *asking around*. There was one patient that *would* be easily recognized, of course. And that person, she decided, would be tended to last. Hopefully with a short and sweet encounter. *Though most likely not sweet.*

About halfway into her morning medication pass, Ella was walking down a hallway on the upper level of the home, about to descend on the stairs, when she noticed Jane Beckwith on her way up. Ella tucked her head down. So far, since initial day of recognizing her as a fellow employee at the facility, there'd been no more encounters between them. Yet surely, she had to have known the day would come. But the uncertainty of how it would all unfold made Ella feel off kilter. The meeting-up, when it happened, could very well produce a concatenation of events.

Ella held her breath as Jane got closer. Maybe they could walk by one other in peace. With only a simple nod of acknowledgement between staff. No deep digging into who was who—personal information and such. But the pausing in footfalls were seconds too long, moments after they passed each other by.

"Eleanor Hurley?"

Ella felt her heart stop. So much for incognito.

"Eleanor?" The name came at her again.

Finally, Ella turned around. Only to find Jane's over-done eyes studying her. Ella gave a half smile. "Yes…Eleanor…or Ella as most seem to call me."

Jane's mouth dropped. "Thought that was you. Wasn't sure though… something's different about you. Maybe the hair. Jane Beckwith from school." Her brow narrowed. "Wasn't sure if you remembered me."

Oh, she remembered, alright.

Ella nodded. Cleared her throat. "Now that you mention it. I thought you seemed familiar."

Jane continued studying her, appearing to make observations, scrutinizing, probably searching through her brain for ill-gotten encounters from the past. But if Ella expected any sort of apologetic expression as a result, she received none. The stare-off continued with no real satisfying result. Jane was hard to read. Would all be okay between them now that they'd reached this adult phase of life? Ella just couldn't say. And anyway—just how long before Jane would spill the beans to her old pal BJ? Yet another thing that Ella couldn't predict—surely it wouldn't be long, though. For the time being, however, she needed to scoot. She could already feel herself getting behind for the day.

Ella held up the bag in her arms. "Well…gotta go. Duty calls," she said. Inside, she was feeling anything but the confidence her voice held. Making her way down the stairs, heart beating in quick staccatos, for the umpteenth time, she questioned why exactly she had agreed to the transfer at the convalescent home. Was it worth all the headaches, leftover from childhood, that were coming her way?

She turned down the first hallway to her right. Having done her research, Ella knew Benji's room was on that wing. The idea did nothing to calm her nerves. Pushing the idea of their inevitable confrontation to the back of her mind, she concentrated on the others in her care. She'd find who she could find and then make her way to the cafeteria, where many were certain to have already gone. Who knew where Benji even was at that point in the morning? Possibly no longer on the hall as well, but she couldn't be sure.

After locating five more patients from the roster, Ella thought she'd give a quick peek into the room she knew was assigned to Benji, before carrying out the earlier plan of seeing who she could round up in the dining area. The door squeaked as it opened, causing her to suck in a breath. She wasn't meaning to wake him—just an impromptu check before continuing on her way. The room was dark and at first glance all she saw was an empty bed. But then something caused her to scan left, and she realized there was another bed tucked away in a corner, a variation from the quarters she'd encountered so far. In most rooms, the beds were lined up, side by side. Another perusal told her this bed held a mound of covers. The occupant was still there. Not knowing if it was Benji or a roommate, she began to ease her way back from the doorway.

"Hey," a voice from inside spoke into the dim lighting of the room.

Ella froze. It was Benji alright. "Hi...sorry," she whispered back. "Didn't mean to wake you. Administering medications. I'll come back."

"Ella?" The voice came at her again, somewhat sleepy.

Out of the recent-encounters section of her brain, she recalled the unsettled conversation in the physical therapy room the day prior. The volatile temper and harsh words that had come at her. Was she ready to face that creature again? If only she could gather the daily medications, slip them quietly into a cup, and leave them at bedside. Then tiptoe back out the door.

From across the way, a dark silhouette moved in front of her. She could tell Benji was sitting up in bed. Inwardly, she sighed. She might as well get it over with. "Yes, it's me," she answered. "I have your morning pills. Can I...is it okay to bring them in now? Or would you like me to come back?"

There was more shuffling amidst the bed linens. "So, you're my nurse today then?"

"I am." Ella held her breath, not sure of how the news was going to be received, considering.

"Okay." There was a pause. "Now is fine."

Ella tried to interpret the tenor coming from the shadowy recesses of the room. Nothing screamed out hostilities. But there were no undertones of enthusiasm either. Just as well. Professionalism was best being played out between them. Maybe he was finally coming to that realization.

"Alright then. Just give me a few minutes and I'll gather what I have for you." She left the room and found the nearest nook to sort out what had been prescribed, announcing her return by the squeaking of the door. Through the barely-there lighting of the room, she made her way to his bedside, careful not to trip over an array of scattered items on the floor.

Ella could see movement coming from the corner. "Do you need a light?"

"That would be helpful."

A few seconds later, a lamp was lit at bedside, casting a dim glow over the room. Offering assistance in navigation, but not so much so that it could be considered blinding. Still, when her vision shifted to Benji, she could see that he was squinting, wiping his face, still fresh from sleep. She took in the locale. Clearly, there'd been personal possessions brought in from home. It was a stark contrast to the hospital setting—all white walls, florescent lights and metal cabinets. Had his parents delivered them? Friends? She hadn't recalled seeing his family at War Memorial, but then she hadn't been with him every second, so it had been possible.

"Better," he asked.

"Much."

The air held a subdued quality as she finished preparing the medications. Ella supposed there could have been a thousand reasons as to why, notwithstanding, the last encounter in the physical therapy department. But she was just there to do her job. She handed him a cup filled with a concoction of things meant to heal the body and mend the mind. Taking a large swig of water, he swallowed it down. The conversation was kept to a minimum, though not considered hostile in any way. Ella tried to tell herself it didn't matter. That it was for the best—the muted environment filling the airspace. Besides, he was probably tired. But somehow, it was the chance of apathy resonating from him that prickled her skin.

Still, when she left the room—Benji reaching for the table lamp at the same time—she couldn't help but wonder if it was his eyes she felt on her back, watching her leave. Two thoughts went through her mind as she stepped through the doorway, back out into the hall: Shouldn't he be getting up for the day, instead of hunkering back down? Shouldn't he be heading for breakfast? She hoped he wasn't travelling down a road toward depression. And then, subsequently, why was it, she wondered, that the idea of him watching her sent a shot of adrenaline spiraling though her veins?

The following day, Ella found Benji to be on her roster again. What happened to Ms. Kijak's *we don't have the luxury of having the same group of patients two days in a row* theory she wondered? For some reason though, she wasn't at all surprised. Given their recent history together, it seemed they were fated to end up as nurse and patient—for whatever reason. It was just one more cross in life that she'd been given to bear.

Whatever the case, as the morning progressed, busy as it was, she couldn't afford the luxury of being concerned. Two patients on the same hallway had come down with fevers, lethargy and respiratory symptoms. The rounding doctor hoped that it was not the flu, but under the umbrella of caution, they quarantined the wing. This meant a whole new set of residential measures that needed to be implemented at the facility, which Ella did her best to assist in, along with her daily nursing duties. By mid-day, she ended up transferring the first patient that had shown symptoms to the hospital, so they receive more focused care. By then, she'd only had a brief encounter with Benji in the cafeteria, handing over his morning medications on the fly, while transporting a cart full of breakfast trays on the way back to the hall.

The next time Ella went to check on him, she discovered he was nowhere to be found, and thought it odd. After two sweeps through the building, she began asking around in the cafeteria. Had anyone seen Benjamin Marek?

"Have you tried outside," one of his dinner-time cronies asked.

Outside-Ella wondered. She hadn't known it was allowed. Apparently, it was—for the more mobile patients, including the wheelchair bound that could navigate on their own. And yet with the winter temperatures why would anyone want to go out there just to stagnate in the cold?

"A tad nippy wouldn't you say?" Ella straightened her nursing cap from a burst of icy air. She had found him, as she was told, outside on the back veranda, adjacent to a garden. One, she decided, that held much promise for the summer months ahead. But for the time being, it felt forsaken and lonely. And just plain cold. Benji cocked his head, half turning around. Studying her for a couple seconds, he offered a slight smile.

"You could say that."

He faced back to where he had been originally looking. For a handful of moments, there was silence, save a far-off whistle from the wind. "Feels good though." His voice broke through the stillness. Ella took a few steps closer. "Wakes you up somehow. Reminds you that you're still alive…know what I mean?"

Did she know what he meant? Not really. Not in the way that he was thinking—after what he'd been through. Being in the war and all. Yet, in other ways, she supposed she did. She had issues of her own. Each day was a struggle to forget. Or an effort to remember—how to live. Ironically enough—Benji had been helping her with the latter part. Though she wouldn't often admit it—especially to herself.

"In a way…I guess I do," she finally offered. It was the truth.

"There is nothing like it…the cold on your face."

Ella shivered and wrapped goose-bump covered arms around her torso. She had stepped outside without a coat, thinking only of making a quick check on a patient. Benji noticed the action and broke into a grin. "Or on the rest of your body, I suppose." Ella laughed even as she spoke.

Benji looked around, then gave a quick scan of his own attire. It was as if he was searching for something to give her—a way to warm her up. In the end, he lifted his arms up from the sides of his wheelchair. The action lasted only a second or two before he rested them back down again. What was he suggesting? That he wanted to take her in his arms as a means to offer comfort? *Mostly likely not.* But Ella's pulse tripped with the thought.

"Come to think of it. You *are* starting to look a little too cold. Freezing, really."

Ella shivered again. "Yeah…I only meant to check on you. I couldn't find you and someone suggested that you might be out here. I see that you're fine though…and I don't blame you for wanting to catch some fresh air. Cold as it might be. I didn't know that it was allowed… patients coming out-of-doors. But I'm glad that it is. Glad that this place offers some freedoms that the hospital didn't." Ella pointed toward the back entry door. "Well…I do believe I'll be returning inside…but do you need anything before I go?" *Forever the good nurse.*

Benji nodded, "No, I'm copesetic here." Swiveling in his chair, he began the preparation of facing the cold, winter breeze once more on his own. Ella gave her own nod in return, knowing that by then his back was to her, attention once more focused on the expanse of the outdoors. Her boots made a crunching sound as she retraced her steps over the veranda.

"Wait," she heard a voice over her shoulder call just as she reached for the doorknob to the home.

Ella went still in her tracks. Maybe there was something he needed tending to after all—a medication of some sort. Or something along those lines. None-the-less, less valiant thoughts made her heart begin beating hard against her chest.

"I could let you use my jacket," she heard the voice say. "If you wanted to that is," then offered in follow-up. "I mean…if you wanted to stay outside for a little while longer." The last few words were spoken in a quiet tone, so much so, that Ella found herself straining to listen. Finally, she turned back around.

The blue eyes she saw looking at her sent a warm flush over her skin in-spite-of the cold air. What was happening? She sucked in a breath. "I…ah…I better…thank you for the gesture…but I better get back inside. Yeah," she wagged her head. "I better not." She knew it sounded like she was fumbling for words. *What had become of the confident nursing portrait that she liked to portray?*

But if Benji noticed the bungling, he never let on. He just kept looking at her in a way that was doing all sorts of inappropriate things to her insides. "Okay, then," he eventually said, releasing her from his sightline.

Ella took a two-second count to compose herself. Then, with a shaky hand, turned back to reach for the door, feeling fully confident of one thing. All the progress she had been making in moving forward toward professionalism and *not* entertaining the idea of relationships with her patients had just been erased away in one short conversation.

CHAPTER 20

Ella had butterflies in her stomach the following day as she went about locating Benji for morning med pass. It was official—they still had a connection. They had told each other as much in the look that had passed between them out in the garden on the shift prior, with the frigid temperatures of old man winter swirling through the air.

And to think she had been working so hard to keep it at bay. To outright deny the feelings they shared. But somethings just weren't possible—and this was one of them. And besides, she was worn out from trying. Why deny it any longer? Why not kindle a relationship with one another and let the chips fall where they may? Years had come and gone since high school—would anything bad actually ever come of him discovering who she really was?

It was a risk Ella decided she was willing to take.

But when she found Benji in the hallway on the way to the cafeteria first thing, something seemed off. She couldn't put her finger on it. It wasn't that she found him to be unfriendly, just subdued. On the other hand, there were moments carried over from the day before as she filled his medicine cup where he caught and held her attention with his eyes. So it wasn't that *those* feelings had faded on the overnight. The looks he sent her, were enough that she could, at times, feel a blush working its way onto her cheeks. So much so, she had to work at hiding it from the other patients that were lining themselves up to navigate the breakfast procession. Still, in-between all that, the restraint was still there, bordering on melancholy.

After Benji, Ella moved on to the next person in line. John Bouchard, one of Benji's chums from their initial encounter in the cafeteria. "Whatcha got for me," John asked as she sorted through pill bottles. "Anything fun in that collection of yours?"

Ella continued separating concoctions and filling up the medicine cups from the list of medications prescribed to Private J. Bouchard, then glanced over her shoulder. "Depends on what you consider fun. Is a laxative entertaining enough for you? I think there is one with your name on it right here." She held up a brown bottle.

John's cheeks turned from pale to red. Some of the others in line began to chuckle. Ella struggled to keep her face straight. Over John's shoulder, she could see Benji looking on. Their eyes met and held for a few seconds, and she felt something swirl down low in her veins. Yes—the attraction was definitely still there and brewing strong.

Moments later though, something else flashed over Benji's expression and he focused his gaze elsewhere, seemingly at nothing in particular. Just away. Far from the activity and conversation at hand. Ella pretended not to notice. Working hard to stay focused, she concentrated on her current list of patients. Shorty was next.

"Go get your meds," someone called to him from further up in line.

"I will…geesh, back off," Shorty answered back.

"No…I mean get out of line and go get them—" The someone who was talking looked over at Benji for a reaction—a mark of approval. But Benji was still distracted, staring off.

"I'm not getting out of line…I'll lose my spot."

"You won't lose your spot. Someone will save it." The person addressing Shorty elbowed the guy next to him. "We'll keep it saved for you, won't we fellas?" A few chuckles ricocheted throughout the line. Again, a glance was offered toward Benji.

But nothing.

Shorty swiveled around to take in the entirety of the line, which was now snaking halfway around the cafeteria, then shook his head vehemently. "No way…I'm not going anywhere."

Once more, the person initiating the exchange cast his eyes in the direction of Benji. Clearly, he needed the approval of his leader. It was fast becoming evident that without the *leader's ok* over the state of affairs, his words were losing effect. The whole thing might go bust. And then it would be score-one for Shorty.

"B—" The guy in line called out. Ella felt herself freeze. *Was he addressing Benji?* Because it sure sounded an awful lot like he was saying *BJ*, and the echo of it wasn't settling well across her shoulders. Sure enough, it was Benji he was talking to. He turned his head in the direction of those further up in line.

"What's buzzin cousin?"

The guy smiled, relief evident in the turn of his lips. Finally. He had Benji's attention. *Oh, great leader you have answered.* "Shorty here needs to step out of line and get his medication from the nurse wouldn't you say? Shorty has other ideas to say about that. He is declining the invitation. Tell him B."

By all appearances, Benji seemed uninterested in the banter. In delayed reaction, he opened his mouth to speak, but Shorty interrupted. "I said I'm not going anywhere. I'm not stupid. You fellas are not going to save my spot if I do. Just look at that line."

"Shorty." Finally, Benji was engaging. His eyes took on a semblance of attentiveness, if not a slice of impishness. "Listen to Larry. If you want your meds…you should probably go get them."

Ella looked up from where she'd been quietly preparing the pills and tinctures that were on shorty's list of prescribed treatments. With ease of movement, she walked over to where he was standing in line, a panicked expression still on his face. She held up the medication cups in offering. "You don't have to go anywhere, Shorty," she said. "Here… take these." She lifted an eyebrow in Larry's direction before turning to look at Benji, sending him an eye roll and a shake of the head.

Benji did his duty by offering back the look of having been heftily chastised, all-the-while a playful spark flickered in his eyes. "Or stay right where you are, Shorty," he said. "Good choice."

The remainder of the morning passed in a blur of busyness for Ella. Thankfully, no more patients had come down with the respiratory symptoms of those being contained on the east wing, for the purpose of ruling out the flu. But the ones that were sick needed extra tending to, taking up the majority of her time. Before she knew it, it was lunch hour—time for tracking down her more mobile patients in-order-to administer noon medications. Many were in the cafeteria or well on their way, some still lounging in the rec room, catching a game of pool or a round of cards prior to heading over.

Benji was there as well. Already having gone through the lunch line, he was sitting by a group of cronies near the davenports in the far corner of the room. Without trying, Ella's eyes were drawn in his direction. Mostly, because he was her patient, and although he wasn't due to receive meds, she needed to visually check in. But for other reasons as well. He didn't notice her looking, and she stayed for longer than intended in one place, watching him for a few minutes.

Similar to earlier in the day, she noticed he seemed unengaged with those around him, frequently staring into space, eyes drawn to the window, or to no particular place at all. Several times, those sitting with him attempted to make conversation, which, on most days, Ella was sure would have been met with success. Benji was nothing if not a social creature by nature. Though not always in a productive way.

But for the moment, that seemed beside the point.

Watching him for longer than she would've liked to admit, Ella stirred herself into motion, continuing on with the med pass, making a checkmark on her column with each one completed. After administering a pain elixir to the last patient listed on the clipboard, she prepared to go find Sophia, the young girl who helped out at the front desk before and after school, sometimes extending her hours until well into the day—all in the name of doing her part for the war. The home was short on certain supplies for dressing changes and Sophia, she was told, would be the one to place the order.

It was time to quit worrying about Benji, she told herself even while heading toward the rear exit of the room. Other things needed her time and attention as nurse on duty. But when she noticed movement from the corner of her eye, turning, she found Benji wheeling himself toward the main entrance of the cafeteria, and it made her take pause.

Why was he leaving the lunchroom early, she wondered? And why was she convinced it had everything to do with his melancholic mood? Ella knew she shouldn't concern herself over it. Knew she should continue on as planned—go and find Sophia, put in her order for supplies.

But instead, found herself heading down hallways that led to the furthest wing of the house. The section that belonged to Benji. The closer Ella got to his room, the more her steps slowed. She knew he was just moments ahead of her. The floorboards were practically still hot from the friction of his wired-spoked wheels. When she reached his room, marked by the growing familiar number 136, Ella hesitated before knocking. The door was shut—she should probably just leave him in peace.

But a loud noise coming from the inside the exterior walls made her have second thoughts.

Maybe, she SHOULD check in.

"It's open," a defeated voice answered the soft rapping of her knuckles against the wooden slats of the door. The hinges squeaked as Ella poked her head though the frame. She found Benji sitting on the edge of the bed, wheelchair hovering on the side, having just recently transferred himself. What was the loud noise, she wondered? Glancing around, she discovered a disheveled hardcovered book in the middle of the floor, as if it had been thrown.

Benji's eyes greeted her with a measure of surprise as she let herself inside. "What's cooking," he asked with a narrowed brow. Her presence had caught him off guard. He'd been expecting alone time—and now here she was.

But was solitude what he really needed? Clearly, there was something on his mind. Was it anything she could be of help with? "I just...I saw you leave from the cafeteria. And I just wondered...is everything okay?"

"What...can't a fellow leave the lunchroom when he's finished eating?"

Ella flinched, but only a little. What were nurses if not made of tough skin? "I suppose...that's accurate, but I also have noticed that you don't seem yourself today."

Benji adjusted himself on the bed. "Is that true...how so?"

"You seem quieter than normal, less interactive with people. I've noticed you staring off like something is on your mind."

Ella was met with silence. The muscles in Benji's jaw twitched as he looked away, giving her fair warning of a sour mood percolating just below the surface. "What exactly," he said, jerking his head up, meeting her eye, "do you know about not seeming yourself at any given time of the day? What is it that you've been through that gives you the right to come in here and judge my mood of the hour?"

This time Ella flinched with greater measure. *How dare he talk to her that way when she was only trying to help?* And yet at the end of the day—she was still a nurse. She needed to keep a professional stance. But she was getting very sick of his swaying dispositions. One minute happy—the next blowing up in the physical therapy room. Joking with the guys—then throwing around words of anger at the drop of the hat. Light-hearted and engaging with the staff (AKA herself)—then temperamental and pensive, staring off into space in a winter garden, wanting to be alone. She could feel her blood pressure rising, the tell-tale sign of its manifesting in the reddening color across her skin.

What did she know about hardships in life? What adversities had she to endure?

Oh…if he only knew!

"True…I have never served in the war. I have never been through the same circumstances as you. How horrific to suffer at the hands of the bombing…to see what you've seen. But I also know this…sometimes you have to try."

"Try?"

"Yes…try!"

"I fail to see what you mean."

Ella sighed. How could she explain? She wasn't entirely sure of her own meaning. Or even that what she was getting at would work in the end. But if there was a flicker of hope, a possibility that it *could* work, then *trying* was the only way to set it in motion. "What I mean is… some people are their own undoing. They sabotage their own healing. Instead of trying harder, with concentrated determination, they get mad and quit."

Benji opened and shut his mouth twice, gulping air, as if to swallow back anger. His cheeks were filling in with a hue of red. "So, I can assume by *some people* you are referring to me. I can tell you…you have no idea what I'm going through here. None."

"Maybe not," Ella set her chin, eyes flickering with fire. "Or maybe so," she said under her breath. "But I've been watching you…sometimes you make excellent strides, moving forward, walking, good vision for days…so I know you are capable. I know you can do it. But then when the least thing sets you back, you get mad and quit trying. You act angry at the world. And that isn't going to solve any problems…least of all yours."

"*Maybe so?*" Benji furrowed his brow. "What do you even mean?"

Eyes widening, Ella cleared her throat. "Nothing…you're right. That comment wasn't relevant here." The things she'd endured in her lifetime—apples to apples, it wasn't on par with the topic at hand. Even as she thought these things though, a measure of frustration shot through her veins. Would that remark be the only thing Benji took from their encounter? If so, it was only a deflection. One more way to avoid the truth—of trying. The idea of himself *trying* to get better.

Benji's jaw twitched with irritation and Ella prepared herself for another lambasting. Of all the reasons she wasn't equipped to be his judge and jury. Of how she knew nothing about trying and not trying or being confined to a wheelchair. Instead, he lowered his head. *This, she wasn't prepared for.* She held her breath.

What to say? What not to say? Caught in a web of uncertainty, Ella remained quiet while Benji fixed his vision on the floor.

Running a hand over his face, then though his hair, a modicum of stillness filled the room. Long seconds passed, feeling like minutes. Finally, he looked up. "There are things you don't know about me," he said in a defeated voice. "I'm no damn hero. Not even close."

Another period of silence. "Alright," Ella breathed. *She could argue to the contrary. That he was fighting for their country, for freedom, for fellow humans to have liberation from the atrocities being committed across the globe at the hand of Hitler. That was true heroism if there ever was any.*

"I try to put it in the past…but it's not…it's not going there."

"The past wasn't that long ago. Time heals…they say, anyway."

Benji trained his eyes on Ella, staring hard, as if studying her. As if she was triggering something in his memory. Or maybe he was looking straight through her. Afterward, he shook his head as if to clear it. "I have a feeling *this* past is going to last forever. It feels like it already has."

"For what it's worth…I wish you wouldn't have had to endure that." Ella walked noiselessly to his bed and sat down.

Benji sighed. Looked over at her, and then out into his room, regarding nothing in particular. Similar to what he'd been doing throughout the day. "It's haunting me…I can't quit seeing his face."

"Who's face?"

"It was a boy…a young boy. I couldn't save him. I *didn't* save him. And now he's gone and here I am, still alive, and for what reason? It should have been me that died…not him. His family could still have him…He'd be part of their life…Instead I'm walking around free." Benji glanced at his legs. "Not *even* walking…I'm sure they hate me."

Empathy filled the expression on Ella's face. She reached out to lay a hand on Benji's arm and then seemed to think better of the action, resting it on the bedcovers instead. "War is an awful thing," she said. "I'm sure you did your best. You were caught unaware…sabotaged… the bombing. It's a tragedy what you had to endure…all that you went through. That little boy was a causality that you can't beat yourself over. I know his family wouldn't want you to. It sucks. The whole thing sucks…that he died. That many more died as well."

Benji kept his gaze fixed on somewhere in the room. Ella wasn't sure if he was even listening, until finally, he nodded his head. Though she wasn't sure the gesture was made as a testimonial of agreement with what she was saying or from a crushed spirit. For a few minutes they sat there in silence. It seemed he had bared what he was going to and now had nothing more to offer.

Ella repositioned herself on the bed. Cleared her throat. She felt like more needed to be said. The conversation hadn't ended with the resolution that was needed. But where to start? "I ah—" She started then stopped. Taking a breath, she tried again. "I know something about loss too. About how much it hurts…and keeps hurting. How it feels to take the responsibility of it on yourself." She paused for a two-second count. "But the thing is you can't quit…you can't quit living or what is the point? What is the purpose? You just…you have to go on."

At that. Benji turned in her direction. Watching as she talked, he seemed to hang on her every word. It appeared she had finally gotten through—at least a little. She had touched a chord that resonated deep within. They had something in common after all—a sense of deep loss. Maybe it would be a place that they could grasp onto together, that *he* could grasp onto—start the healing process.

"I'm sorry," he said, looking her directly in the eye. "For what you've had to go through."

"You…you don't have to be sorry," she answered back softly. The way he was looking at her, with so much sincerity, like he meant every word—she felt it to the core, a deep connected feeling. It was one conversation—but so much had been accomplished. There was a new level of understanding between them.

Benji nodded.

Ella swallowed. All of a sudden, the air around them was changing. That *feeling* was taking over. Pulling them in. Drawing them together. Like so many times before. She knew she shouldn't have followed him to his room. Shouldn't have put herself in this situation. But here she was—and she couldn't look away. But she had been concerned for his mental wellbeing. Had only wanted to help.

Or had that been the only reason?

"Thanks for listening," Benji said in a subdued tone. "You—" He shook his head. It seemed the space between them on the bed was melting away. Ella wasn't sure who was moving, him or her—maybe both. It felt like slow motion. "Sometimes I don't know what I would have done if I hadn't met you."

Ella felt an electrical jolt shoot through her veins, making pieces of her heart spring to life. The truth was, she felt the same way about him. But it felt so good to hear him say it. At the same time, something twisted in her stomach. *If he only knew who it actually was that he was saying this to.*

She brushed the nagging thought away.

"Benji," she whispered. Just saying his name, using the familiar form she had constructed to address him—*Benji*—helped to push thoughts of BJ Marek away. He didn't exist.

Benji moved closer, erasing the few feet that held them apart during their discussion. Reaching for her head, he cupped his hand, and brought her face forward. Every part of her body came alive as his lips swept over hers. So soft, barely a touch.

He leaned back. Looked into her eyes. Ella shivered, her lips opening slightly, waiting, hoping for more. A thousand things seemed to pass between them in that brief collection of moments. "Ella…babe," Benji breathed as he tipped forward again. Enough waiting! It was clear where they both stood. That they no longer wanted to pretend. They no longer wanted to be apart.

This time when his lips met hers, there was no hesitation, only a sense of urgency. They both wanted this, wanted each other. Couldn't get enough. They had faked indifference for so long—had worked so hard to hold their feelings at bay. But right then, being together, all that was gone. There was only each other. That moment. They kissed like they never wanted to be apart again.

Resituating on the bed, they lined their bodies up, pressed into each other, wrapping arms around each other, reaching, hanging on. Benji ran his hands up and down the length of Ella's back and she shivered. His touch felt so good. Being that close to him felt so good.

She too, started exploring his body, hesitantly at first, then with more brazenness, fingertips traveling over his spine, then the muscles of his shoulders and back. She had been attracted to him for so long—shortly into his hospitalization, if she were to admit the truth. Had it begun as an infatuation over him being their resident soldier at the start of a war? Possibly. But she knew that it was more than that. There was such a raw beauty to him that she had never picked up on as a child. The way his eyes could look right through you—so blue. His strong body. The cut of his jaw. Chiseled cheekbones. Perfect lips.

Perfect lips. The kissing was making her come undone. Throwing her off kilter. And she only wanted more. Benji reached inside her nursing pinafore, and she sucked in a breath as his hands made contact with her skin. She knew she should be pushing him away, slowing things down. Instead, she reached for his shirt, pulling it from his waistband. His bare physique felt glorious underneath the nerve endings of her fingertips. And he liked it too—she could hear his breaths coming quicker, matching her own.

Where were they headed? She couldn't think straight. She just didn't care. It all felt so good. *And maybe a little wrong.* But mostly so—damn—good! By then, Benji's hands were all over her and she was letting him, doing her own fair share of exploring. "Ella...you're so beautiful," he whispered, laying her down on his bed. The skirt of her uniform was pushed up. He was straddled on top of her, getting ready to pull off his shirt.

Just then a noise at the door drew their attention, sending everything to a screeching halt.

The doorknob began to turn.

With deft movement, Benji sat up and Ella jumped to a standing position, all the while both tucking clothing into place, smoothing hair, wiping mouths. By the time Benji's roommate entered the room, they were suitably put back together, save the glimmering look in both of their eyes.

Ella held up a glass of water that she had astutely found on Benji's bedside table. "Well, if you are sure you are feeling better...I'll leave now," she said. With a slight tremor betraying the movement of her hand, the glass was passed into Benji's grasp. "Make sure you drink plenty of fluids. Rest if needed."

An almost indecipherable smirk formed on Benji's lips. "Yeah okay... but I'm pretty sure I am feeling better now. Much better, actually." He sent her a wink while his roommate busied himself on the other side of the room.

Ella worked hard to present a professional demeanor, nodding as she offered a serious, congenial smile. On the inside though, she was grinning from ear to ear as she slipped through the door to resume the rest of her nursing duties for the day.

CHAPTER 21

"Can you help me out over here? My patient is acting a little sluggish after eating and I need to get him into his chair and back to his room."

Ella looked up from the patient she was tending to in the cafeteria and found Jane Beckwith walking her way, calling over to her. "Yeah, sure, I'll be right there," she nodded back. Giving a discreet glance around the dining room, she looked for Benji, a type of nervousness settling over her.

It was noon at the convalescent home and Ella had been in the cafeteria, tracking down patients for midday medication administration, helping the indisposed to set up their trays so they could feed themselves, sometimes lending a hand in feeding the ones who couldn't, due to lack of use of an extremity or worse yet, an amputated hand or arm. Soon into the meal, Ella had noticed Jane Beckwith coming into the room, wheeling a patient. Jane dressed in full regalia—fancy looking nurse's uniform, plentiful makeup and bouffant hair. A wave of nervousness had passed over Ella right then and there.

Since beginning work at the home, she had rarely run into Jane, and besides a few closeup encounters, it had been mostly at a distance. Seeing Jane then, all the reasons for not wanting her around crept into Ella's head, crushing her windpipe, making it hard for her to take in a good breath.

The desperate part of herself was telling her psyche to make an excuse for leaving the cafeteria, *Sorry, but she would have to get someone else to help her.* Then make a mad dash out of the room, go anywhere, somewhere far from any chance of interaction with Jane Beckwith— coupled with the chance of Benji being in the same place, sharing the same scenery, having access to the same conversation.

Benji. Her Benji! A memory, reminiscent of their last secluded encounter together in his room came flashing into her mind. How much they had shared together. How their relationship had fast forwarded to another level. Goosebumps covered her skin at the thought. A few days had passed by, and it was the first scheduled shift since their intimate time together. She'd only a brief interaction with him during medication pass earlier that morning, and that was with several others looking on. Still, all the good feelings had been there, even with many other patients in the vicinity. Clearly, the deal had been sealed between them—they were completely sweet on each other.

Maybe in time she would feel comfortable enough to talk about their past together. Maybe by then they would be so deep in a relationship, so deep in love, that it just wouldn't matter. Maybe he would tell her he was sorry. Maybe she would forgive him. Maybe he would never be that person—BJ Marek—again. *Maybe.*

The goosebumps that peppered her arms quickly transformed into skin pricks as she imagined him to be somewhere in the room. Somewhere within hearing distance from her and Jane's interaction. An interaction where Jane could start discussing the particulars of their time spent together back in school.

"You coming?" Jane was starting to transfer the patient on her own. Ella couldn't have that. He looked heavy and like he didn't move very well. She didn't want anyone to get injured, not even Jane. With one more perusal of the cafeteria, she stopped what she was doing and made the jaunt over, heading in the direction of Jane.

"Is he okay?" Ella eyed the patient they were getting ready to help into the mobile chair. He was looking a little glassy eyed, a little out of touch with the world around him.

"I think he'll be fine. I just need to get him into bed. The pain killer he took before lunch…it might have been too much. He just needs to sleep it off."

"Okay…if you think—" But right then the patient slumped to the left. "Whoa," Ella lifted the man back into sitting position. "You okay—"

"Mack…his name is Mack."

Ella shook his shoulder. "You okay Mack?"

Mumble mumble mumble "—I'm 'kay—" The patient made an attempt at sitting a little straighter, eyes opening then drifting shut again.

"Come on Mack...wake up for us," Jane cajoled. "We are taking you back to your room, but we need your help getting into the wheelchair."

While Mack made another attempt at opening his eyes, the sound of laughter caught Ella's attention. A patient sitting at the table was looking on with interest, chuckling to himself. "He likes his morphine alright...that Mack."

"Come on Mack." Jane was shaking him now. Ella was beginning to experience a flash of concern over the patient's lack of responsiveness, when something caught her attention from the corner of her eye.

Benji entering the food line.

Ella's pulse rate doubled in tempo. She just knew something like this was bound to happen! *Dammit, Mack, move...NOW,* she wanted to say. Instead, she grabbed the wheelchair bringing it closer, her back turned to the parade of patients who were busy getting macaroni and cheese, green beans and canned pears dished onto their trays. Benji as well, she could only assume. "I tell you what we're going to do," she said to Jane." We'll get this chair as close as we can and lift him ourselves. I don't think at this point he's capable of helping much, so it's going to be up to you and me. The sooner the better. I think you're right...he needs to get back to his room, back to his bed." *Pronto!*

For a second or two, Jane looked somewhat unsure. Did she think they couldn't make the transfer by themselves at that point, with the patient clearly unable to assist? Or was she worried that there was something more going on there than mere sleepiness from the pain medication? Ella glanced over her shoulder to the food line. Benji was continuing to make his way through. Closer and closer. Any time now he'd be scanning the cafeteria, looking for a good spot to sit. "Okay... yeah, let's do it," Jane finally said.

They had to tug the seat Mack was sitting on into a cockeyed position in-order-to get the wheelchair wedged in nearby. When they were through, Ella could feel herself sweating. Was it because of the effort she was expending or because of Benji of being in the same room with her and Jane? Surely by then, he was nearing the end of the food line—if not already through. "Okay…help us out here, Mack," Ella said, stepping in front of his chair.

Jane was on the other side. "Yes…help us out, Mack." She turned to Ella. "We'll count to three…then make the transfer."

Ella nodded. "You count." Mack's eyes drifted shut once more, his skin looking pale. *Was he really going to be okay?* Was *she* going to be okay? Where was Benji? Was her own skin pale too? Most likely not, because she felt flushed. Hot. Shakey. *Far from pale.* Blowing out a breath through pursed lips, Ella re-focused on the patient.

"One two three," Jane said aloud and before Ella knew it, they were lifting, moving, shifting dead weight. Mack landed with a thud into the wheelchair, haphazardly wedged, but safe none-the-less. Ella met Jane's smile of success with a nod of her head.

Now if only to escape.

She gave one more glance at Mack and found his eyes had popped wide open, the coloring back in his skin. By all appearances, he looked much better. Still, only moments before, it had appeared as if he was circling the drain. Maybe it was just the pain medication after all. But then again, maybe not. "You'll have the rounding doctor take a look at him won't—"

But Ella's words froze in her throat. Out of the corner of her eye, something was drawing her attention. Blue eyes peering out over the cafeteria, a filled tray balanced in one arm, looking right at her and Jane, taking in the situation. Or was it something more she felt, staring her down? A studying of sorts. A deep analysis.

Ella couldn't look. Couldn't face the possibilities of the thoughts going through Benji's mind—didn't want to. Bending down to Mack's chair, she began straightening him out a bit, making him more comfortable for the ride back to the room. And then—the plan would be—without turning to look back at Benji, she'd stand up and go—make a beeline for the door. Crisis averted. *Hopefully.*

But something stopped her strategy from getting carried out as intended. Was it the pull of her vision in Benji's direction for one more quick look? Was it the sound of Jane's voice coming at her, momentarily averting her attention away from breaking into movement? Or was it the collision of both?

"Yeah, sure...I'll have the doctor check him out. Thanks for the help, Eleanor," Jane said as she began propelling the wheelchair into motion.

Eleanor.
Eleanor Hurley!
From back in the day.

The name screamed loudly in her ears, echoing around the cafeteria, ricocheting off the walls.

This time, when Ella's eyes found Benji's, it wasn't for just a quick glance. His expression held them there—an immobilization of time and space melding their psyches together. The confounded look crossing over his face. A donning of truth. The lifting of the brow. The freezing of the cheekbones. The drop of the jaw—before setting rigidly into place.

Ella saw the moment horror filled his eyes and knew it was a reflection of her own. Complete recognition skidded across his features. Shrieked loudly into the air around them. *Eleanor Hurley, indeed.* The coloring of his skin turned pale. He looked white as a ghost. Lunch tray beginning to slip in his grasp, he re-shifted the hold to keep it from tumbling to the floor.

Running seemed like the only option. But Ella knew it was too late for that. Benji set his food down at the nearest table, a cursory toss, and began rolling over, his gaze never once leaving Ella's face. The look of aversion he was sending made her want to melt into the tile beneath her feet. But it was too late for that.

It was too late for anything.

"Eleanor...Eleanor Hurley," he said on approach. He still looked stunned. Shock mixed with disdain. "Well, isn't this a fine thing. I thought you looked familiar somehow. But I didn't place you...until just now. He studied her some more through narrowed eyes, nose curling into a sneer.

Ella's stomach began to churn. She wanted to puke. To have someone look at you with so much scorn. Like you completely disgust them. *Someone you were falling in love with.* But this wasn't the person she had been smitten by. No—this was someone else.

She knew *exactly* who this was.

"Wow," he paused. Shook his head. "I'll admit…I was fooled. Your hair…it's so much longer…lighter. You look quite a bit different than I remember. I didn't place you. But now I can see it…clearly."

Ella felt her face heating up. "I wasn't trying to fool anyone," she said, her voice shaky. *Or had she been?* She had figured out who *he* was—had known his true identity for some time. And yet hadn't disclosed her name. Things weren't cut and dried though. It had all been complicated. There were hearts on the line. Or hers at least. The way Benji was looking at her right then, with so much contempt, it would be hard to believe there had ever been an iota of feeling in his heart towards her.

But it wasn't like she had been trying to purposely fool anyone. *Except maybe herself.*

"Well either way…you did a good job."

"Like I said…I wasn't trying —"

If possible, the sneer grew even greater, eyes tightening into slits. "Wait a minute…do you even know who I am?" The voice coming at her was nothing short of incredulous.

Ella sighed in defeat. "Yes…I know who you are."

Say it. Say my name then, his expression seemed to scream, all-the-while while staring her down.

"BJ Marek," she spit out. Her voice sounded small and pathetic. She almost choked on her words.

BJ Marek who I hate from school!

CHAPTER 22

~1935~

The cinder track stretched out, long and curved, encompassing the field. The path to victory lay within its lanes, the defining stripes blocking out the competition. Focus and concentration pulsed a mantra from the starting blocks, Eleanor Hurley's heart beating in sync to its time. She could do this. She *knew* she could. The power of the win rested in the strength of her legs, ease of movement within her torso, fast swinging arms. Sheer determination.

She was fast.

Plain and simple.

A fact that hadn't been acknowledged by many.

She knew it though. Deep in her heart. With every step she'd taken during impromptu races at recess, and in gym class. It was always the tips of *her* shoes that crossed the finish line first. But she wasn't one to brag. And it seemed the like the kids were always holding others higher in their esteem. Those that *did* like to toot their own horn. *Mary Fortin—she is so fast! Elizabeth Bouchard—she's going to win everything!* Ella had heard it over the years, on the playground, throughout the halls, in the lunch line. And she'd beaten them both. Mary *and* Elizabeth. More than one time each.

In years prior, it had been Jane Beckwith. Jane was clearly a star. *No one was faster than Jane.* But Eleanor knew differently—even though Jane was two years older and by all means, quick. Eleanor had beaten her fair and square that time on the football field when the entirety of the student body had raced, several grades at once.

Eleanor dipped her body to the ground, heart thudding loudly in her chest. It was the big track day. Junior high meet. Now was the time.

186

Proof of a win would be in the judge's hands with the breaking of the victory string. No more hearsay during an off-the-cuff competition at recess. No more *he said, she said.* This wasn't a popularity contest. It was just the real thing. It didn't matter who boasted what—people could talk all they wanted. But the actual truth was—whatever transpired that day on the track.

At any rate, whatever the results were going to be, the clear confirmation of a victory would be acknowledged in less than a quarter of a minute.

Eleanor waited with deep anticipation for the sound of the gun. *Tick-tick-tick*—heart thundering in a steady rhythm. *Focus-align-calibrate*—brain reeling nerve signals into place. *Bang!* The reverberation of the sound catapulted Eleanor into motion. Jarred like a rocket, she set off for space. All legs and arms, body thrust forward to break through the wind. It was just her and the light thudding noise of her shoes hitting the cinders below.

Sheer speed.

Faster and faster.

But she wasn't running in solus. There were people close by—other contenders. The airstream from their bodies filled her senses as they stayed in her wing-space. A reminder that she needed to give more effort, hasten her speed, press harder.

Puff puff puff. Thud thud thud.

Legs moving quicker and quicker.

Home stretch—the thin line of the victory string within clear view. High gear kicked in—a deep reaching for every ounce of effort expended.

Pounding footfalls later, the others fell way. Eleanor was on her own again. Loud breaths alone in the wind. Ten more steps and the rope was broken, pushed away by swinging arms raised high into the air.

There was no doubt about it—she had won the race!

Exhilaration shot through her veins as she paced her lane, mouthfuls of inhaled air coming up from her throat. The track and adjacent field became a whirl of movement. People everywhere—collecting times, some gearing up for next races, runners landing in beside her, completing the heat. Eleanor took a few moments, allowing her body to unwind. On the inside, she was grinning from ear to ear. Did anyone notice? Did anyone care? For a split second her eyes rotated to the sidelines, and she found herself wishing her parents were there to witness the win, but she knew they were busy working. Or in her dad's case, drinking.

If only Thomas could have been present.

Swiveling back to the infield, a blur of blue and white movement swept through her vision. High schoolers, dressed in Blue Devil apparel, helping out for the day. She had known this was common practice. And expected. But somehow it hadn't entered her thoughts just who those students would be, or even that they would be there, really. That their presence would have any effect on her at all.

But right then, seeing BJ Marek across the way, his usual subordinates at his side, Jane Beckwith being one of them of course, she couldn't help but stick her chin up a little higher, hold her head a little more aloft. Had they seen? Had they been witness to her win? Inside, for some reason, she really hoped so. Actually—in unforeseen desperation. With sudden, pressing need, she secretly wished BJ and Jane had been privy to her crossing the finish line in first place. That they would pay her some heed. An acknowledgement of her being on top.

But if they *had* noticed she would never know. As far as Eleanor could tell, Jane Beckwith, busy cavorting with all her friends, never once looked her way. And when BJ did catch her eye—it was only to give his typical dirty look.

CHAPTER 23

(Benjamin Marek requested another nurse.)

Dear Thomas,

What has been, what could have been, what has to be— all circulating on the prison wheel of my mind.

~E

CHAPTER 24

Ella stared at the roster. Included on the list was the same group as the day before at the convalescent home. Except for the patient named Benji—*Benjamin Marek.* Her fingertips froze on the paper. Why would this be? If she was being assigned to an entirely different group, then it would make sense. But he was the only one missing.

Except deep inside she did know.

Sifting through the other assignments, she began comparing names and groupings. Had they decided to divvy up the patients in a different order? Maybe based on difficulty of the assignment? Maybe they figured, based on workload, things needed to be shuffled around a bit—evened out. It made sense.

Except it didn't make sense.

Apples to apples—the various assignments appointed to Ella since arriving at the convalescent home had all offered the same level of complexity.

She continued sorting through the sheets, searching for some type of discrepancy. But the combinations all seemed to be the same, typed neatly in order, just like always. Save one page where the name Benjamin Marek had been scribbled in at the bottom. With shaky hands, Ella speed read down the column and found the patient's name—Mack— that she had been helping Jane with in the cafeteria on the same page. *So that was it.* Maybe Benji was his replacement. Or was he? Mack's name was still on the list. So obviously still at the facility. And yet Benji's name had been added under his.

"Excuse me, Ms. Kijak," Ella called out, having found the administrator in the hallway. She couldn't let it go.

Ms. Kijak turned around. "Yes?" She eyed Ella on approached. "How can I be of help?"

Ella cleared her throat. She couldn't help but be a little intimidated by the stern expression that was staring her down. *All business, indeed.* "I...ah—" She lifted the paper that contained her list of patients for the day. "I was just wondering...I noticed that one of the names has been removed from the assignment I had yesterday...and I wondered if something happened to him...or if you knew why."

"Ah...yes. I presume you are speaking of Benjamin Marek?"

Holding her breath, Ella gave a nod.

Ms. Kijak paused as if trying to sort through her words, searching for an appropriate way to say what she was about to say. "Yes...he...well, I don't really know how to deliver this. He requested that going forward he not have you as a nurse."

Ella felt her face go red. Though with embarrassment or anger she wasn't sure. What all did the administrator know about their untoward relationship? Did Ella owe her an explanation or the possible reasons Benji had put in the request? Did she want her side of the story? And what *was* the story exactly? What all had been said on Benji's behalf? Should she ask?

Of course, Ella knew the real reason for the withdrawal dated back to childhood. But had he given other explanations, in-order-to push her under the bus? Would he exploit their love affair to others, making her seem like the guilty party? Because that would certainly be a BJ Marek thing to do. Always the mongrel. *Dastardly nurse, aggressively hounding the suffering patient, taking full advantage of the situation.*

"Oh...okay," she spit out, unable to hide the shock in her words. Or was it grief? A combination of anger mixed with pain. Held in limbo, Ella wondered what she should say next. But Ms. Kijak's face, looking down at her, didn't appear to require any sort of explanation. The matter had been simply stated as if this type of thing happened on a daily basis. *By-the-way, there has been a change in your assignment. Patient doesn't want you anymore—have a good day.*

But Ella couldn't help but wonder as the administrator turned to walk away, continuing on down the hall, if it had been an element of pity she had witnessed breaking through the austerity of her eyes.

The rest of the workday went by in a blur. It was always there in the back of Ella's mind—the hurt and complication of it all—but she had other things to do. The daily routine of tending to the patients was plenty on a good shift. But it seemed that day in particular the needs had grown: a stroke victim whose blood pressure she had a hard time bringing down, an injury to one who stubbed their toe getting out of their wheelchair, the foot continuing to swell and discolor during the day—enough that they needed to send out for x-rays. And finally, an irritated patient who was psychologically needy on the average day, began escalating out of control in the rec room, threatening everyone around him with a pool stick. It took the aid of several employees, including the rounding doctor, and a prescription for a sedative to calm him down.

Then, just past two p.m. well after lunch hour, Ella was summoned to Jane's wing to help out. Jane's patient from the day prior. Mack, sleepy after taking pain medications, had apparently not recovered. In fact, he had gotten worse instead, needing to be sent to the hospital for further evaluation and treatment.

Hastily catching up on her own work, Ella was making her way over to Jane's wing, when Sophia, the teen helper from the front of the home, flagged her down. Ella was about to offer an apology for being too busy to stop, running along with a quick wave of the hand instead. But there was something about the empathetic look on Sophia's countenance that made Ella take notice.

"Sorry for the day you're having," she said in her typical soft voice. Faint-sounding enough that it took a few seconds for the words to register in Ella's ears.

In domino effect, her own answer was delayed. "Oh...oh yeah, thanks. You can say that again. It's a busy one alright." *Not to mention discouraging and disparaging.* But Ella wouldn't go there.

"Yeah...busy for sure. Its nice of you to help Jane out." Apparently, news had spread that Ella was on the way to check on Jane's patients while she was busy getting the declining, Mack, ready for send-out. Clearly, Sophia knew the ins and outs of the assignments. Who did what—where, the goings on of the day. But then that would be expected.

It's what she did—assisting with the directing of people here and there, helping out on the fringe of things.

Ella nodded her head and glanced at the clock on the wall behind the front desk. She really needed to get going.

"And," Sophia started, then stopped. "I wanted to let you know I'm sorry about the start of your day too."

The start? Ella's ears perked up. She eyed the sympathetic expression on Sophia's face. "Which...what part exactly," she asked.

Sophia's lip curled downward. "You know, with the change in assignment and all."

Ella continued to watch Sophia's expression as something dawned on her. *Of course.* Of course, Sophia knew. But who else knew as well? Most likely the entire facility. After all, the place wasn't *that* big. Ella tried to ignore the pain that was finding its way to the circumference of her heart. Busy or not, it was still there, buried beneath a pile of patients, pulling at her in every direction. "Yeah...that. Patients request other nurses sometimes. It's bound to happen."

"And it does. But that Benjamin—" Sophia shook her head.

I'm hearing you loud and clear, Ella wanted to say. "Yes...that Benjamin," she echoed, sending a grim smile. It was the most she could offer on the matter. Inside, her stomach began to churn. "Well, I suppose...I better—" She motioned to the hallway and began edging away. A few steps later, she turned back around. "Thanks though, Sophia...I appreciate...thanks."

Speaking of *that Benjamin,* Ella knew full well he had been transferred to Jane's list of patients. On first hearing that Jane needed help, she tried not to think about that *minor* detail. In fact, she was busy enough with her own group and then mildly overwhelmed enough with the request of lending more aid in Jane's direction, that at first the thought didn't even occur to her. And then when it did, a deviously bitter memento flashed through her head:

Well, well, can't get rid of me that easily—Benjamin, Benji, BJ—

With a defeated shake of the head, she wiped away the notion away. He had requested not to see her, not to be in her care. And see her, he wouldn't. It was late enough in the day—anything provided to him by nursing would have already been completed. She would focus on all the other thousands of tasks that needed her attention and avoid him entirely—as he wished.

The last hour of the day Ella faltered on her decision. To her relief, she hadn't seen Benji for the entirety of the shift, unusual as it was in a facility that size. But as changing of staff approached, it was common practice to perform one last cycle of rounds. Jane was still busy, playing catch-up after sending Mack to the hospital and Ella reasoned that it would only be right to round on her roster along with her own.

It was her ethical responsibility to include Benji on that list.

As Ella went through the building checking patients off on the clipboard, she kept a peripheral lookout. If she just laid eyes on Benji— *no interaction, mind you*—she could report in that all was well with the entirety of the group. Done deal. Mission of helping complete.

Final few minutes of the day, Ella felt the timeclock's looming approach, less sure that she would be able to report in on this particular patient. Having scaled the hallways numerous times during the last hour, while doing final tally, he had been nowhere to be found. Not hanging out in the cafeteria, not shooting-the-breeze with the guys in the rec room. Not even outside ruminating in the winter garden. Though she'd only given a quick peek out on the cold veranda.

Ella knew there was a strong possibility he could be holed up in his room but wasn't going to go there. It's where she was drawing the line. Still, she needed to check him off the list to give a comprehensive narrative. What to do?

Thankfully, at the last minute, she saw Shorty coming down the hallway. "Say, Shorty, could you do me a favor?" She regarded him imploringly. "I'm rather busy at the moment, winding things up. Could you knock on door 136 and make sure all are accounted for in the room? That everything is okay."

Shorty looked at Ella strangely. But did as she requested. Ella had come to his rescue not long ago in the lunchroom in front of the guys. Now he would come to hers. Though he wasn't sure as to the how exactly, or why.

Ella heard the wrapping sound of his knuckles against the wood and held her breath as Shorty went in. Returning, less than a minute later, he found her making busy, buying time twenty-five feet away. Out of hearing or seeing distance, should a certain occupant of the room have come to the door. "Everyone is present and accounted for in room 136," he announced. "I don't know...far as I can tell, they look okay to me."

"Okay...alright, thanks, Shorty." Ella flashed him a smile, letting out a breath. "That was a big help." As far as end-of-the-day reports go, it would have to do.

But it did nothing to calm Ella's spirit inside. If anything, only added to the weight of everything she was feeling. Benji was there alright, present in the building, only a few feet away—but the line had been clearly drawn. With a seething heart, and a mix of deepening sadness, she made a decision. She knew what needed to be done. What she needed to do.

Head hung low, the ornate trim of the wainscoting turned into stripes as Ella made her way from the convalescent home late that afternoon. Lengthy strips, elongating and stretching—connecting with the grout lines of the tiled floor in the entryway. And finally, the handrailing on the front porch.

Down the sidewalk she went as the stripes folded in on themselves, splitting and fragmentating. Ella kept walking, one foot in front of the other, further and further from the building. This she knew, as sure as breathing—was the last time transportation would take her to the address listed on the mailbox out front.

On her way to Maple Street, she asked to be let off at 311 W. Spruce. War Memorial Hospital. With slow steps, she walked through the front doors. Pausing, she took a look around, breathing in the sterile smells, so well-known to her senses. It felt like coming home. Almost to the point of bringing tears to her eyes. The sentiment of it all confirmed the decision that rested firmly in her mind. *Now to find out whether the powers-that-be concurred.*

Crossing her fingers and whispering a prayer, she began making her way down a well-acquainted hallway. Then the next. And the next. Becoming somewhat shaky, her footfalls arrived at the central nursing desk that housed her assignments for the past few years. What would the reaction be to seeing her return?

"Why look who we have here ladies?" Florence the ward clerk was the first to visualize her presence. "How *are* you Nurse Ella?"

A weak grin, edged in relief, escaped from Ella's lips. "I'm doing okay." Reaching a hand to her head, she smoothed back her nursing cap. "Honestly, it's been a long day. But it sure feels good being back here. Nice seeing you, Flo." She glanced around, her eyes landing on the doorway to ward-four. "Has it been busy lately?"

"Mostly…but off and on. It's nice seeing you too young lady. Just stopping by for a visit?"

"Sort of." Her eyes continued scanning. "Is Gladys Bukowski around the premises?"

"Did I hear my name?" A gray-haired, plump lady who looked to be in her sixties rounded the corner. At the central nursing desk, she paused mid-step. "Ella Hurley…I thought I recognized your voice. Nice to see you. How *are* things?"

"Gladys." Ella's smile widened at the lady who formerly been her head nurse. "Wish I could say copasetic…but—" She let out a sigh. "Could I speak with you a minute?"

Glady's eyes took an introspective air as she studied Ella's face. "Of course. I have time right now actually. Want to follow me to the office?"

The door shut behind them and Ella took a seat. Gladys leaned against her desk. "What is on your mind? How are things at the convalescent home?"

Ella hesitated, experiencing a measure of imprudence. Was she being indulgent and immature coming there? Particularly in the light of the war and all. *What to say—what not to say?* Suddenly she felt overwhelmed with indecision. What, in all actuality, was the right thing to do? Shouldn't she just stick it out? It wasn't too late. No resignation had formally been put in. *Ugh!* She glanced at the hands that were folded in her lap in-order-to stop their shaking. Then looked back up. "I'd like to ask for a transfer back to the hospital," she finally spit out.

There—she'd said it.

For a moment, Gladys Bukowski paused, seeming to take in what had just been said. "So then...things aren't going well there I take it?"

"No...yes...not really." Ella sighed. "I just feel ill-suited...like I was of more use back at here at War Memorial."

Gladys studied Ella's face some more, her eyes seeming to say—*Is that so?* Clearly, there was more to the story, but if Ella wasn't ready to share—then so be it. Maybe more information would be elicited at a later date, when she was ready to disclose. "If you are sure...then yes, certainly the transfer back can be arranged. Possibly Linda will be willing to go in your place. I heard she was contemplating the convalescent home. I'll speak with the administration to make sure everything is in the clear. But consider it done."

Ella felt a sense of relief as she stepped back out into the hallway—mixed with an unshakeable melancholy. It felt like a big, warm hug, knowing that she could come back to War Memorial. And yet the very reason she was returning—in juxtapose, leaving the convalescent home—felt like a gaping wound that wouldn't easily go away.

Coming upon the central nursing station, she peaked her head into ward-four. Long rows of white metal beds, just like she remembered. For a few minutes, her eyes took it all in, sending conflicting messages of calm and affliction to her brain. She was about to pull herself away from the doorway, when she heard her name being called from the recesses of the room.

Pausing, Ella turned back to find the smiling face of Lillian peaking from behind the wall, storage unit. "Well, aren't you a sight for sore eyes," she said to her.

"Lil." Ella smiled back. *Her best nurse friend.* "It's good to see you." An amiable sense of respite washed over her. "Better than you know."

"What are you doing here? Come to pay an old pal a visit?"

Ella swallowed, feeling somewhat sheepish. "Kind of...but also... I've come for my old job back."

"Really. The convalescent home wasn't for you?" Lillian paused, eyes widening. "Or does this have something to do with a certain soldier that resides there? Say, one that was in your care here at the hospital as well."

"I'm not—"

"Wait…you don't have to say anything at all. I'm sure you'll tell me all about it in time. And actually…you don't have to explain much…it's all there in your eyes. You fell into a complication, didn't you? Don't fret much over it, El…it can happen to the best of us. Anyway…personally, I will be more than happy to have you back around this place. Their loss is our gain."

Ella kept Lillian's words as a mantra in her head as she continued the rest of the way home. A sort of balm for the soul. And she needed it—because a part of her wanted to fall into a deep pit. It hurt more than she wanted to admit—Benji's rejection. But this was a different time in her life, no longer the growing up years. And she wouldn't wallow in the misery he'd sent her way, as she had for too many years. She had done the right thing, Ella realized—leaving the shadow of his presence at the convalescent home. Because one thing was certain, she would no longer subject herself to the perpetual pain Benjamin Marek was always so ready and willing to send her way.

Dear Thomas,

Dearest friend I'll ever have.
Dearest friend I'll NEVER have
again.

~E

CHAPTER 25

The winter months passed, February fading into March, but the cold weather typical of the north hung on. Conversely, Ella let go. As well as she possibly could. Digging back into her job at War Memorial Hospital, with sheer determination, she pushed the whole thing with Benji and the convalescent home to the back of her mind. The rest of Ella's life needed her to be functioning in the present tense—her household (particularity Chance), her friends (particularly Siobhan), the war effort (particularly everyone that was joining with her, laboring for the cause).

"Should we see if we can drive inside?" Siobhan's voice spoke over the tinny blast of big band music coming from the car radio. Turning off Easterday, she edged the Mercury Club Coup closer to the Fort Brady entrance on Ryan Street, while Ella rode shot gun. *Sault Ste. Marie Military District.* The sign in front of them stood out in bold lettering. The girls had a double date planned. Siobhan's love interest and soldier tenant from the overhead garage apartment, James O'Malley, along with one of his fellow comrades from the service.

Ella wasn't at all sure about the arrangement but had reluctantly agreed. *"Don't be a crumb. It'll be fun,"* Siobhan had told her over and over again. In form of persuasion, she had even talked her parents into use of the family vehicle. *"Okay…okay, don't flip your wig…I'll go,"* Ella had eventually conceded, looking into the face of a beaming Siobhan.

"Remind me again why we need to go in?" Ella fiddled with the knob of the radio, turning it down a notch so she could hear. "I thought they were meeting us at the bowling alley?"

"True…they are, but Surf might be picking up Johnny first. If we spot them up here, we can give them a lift and ride together. Wouldn't that be fun?"

Ella eyed the gate, watching military vehicles coming and going from the entrance. Her face held a measure of skepticism. "I suppose… if you'd like, but if they said the Soo Bowling Alleys then that's probably what they meant." Though, truth be told, Ella wouldn't have been too upset if the date had gotten cancelled entirely—due to miscommunication. In the end though, Siobhan relinquished the idea of wanting to go inside the military base and went with the earlier plan, aiming the car in the direction of Easterday Hill.

Across the street, the makings of construction caught the girls' attention as they pulled away from the fort. Building after building, all parts mortar and wood, in the process of being erected into barracks. Out of nowhere, Melvin Hurley's voice echoed in Ella's head, competing with the music from the radio speakers. *"It says here,"* he'd shaken the newspaper for emphasis, *"Uncle Sam is building twenty more buildings to house the troops…opposite Fort Brady. That means room for more soldiers. Great…just great—"* That was all just before spilling his drink, demanding afterward that Grace clean up the mess.

Driving through a flurry of downtown activity on Ashmun, with soldiers outnumbering the civilians on the sidewalk, they rounded the corner to Portage Avenue. The Soo Bowling Alleys would be just up ahead. Nearing the waterway of the St. Mary's River, Ella's head turned toward the Locks. It was hard to believe that they were already up and running for the season. It was still so cold outside. In years prior, April had been the month set for the grand opening. But the war, and the demand for iron ore—the Locks being the main shipping source—had deemed that they set things in motion as early as possible for the season, the stately presence of the William G. Mather making the maiden voyage for the year. How grand the ship had looked forging through the waterway on that day, chunks of ice peppering the surface of the waves, people from town cheering on at a distance.

Ella would've liked to have said that the Locks being open brought some semblance of normalcy to the city. But that year were the reminders that things were different. No longer a tourist destination, the civilians were kept at bay—as they had been since the stirrings of the conflict in other parts of the world. But now that the U.S. had officially joined the fight, added were military guards on any passenger watercraft that passed through the gates of the rising and dropping water levels. And steel mesh nets were positioned above the upper lock gates and below the lower ones to intercept the possibility of incoming torpedoes.

No things weren't the same at all—for more reasons than Ella cared to think about. Not the least of, one that she worked hard to keep buried on a daily basis. But she wouldn't allow her mind to go there—not that night. Siobhan had worked so hard to set the evening up and Ella would participate as if having a jolly good time came as naturally to her as it did the next person. Besides, she would do well to remind herself, pain and hardship were a part of her life—always had been. Or so it seemed. For her it was like breathing, close as it was to her heart. Better to learn to live with it and just keep going.

Otherwise, one could feel themselves being sucked down into the doldrums. And Ella refused to go there. But beyond the one big problem in Ella's mind, there were other things going on around town, holding her attention, drawing it away from the more deep-seated nuances. Like her little brother Chance's anxiety over the newest notice posted in town that spoke of **Deadly Danger.** It was a warning to the general public that the district was heavily armed and ready for action. Should there be an air attack, hundreds of bullets and shells would be shot into the air, plummeting back to the ground seconds later. This falling ammunition risked penetrating the roof of civilian housing. It was imperative that at the sound of anti-aircraft fire everyone take shelter in the same way they would for a bomb.

Or the edict for *lights off at night* and the use of blackout curtains, so that the city wouldn't be easily detected in a darkened sky, making it an easy target for bombing or gunfire. Every evening that the lamps were turned down low at the Hurley household, Chance's eyes would grow wide, and he would start asking questions. *Was there going to be bomb tonight? How did they know it was safe to stay upstairs in their bedrooms? What if an explosion happened while they slept, and it was too late to get to safety?*

All good questions.

And ones that required lots of reassurances. None of which came from a drunken father and very few from a withdrawn mother. So, the answers fell to Ella—which she gave often, buoyed by plenty of falsehoods, fallacious soothings that made them all sleep somewhat better at night. But children were nothing if not resilient. And Chance made up for his nightly anxieties by playing heartily during the daytime with his buddies out in the snow-covered streets in front of the house. Which, now that it was heading toward spring, were finally showing signs of melting, little spots of asphalt peeking through the packed ice.

Sure enough, James and Johnny were already at the Soo Bowling Alleys by the time the girls arrived. Siobhan's face lit up the minute she saw them waiting at the entrance. "Greetings, Surf," she called out, her car door slamming in the background.

"Now there's a fine dame if I ever saw one," James said back, his eyes never leaving Siobhan's. Rushing toward him, she came in for a kiss that didn't end any time soon.

"Why don't you two get a room already," the guy who had been standing beside James said with a smirk. Ella rolled her eyes and glanced away. No doubt about it, her friend Siobhan had found *something* in James O'Malley. But was it true love? Eventually, the enamored couple broke apart.

"Forgive me, sir and ma'am," James said breaking into a grin. "Allow me to introduce you to each other. Johnny this is Siobhan's friend, Ella."

"Best friend," Siobhan broke in.

"Excuse, me...best friend. Ella, this is my pal, Johnny. May you two have half as much fun as my gal, Siobhan and I are going to have tonight." James gave Siobhan a wink.

Ella gave Johnny a look that she knew included a poor attempt at a smile. Inside she grimaced. What was wrong with her? Her thing with Benji was fading into the past. *Distant* past as far as she was concerned. She needed to move on. And the guy, Johnny, standing outside in the crisp evening air was regarding her with all smiles. He had handsome cheekbones and a welcoming demeanor. She could definitely do a lot worse. Taking a breath, with resolute determination for a fun evening, she stepped it up a notch and gave a flirtatious flash of her eyes. "Nice to meet you…Johnny. I'm ready for some bowling. How about you?"

The first round of games took off with a ceremonial *May the best duo win!* They had broken into teams. Couple against couple. Drinks were served and the spirits were high between them, the sound of the Nat King Cole Trio playing in the background. Ella was glad she had worn a pair of slacks to maneuver the wooden floor of the lanes. And apparently Johnny was glad she had too. By the time they were halfway through the frames of the first bowling game, he had given her a few looks that made her cheeks blush red. And truth be told, she thought he didn't look too bad stepping up to the lane himself, pants fitting just right. Though she hoped her eyes weren't vagrantly betraying her thoughts in the same way his had been.

It was a jovial outing indeed.

But even through all of the merriment, it wasn't long before the talk between the foursome steered toward the conflict that was going on in the world. Rumors and reports of the atrocities being committed in Europe—the loathsomeness of Hitler. And the doggedness and trickery of the Japanese in the Pacific Theater. Eventually, overseas topics exhausted, the focus turned to the crusade of the war on a more local level.

"How about the 399th Barrage Balloon Battalion arriving?" James' eyebrows lifted as he asked the question.

"Now those things are impressive," Johnny cut in.

"Tell us more about them." Siobhan's eyes popped wide.

"Oh…you'll soon learn. You'll see them alright. Won't be able to miss them floating around in the sky…all over Sault Ste. Marie. They have the battalion set up in Pullar Stadium for the time being…they say one balloon takes up the whole floor of the ice arena."

"Wow…that sounds impressive. But I fail to see how they will help exactly."

Ella gave a nod toward Siobhan. Her words had echoed Ella's thoughts exactly.

"Babe…I can tell you how. They will prevent low flying planes from being able to bomb. The goal would be for the aircraft to get tangled up in the balloon. A balloon filled with hydrogen gas, mind you. They will place them all around town. Imagine…good year blimps everywhere. The would-be planes would soar in…and then… whoa…too late… crash—"

"Okay, Surf…I can see that. But who is the ace that will control these things? What will stop them from just floating away?"

James laughed. "They will be held down by long steel cables. Trust me, they'll stay put. They won't be going anywhere."

The girls looked at each other, eyebrows raised. Shaking their heads, they let out a half chuckle. "Well, a sight to be seen for sure," Ella said.

"Indeed," everyone agreed. From there, Siobhan and her James went back to frequently holding each other's gazes, nonstop hands all over each other, lost in their own conversation, while Ella tried like everything to seem interested in Johnny.

But something wasn't quite working for her, and she couldn't put her finger on it. She had already determined that he was a dreamboat— or close to it. *And my, but she was trying!* After too much flirtatious effort, most of which seemed forced, she was actually *relieved* when the discussion from Siobhan's side of the table ended up taking a turn once more toward topic of the war.

"Hey Ella," she called over their array of half-finished glasses. "Have you heard they are taking volunteers to be aircraft spotters? All around the clock. I'd do it…wouldn't you? I say…sign me up. What do you say…maybe we can do a posting together?"

Ella didn't have to think twice. "Sure…I'll do it." *As long as Chance had what he needed on the home front*, she quickly reminded herself. "Is that what I keep seeing going up around town? Stations to watch for foreign aircraft?"

"That and antiaircraft machine guns. They've been installing those too, especially along the canal," Johnny answered, offering Ella a look. Somehow, she had a feeling that he was trying to impress her with the knowledge. In return, she nodded and smiled appreciatively, hoping the night wouldn't seem like a *total* dud for him. *She just wasn't his gal.* "And…let's not forget about the large searchlights they're putting all around," he added, taking note of her interest, a certain light appearing in his eyes. Inside, she grimaced.

"I just wasn't his gal," she told Siobhan a few weeks later. They were sharing a soda at Arbuckle's.

"Poor Johnny." Siobhan smoothed her long, dark hair, fashioning a mock ponytail at the nape of the neck. In the aftermath, her high cheekbones declared their beauty, causing a customer passing by their table to do a double take. Failing to notice the look, Siobhan didn't miss a beat in the interchange. "You broke his heart by the end of the night. Poor Fella. But not to worry. He bounced back…shall we say…and is on to the next dame around town. According to what Brenda's been saying…Brenda, the lucky new gal…you missed out. This…according to Surf."

Ella laughed. "Good…good for him. Good for *her*." Lucky or not lucky, it still didn't change the fact that she didn't feel ready. Not ready for Johnny or anyone else. Hopefully *someone* else though— sometime. She couldn't say no forever. *Could she?*

"He's so smitten," Siobhan continued. "He hasn't even been going fishing with Surf and the gang of soldiers that like to go over to Sugar Island."

Fishing.

The word travelled through the air to settle deep onto Ella's chest.

Her mind began to swirl, a panicky feeling settling over her skin. A sensation surrounded her like she was being pulled under—far away from her present surroundings. She shook her head to free her thoughts.

"Did you hear what I said…what I've been saying?" Siobhan's voice came through a fading tunnel, landing with effort on Ella's churning ears.

"What…what, yeah," Ella forced herself to answer, pinching an arm for the needed effect. It worked, just as it had in times past. Once again, her focus returned. She sent Siobhan an encouraging grin, though her voice was a little wobbly. "As you were saying?"

"What I was saying was…I finally went there too. To Sugar Island. Took the ferry and everything. Surf took me there…fishing. Just him and I. He kept saying he was going to…and he finally did. We had so much fun. It was a wonderful time. Of course, everything is killer diller when it comes to my Surf." She took a drink of her soda, her eyes momentarily glazing over, reminiscent of an inappropriately happy thought. "Didn't even know there were gun emplacements over there on the island. Three of them. Did you know that?"

Ella shook her head.

"Surf showed me around. Just as close as was allowed, of course… or maybe somewhat closer." She laughed. "They are up on the most elevated parts of the island."

"I believe it. The gun emplacements truly are popping up everywhere. And what about those balloons?"

"Yeah…I heard I missed out on the one that came down on your street," Siobhan answered. "It actually happened while I was over on the island can you believe?"

"I'm telling you, Siobhan…if that wasn't a real humdinger!" Ella thought back to Chance running in the front door a few days prior, face flushed, words running altogether. *A balloon. The balloon.* He could barely get the words out of his mouth.

"What balloon?" Melvin had narrowed his gaze, eyes squinting from the easy chair.

"Downcamedownfromthesky."

"Slow down, Chance." Grace slid into the room. A rarity for her. She never purposely entered any conversation those days. But this was different—something big. Ella could tell. And besides, seconds before there *had* just been a big swooshing noise coming from the out of doors, backing up the urgency in Chance's voice.

Chance took a large breath. "One…one of the big balloons…just popped…landed on our street…just…just further that way." He pointed in a westerly direction. "I saw it. I actually saw it coming down." His countenance was filled to the brim with animation. "It was killer diller!"

Grace's eyes grew wide, matching the expression on Ella's face. "Oh my, Chance…did anyone get hurt? Are you okay? Thank God you're okay."

"I'm okay," he answered, nodding his head vehemently. "But it landed…it's on someone's house. It's still there!"

"Damn rubber cows," his dad interjected, coming to life in his easy chair. In follow-up, he took a large swig from the glass that rested haphazardly in his hand.

"Do you want to see it? Want to see?"

Ella was already grabbing her jacket. Of course, she wanted to see. Even her mom wanted to see. Moments later, they were out the door, the sound of Melvin's voice slurring on and on in the background.

"Stupid balloons. No use for them. There's an article in The Evening News every other day reporting on all the havoc they are causing around town. Interfering with the power lines. Interfering with everything. Now this happens. Need to get rid of them, right along with all the damn soldiers I say."

It was a short jog down the Maple Street to the scene of the excitement, with a hard to miss location, the gathering crowd giving the whereabouts away. Chance had been spot-on about the deflated balloon alright. There it was, draped over the house—a collapsed circus tent—right where it landed, parts of it still tangled between the tree and power lines in the front yard. *Oh my,* thought Ella, echoing her mom's sentiments from earlier.

"Oh my," said Siobhan, as she sat listening to Ella recite the tale of the mishap while drinking their sodas at Arbuckle's. "And what was it that Surf had been saying about those things…*oh they'll stay put for sure.*"

"Yeah…*they'll stay put for sure,* alright," Ella echoed. "Not that one though, apparently. Or several others either, from what I've heard." The sound of the girls' laughter followed, transitioning them into the next topic of discussion. And then the next. And the next.

Over the next few weeks, it was several more times that the girls got together, catching up on anything and everything, as friends often do. Mostly, discussing the latest on Siobhan and Surf's relationship and the lack-thereof concerning Ella's. But Ella was nothing if not astute on changing the topic, when it came to her. Especially concerning her love life. Eventually, it would fall into place—and that was that.

Before the girls knew it, several meeting-ups had taken place and the tail-end of winter transitioned officially to Spring, ushering in late-April's arrival in Sault Ste. Marie. In the entirety of the United States, and the rest of the world too.

After December's devastating attack on Pearl Harbor, President Roosevelt had ordered that the tattered pacific fleet be given over to the command of Admiral Chester Nimitz. Subsequently, Nimitz took on Edwin Layton as chief intelligence officer. This, in-spite-of Layton's misgivings of having let the fleet at Pearl Harbor down by not detecting the strike of the Japanese.

But Nimitz had faith in Layton. So, that, along with his own sheer determination to step up the game of anticipating Japanese strategy, made Layton all that much more aimed toward success in the world of secret intelligence. Without which—it would have been extremely difficult to lay challenge to the Japanese, daunting as they were in their own grouping of ships.

As ordered, within a few months of the bombing on the Hawaiian Islands, the cracking of the Japanize code, deciphering and interpretation of radio messages, was increased two-fold. Simply put—The President of the United States demanded he would be told *today* of what the Japanese would be doing *tomorrow*.

By using that codebreaking intelligence, the United States Navy knew that a big attack was being planned somewhere in the Mid-Pacific: a port in Papua, on the big island of New Guinea. And then in Tulagi, a small island at the end of the Solomons, where the Japanese wanted to erect a naval base. The invasion would endanger the seafaring supply chain between the U.S. and Australia.

The voice transmitting through wooden radios all across the Soo was reporting the news. ***The U.S. was engaged in a conflict on the Coral Sea***. Aircraft carriers against aircraft carriers. War-planes against war-planes. A first for conducting such a battle that way. The fight raged on. Then, May 8[th,] intensifying in magnitude, with both sides attacking at the same time, the conflict came to a conclusion. Once again, America suffered its losses.

But this time, the Japanese, even more.

And for the U.S. Naval Officers—there was peace in knowing that this time the melee had lacked the debilitating element of being caught off guard.

Oh, the victories and sadness of war, thought Ella when she learned of the gain. The victories always overshadowed by the underlying sadness of the losses created in battle. Even the taking one, single, solitary life.

But how many more were the atrocities being committed overseas by the hand of the German regime? How mis-conceived were the alliances between those countries joining with them in supporting the loathsomeness of the invasions? How many were the lives being lost each day through starvation and deathcamps? No, not a single, solitary one—**but thousands and thousands**.

And so, the war forged on.

The complexity of it all was overwhelming.

To Ella though, for the time being, sadder than the thought of war, was the update she had received while spending her latest afternoon out with Siobhan. Oh, the misery of the tears that had been shed on her shoulder while she learned the news, causing the information of the Coral Sea victory to fade into the backdrop. James O'Malley, Siobhan's soldier, her *Surf,* was to be shipped out the following day, for a new assignment. As to where—like Siobhan had been warned early on—he wasn't allowed to share. Though Siobhan strongly suspected Europe.

Dear Thomas.

At night I count the stars.
When I finally number them all,
it will be the tally of how much I miss you.

~E

CHAPTER 26

A few more weeks passed, and mid-May arrived. With it, the declaration of "M-Days" in Sault Ste. Marie. Held on the 15th and the 16th, they were commemorative events designed to reflect the efforts of the military working closely together with the growing civil defense in the area—civilians responding against the threat. The kick-off for the events was a downtown parade of colossal proportions.

Winnowing through the crowds, Ella searched for a spot on the sidewalks of Ashmun Street to watch the military procession as it marched through. A downtrodden, Siobhan, half-heartedly followed along at her side. The gathering of people to sift through was layers deep. Ella had never seen anything like it. The anticipation of the assembly was contagious. Caught up in the excitement, she found herself wondering how Chance was reacting to the whole thing. With childlike enthusiasm, no doubt. Ella had separated from him back at their house on Maple, his pal, Kip's family picking him up to ride with them. Hopefully they had found a good spot to view the festivities, in particular the military march. And what of her parents? Would they show at all?

"Isn't this something," she asked Siobhan, while peering down the street, looking for the first traces of soldiers in formation.

"I suppose." Siobhan's voice was deadpan.

"You suppose?" Ella took a moment to search her friend's face. She had been trying like everything to cheer Siobhan up for the past several days, with seemingly very little luck. She had hoped the festiveness of the parade would be just the thing. Never had she seen her friend like this. Maybe it was true love after all. There could be no argument that Siobhan had entered the doldrums since the moment of discovery that Private James O'Malley was leaving town. Falling even deeper into them after his train had officially departed. Ella nudged Siobhan in the arm. *Chin up*, her expression conveyed.

Siobhan took a sweeping glance around. "Okay it's something." She faced toward the northern portion of the roadway. The beginning columns of marching soldiers were visible and becoming clearer by the moment as they headed in the girls' direction, coming south from Portage Street. "But I also know, no matter how many soldiers pass by where we are standing, the parade is still going to be one short."

Ella reached for Siobhan's hand and gave it a sympathetic squeeze. "I know," she said. A moment passed by. "But—" A pause fell between them.

"I know…I know…but I'm going to make the most of this day and fully participate in the fanfare. When will I ever get to be part of something like this? And to think… all this…right here in our little old hometown of Sault Ste. Marie way up here in the north?"

"Exactly."

Clip-thud. Clip-thud. The rhythmic sound of marching grew closer. Soon, the parade was upon them. Row after row of soldiers in full dress, rifles positioned over left shoulder, faces focused straight ahead in *"at attention"* posture. The buzz of the crowd grew. It was truly a moment to be shared.

Clip-thud. Clip-thud. The streaming of soldiers continued, walking right passed where they were standing in front of Cowan's Department Store. For a moment, Ella leaned around the person beside her to get a better view of the street, to get a better picture of what would be coming their way. In awe, she sucked in a breath. The procession was continuing down Ashmun, as far as the eye could see, all the way to the water, ostensibly having no end. The news paper hadn't been just whistling dixie. *Oh, the magnitude!*

"Excuse me miss," a little voice lifted up to Ella's ears. She looked down to see a young lad squeezing in through the conglomerate of people on the sidewalk, edging toward the street. "Just trying to see the soldiers in the parade."

"Of course." Ella stepped aside and smiled at Siobhan. The boy reminded her of Chance. She moved sideways and allowed him to enter the space in front of her. The groupings of soldiers carried on, all in formation, six deep and several wide, followed up by ten-foot gaps where the American flag was inserted, flying proudly in the breeze.

Then, more of the same.

And more of the same.

"This is so awesome," the boy shouted with enthusiasm. "I want to be a soldier when I grow up." He looked up at Ella, making sure his declaration had been heard. She froze—vision connecting with the wide eyes that were watching her face. It hadn't been Chance he reminded her of after all.

But Thomas.

So much like Thomas.

Would Thomas have been a soldier—had he grown up?

Then, another thought occurring to her, she began to look around. Who was watching out for this boy anyway? *Who was making sure he stayed safe?* "I can be a sort of soldier now," the animated voice continued on. "I've been helping to gather metal for the war. I'm a young soldier helping out."

Ella patted the boy on the head. "And what a great soldier you are," she said. His zeal for helping socked her in the heart. *And oh, his demeanor.* So much like someone she remembered from years past. Once again, she glanced around in search of a parent or guardian of some sort. So many people—hoards and hoards. All attending that day's event to show their support, because, just like the Thomas-look-alike, in some way, they too wanted to help. Many already were—helping. Stepping up to the work force, putting in several hours of overtime. The young, participating in drives, gathering scrap metal that could be used for armory. Preparations around town being made to grow victory gardens in back yards, in-order-to increase food production. The use of ration stamps, without complaint.

Looking up, Ella saw a lady pushing through the crowd. "Theodore... Theodore," the lady called out, her eyes searching. The boy in front of Ella poked his head around her leg, lifting an arm into the air. "There you are," the lady gasped. Relief was evident in her countenance. Reaching for Theodore's hand, she weaved him back from where he'd inserted into the line of people standing curbside. "Sorry," she mouthed to Ella while backing away.

"No problem," Ella said back. She felt a little dazed.

"You okay?" It was Siobhan's voice, next to her, after the boy had disappeared from sight.

Ella shook her head. "Me? Yeah, I'm okay" she looked twice at Siobhan. "What about you?"

"Oh, just hunky-dory."

Ella's eyes fell back on the street. "Have you ever seen so many people though? Did you even think something like this was possible? Such a display of military might." By then, the Civil Defense personnel were marching by. "And look at the volunteers…can you even count how many?"

"Actually, I have been loosely numbering them in my head. Hundreds and hundreds, I'd say. Wouldn't be surprised if it's upwards towards one thousand, even."

Clip-thud. Clip-thud. The sequence of military soldiers and volunteers continued to trek by.

"He hasn't even written me yet though, El."

Ella bit her lip. Siobhan may have been counting the persons in the parade, but apparently she was also multitasking. Clearly, her mind was somewhere else, far away, as well—overseas in Europe. "Siobhan," she said. "It hasn't even been that many days since he left. Surely a letter will take some time to get here. He will write. I know this is hard…but you have to take heart. And remember to pray for him…daily."

"Or even more often than that."

"True."

"Eight hundred."

"What?" Ella glanced sideways.

"We are up to eight hundred on the civil defense tally by now."

"Oh…oh, wow." Ella faced back to the parade. "Impressive." *And— multitasking for sure*, she thought.

"Better that he left here anyway. He never did like all the snow. And we've had so many late snowstorms this spring. Better that he got away from all that."

Ella shrugged. *If you say so.* But she knew Siobhan wasn't buying into her own theory on that one for a moment.

"Nine," Siobhan interjected suddenly, returning to the count.

"Nine what?"

"We are up to nine hundred. See I told you...there was going to be close to one thousand and I was right."

And so, the conversation went for the next several minutes, bouncing back and forth between the topic of James O' Malley and the particulars of the parade.

Clip-thud. Clip-thud.

Ella felt a stirring in the air, interrupting her and Siobhan's banter, the crowd all around pointing. *"It's Governor Murray Van Wagoner,"* someone said. In rippling result, many others began echoing the same. *"We didn't know he was going to attend."* In domino effect, similar sentiments were beginning to pop up in rapid-fire motion to the right and to the left. *What was this?* Ella strained to look, but it was hard to visualize anything with the column of soldiers blocking her view across the roadway. A few moments later, a clearing came between groupings, and she could see exactly where they were pointing. Sure enough—there he was. The Governor of Michigan, in attendance of the "M-days" parade. A cause for excitement, for sure.

"And beside him there...I do believe that is Colonel Furlong, Administrator for Michigan Civil Defense," another person spoke into the crowd.

At that announcement, another wave of excitement rippled along the sidewalks of Ashmun.

Clip-thud. Clip-thud.

Ella settled back in to watch the procession, still in awe over the sheer enormity of it all. Here and there she continued to catch a glimpse of the governor between the rows of units marching. It was a proud day indeed and quite something to be a part of.

But as she kept catching glances, along with the others, at one point, it wasn't the face of a Michigan administrator that caught her eye from across the street, but an apparent apparition tucked neatly into the crowd. The facial structure of a person that was all too familiar.

Out-of-nowhere, her heart jump-started in her chest, beating at a runaway gallop. *What was going on? What was she seeing?* All air exited from her lungs. *It couldn't be.* She breathed loudly. *Or could it?*

The next grouping of soldiers quickly filled in the gap of her sightline, once more blocking the view. Still, Ella's heart pounded as she waited for the next opening to appear. A chance for another observation through the crowd.

Clip-thud. Clip-thud.

Soldier after soldier.

Then, finally, after what seemed like an eternity—another gap in the procession.

But this time, there was no-one and nothing that resembled what she had thought to have witnessed minutes before. No one that remotely resembled *Benjamin Marek.* What had she even been thinking? Benjamin Marek was not there at the parade. More than likely her former patient was still back at the convalescent home, rolling around from room to room in his wheelchair, busy hating her like he always had.

What was it about that days' festivities though that was playing such tricks on her mind? First the boy who looked like Thomas, then the ghost of Benji in the crowd. Shaking her head to clear all troubling thought, Ella glanced at her watch, and then back to the street. Forty-five minutes since the first members of the armed services had begun their trek up Ashmun, and one block away, she could see the tail end of the procession coming their way.

The observance of "M-Days" faded into May's remaining weeks. And all that was left was a down-hearted Siobhan, still distraught over the departure over her soldier when all the rest of men in uniform had been christening the downtown streets, parading proudly around city. Ella listened and listened to her friend, meanwhile burying feelings over the soldier *she* once knew.

At home on Maple Street, the airwaves played updates about the war, while her dad argued from his armchair, liquid sloshing from his glass, as he waggled his arms, bringing home point after point. When the radio wasn't on, it was the "M-Days" events that he harangued on about. *"That stupid excuse for a parade was useless,"* he lashed out on repeat for at least a week after the whole thing was done and over.

How would you know," Ella wanted to ask. *You didn't even show up for the event.* Instead, she bit her tongue, thankful for the discovery of her mom's attendance. And then, of course, Chance, excited-as-could-be, talked of nothing else. The soldiers all marching in sync and the large machinery displayed around town were his favorite parts. Often, in follow-up, he paraded around the house, dressed in mis-matched green clothing, scavenged from his closet, face at full attention, toy rifle slung over his shoulder.

At the sight of him, Melvin would roll his eyeballs into his head, take an extra big drink, and drone incessantly under his breath.

Of late, the voice from the wooden radio receiver in the living room spoke of how before World War II, battleships ruled the waves. But it was a new planet, with newer technology. And warplanes were fighting the war upfront and center. Unfortunately, the atrocity of Pearl Harbor had proved that to be all too true. The warplanes, taking off from Japanese carriers at sea, had been able to do more extensive damage than the firing of weaponry from the deck of a battleship alone.

Yes—the flying of planes was key. This was once more brought home by the battle that ensued on June 3rd. United States Navy spy planes detected a Japanese fleet getting ready to attack west of Midway Island, amidst the planned Japanese attack in the Aleutians. Prompted by the sleuthing machines of the airways, U.S. bombers were launched in early defense.

Though the ships were missed in the detonations, early the next morning, another spy plane took off once more for the skies. More of the Japanese fleet was spotted. Albeit, northwest of Midway. An armada similar to the one that had sustained the surprise attack on Pearl Harbor.

But this time, instead of having the element of surprise on their side, they were met with U.S. carriers. Armed and ready, with the information relayed by the scout, American warplanes took off from the flight decks in the early a.m. in order to intercept the Japanese pilots who were plotting their attack.

Full scale battle ensued over the next three days.

Dive bombers. B-17 bombers. Torpedo bombers. Fighters.

U.S. Navy Task Force. Imperial Japanese Navy Mobile Force.

Submarines patrolling beneath the depths.

In the end it was the Dauntless dive-bombers from the USS *Enterprise* and *USS Yorktown*—U.S. Naval vessels—that secured lethal strikes on the Japanese fleet, doing the needed damage to secure a great American victory.

Radios, newspapers, and Movie Theatres all across the country shared the news with a celebratory tone. But when Melvin Hurley picked up his copy of *The Evening News* to read of the win, he seemed anything but appreciative, mumbling curses, sometimes shouting them. As far as the rest of the Hurley household, they quietly applauded the victory in their hearts, with Chance—not so quietly—stepping up his "M-days" parade routine, dressed in full regalia.

CHAPTER 27

A few days later, just after sunset, the sound of ships saluting as they chugged through the channel, filled Ella's ears. A deep baritone blast followed by the bright blare of tenor, coming in from her open window. One going west and one headed east. She imagined how close in proximity the liners were to each other as they lumbered through the deep splashes of water that made up the channel. Two cargo carriers in route to a destination, taking up the entirety of the waterway, one having gone through the Locks—one about to enter.

Shortly thereafter, she decided to retire early for the evening.

Falling rather quickly asleep, she entered into a dream.

It's just past dusk, the sun having left a faded amber glow in the sky. Ella is somewhere close to her home on Maple Street, when she sees a young boy breeze past her. In an instant, something triggers in her mind. There is something about this boy—a certain type of significance. He is of some importance to her. This, she knows for sure. Oh, yes, of course—it is Chance, her brother. She makes a decision to follow him. But the closer she gets on his on tail, the realization sets in—it isn't Chance at all. The hair color is too dark. Still—it's someone of significance. Of this she is convinced.

Taking in her surroundings, she realizes where it is that they are heading. On the northerly streets just east of downtown, they are in route to the Locks. **The Locks!** *A buzz of alarm fills Ella's veins. A type of urgency. All at once, she knows exactly who it is that she is following.*

Thomas.

Her other brother.

Beloved Thomas!

She needs to hurry up!

Needs to catch up.

Having picked up her speed, she realizes the effort is futile. There never seems to be an increase in momentum with the energy expended. Still, she follows. Through alleys. Turning down side-streets. Crossing sidewalks that transform into gutters. Over bridges. Amidst throngs of fisherman casting lines.

Line after line after line.

But no matter how hard she tries, the shadow of the boy remains the same amount of distance ahead. Close enough to see. Too far to catch. Still the exigency stays with her. She can't just give up. Won't. Just when she thinks she can't take another second of not being physically able to close the gap, the figure in front of her changes, morphing before her eyes.

Ella's heart stutters in her chest.

No longer small in stature, the person is now her own age, another familiar that occupies a big space in her mind.

Benjamin Marek. Soldier extraordinaire.

Now she is chasing Benji.

The clippety-clop marching sound of the "M-days" parade suddenly emerges into the background.

Street after street after street—water approaching just up ahead. The Locks is still their destination.

Why is the male figure running from me anyway, she wonders?

And why is she chasing him?

But in-spite-of the questions, an innate need is there, pulling her in Benji's direction and she keeps going, following after his disappearing form. It's as if it is still Thomas that ultimately she will discover when the pursuit is concluded. Benji is only a means to an end.

Or is he?

Who is she chasing really?

The enigmatic cat and mouse game goes on and on, seemingly lasting forever. Street after street. Eclipse after eclipse. By the time they reach the waterfront, Ella is starting to feel exhausted. By now, she is side by side with the channels of the Locks and the person she was following has completely disappeared from sight.

For a moment, Ella feels disoriented, not remembering why she is there to begin with. Spinning in a circle, she takes in her surroundings. Seconds later, a pair of ocean liners come into view and a stirring of significance resonates somewhere in her soul.

Concurrently, the sound of fog horns reaches her eardrums.

One salute. Then two. Followed by a series of several more. Coming in tolerable decibels at first, they keep getting louder and louder with each blast. Detonating into the air, they begin bouncing off the horizon, forcing Ella to cover her ears.

The ferocity of the noise is becoming a power in its own right, causing her to act. Ella looks to the channel and notices the gates of the Locks have closed. The wooden walls encompassing the water are beginning to show a darkening stain around their upper rims, a clue that the levels inside are starting to change. Ever so slowly, the water is beginning to drain.

A pressing need takes over in Ella's brain, matching that of the cacophonous horns signaling all around her. At once it hits her that whatever it was that she was looking for—whoever it was—she'll now find it. Lying at the bottom of the lake-passage, inside the emptying basin of the Locks. If only the water would continue to drain at a faster rate!

Finally—but certainly not fast enough—the last of the liquid empties, making a loud sucking sound, similar to the funneling effect of bathwater once a tub plug has been pulled. Towering over the edge of the platform created for viewing of boats passing though, Ella peers into the gaping hole that has been formed from the depleted water basin. Surely now she'll find what she has been looking for, she imagines. Surely now her mind will find some type of resolution.

At long last, a type of peacefulness will transcend over her life.

But all that she uncovers, plastering the bottom of the barren waterway, are piles and piles of dead fish.

CHAPTER 28

It was a warm, summer day, welcomed in the north country where much of the year is spent enveloped in cold, sometimes frigidly so. Chance had been taking advantage of the weather, outside playing street hockey with his friends for nigh onto several hours. Wanting to take a break, he headed back in, trading activity for refreshments. It was his pal, Kip, following him to the house, door slamming behind them, who had suggested a trek into town for a tasty treat, which Chance quickly jumped on the bandwagon for.

And Ella thought—*why not?*

It was her day off and though she had signed up with Siobhan to do volunteer aircraft spotting, for the next few hours she was free. Besides that, who else was going to take them? Not her father that was for sure. He was, by that time, passed out in the armchair, from having started drinking earlier in the day. And their mom was already in town, busy at work. But the chances of Grace taking them had been slim to none anyway—it seemed she never had the energy or the motivation for things like frivolous excursions anymore and hadn't for some time.

But school was out for the summer and what was summer for, if not a little fun. An opportunity to enjoy the pleasant temperatures, while immersing in the out-of-doors. So, Ella said, "Why not."

The walk to town was filled with two boys galivanting, running, then sauntering, exploring, pushing and shoving. Anything but keeping a straight line. Ella couldn't be happier than to watch them having so much fun. *As all young boys should have opportunity to do.* Beginning at their address on Maple, the trio crossed Bingham and turned onto Ashmun, working their way south.

Once on the centralized streets of downtown, activity came to life, with pedestrians and soldiers perusing the sidewalks. Streams of cars putzing down the main thoroughfare, some parallel-parked along the store fronts. Looking for a safe place to cross, the trio made the switch to the sidewalks on the west side of the street. Just up ahead, set among a row of multi-story brick buildings, was a long, striped awning and a sign that read F. W. WOOLWORTH CO.

"Hey, let's stop in to see, Mom," Chance said, casting his eyes upwards to browse the inscription.

For a moment, Kip's face fell, and it looked like he was going to protest. After all, food was top priority for a hungry stomach. "Maybe for a few minutes," Ella interjected, that seeming to satisfy.

Locating Grace inside the store working a cash register, they waited for the line to clear, before approaching. A smile lit her face at the sight of them, in-spite of the underlying melancholy that seemed so much a part of her demeanor. Chance ran to give her a hug, Kip delivering a friendly wave. Ella offered a warm grin from the sidelines.

"Hi, Mom," Chance bestowed in an enthusiastic voice. "El's taking us downtown for ice cream. We wanted to say hello."

"Well, hello there," Grace answered back. Obviously, he had made her day. Still, she gave a nervous glance over her shoulder to see if anyone was entering her line. But all was clear for the time being. So, they spent the next few minutes making small talk, mostly the boys jabbering on about their day. Or this or that cool item on the store shelves that fell within reach of their eyes, while the ladies looked on with smiles, short, interjected retorts, and nods of the head.

After finishing the impromptu visit, back out on the sidewalk, they were continuing to walk in a southerly direction when Chance pulled on Ella's sleeve. "Hey…how about Arbuckle's? Aren't we going there? We are on the wrong side of the street."

"So, it's Arbuckle Drug we've decided on then?"

Both boys nodded their assents, people coming and going all around them.

"Well then it's Arbuckle's we're off to. You're right though we have to—"

But Ella's words sharply disintegrated, her sentence getting swallowed into thin air. Just up ahead, an illusory figure seemed to be crossing her line of vision, blocking all thought. Her mouth went dry as she tried to sort out what exactly she was witnessing. *Who*—she was seeing.

"Benji," she said aloud. But it was more of a whisper, spoken only to herself.

The person in question looked as dumbfounded and shocked as herself and Ella realized that the both of them had frozen into place, no longer continuing their steps in an onward motion. Chance and Kip, ignorant of the situation, kept going, ardently in search of a crosswalk. Stopping abruptly, they turned back to look at Ella. "Are you coming, Sis?" Chance's eyes were round and inquisitive.

Ella brushed him off with a lift of an index finger. A gesture, of which, later, she would have no recollection of doing. But the sound of her brother's voice—it was enough to break the spell. Ella began inching forward. As well as did the phantom person in front of her, dooming them to intersect in a matter of several short footfalls.

The closer she got, the more realization set in. It really *was* him. Benjamin Marek in the flesh. *With no wheelchair in the vicinity.* How could it be? A flash of the "M-Days" parade came floating through her mind and she thought *maybe it really had been him she had gotten a glimpse of through the crowd after all.*

"El—" The word seemed to stick in Benji's throat as it left his mouth traveling through the space between them. *Ella? Eleanor?* Ella wondered which connotation of her name he meant to say. Or if he even knew. Was he confusing who she was in the same way she had been him since discovering the truth of his identity? There was a part of her that wished he would just spit the rest of what he intended to say out. Because the label that he addressed her by—it would let her know where she stood for the moment.

It seemed she wouldn't be that lucky.

Benji appeared as flustered as he was in shock. "This…it's been a while," he continued, somewhat shakily, with no clarification of name.

Ella gave a curt nod. She didn't know how to react—visibly at least. Inside, her brain was in a whirl, heart beating fast. To say an encounter on the sidewalks outside of a medical setting was unexpected and overwhelming after everything that had gone down between them, not only over the winter, but during the course of their lifetime, was an understatement. She wondered whether a brief trade of greetings would be the sum and total of their exchange. A hello and goodbye and off they'd go.

But there were so many questions going through her mind.

"It has," she finally said, letting out a sigh.

At the sound of her voice, he looked directly at her, focusing, seeming to peer into her eyes. Almost as if startling. Had he not expected her to answer back, then? Truly, if she thought about it—she had good reason not to. The way he had easily dismissed her as his nurse, when he found out who she was. *Had dismissed her from his entire life.*

"So...ah—" He seemed hesitant. Cautious. But not hostile at least. There was no trace of arrogance in the blue of his eyes. It caught her off guard. Another tailspin for her mind. Just how was she supposed to react to seeing Benjamin Marek out on the street? A big part of her wanted to curse him and run. Or at least find a crosswalk and carry on with the plan of getting ice cream. Glancing away, she caught sight of Chance and Kip some feet away, entertaining themselves by pointing into the Gambles storefront window. Instinctively, they were allowing her some space. "—how have you been," he finally spit out.

*How had **she** been?*

"I'm...I'm good." Ella reached to smooth her blond, teased hairdo, a new style she was trying. His eyes followed her hand. Once again, she felt thrown off guard. Clearing her throat, she fought to center the framework of her thoughts. "But what about you? Clearly you are doing...well. So much better." She felt her voice slipping into professional mode and realized that was the perfect solution. Perfect way to treat the situation—as a nursing professional who cared about the outcome of a previous patient. A sense of relief swept over her bones as she felt herself getting ahold of the moment.

"But what happened though," she wanted to add. *"What happened to make you able to walk?"*

It was almost as if he had read her mind. Or as if she had spoken her thoughts aloud. "I am." He pointed to his legs, which appeared to be perfectly strong. Capable of anything. Which, if Ella was to admit it—matched the rest of him. Overall, he looked robust and good. Healthy. *Handsome.* She fought back a blush at the last thought. Thankfully, Benji seemed not to notice. "You are probably wondering about me walking I assume."

Ella couldn't hide the enthusiasm in her voice. "I was…wondering. I can't believe it…I mean it is such good news. So good to see this!" *A nurse verbalizing inquisitiveness after weeks of investment in a patient.*

Benji laughed. Her zeal was contagious. "I feel the same way. In fact, I couldn't feel better." He blinked. "Well, mostly at least." He cleared his throat. "Anyway…I suppose you want me to give you the dope."

"I do…I mean, how did it all come about?"

"Well…it's simple, really. There was a certain someone that once told me I needed to try harder. Stop feeling sorry for myself…fight through the mental block that was preventing me from getting better."

Ella sucked in a breath. "Really…a certain someone? How brazen of that person…to just up and give advice like that. I supposed it could seem kind of cold-hearted in a way." She paused. "But if it worked… then—"

A slight grin formed on the corner of Benji's lips. "Then in the end it could be considered caring, not cold. Right?"

Ella nodded slowly. She felt a taken aback. "So…you decided to take the advice and here you are?"

"I wish it was that easy…or that it fell in that order. Being honest… at first, I started trying harder just to prove a point. It felt like I was doing all that I was doing out of spite."

To spite who, Ella wondered. But she was pretty sure she knew.

"But then, pretty soon I started to see results and spite turned into sheer determination. I was feeling so left behind. I needed to catch up and get out of that place."

Left behind by who, Ella wondered. Another question—this time with an answer she was less sure about. But if—say—it was her he had been referring to, leaving him behind, then maybe the best thing she ever did was exit the convalescent home.

"I began to focus and work really hard to improve physically and mentally. And, well, after a lot of hard work…here I am."

Ella's eyes widened as she shook her head in wonder. "That's quite a story. A testament to hard work, indeed. Glad that your hard work paid off. You're on the beam, Ben…Benji."

Benji pressed his lips together and gave a slight nod. Afterward, a pause fell between them. Ella wondered what to do next. Their conversation was over, she supposed. They had seen each other, addressed the shock in their own minds, recovered enough to go over the details of his obvious recovery. And now what more was to be said? He would go his way and she hers. The past they shared would be left behind at the medical facilities where they had interacted together.

Or in the hallways of a brick school building.

A wave of discomfort flitted across her shoulders, and her eyes flickered away, turning once more to find the boys. Though still in front of Gambles, their behavior was digressing, including a repertoire of pushing and shoving, darting into the path of pedestrians. "Hey…El," Chance called over, seeing her eyeing them. "I thought we were getting ice cream. What happened to Arbuckle's. We found a place to cross over."

Kip looped his arm over Chance's shoulder. "Yeah…I'm hungry," he echoed.

Ella chuckled as she watched Benji taking in the situation. "Don't mind my brother and his friend," she said. "But I do think they are getting a little impatient with me. We were on our way for ice cream. I promised them."

Benji looked confused, his brow narrowing. "Your brother?"

"Yes…I have a younger brother who came along later in life." *Apparently, he hadn't known. And why would he, really?* She was sure BJ Marek had spent very little time contemplating the home life of the Hurley household over the years. "Chance…or Charles rather. But we call him Chance."

For a few moments the expression Ella witnessed taking over Benji's countenance spoke of uncertainty and disorientation. A regular tailspin, followed by a glazed-over, far-off stare. *What was going on?* Finally, he shook his head, snapping out of wherever it was that he had gone. "Oh, okay…yeah, Chance…well copasetic. I didn't know."

Ella fought back a frown. The whole thing felt odd. But there was so much about Benji she didn't know, actually. And what she did—it wasn't always good. Or *mostly* wasn't good. It was possible seeing her brother had triggered something inside himself. He had once mentioned that he felt trauma over a young boy in Hawaii that he hadn't been able to save.

"Well…I suppose…I better—" She pointed toward Chance, to his friend. Easing into motion, she began sidestepping away. "Nice seeing you."

"Wait," Benji called out as the distance between them grew.

Ella almost jumped. Stopping all movement, she tilted her head in question, looking back in Benji's direction.

"I mean…I've told you how I've been…but what about…how about you, personally? You haven't told me how you have you been."

Ella narrowed her eyes. *Fair enough.* But even so, a surprise coming from the Benjamin Marek she had last encountered at the convalescent home. From the Benji, who had, by all forms of the imagination, transformed back into the BJ Marek that she once knew. To tell her all about his own success—that could be considered a typical BJ behavior. A demeanor that she had encountered more than once throughout the years. But for him to actually give two cents about her? That was catching her off guard.

She smoothed her summery dress. "Me? I've been…okay…good. Yeah…I'm doing just fine." She'd admit to nothing else, of course. Not to him.

Benji regarded her, blue lenses piercing through sunlight on a busy street. "Well, you look good. Just swell, actually."

A blush crept onto her cheeks. So, she was Ella then—*or so it seemed.* This was the Benji she had come to know at the hospital. It was an unexpected phenomenon after all that had gone down between them, after all the time that had passed. It was a crazy feat, really. BJ Marek knowingly admitting aloud for the very first time that, one, Eleanor Hurley, *looks good.* Stop the press! *Please,* someone—record it in a news article. If only his forever cronies could be there to attest.

Ella felt slightly shaky hands reaching for her hair once again, smoothing it down. Seemingly of their own accord. Why was she so nervous? Why were her thoughts going there—scattering to all sorts of places? Some of them dark. But she knew the answer to that question—there had been too many ups and downs.

Don't pick her…We don't want that one. She's worthless.

He had, and continued to, affect her life in so many ways. Dominated it. Always had.

Would he forever, then?

She hoped not.

"Thank you," she said, willing her voice to not sound mousey, insecure, smitten.

"A new hairdo," he asked.

"It is." She smiled, feeling herself snapping out of the angst. Life was better lived when participating in the here and now. A lesson she would be wise to take hold of. Ingest deeply. "It's summer after all. What a better time for change in the north country wouldn't you say? Embrace the new season and all that."

"I can't argue with that." He rotated in a semi-circle, taking in his surroundings. "And what a great season it is. Beautiful weather…perfect today. And—" He stopped talking. Stopped moving.

"And what?" Out of nowhere, goosebumps began developing on Ella's skin.

"Well, it just occurred to me…it's the first time I've ever seen you without your nursing attire on. Don't get me wrong…not that I didn't appreciate the uniform…but today, I don't know what it is, but you look especially lovely in real clothes if you will."

"Oh." The goosebumps began to spread. *Tenfold.*

My, my, the compilation of good feelings spiraling through the veins, thought Ella.

But to say that it was the first time, he had seen her without nursing attire on—Ella knew that simply wasn't true. Still, she couldn't argue with the way his words were making her feel.

"And you," she said, returning the volley. "It's the first time I've seen you up and walking."

At that, Benji beamed. "So, it is." He held his arms out, like a cross. Did a little spin, pride emanating from every part of his demeanor. "Looks good on me…wouldn't you say?"

So much cockiness. Ella shook her head and laughed. But even as the words left her lips, she knew deep down—they weren't true either. She had been watching Benjamin Marek walk around for years and years.

CHAPTER 29

After depositing the syringe she had been using on a metal tray, Ella covered up her patient with a blanket and began wheeling a cart with the leftover supplies down a long aisle of beds. She was at the hospital, working her regular shift. But her thoughts were anything but regular. Since running into Benji on the streets of downtown, her mind had been able to concentrate on little else. It had been such a shock to see him! And then to witness him up walking, participating with life—as if all were normal. In a million years, she couldn't have imagined it prior to that day. It was as if she had expected him to live out his years at the convalescent home, wheeling around in a wheelchair, doing what he needed to just get by. Simply existing.

Nurse to patient—she was happy for him.

But in all actuality, according to their last encounter together at the convalescent home, she *was* no longer his nurse. Hadn't been, in the end. He had taken care of that all too well. And yet, seeing him back out in real life, away from the medical setting, away from all the memories, everything had come at her from another angle. A confusing angle, if you will.

The way he had treated her out there on the sidewalks, across the street from Arbuckle Drug—with complete decency. With none of the recent past surfacing, or the deep past either. *Well, maybe some of the recent past.* It seemed there was still *something* there between them. If nothing else, an innate attraction. But that only added to the puzzlement. Last encounter they'd had, he'd more than revealed the coldness of this true self. His true feelings. *BJ Marek at his finest.*

He still loathed Eleanor Hurley indeed.

During the encounter downtown, though, he didn't pay homage to her true identity. It was like he'd already forgotten. She was just Nurse

Ella. He seemed light-hearted and personable. Friendly. As if she were his equal.

Eleanor Hurley was *never* his equal.

But Nurse Ella and Eleanor Hurley were one and the same. There was no way to divide the two. If Benji didn't care for the earlier version of her, in the end, there was no real way he could care for the person she was in the present.

It was as simple as that.

All else was just blither blather floating around in the wind. She needed to brush it away, so it didn't keep getting in her eyes. *In her heart.*

The principle could be applied in the same way to him then, she realized, as if confirming the thought in her own mind for the very first time. BJ Marek and her patient, Benji, were one in the same. If she hadn't cared for the earlier version of him, there was no real way she could care for the person he was in the present.

It was as simple as that.

And who was he in the present anyway—someone who vacillated between thought patterns and behaviors? She was never sure which version of him she was going to get during each encounter. The whole thing was exhausting. She knew one thing for sure. She was done. Regardless of running into him on out there on the street, she needed to forget it all and move back on with her life.

The release of that thought allowed Ella to carry out her day with renewed purpose and focus, giving the patients what they deserved from her undivided attention: antibiotics for cellulitis of the legs, increased IV fluids for an acute kidney injury, preparations in sending two gallbladder attacks into surgery, and the care of a young child who'd been vomiting for three days.

The morning passed by, and Ella was happy with way it had gone. Caught up with tasks and patient care, she left the entry doors of ward-four, heading toward the central nursing desk. Shortly, it would be time for lunch. *"So good to see him again,"* she heard the ward clerk say on approach.

"I know…and he looked so good," Josephine, a nurse assigned to ward-two, answered. She was leaning against the counter twirling a strand of hair that had escaped from her nursing cap, while the clerk was sorting through a stack of papers on the other side of the desk. Sorting—but mostly talking. "And to think a few months ago, he'd been near death. Swollen up, bruised, and unrecognizable."

Ella went still in her tracks. *Who were they talking about?*

"Maimed soldier. But no longer, as it would appear."

At the word *soldier*, Ella's heart began to beat a little faster.

"Nice to learn of a success story. We need a little of that these days. Something positive to cheer us up a bit. So much going bad…with the war and all. With all the stories floating back from Europe. Good of him to stop by and visit. That boy is on-the-beam."

"A regular ace," the ward clerk agreed, while grabbing a fresh stack of papers and then setting them right back down in the same spot. "Good to see him. And…up walking around too."

Ella couldn't take it, by then her heart was heading toward a runaway galloping. "Sorry to interrupt," she interjected, "but who are you talking about?".

"Oh…hi, Ella." Josephine pulled away from the desk. "Didn't see you there. We were talking about the soldier that was here at War Memorial last December into January. You remember him, don't you?" She paused, eyes opening a bit wider. "What am I saying…of course, you'd remember him. If I remember correctly…it seems like he spent most of his time in ward-four. Benjamin was his name."

The breath left Ella's lungs. Nodding her head, she tried her best to keep composure. "Yes…I remember him. He…did you say he was here? In the building…recently?"

"Yes." Josephine smiled wide. "Not too long ago, actually. But I believe he is gone now. He just left."

"Did he—" Ella stopped, then started again. "Did he mention what he wanted? Why he was here?"

"Just to visit," the ward clerk chimed in. "He was a patient here for so long. I think he was just stopping by to pay us his thanks. As I'm sure you remember, it was really touch and go for a while. And to think he's doing so much better. So good to see him."

"Yes," Ella nodded. "I'm sure it was.

Disappointment flooded over her like uncontrolled rapids of a deep, murky river.

Somehow, she had just missed him.

But why had he even actually been there? Was it really just to visit? He knew she worked there—*of course*. But seemingly hadn't asked about her. Yet was willing to risk running into her. Was it all a coincidence? Was he just paying thanks to the facility after all? And yet she had been such a big part of his stay—*not to even ask if she was working?* Had he gotten to see Dr. Northcott? The questions twisted through her mind like a tornado gaining strength.

She took a big breath, to get a hold on her emotions. All the cross-examining in the world wasn't going to solve what she didn't have answers for. Taking a moment or two to disregard what could have been had she only arrived at the central nursing station a few minutes earlier, Ella brought her focus back to the present. Afterward, all that was left was a subdued feeling of melancholy. Of which, she quickly reminded herself, couldn't be permitted to take hold, after resolving to *let go*, only hours ago that same morning.

Taking a series of back hallways, she headed toward lunch. *There was nothing that a few morsels of food couldn't cure*, she realized as hunger pangs began hitting out of nowhere. Having had a busy morning, there hadn't been time for morning breaks or snacks. Rounding the last corner before reaching the breakroom door, she stopped in her tracks. Behind her, she heard a stir in the air.

"Ella...El—" came a voice, calling from over her shoulder.

The heartrate that had been tripping at a fast-paced minutes earlier, began once again re-gaining speed. The deep tone that was coming at her ears was all too familiar. Lifting a hand to her chest, she turned around. "Benji," she breathed. *"You're still here,"* she wanted to add. "What brings you here," she asked instead. *He hadn't left after all!* She felt it all the way to her toes.

Suddenly, she was beyond happy.

Seconds later, she reprimanded herself. *This is stupid,* she thought. She needed to quit feeling so enthralled in spirit. When was she going to learn to back off—back away? Leave it all where it last was—which was nowhere, according to vivid memories.

"Just came by to pay a visit." Benji ran a hand through his hair. Ella couldn't help but notice how good he looked. The style of his cut— shaved close at the ears, bangs hanging over his eye, when he didn't push them away. *Which he just had.* The design was nothing like the hospital hair that she'd grown used to.

She swallowed hard.

And his outfit—the way it fit him now that he'd gained back a healthy weight, looking fit like he'd been working hard at physical labor or exercising in some way.

"I spent so much time at this place." He gestured, while starting to talk again and Ella reeled her thoughts in, training them on what he was saying. Instead of his appearance. "I wanted to tell everyone hi... and see what this place looked like while standing on two legs."

"That's nic—" Ella started to say.

But Benji wasn't done.

"And to apologize." He lifted blue eyes to look directly at Ella. "To you especially," he added, his voice going quiet. "Since you were my nurse so much of the time. I wanted to apologize for the way I acted as a patient. There were times I was a real ass. I know I was frustrated and depressed...but there is no excuse."

Ella's breath caught in her throat. The last thing she ever expected to get from Benjamin Marek was an apology—for anything. And yet the remorse he offered—in Ella's mind, it only addressed part of what needed tending to. True, he had been a moody patient, which, at times, had been hard for the staff to deal with. And sure, she really *had* been the one to experience this first-hand much of the time. But the greater issue, as far as she was concerned, dealt with another matter entirely. The way he had gotten rid of her as soon as he discovered her true identity. *What was his excuse for that?*

"Thanks...for the offering," she said. "It's appreciated." There was no way she'd be bringing up the other issue for discussion—*ever.* For a two second increment there was a pause between them with his eyes holding hers. Eventually, Ella cleared her throat to break up the moment. Before she felt herself getting sucked in. *And to what?* Clearly, this was a professional gesture on Benji's behalf and nothing more.

In-spite-of what she secretly longed to hear from him in the way of an apology—still what he'd said was nice. Welcomed. After the admission had been offered, he began to look antsy. Like he wanted to leave, maybe. Like—*enough said* on his part. He'd done his thing. Accomplished what he set out to do. Ella lifted a hand toward the breakroom in-order-to offer respite. "Well...I suppose. It's my lunch time." She bit her lip.

"Oh...oh yeah, okay." Benji startled into motion. He began backing away, an uneasy smile finding its way to his lips. "Bye, then," he added, his voice sounding strangely different.

Ella nodded. "Bye," she answered back. Inching forward, she proceeded in the direction she had been heading earlier. Having just reached a hand toward the doorhandle of the metal, breakroom door, she heard her name being called out again. Once more, she paused.

"By the way...I also wanted to tell you...it was nice seeing you again...running into you downtown." He paused. "Seeing you here today too."

All the last second uneasiness—was it because of that, she wondered later. Had he been nervous to tell her he was happy to see her again?

Four days later, after three more shifts at the hospital, Ella heard her name being called out yet another time. On this occasion, she was in line at Central Savings Bank, downtown on Ashmun. It was payday and now that Melvin was no longer working, it was important that her check be deposited in a timely manner, allocating it toward needs of the family. With each new earnings and each signature on the dotted line, she felt a margin of resentment toward the person's whose money she was replacing. The individual who was at home, either with glass of liquor in hand or sprawled out somewhere snoring. Or else hanging out at the Belvidere Ships Tavern as was the growing pattern of late. Anywhere, but at work.

The second she heard her name, Ella went still in her tracks. She'd been fixated on the teller in front of her, beckoning "*next*" as the line moved in slow progression. But the moment the familiar ring of the deep tone reached her ears, the banker's words became superfluous noise in the background.

Slowly, as if floating, Ella turned around.

And there he was, as she knew he would be after hearing the voice, but the way he was looking at her with such interest woven into his expression, lips formed into a smile, the reaction that sifted through her insides was anything but expected. Suddenly she felt weak. Dizzy. Giddy even. For a quick moment, she thought to chastise herself for allowing these types of emotions to take over—but then a stronger force grabbed hold and all caution fell to the wind.

"Hi Benji," she said with a smile. There were a good handful of people between them making any type of conversation difficult, so she prepared to turn back around, albeit with a heart beating hard against her chest.

"Wait for me when you are done...will you?"

The request caught her off guard. "Okay...yeah," she answered mid-turn. "Yeah...I could do that."

By the time Benji had gone through the line, Ella had talked herself down from the bungle of nerves that were flummoxing her body while she waited for him by the tiled entrance of the bank. Once again, his eyes regarded her with a type of open affection as he made his approach. Ignoring the reaction that was being stirred up in her body, she allowed a grin to take over her lips. "Well...well, three times in one week. This is something," she offered playfully. "If I didn't know better, Benji, I'd say you were following me around town."

The comment enlisted a few chuckles from those in line who were within hearing distance. Inside, Ella was checking herself. *Had she really just made a flippant comment like that toward one, BJ Marek?*

"Well...technically it's been eight days since I first ran into you. So that's not really considered a week." Benji's retort held a lighthearted tone, but Ella noticed a trace of pink splayed across his cheekbones. "But who is counting...right?" At that question, he held her gaze for longer than was necessary.

And all at once, it was she who was blushing. She could feel it from the top of her blond hair that was pulled back into a ponytail, down to her sandals—this thing between them. It was still there. *Something* was there. Taking hostage of her senses, it was playing havoc with her insides.

"So," she said, letting out a breath. Benji's eyes found her lips, following the sound that had just escaped from them. *Ugh!* On the inside, she wanted to kick herself for not being more discreet.

"So," he said, shoving his hands the front pockets of his slacks. His gaze traveled back up to meet hers and once more the irises of their pupils locked. Ella felt a tingling sensation spreading throughout her body. *What was this?* They were acting like they were juveniles—all tongue tied and dewy-eyed. Like they were in high school or something.

High school!

At that thought, Ella felt a panicky sensation surge through her veins. Working hard, she tried to block it out. And yet, there were the bluest eyes she had quite possibly *ever* seen, looking at her like she was the best thing *ever*. So many conflicting emotions. How did it all compute?

"Must be banking day." Benji's voice came to life, interrupting the unwanted thoughts. They both laughed a little.

"Yeah…must be." She glanced down at the paystub in her hand and for a moment wondered if Uncle Sam paid the soldiers that had been injured and sent home to recuperate. Was that why he was there—to deposit his own check? And if so, was the compensation enough? Compared to the giving of one's life for their country—left to live out remaining years with permanent disabilities? And yet by all appearances, the way Benji looked, it seemed he was bouncing back. Healing—*or healed, rather.*

Very well, in fact.

At this last thought—once again, Ella felt her cheeks growing pink. Because—he *did* look good! Great, even! But did she really have to blush? Such a physical betrayal of all that was going on in her mind.

Simply put—*she was acting like a mess!* What had happened to all the professionalism she once knew how to claim?

"Well, it's a good thing that the hospital pays you for all the work you put in there. It is sure well deserved. I, for one, got to witness firsthand all the running around you do while on duty. All the different directions you get pulled throughout the day." Benji's voice softened. "Not to mention all the lives you save."

Ella's eyes widened. "I don't know about that—" she started to say.

"Mine for instance." He hadn't finished.

Ella's breath caught in her throat. "I mean—"

"I *do* know that for a fact, Ella. Look at me now." He lifted his hands,

Oh, she'd been looking.

"True…but what happened to hard work and determination. Don't' you think that played a big part? Every part, really."

"That…and a certain hospital staff member that forced me to take a look inside…find the grit I needed. Say…one certain nurse."

"Okay…alright, if you insist on seeing it that way…saying it that way, then I'll concede if it makes you happy. But—"

"But what?" Benji's eyes narrowed. His head was tilted. He bit his lip.

"But what was he doing to her" she wanted to ask. She was feeling all kinds of dizzy. Standing there with him in the lobby of the bank, lines of people coming and going while the two of them were doing— what? Smiling at each other, giving looks, holding gazes, blushing. Oh my—was she brazenly flirting with BJ Marek out in public? And was he giving it back in equal parts? Or vice versa? Was that why so many of the patrons were giving them glances, stifling cheeky grins as they passed by? Could anything be more obvious?

"But if you're going to talk about saving lives…then let's talk about you."

Benji looked confused.

"What about you going to war…fighting for our country," Ella offered in clarification. "Joining the cause…collectively working toward saving those overseas who are getting taken over by a vile regime, while protecting our country at the same time. I'd say you are the one who is saving lives here."

In a flash, all the light left Benji's eyes. His expression froze, save a tiny muscle in the jaw that began to twitch. For a third time during their encounter, Ella felt an overwhelming sensation from her head to her toes. But this time it was more like whiplash. A shock to the system. A sense of dread.

Something was going terribly wrong.

What had she said *exactly* that was creating the turn-about?

Clearly, it was the saving lives part. Did he really not want to take credit for such a thing?

"I mean," she started to say. *What **did** she want to say?* Because, Benji was saying nothing. It seemed there was no good place for the conversation to go from there. Maybe she should just politely excuse herself and be on her way. Obviously, there was a hurdle between them that she was incapable of figuring out. Maybe somehow, they had just circled back to square one—though she didn't know how or why. Maybe she never would. Maybe, just maybe, it wasn't meant to be, after all. End of story.

Shaking his head, as if to clear it, Benji forced a smile. A two-second pause came and went, and the turn of his lips appeared more natural. The glow in his eyes all but returned, eventually restoring to full volume. "Well...since we have such obvious gratitude toward one another's professions...why not repay each other somehow...say, by going out on a date together?"

Ella didn't think she could be any more stunned than she'd been earlier in the conversation. But once again, she was wrong. Somehow, there had been a recovery on the part of the opposite party—*and how!*

A date with Benjamin Marek?

Was this a trick?

All at once, a lifetime of memories came spinning through Ella's mind as if on a movie reel played at the theatre, during the downtown show. Without warning, a measure of panic shot through her veins at record speed. All the dizziness from earlier had returned, making it difficult to think straight.

"You okay?" Benji directed the question with unease evident on his brow. "Bad idea, then?" His face fell, slightly.

"No...I—" Ella tried to pull herself together, willing years and years of inundating thoughts to go away. She looked up at Benji and found the bluest eyes, focused solely on her. So much affection emanating from them. So much care and concern. It was almost as if she had made up the rest—the entire history they shared together. "I think that would be fine," she finally uttered aloud. "Yeah...that would be a good idea."

"Copasetic." Benji was beaming, relief evident in the whole of his demeanor. "Do you work tomorrow?"

"No. I'm off."

"Great...then I'll pick you up six p.m. sharp."

Ella couldn't breathe. "Okay," she nodded. Then looking up, saw several smiles from the patrons in line for the teller's window. Those that were currently waiting, had overheard the entire conversation. And looked like they couldn't be happier about the results.

But the bigger question—was she?

CHAPTER 30

"Why do you look so fancy?" Chance darted around the corner, peering into the bathroom as Ella put the finishing touches on her hair and makeup.

Did she? Look fancy? Too fancy? She hoped not. The butterflies in her stomach started up, fluttering madly, getting tangled up with one another. She smoothed down the floral, sleeveless dress she had picked out, eyeing the way it accentuated her small waste, flaring just below. "I don't look fancy," she protested.

"I'd say fancy. Where are you going anyway?"

"That's none of your beeswax."

"How come?" Chance crinkled his nose.

Ella hesitated, eyeing the suspicion in her brother's eyes. How much to explain when she wasn't completely confident about the situation herself. "Out with friends," she finally said, applying a bow to the back of her ponytail. One friend, really. Or was it a foe? Who was Benjamin Marek, exactly—her said date for the night.

"Where to? Must be somewhere swell." He wasn't giving up.

"Actually, I'm not sure. We'll see where the evening takes us, I guess."

Chance performed an eyeroll, a frown finding its way onto his face. "Well…I'm bored. There's nothing to do around here."

"How about Kip? Why don't you see what he's up to?"

"Gone. Left for Barbeau with his family to spend a week at their summer cabin."

"Okay…well then, how about some of your other friends from the block?"

"I don't know…maybe." Chance looked less than convinced.

"It's better than sitting around here all evening, moping." Ella grabbed a light sweater and her handbag as the sound of a vehicle made its approach, slowing down in front of their house. Hurrying to the hallway second-floor window, she peaked out. Sure enough, there was a Packard Clipper parked outside, though she couldn't see the occupant through the shaded glass. Placing a kiss on the top of Chance's head, she made for the stairs. "I think it's a great idea. Go see about Bobby or Betty."

With that, Ella headed for the door, hoping her quick movement and ornate attire wouldn't catch her father's attention on the way out. But she needn't worry. He didn't stir, let alone lift an eyelid as she breezed through the living room, three feet away from where he was lounged.

Benji was just stepping from the vehicle as Ella made her way down the sidewalk. His eyes widened at the sight of her. "Wow…you look lovely," he said. And for a two-second count their gazes locked. The butterflies from earlier started up again, but this time for different reasons. Ella broke the moment with a smile.

"Thank you," she said. So, she wasn't being too fancy after all. Suddenly she was glad she had gone with the floral choice. "You look nice yourself." And he did. Shirt and slacks fitting just right. The way his hair was slicked back on the sides, bangs falling repeatedly over one eye like they did. Letting out a deep breath, she slid into the front seat, while he went back to the driver side.

Once inside the vehicle, they turned to look at each other. For a modicum of a moment, time stood still. Benji bit his lip. "So…were doing this. Can't believe were really doing this." It was a hell of thing to say on a first date. But Ella got it. *Exactly*. They had been through so much. And yet here they were—together. Finally. If anything, the statement, set her at ease. There was no sense in pretending they didn't have history between them.

Ella nodded. Their eyes were still affixed. "It appears we are." She swallowed hard.

"So," he said.

"So," she breathed, finally breaking away. Afterward, patting the dash. "Nice ride. Is it...is this yours?" She couldn't imagine.

Benji laughed. "No...my dad's. But mine for the evening."

"Well...where to?" He hadn't started driving yet. It seemed they were still wrapping their heads around the moment.

"I was thinking Manhattan Café."

Ella had seen the advertisements. Had eaten there on occasion when the money was available. *Steaks, chops, spaghetti, and regular meals at popular prices.* And now she'd be eating there with Benji. A little flutter rippled through her insides. "I'd like that."

Benji eased the Clipper into motion, and they started off down the street. Driving over to Portage Avenue, they parked and walked to the entryway of the restaurant. An aura of allure enveloped Ella as she glanced over at her date. He looked so handsome. And she—well with the way he kept giving her the glances—she figured she must look pretty good too. It certainly felt that way. Everything seemed perfect.

And she had non-stop goosebumps to prove it.

After getting seated, she picked spaghetti from the menu, and he got a chop and potatoes. The food was delicious. And the company even better. Though Ella found it was hard to eat when butterflies were occupying the space where food normally goes. Sitting across from each other, they kept catching one another's eye. Between bites, between conversation, during conversation. Sometimes pausing mid-line. Thrill after thrill kept finding its way to the pit of Ella's stomach. All the attraction that had begun to flame during his stay at the hospital was still there, seemingly reaching a crescendo.

This was no first date.

Yet, in a way, everything felt brand new.

Completely unexplored.

After dinner, they walked unhurriedly to the car, neither seeming to want the night to end. Reaching the passenger side, Benji made like he was reaching for the handle to let her in, but instead he stopped, Ella wedged between him and the door. Noticing the pause, Ella turned to face him. There was something about the look he was giving that made her catch breath. He was so close. Her mind flashed back to their time in his room at the convalescent home and once more goosebumps covered her skin. Was he about to kiss her again? She could feel her lips parting as if of their own accord. Benji didn't miss it. His eyes dropped to her mouth. A two-second count ticked by, and he seemed to be leaning closer.

Then, sucking in a waft of air, he stepped back.

A wave of disappointment swept over Ella.

"Would you...ah...do you want to go for a ride before heading back?"

'Um...yeah...sure." Ella felt off her guard, undone. Marginally disappointed.

After she got in, he slid into the driver's side, and they took off. Leaving the downtown, they started heading west, putting behind them the busyness of the city. They streets grew quieter as they drove, and they did too. The conversation had been flowing over dinner. Non-stop chatting and light banter—*between the looks.* But this was something new. Not in an awkward way. More like an unspoken attraction that was brewing.

What were they going to do about it?

Every now and then, Benji would glance over and offer a smile. Lips turning upward, Ella wondered whether the return gesture she was giving bespoke of all the nerves that were playing inside her body. Or if he could hear the wild sound of her heartbeat. "Have you been out to the Shallows much?" His voice broke the silence. There was something about the tone that was different. Subdued. Softer than normal.

"Not much."

The quiet resumed, except for the sound of the Glenn Miller Band playing in the background.

"Is that where we're headed?"

Pursing his lips together, he nodded. "I thought so." He looked over at her. "You okay with that?"

Okay with what?

Why did she feel like it was a loaded question?

But the answer was—yes. *Yes, to everything!*

No matter the question. *Oh my—*

Damn—she was losing her mind.

Parking in a wooded area on the edge of the water, seemingly far from the rest of the world, Benji shut off the ignition. "So…this is it." He turned toward her. "Do you like it?"

"I do," she breathed. *And I like you. God help me. So, all this surrounding us is secondary.*

Benji reached a hand to her face and ran a soft touch down her cheek. Ella got chills. "I'm so glad we ran into each other again."

"Me too." Her voice came across too soft. Something shifted in his eyes.

"Ella," he mouthed. Once more it looked like he was leaning in. Once again, he stopped. Afterward, he began straightening around in the driver's seat. "Do you want to walk down by the water?"

Yes, to everything!

Leaving the vicinity of the parked car, they started down a foliage-lined path. He reached for her hand while they were walking. "Is this okay," he asked again.

She nodded and smiled. He gave her palm a little squeeze. Reaching the water, they stopped to look out over the draw of the waves as they pushed to shore. "Very relaxing," Ella said. But the tempo of her heartbeat was saying *that is a lie.*

"Yeah…I come out here sometimes to think…to relax."

"I can see why. I've been out this way on occasion, but never to this spot."

After that, silence fell back over them, and they resumed their laid-back stride along the lakeshore. On the inside though—nothing was quiet in the least. It seemed the further they walked, the greater the thickness in the air. An unsettled wind current stirred in the space between them. It grew and grew until it had no place to go.

"El—"

"Benj—"

They both turned at once. Nervous laughter lifted into the air.

"You first," said Benji.

But Ella shook hear head. "No…you."

He stared hard. Shook his head one time. "You are so…so beautiful." This time when Benji leaned in, he didn't pull back at the last second. It was just a soft touch of the lips, but it delivered all that was needed. The shivers were immediate as they consumed Ella's body. She let out a small breath that sounded more like a gasp.

At that, Benji did pull away. But it was just to look into her eyes. A look passed between them that spoke of something deep. An innate connection. *I want you so much.* A groan escaped his lips and he leaned in again. This time when he put his mouth on hers the softness transformed into a type of urgency. In an instant, they reached for each other, arms wrapping, hands pressing, fingers sliding through hair. It had been so long since they'd been together. They'd had a taste of how good it could be back when he was her patient.

And had been starving since.

The kiss continued and their hands continued reaching. Exploring one another's body. His felt so hard under her fingertips. Hers so soft. He was touching her in places he hadn't before, and it felt so good. She never wanted it to end. Didn't want him to stop. The sound of exhaling from her lungs grew louder. Or was it his? Would it really be considered air exchange at all? A type of desperation set in.

Finally, he eased away, both of them catching their breath. For a moment neither of them spoke—couldn't speak it seemed. "And what was…what were you going to say," Benji asked, his voice caught between a whisper and soft laughter.

Ella took a step back. Pressing a hand to her swollen lips, she grinned. "You know…somehow I can't quite remember."

"You—" Benji wrapped an arm around Ella and pulled her head against his shoulder. "I'll bet you can't." This time when they began walking, it was side by side, her body pressed into his, a subdued feeling enveloping their gate.

But when they arrived back to the Packard Clipper, one look between them, after settling into their seats, and they were reaching for each other again—all thoughts of placidity forgotten. This time stepped up a notch from what it had been on the sandy trail of the lakeshore. Ella could no longer think straight. This thing with Benji—it had been building for so long. Ups and downs. Past or future. Right or wrong. All she knew—what she was feeling for him right then and there—it was stronger than anything she had ever experienced. And against all inklings of better judgement—she just couldn't say no to that.

The date at Manhattan Café with time spent afterwards at the Shallows was followed up by another date. And then another. Soon it seemed they *were* dating. Like they were a thing. Ella could hardly believe it. In what world could she ever have imagined she'd become a couple with BJ Marek. Sure, all was not perfect. In many ways, to Ella, it felt like she was *sneaking* out with BJ Marek. Because there was no way she would tell Siobhan. Nor, really, her parents. They'd heard the stories over the years through tears on the home front. And Siobhan had witnessed them firsthand—at school.

But this wasn't BJ Marek from back in the day. It was the soldier who had given of himself at Pearl Harbor, who she had personally nursed back to life. *Benji.*

Her Benji.

Except he wasn't *just* Benji. And she knew it. But it was easy to forget when they were together, caught up in looks, touching, always reaching. Finding ways to take it to the next level. They couldn't get enough of each other. It wasn't just physical either—though she couldn't deny he made her crazy that way—they laughed together easily, had fun, talked effortlessly of the most mundane things.

More and more, he was seeming essential to her life.

Somehow—in the future—she'd have to think of a way to break the news to the others who were essential in her life as well.

"You're a real doll…you know that?" They were lying together, tangled up in the bed of his childhood home. His parents were gone for the day. Nestled on the other side of Easterday Hill, opposite from Siobhan's residency, the Marek home was in a neighborhood that spoke of money. Standing proudly with rows of other brick houses, it faced down on the city, watching over its comings and goings. "What would I have done without you?" He squeezed her bare arm and began running the tips of his fingers up and down her skin. She was clothed only in his tee-shirt, he a pair of shorts. "Let me rephrase that. What would I *do* without you?"

Ella lifted her head off his chest and placed a kiss on his cheek. "Very true." She leaned back, while sending a wink. "I'm not sure what you'd do?" He pinched her side, and she giggled a little. On the inside she was thinking the same thing. *What would I do without you?*

They'd been spending so much time together. When they were apart, her body physically hurt from missing his touch. Everything was so new for her. and she craved it like a drug. Craved him like a drug. In her mind, it was still a bit tricky making it all work between them. There were things they still weren't discussing. But somehow, they were making it work. *And how.* When they were alone together, he said such nice things to her. Made her feel like she was the most beautiful, needed creature in the world. It felt like they were falling in love.

He even came over to her house on Maple Street. Though that part was a little awkward at times. But her parent's lack of involvement helped to avoid any confrontations. Clearly, they didn't recognize Benji. And mostly they stayed away when he was visiting, her mom retreating to her room, her dad retreating to the bottle. Only Chance refused to stay at bay, involving himself in their activities and conversations at any given opportunity. Though Benji seemed a little standoffish and taken aback by Chance, especially at first, he eventually began to warm up, interacting on certain levels. *And how could you not with Chance?* He just had that way—a certain charm that sucked you in.

"Seriously though, El...you are so perfect for me." Benji began stroking her hair. "It's weird," he paused. "Sometimes when I'm with you, I forget who you really are...or that I knew you in elementary school, in high school...in *any* school." He leaned down in slow motion, as if lost in some thought and placed a kiss on the top of her head. "Most of the time...to be honest...I just don't think of you that way... as someone I used to know."

Ella froze. This was the first time he had addressed the topic of *them* in the growing up years—of who they were in times past. Since his original discovery of their history together with Jane Beckwith at the convalescent home. *What was to be said next*, she wondered. Was his query the catalyst for a more serious discussion? And what of him saying he didn't think of her as Eleanor Hurley—because that is who she indeed was. Although Ella would be first to admit, she, at times, couldn't reconcile the Benji beside her as being BJ Marek either. Nor could she bury the truth that she was the queen of wanting to forget. There were things in her life—significant things—that she wished she could erase from her memory on a permanent basis. Or simply go back and change.

"Benji...I think—" There was so much she wanted to say. It was time to broach the topic. Take a painful trip to the past.

"I just can't help but think about the future though," Benji started talking again, causing Ella's words to catch in her throat. What was he about to say? Obviously, the future held as much weight as the past. For the moment, all thoughts of their childhood would have to be put on hold in her mind. She was all ears. "I can't help but wonder what it is that I'm supposed to do next," he continued. "Sometimes I feel like I'm just immobilizing. I can't just keep doing nothing any longer. Should I begin working? Is it time? Should I go to work for my dad in his excavating company? Take a job in factory...put in lots of hours like others are doing to help out the cause? Or—"

"Or what?" Ella's heart began thudding loudly in her chest.

"Or should I go back to work for Uncle Sam? See about re-enlisting."

It felt like a dagger to Ella's chest. Why did she know he was going to say that? Though, hearing the words in a sentence, coming from his mouth hurt more than she could have expected. "Okay—" She couldn't hide the disappointment in her voice. Her lips turned into a frown.

Benji shot a look in her direction. Studied her face for a few moments. "Hey," he said, reaching up to brush a lock of hair from her cheek. "Even if I do go back in. It won't be the end of us. I will take you with me in my heart. Hopefully in picture form too," he added with a chuckle. Then grew serious again. "My guardian angel nurse, who brought me back to life. You'll go with me always." Resituating himself onto an elbow, he peered further into her eyes. "If I do go back in, you'd wait for me to come back here at home, wouldn't you? Say yes. Please, El...tell me yes."

Ella's expression turned into a pout. "Well, I'm not going to lie. I don't like the idea. One bit. You were just injured and now you are finally better. It will be hard to not think of the what ifs if you go back there. It will be hard not to worry."

"That's the thing though…I did make it out of there safely. Well, not exactly safely…but I'm doing better now…I still have more to give."

Ella thought of Siobhan. Of how much she hated to see her soldier go. Her *Surf.* Of all the sadness she carried with her, all the angst, biding time until she could see him again one day. Until she could fall back into his arms. Now, much against her will, it seemed Ella would finally be able to relate. Biting her lip, she turned away.

"I'd miss you," she sighed.

"Awe," Benji said, reaching for her face, turning it back toward him. "I'd miss you too. You're really starting to get under my skin. You know that?" He tweaked her nose. "But I promise it wouldn't be forever. And besides, who knows what they'll say. I can't guarantee they'll let me back in. There are certain standards. Certain criteria. But…if they do, I'll come back…to you. Because I can see it now…you are my future. That is…if you can see me in yours."

Ella didn't know if she should smile or sigh at that. Laugh. Or cry. *How to answer that exactly?* But Benji took all decisions away as he leaned in, pressing soft lips against hers. "Oh…El," he whispered. Resituating himself in the bed, he placed his other elbow on the far side of where she was laying, straddling her with his body. Placing weight on his dominant side, he freed up a hand to find her leg and began running it slowly up, farther and farther. She gasped and her hands slid around his back, pulling him closer. The tee-shirt that she was wearing—his tee-shirt—was getting bunched up, baring more and more skin as she pressed into him. Her mind fell into a delirium. All she wanted was the pressure of his mouth to grow. The pressure of his body against hers to grow. For him to bring her to a place where she didn't have to think about the past that she wished could be wiped clean from him. Or the future that she desperately hoped would be filled with him.

Dear Thomas,

You are gone now, forever; God rest your soul.
But they who are responsible, no vindication, no console.

~E

CHAPTER 31

Benji grabbed Ella's hand as they exited the Soo Theatre together on Ashmun. "I felt for the poor chap, didn't you?" He shot a glance at her as they began walking down the sidewalk, his bangs falling over the brow, her locks, loose, blowing in the wind. "Double-crossing boss had it coming to him." Benji raked fingers through his hair in gesture of combat with the blustery air.

Ella nodded her head in agreement. They had just finished watching *This Gun for Hire* starring Alan Ladd. "Payment in marked money? I'd say he had it out for him. Double crosser is right. Imagine the surprise each time you bought something, and you started getting traced as a perpetrator. Completely unbeknownst to you."

Benji squeezed her hand and they kept walking. Breeze blowing all around them, they talked over the particulars of the film. Ella kept remembering the opening, played prior to the main feature—wondering if the obligatory war propaganda had affected him in anyway. But, at the time, aside from going still in his seat, there'd been no other clues on his thoughts over the matter. And if he wasn't mentioning it, then, Ella wouldn't be bringing it up.

Moving in a northerly direction, they kept a slow pace, heading for Kresge's. They were in no particular hurry for the evening. The loose plan was—grab a sandwich now that the movie was over and then head to the water's edge, waiting for dusk to fall. Doing whatever they could find to do—wherever. As long as it included spending as much time as they could—together. It seemed to be their plan—every chance they got. Remaining in each other's company.

They were settled into their seats, in the middle of eating ham sandwiches, when Ella noticed Benji growing quiet. Taking a sip of her coke, she glanced up to find him starring off, deep in thought. "What is it?" Her voice came across muted, matching the apparent new mood.

Benji snapped to. Caught her eye. Pausing for a few seconds, he bunched up his lips. Half pout. Half admitted discouragement. "Well... might as well tell you. I found out earlier today...they aren't accepting me back."

"They?"

But Ella felt she already knew.

"Uncle Sam. The Armed Forces. They said I couldn't return." The defeat in his eyes only lasted an iota of a second. Still, it was there, privy only to those who knew best his trained reactions.

But Ella couldn't help it—she was anything but sad. With every effort, she worked hard to keep her secret joy at bay. Last thing she wanted, was for him to leave town. "Did they give you a reason? Did they say why? I mean you look very good to me. Strong. Fit." *What was she saying?* To the naked ear, it almost sounded as if she was encouraging this thing.

"Apparently there is more to it than that. Though I may look physically capable on the outside, they have to account for all the other issues I've been through. Not walking. Not seeing. All those things. They are considering them to be psychological symptoms. And though I am doing better. It hasn't been a long enough time to say for sure—"

"To say for sure that what?"

"To say that I've been completely healed. That I won't relapse."

Ella folded her hands together. Pressed her lips into a thin line. "I'm sorry, Benji. I don't—" Her words were sticking together.

Benji's eyes narrowed into two slits as he searched her expression. Afterward, he let out a chortle. "Ha...you're not sorry at all...be honest." Shaking his head, he began to grin.

Ella felt her shoulders relax. "No, I—" She started. Then stopped. "Okay...I admit, being honest, I don't *want* you to go away. But I also want you to be happy though. So, if that's what you feel was needed... to re-enlist...then I'd—" Suddenly, her mouth felt dry. She took another sip of her coke. Benji's head was cocked, watching. Waiting. "Then I'd learn to pray really hard...and also probably worry too much."

"Well don't worry about the happy part…I am plenty happy here with you." He held her gaze. Then, raking fingers through his hair, straightened in his chair. "It's okay that it didn't work out. I just…I had to look into it though. I had to try. I couldn't be back home while others were still out there. But—" His facial expression transformed, taking on a lighter tone. "Now…I'll go to work for my dad…find ways to volunteer for the cause. It's what I'll do." *Simple as that.*

But was it? That simple?

"Okay." Ella let out the word slowly, all sorts of questions filtering through her eyes as she peered across the table.

Benji reached over to pat her hands. "No…really. It's okay." He met her scrutiny with a smile. And it seemed so genuine, she could do nothing but breathe easy. Drop the tension in her shoulders. Get re-sucked in by the light of his blue iris's.

Still, it would be a lie to say she was surprised that he didn't seem more disappointed over the matter. But if he was on board with the latest plan for the future, then so was she. Lifting her sandwich, Ella began eating, picking up where she'd last left off. Benji followed suit.

Soon enough, they fell into light banter between bites. Including pointed stares, alternating with jokes and laughter. Finishing, the last of what was on their plates, they opted for ice cream to top things off. They weren't particularly still hungry, but it just sounded good. And with all the rations going on, not every day did they splurge on treats.

Afterwards, stepping back outside into the evening air, they continued with the talked-about itinerary of heading toward the water to finish out the night. Except that with the forecasted wind gusts, the temperature seemed a bit nippy. Ella needed to stop by her house on Maple for a jacket first.

It always felt weird bringing Benji to her family home. Benjamin of the past and Benji of the present just didn't mesh well together. There were never any formal introductions with the parents. No talking of *remember when this happened—remember when we did this as kids* as you'd expect from two individuals who'd grown up in the same town together. No stopping to deliberate over family portraits from the past.

Just a few nods and the making a beeline for the bedroom. Barring Chance intercepting them in route.

That evening was no exception.

They were almost to the staircase door, when Chance's voice increased in decibel. "I scored three goals in street hockey today." He was at Ella's heels, supposedly talking to her, but his head was turned toward Benji. The information was clearly directed at him. "And they had Archie on the other team blocking the net and I still did it. Wham." He made like he was swinging a hockey stick. Ella glanced at Benji and held back a smile. This one's for you she told him with her eyes. Chance had been talking incessantly since they walked in the front door, all souped-up on energy, bouncing as he went. Following as they went.

"That's swell," Benji inserted, lips turned up at the corners. He bumped a playful fist to Chance's shoulder. "You're a real ace." The smile lasted for prolonged moments. In-spite-of the awkwardness the Hurley house presented. In-spite-of the anxious darting of his eyes when they had first entered. In-spite-of the way he took in the living area and the pictures on the walls as if entering the home for the first time. But it wasn't—his first time, nor a first date—and this confused Ella a little. *Why did he still seem so ill-at-ease at times?*

They could still see the beaming smile that Chance wore at that remark as the pair headed for the stairs. "We're going out for a while, Chance." Ella told him. "Just grabbing my jacket."

Up in Ella's room, they shut the door and Benji immediately pulled her in for a kiss. Pushing her against the wooden slats of the door, he leaned an arm against the frame, lips pressing against hers. Breath catching in her throat, she melted into him, feeling a rush of the unexpected. And as always, the thrill of his body against hers. Along with the urgency of his mouth on hers. She just couldn't get enough. He either, it seemed. Freeing a hand to find the curve of her hip, he slid a cupped palm over to her bottom, fingers pressing. Something like a whimper left her throat. On the inside she wanted to shake her head in disbelief—she was completely shameless when it came to him. So needy. So in-tune to his every touch.

Benji groaned and pulled away. He touched a finger to her lips, drawing her bottom lip down, looking right into her eyes. Both of them were catching their breaths. He shook his head one time, breaking the gaze. Then eased her away. "You'd better grab that sweater you were talking about or very soon we won't be going anywhere."

Ella chuckled, lifting a hand to her swollen lips. "Jacket...I'm grabbing a jacket. But I just need to use the lavatory first." Straightening her dress, she reopened the door that had just felt the weight of her body leaning against minutes before. "Be back in a jiffy," she said with a wink, peeking her head back in for a quick second before exiting into the hallway.

A quick second turned into lengthy minutes, and it felt like a long time had gone by when Ella returned to her bedroom. She hadn't meant to—but somehow time had just gotten away from her. "Sorry... I'm back," she said with a breathless rush, bursting through the door. "Ready."

Lifting her eyes to Benji's, she expected the welcome-back look that was sure to be waiting for her on return. Inwardly, she prepared herself for the euphoria, knowing she shouldn't give into it, shouldn't linger on his gaze for one second. Or, like he'd just said before—they might not be going anywhere anytime soon.

But would that really be so bad?

Instead, what she found looking back at her was no stare at all. It was just an aloof Benji, with no eye contact, gaze focused away. Ella went still in her tracks, heart beginning to explode in her chest. *Something had changed.* Something was going on. She could feel it bouncing off every part of her nerve endings. The discomfort in the air was palpable. "Benji?" Her voice was just a whisper as it ricocheted against the walls of the room.

After a two-second delay, Benji turned in her direction. "Okay... ready," he asked, shaking his head as if to free a thought. Or possibly many thoughts—by the way it appeared. But in-spite-of the apparent attempt at a reset, the reflection of his eyes was dull, holding none of the playfulness, endearment, or lust from earlier.

He had the Packard again and Ella situated herself in the front after Benji opened the door, still performing all the things a guy is supposed to do on a date. Chivalry at its best. But what had seemed like grand gestures and impeccable nuances on dates past, somehow just felt like going through the motions. Suddenly, there was no warmth behind the touch. Ella didn't know what to do. *Cut to the chase and ask what was wrong?* For some reason she just couldn't. She'd never been one to dig deeply into things, question motives for behavior.

Though she'd never really been in a serious dating relationship either. Always, with her parents' moods, she'd learned to avoid confrontation. There never seemed to be any real solutions to Melvin and Grace's problems—so why delve in. And with Siobhan—well, when Siobhan got mad, Ella just found it was better to give some space, a cooling period, allowing her time to come back around when she was good and ready. It had always worked for them. They were still the best of friends.

But things were much more complicated when it came to Benji.

Ella glanced over at his profile. They were driving down the street. But where were they headed? It seemed they were coasting down Ashmun, turning onto Portage, and circling back. Over and over. This wasn't like him. Certainly, not the usual pattern they had fallen into. What happened to parking down by the water? Holding onto each other like they never wanted to let go. Exploring each other's bodies like they could never get enough.

"I got my jacket. Are we stopping anywhere?" Ella had to speak loudly over the music in order to be heard. Another atypical thing—playing the radio at high volumes in-order-to drown out the possibility of verbal exchanges. Her heart was thrumming in her ears, at increased decibels, louder than the words coming from Jimmy Dorsey's *Tangerine*. Her head began to swim. *Really—what was going on?* From her sideview, Ella could see a tiny muscle working in Benji's jaw. Clearly, he was on edge. A bad feeling was resting on her chest. She wanted to reach over and lay a hand onto his leg, settle him, have a serious conversation. But then, thought better of it.

He let out a yawn, finally bringing his eyes in her direction, albeit briefly. Ella held her breath. Was it a yawn of boredom? Or a yawn from being tired? Either way, it left her feeling off kilter. "You know," he said, biting his lip. "I thought I was up for stopping somewhere tonight but I'm starting to feel a little beat. Hope I'm not catching something. I think—" Pausing, he flicked another look in Ella's direction. "I think I'll drop you back off and call it a night."

Catching something? She narrowed her eyes. What on earth could she say to that?

But somehow, Ella had a feeling that wasn't it at all. Nodding her head, she sat silently while he drove the car back to Maple. All-the-while, her heart was sinking in her chest. Something was going very wrong. She could feel it—in her brain. And in her soul. It was an all-consuming sensation. She couldn't let it go. "Benji," she said as he came around to open her door, after pulling up to the curb. "What is—"

But she didn't finish. He was already headed back to the driver's side. "I'll be in touch," he called over the roof of the car, offering a smile. But the gesture didn't quite reach his eyes. Ella felt stunned. She couldn't breathe. Clutching her chest, she watched the Packard Clipper drive away. *What had just happened?*

What had gone down between them that was serving as the catalyst to dissolve their newly budding relationship? Because she was just sure that was *exactly* what had just happened. Ever since she'd used the lavatory at her house, he'd been a different person, lacking the warmth typical of the Benji of late. And then in the car, somehow, he'd been aloof and anxious at the same time. Like he wanted to be anywhere but there with her, trapped alone in such a small space. No affectionate smiles, no caressing touches, no breath-stealing looks.

Ella all but ignored Chance's incessant chatter as she made her way into the house and up the stairs to her room. "Hey...where's Benjamin?" His voice lifted from below as she continued her disheartened gate, step after step, just shy of reaching the top.

"Not sure," she murmured over her shoulder.

"What?"

"Home. I said he went home."

And that was that. She shut the door to her room with a thud and sank onto her bed. Her head was still spinning. She felt sick to her stomach. Completely bereft. She had a very bad feeling about things. Staring into space, for many minutes she saw nothing—save the barrage of ugly thoughts running through her mind. Then her eyes fell onto the floral painted dresser that was tucked into the corner, under the sloping eaves. Scattered atop, were a flood of letters written to her deceased brother, Thomas. Years of them.

Beloved Thomas.

For a few moments her heart took on a new pain. As if often did at just the thought of her departed sibling.

Then Ella went still. She half remembered having the letters there on top of her dresser. Half not. She *had* written a new entry only the night before, adding to the accumulating stack from over the years. But had she left them there afterward, just laying open and scattered? Possibly. But most likely not strewn though. She hadn't been rifling through them—this she was certain. Thinking back to the evening before, she tried to recall the activities of the day that had just passed. What had she done in her room? Had she been looking for something in her top drawer and left the letters out? Even tossing them around in her haste?

But nothing was striking across her mind.

No particular memory that could confirm or deny what she was seeing.

In slow motion, Ella made her way across the wooden floorboards of her room. Over to her dresser. Gingerly, she began leafing through each piece of paper, picking them up, gathering them into a pile. Edging back to bed, she curled up by her pillow and began sifting through the stack, one page after the other. Reading and crying into the wee hours of the morning.

And mixed into the conglomeration of heartfelt words and memories that lifted to her eyes were thoughts of Benji stamped onto every page.

Days went by and Ella heard nothing from Benji. The bad feeling that had begun the day he cut their date short became a dull ache, infiltrated by moments of panic. Over and over, she ran through a list of questions in her mind. But how to approach him and when. And the biggest question—

Why?

Why had everything changed so quickly?

Her thoughts kept going back to the letters. But in the end, she failed to see the significance. Or the thread that tied them to the reasons he had acted like he had, cutting off all feelings and emotions, leaving her high and dry.

But beneath the assortment of theories running through her mind, a bigger question loomed.

One she feared the most.

A simple, intrinsic explanation.

Was it, because in the end, she was Eleanor Hurley, and he was BJ Marek? And he couldn't get beyond that. If so—for him to take her as far as he had and dump her mid relationship, made him *one cold bastard.*

Ella's next shift at the hospital, it became hard for her to focus, distracted as she was by the unsettled thoughts running through her head. Bottom line—*what had happened?* It kept at her, digging at her psyche, repeating its tainted mantra over and over. A few hours into the day though, the severity of illnesses that surrounded the patients brought her brainwaves back into focus. She had no choice but to narrow her attentiveness, tending to medical scenarios that required her undivided concentration. And for a while she *was* able to forget. Mostly.

Until the end of her shift when she was loosening her nursing cap, preparing to walk out of the hospital, and the nighttime ward clerk handed her an envelope with her name written atop.

What was this?

Her eyes darted all around.

But there was no one in particular that stood out as the sender.

Once more, a bad feeling began circulating in her chest. Her heart rang out in sharp staccatos as she turned her attention back to the letter. With shaky fingers, she peeled open the sealed flap and began to read.

Ella~

I'm sorry to say this in a note, but now isn't a good time for me to have a relationship. Thanks for everything.

My apologies~
Benjamin

What?

Ella could hardly believe what she was reading. *That was it?* That simply, that quickly, it was over? *Just over?* The whole thing? No more of an explanation than that? Her blood began to boil. She felt weak in the knees. This type of thing was so typical of the BJ Marek of the past. She should have known. What happened to him telling her she was his future? That he was plenty happy with her. What happened to him saying that she had saved his life? Did that no longer count for anything?

So that was how it was going to be, then!

A life for a life.

Only, Ella knew that wasn't the true interpretation of how the old adage went.

In this circumstance, it wasn't a fair exchange.

The difference being—she had saved a life.

And he had just destroyed one.

CHAPTER 32

The wind blew a frosty blast of air at Eleanor as she huddled at the back of the football field. *Home of the Blue Devils.* Pulling her wool coat around her shoulders, she ignored the chilly temperatures, uncharacteristically low for the fall—even in the north. Though for some it might be putting a damper on the festivities of homecoming week, to most it was just a minor inconvenience. *The show would go on.* Excitement was still in the atmosphere. They would just dress a little warmer. Or put up with a few minutes of icy air on bare skin—should you be lucky enough to be one of the pupils representing your class on court.

For Ella, exposing skin wasn't a problem. She hadn't been nominated to stand out on the field during halftime, hair swirled into a bouffant do, lipstick bright, wearing something fancy. And that was okay. She didn't like being in the limelight anyway. Sure—she'd attend the big game with Siobhan. Drink hot cocoa, eat popcorn, and cheer on the team like the rest of the student body, sitting in the bleachers. But that was still a few days away.

Homecoming wasn't just a one-day deal. It was a weeks-plus worth of activities, chucked into as many classroom hours as could be afforded out of the five days it was allotted. That day, of course—*Sibling's Day.* One would be surprised to discover just how many brothers and sisters actually attended school together. It wasn't uncommon to find students in the upper levels of the school system sharing the same last name. Often, parents had delivered children back-to-back—sometimes, several years in a row.

For Ella, the day didn't hold the same connotation as most. For her, it was a continual reminder poking at the back of her brain of

what could have been. How different homecoming week would have
played out, had her brother, Thomas, been there to participate in the
festivities. Would he have been on the football team? Would he have
landed on court—charming fellow classmates with the smile that she
remembered so well?

Beloved Thomas.

Perched on a bench, tucked beneath the bleachers at the back of the
school grounds, she sat in deep reflection as others partook of activities
and games on and off the field, all created to hype up the big event of
the football match later in the week. In particular, she was remembering
a time at the backyard on Maple Street when she and Thomas were
playing their own sort of football competition, using a round, rubber
ball, instead of the typical spherical shape. Unbeknownst of her own
movements while sitting there, she shook her head, while staring at the
ground, imagining how laughable the situation had been. They hadn't
even been close to reenacting a true game. *The actions of naive children.*

A vision of the flashback had just finished crossing through
Eleanor's mind, when the clammer from a group of students passing by
caught her attention, interrupting all reflective thought. *BJ Marek and
his cronies.* Ostentatious and boisterous as usual. An unwanted entity.
Eleanor shrunk into herself, looking the other way. Focusing hard on
the flagpole from the opposite side of the field, she pretended not to
notice all the pushing and shoving heading in her direction. The smirks
and ill-formed jokes.

Oh, the power of being invisible.

"Look at Hurley…sitting back here by herself." Jimmy Adamik's
voice was loud and confrontational. Eleanor winced. It seemed there
was no escape. *It seemed she wasn't invisible after all.* "What? Why are
you hiding back here?"

Rolling her eyes, Eleanor sucked in a breath. There would be no
point in answering, so she might as well ignore them—best she could.

"Sophomore class needs your help," Jane Beckwith added with a
laugh. "You're not being a spoil sport, are you? Or wait…are you afraid
of losing? Losing to the great senior class." That drew a whole series of
laughter. More arm punches and back slaps.

"Yeah…don't be a crumb." Jimmy spoke up again, elbowing the person beside him. "It's Siblings Day…show some respect. Where is your school spirit?"

"Yeah…some respect."

"Be a lamb. Get off your keister and show some spirit."

"—being such a drip."

The admonishments kept coming. One after the other. The whole lot of them being annoying asses as usual. Eleanor had had enough. What did any of them know about Siblings Day and the heartache of having lost a brother in years past? Gathering her things, she prepared to leave. Go back inside. Or to the other side of the field. Anywhere but there under the browbeating of the BJ Marek group.

Speaking of BJ Marek.

Eleanor lifted her eyes, realizing she hadn't yet received the worst of the demoralizing words that were sure to be flung her way. Those were usually reserved for execution straight from BJ Marek's mouth. His remarks, his looks—they were typically the nastiest. Hitting their target spot on—drawing the necessary blood, they took you down low. Delivered the needed damage to make the devaluation complete. *So, why wasn't he saying anything this go around?*

Bracing herself, Eleanor dared to look BJ's way just as a bunched-up bag of half-eaten popcorn bounced off her shoulder—another peripheral maneuver from the group. But instead of finding the arrogance characteristic of his demeanor staring back, what Eleanor could have sworn she'd seen was a semblance of pain reflected in his iris' as he met her eyes.

A flicker of confusion swirled through her veins.

If she hadn't known better—for one brief moment, it had felt like he was comprehending her angst. All the hurt and bereavement of having to endure Siblings Day when you had lost that someone special in your life. *But she did know better*—because this was BJ Marek, and he wasn't capable of delivering any type of sentiment that encompassed the emotions having to do with empathy or sorrow.

CHAPTER 33

The room felt like it was full of eerie configurations and shifting shadows. Eyes darting in all directions, it took several seconds for Ella to catch her breath. A sense of heaviness settled over her and she reached for her chest. Only to realize the weightiness she was experiencing came from the layers of blankets holding her in place. She was in her bedroom on Maple Street then. Snug and secure in her bed. It had only been a dream.

Another bad dream.

Ella had been having plenty of those as of late. Ever since the last date with Benji, the bad feelings she'd gotten from him had metamorphosized into nocturnal torments. Then increased ten-fold with the follow-up of his formal departure from their relationship, penned officially in a letter. Or note, rather. *Barely a note at that.*

She'd thought about going to see him one hundred times.

And then decided better of it.

She'd heard so many rumors. He wasn't doing so well. Wasn't walking again. Probably couldn't see either. Held up, immobile at home. Depressed. The epitome of a life completely stymied. The trauma from the war back full bore. She just couldn't understand.

What had happened?

He was doing so well. *They* were doing so well—together.

Her heart went out to him. And then got mad at him at the same time. Why wasn't he including her in his problems? She'd helped him before. He'd said as much—she had saved his life. Why was he running from her now?

And why wasn't she going after him?

Because something was stopping her. And she couldn't put her finger on it. Maybe because even though she'd heard the stories of his poor health, she didn't see him in that light. The Benji she'd come to know, was capable of snapping out of it—if he really wanted to.

Maybe that was it. Maybe he didn't want to. Maybe he didn't want her bad enough. *Didn't want Eleanor Hurley at all.*

And there was the crux of the situation.

The one that kept floating around in her mind. In her heart. She couldn't shake it away.

So, she kept living day to day, holding back the pain. Just getting by. Avoiding the myriads of questions thrown at her from a curious Chance. *"Where is Benji? Why doesn't he come over anymore?" "Why do you look sad? Why don't you smile anymore?"*

Doing her best to stay focused at work, she paid close attention to detail when caring for her patients, faking her best attitude with fellow nurses on the ward, Lillian, and others that she rubbed shoulders with on a shift-to-shift basis.

And it worked for the most part, aside from explaining herself to Siobhan. Even with all the distraction going on with her soldier being across seas, Siobhan could tell Ella had something on her mind—she wasn't acting herself. Ella kept putting her off. She knew she needed to tell her about the unplanned relationship that had developed with BJ Marek. But honestly, she was embarrassed. And yet, Siobhan was her very closest friend. Surely after getting over the shock of it all, after giving Ella a stern talking to, she'd forgive her poor decision making and they'd have all sorts of therapeutic discussions over the matter.

Just as they'd had over past years, concerning BJ and the effect of his behavior.

Today was that day.

She would tell Siobhan—finally. Explain all the melancholy conduct. Beg for forgiveness and elicit the support she needed. Ella was both scared and filled with anticipation of the relief that was sure to come. They had agreed to meet at the Locks, spending the next few hours of the day together before volunteering later that evening as aircraft spotters.

Transporting on foot, Ella turned north on Bingham and then headed west onto Portage Avenue. Taking her time, she moved by rote, lost among the tangled thoughts inside her head—the nervousness of telling Siobhan, along with the sorting of convoluted theories involving the relationship that had transpired between herself and Benji. So absent was Ella from her present reality, that she didn't see the group of pedestrians up ahead, congregating in front of the Savoy Café.

Until it was too late.

Without warning, Ella's heart went still in her chest. She couldn't believe her bad luck. The first person she recognized was Jimmy Adamik. Followed by Ed and Rudy, two others notorious for being in the BJ group from high school. And then, of course, how could she miss Jane Beckwith, sticking out in any crowd, with her overdone makeup and profligate hairstyle. There were more, but Ella didn't take the time to tick them off in her mind, identifying them as part of the entourage that always followed along. In an instant, she felt sick to her stomach.

Was it really too late though? Couldn't she still cross the street? Do her best to avoid the collision?

Or better yet, turn back around?

All she knew was, on top of everything—she didn't need this too.

Ella's eyes drifted to the street sign up ahead as she rerouted a pathway in her mind. She could cut over on River Street, creating a detour for herself, and then double back. And since River Street T'd into Portage, it would afford the perfect excuse for crossing over. It was Jimmy Adamik's voice that cut through her thoughts, executing an unwanted interruption for the plan she was concocting. *Leave it to Jimmy Adamik to discover her first,* she thought. To not let an opportunity for skullduggerous behavior to pass him by. It seemed BJ had trained him well.

"What do you know…if it isn't Hurley from back in the day."

The tone of his words sliced through her eardrums like razorblades, and she felt her feet unwittingly freeze in place.

He was like a blood hound, seeking her out. Ensnaring and cornering with his intimidating body maneuvers and demoralizing bark. Then in follow-up, making the delivery to his owner—one, BJ Marek.

Except this time, she knew BJ was laid up in bed.

For a moment the thought offered some sort of respite, giving way for a clearing of the mind.

Rolling her eyes, Ella set her jaw in place, deciding it was not too late to cross the street after all. She would just outright ignore him. Ignore the whole lot of them. But then, Jimmy, stepping a foot to the right as he began gesturing, offered a better view of the entirety of his group.

At once, Ella 's heart all but ceased to beat.

She couldn't believe what she was seeing.

Staring back at her were the bluest eyes she had ever seen.

Cold.

Ruthless.

Unfeeling.

Caerulean iris's, devoid of any emotion that would be considered close to love.

Or affection.

Or fond regard.

It seemed Benjamin Marek was not laid up in bed after all.

He was alive and well, having returned to take his rightful position as leader of the group.

When had all this happened?

Out of nowhere, a strong sensation of pain ripped through Ella's chest. An unbearable hurt that was all-encompassing. For a few seconds she felt physically paralyzed. Followed up by a sort of muscle weakness.

"Marek," she heard Jimmy say. "Look who it is."

All-at-once, years of abuse set at the hand of BJ Marek and his posse came weighing down on Ella as it ran like a movie reel though her mind, erasing any possibility of good she had ever come to know of him.

The only answer Ella could detect coming from Benji's lips resembled something like a snort. And then, a turn of the head, as if to engage with others in his group. Like her presence didn't seem to matter at all. Not in the least. She could hardly believe the callousness in his demeanor. After all they'd shared together.

"Ha…Hurley—" She heard her name echoing among the others, mixing in with jeers and laughter, and her skin began to perforate with tiny prickers. Forcing her feet into motion, Ella commenced movement so that she could carry out her plan by circling away. But the interchange turned into more of a shuffle as Jimmy Adamik stepped into her way.

"Where do you think you're going?" He drew nearer and Ella smelled liquor on his breath. She glanced up at the Savoy Café, realizing for the first time that the whole lot of them had been out drinking together. In a blink of an eye, the ante got upped in her mind with the anticipation of all that could go wrong. This was not high school anymore—things could get a lot worse.

And yet weren't they all adults now?

Shouldn't things actually have evolved into something better with age?

Gathering strength inside of herself in-spite-of the sheer numbers, in-spite-of the hurt that was circulating through her heart with thoughts of Benji's obvious rejection, Ella looked Jimmy right in the eye. "I was just walking down the street, trying to get to where I was headed without you blocking my way. So, if you'll excuse me."

"Ha." Jimmy lifted his brow. "When did you get so sassy? Acting fairly sassy for a dame wouldn't you say?" He glanced back at Benji. By then Rudy had joined Jimmy's side. A little farther away, the others were still involved, joining in on the conversation with sprays of laughter and smirks. Only Benji didn't seem to be all that engaged.

"Dame…my ass," Rudy said, and Jimmy's eyes widened as if a thought was suddenly occurring to him. Afterwards, he began elbowing Rudy.

"Yeah…you're right. This is no dame," he snickered. "More like Able Grable." At that, more laughter emerged. Even Benji looked up.

Or BJ, rather.

BJ Marek looked up.

Ella's face turned red in tell-tale signs of rage and betrayal. *Able Grable?* So, he had shared stories of their intimate encounters with all of his friends? *Of course, he had.* This was no valiant soldier from the war, wounded and nursed back to health, she was dealing with—this was a worm from childhood, dressed up in a grown-man's body.

"Adamik…forget it. Forget about her." Ella's gaze shot to the center of the group. The great Benjamin Marek was finally speaking. Apparently, his cage had been adequately rattled. "She's not worth it," he included in addendum.

Ella's heart sank.

Of course, she wasn't.

Worth it.

How many times had she heard that very same line coming from BJ's lips over the years?

You would have thought she'd learn.

Should it really come as a surprise?

And yet the sound of the words coming from his lips, spoken with such authority on the matter, felt like daggers screwing into the chest.

"Yeah…not worth it," came the anticipated reverberation from the rest of those gathered. Everyone was chuckling, including Jane Beckwith. *So much for professionalism,* thought Ella. If she ever had to step foot into that convalescent home again and interact with Jane under the trademark of work, delivering her nursing services due to shortages, it would be way too soon.

Ella fought with her legs over the idea of providing movement again. But this time when she commenced into motion it wasn't an action enveloped in passivity. No longer an attempt at running away. Pushing past Jimmy Adamik, she parted the crowd with purposeful stride, until she came to face to face with Benji.

He looked a little surprised to see her advance, but quickly hid the expression by putting on a mask of stoicism. That didn't stop Ella from looking him right in the eye. "You know what…B…J…Marek?" Each syllable of his name was annunciated in separate staccatos, loaded with disdain. "You are a complete bastard. Always have been. Always will be." In follow-up to her statement, she thought about spitting on the ground next to his feet, freeing every part of him from her body, from her soul—forever. But then deciding against the gesture, looked back up, eyeing him with every last feeling of discord she felt circulating inside her core. "I've had…*enough* of your worthless ass."

For a two-second pause, Ella could almost imagine that the muscles in Benji's jaw flinched ever-so-slightly, that there was an undecipherable *something* that flickered through his eyes. But it was over so quickly, it hit her that most likely she'd been wrong. Afterwards, all that was left staring back was a semblance of a smirk. One that she wanted very badly to slap off.

Her hand tingled at her side, ready and preparing to make the move. But to steal Benji's own words—he *was not worth it.* At that realization, Ella began to edge backward. All around her, she could hear delayed cheers and hoots mixed in with the signature laughter that dominated his friend-group. *"Damn...Marek...she told you."*

Ella spun around, the whole band of them blurring into a mix of voices and dark shapes. All she knew was, she needed to get out of there. And the only thing stopping her would be some type of physical restraint. But if that had been Adamik and the other's original intent, they were making no move to block her from leaving.

If anything, from all her mind could decipher with the state it had entered, they looked taken aback, a little standoffish. As if she was someone they didn't want to mess with. *If only.* If only she had displayed more of that technique earlier on in life, maybe she'd have suffered a lot less angst at the hands of the BJ Marek group over the years. *Maybe.*

Ella's determination and bravado as she marched away was only an act though. On the inside, she felt anything but put together. In fact, it felt like she was falling apart. The tears, that were hovering beneath misted, half-closed lids, were beginning to drip down her face the farther away she got. It took all the effort she possessed not to break into sobs—thus allowing the consortium behind her to witness the shaking of the shoulders, a dead giveaway, as she made a beeline down the street.

In front of her feet, the cracks in the pavement were rapidly turning into lines.

Lines upon lines upon lines.

All blurring into red stripes at the back of her eyeballs.

Webbing and connecting, until they forged a pattern and a path to follow, turning only when she needed them to, so she could chart a course that would take her to a needed destination. To a waiting Siobhan at the Locks.

Oh, what a mess she'd be presenting to her best friend upon arrival. There would be no chance of backing away from the truth of what she'd been up to with Benjamin Marek. No changing of the mind on how the conversation should go—what to leave in, what to leave out. As-it stood, with the condition she was in, the naked ugliness of it all was sure to be revealed. There would be no way around it.

And hopefully, fingers crossed, after the unveiling, there would be grace extended to cover the wounds.

All around her, the ribbony lines Ella had been following, began to curl and wind, tying into convoluted knots at her sides the further she went. With the detour onto River Street, she had gone left on Water Street, and then circled back on Osborn Boulevard. She was almost to the Locks. The lines, having gone ahead of her, leading the way, were now bunching into a giant ball, erasing the pathway of her footsteps, rending all chords useless, making an impossibility of a return trip.

Leaving her with a feeling of hope.

A hope for strength that would be needed to erase the hurt.

Ella found Siobhan staring at the St. Mary's passageway, watching a vessel going through the gates, smokestack, sinking as it lowered into the basin of the Locks. Sensing her approach, Siobhan turned around. "El—" She started, with happy exclamation. Then stopped, seeing the tear stains on Ella's face.

Taking a few steps closer, she appeared somewhat hesitant on approach. "Hey...what is it?" The words came out as more of a croon.

All-at-once, Ella felt herself breaking into laughter. Half sardonic hilarity—half sob. What a sight she must be portraying, probably half-scaring her friend to death. "Oh, Siobhan," she spit out, wiping her eyes. "I'm a wreck...what a mess I've made this time."

Siobhan's brows widened. "This time? Since when have you been the one to make messes? I believe that responsibility belongs to me."

"Okay...maybe so." *But not always*, Ella thought to herself, remembering one big time she'd screwed up in the past. *That screwup would haunt her forever.* "But this time, I've really gone and done it," she clarified, the tears starting up again.

"Awe...come here," Siobhan said, wrapping Ella in a hug. For several moments they stood there quietly while Ella cried. Finally, she pulled back, and Siobhan began rifling through her handbag. "Here take this." She passed over a balled-up Kleenex. "I promise it's clean."

Once more, Ella began to chuckle in-spite-of it all. Good old Siobhan, she was just what was needed—the perfect comic relief in any situation. But after she proceeded to tell her the details of everything— *what then?*

"So...when are you going to tell me what is going on with you?" *It was like Siobhan had read her mind.*

Taking a breath, Ella froze. Glancing over at the ocean liner, she watched as it sunk further into the waterway. Then shifting away her gaze, she pointed to nearby bench. "Do you want to sit down?"

"Sit down? Really...I need to sit down for this? You're not just whistling dixy. What have you gone and done, El?" The girls settled onto the bench, causing a spray of birds to scatter from the nearby ground. Siobhan leaned in, smoothing back her dark hair. "Okay... give me the dope."

Ella shook her head, still half laughing, half swallowing back dread. "To begin with...do you promise you won't hate me?" Her voice grew somber.

"Hate you? You're really starting to scare me you know."

"I know." The tip of Ella's nose crinkled. "But I need you to promise."

"Okay...okay." Siobhan cocked her head. "If you say so...I promise," she conceded. "I think," she added under her breath.

"So...you remember BJ Marek from high school?" Ella bit her lip.

For a moment Siobhan looked confused. "Yes," she finally said, drawing out the word. "He was a real bugger." Her eyes widened marginally. "Why...what did you do to him? Not that he wouldn't have had it coming...mind you...whatever it was. Honestly...I only wished I could have helped...whatever you did."

"That's the thing," Ella sighed. "It's more complicated than that."

"How so?"

"Do you remember that wounded soldier I told you last winter? The one I was taking care of at the hospital?"

"Vaguely...I mean yes, you mentioned it briefly, one time. It wasn't your typical situation...so I can recall."

"Well turns out...that soldier was BJ Marek from back in the day."

"Really...and you didn't recognize him?"

"Not at first…he was wounded pretty badly. But then later I figured it out."

Siobhan's mouth fell open. "So, what…tell me what happened? Did you give him an extra dose of something…some medicine or something? Please tell me you didn't kill him. Or then again…I can't say that I'd blame you if you did. These things happen…accidents… especially to him." She gave a little cough. "I mean—"

"Oh, I gave him an extra dose of *something,* alright." Ella winced. Clearly, the conversation wasn't headed in the direction she hoped.

"What?"

"Oh, Siobhan, it was something…that is for sure. I fell in love with him…that's what I did. That's exactly what I've gone and done."

For what felt like a few minutes, Siobhan just stared. "I just don't see how that's possible," she finally said, head wagging back and forth. "No, El…no way. Eleanor Hurley, now, listen to me…that just isn't possible."

"But it is." Ella's voice began to waver once more. "Which is why, as you can see…that I'm miserable."

Siobhan, though appearing to be still in shock, slid over as if in slow motion next to her friend. Wrapping an arm around her shoulder, she began listening as Ella spilled the details of their sordid relationship, between bouts of tears and bursts of awkward laughter. The whole time, with brow lifted and eyes wide, questions were inserted for clarification, as was the choice of continually biting of the tongue by Siobhan.

A couple of times, some pedestrians passed by where they were seated, as did a cluster of soldiers in uniform. On each occasion, the girls would pause and feign interest in watching the ship's final descent into the lock basin, Ella covering her face in seemingly nonchalant ways in-order-to hide the distress.

In the end, Siobhan just sighed, giving her friend's arm a little squeeze. "I can promise you," she said. "Each time you are feeling down over this, I will remind you with a list of at least one hundred reasons… all the ugly encounters you and I have had with that scamp and his poor excuse for friends over the years. A little souvenir of why he doesn't deserve the likes of you anyway. Good riddance I say. He never deserved one iota of your attention."

Dear Thomas,

Am I my brother's keeper? Am I my father's keeper?
No—I was neither. And now I have neither!

~E.

CHAPTER 34

True to her word, Siobhan was a great support for Ella. Often reminding her of why BJ Marek was the poorest choice for her in the world, while bringing her to laughter, somehow sparing her the dreaded embarrassments and *I could have told you so's* in the process. Unless they were spun into a wisecrack somehow—which is exactly what Ella needed to keep her spirits up. Making a joke of the whole thing.

Because on her own time, to Ella, it felt like anything but a joke.

Or maybe it felt *exactly* like a joke. Mostly, like—*joke's on me* type of thing.

It was a continual battle to fight back the misery of it all in her mind. Which made her all the more thankful for the efforts on Siobhan's part to keep her spirits up. She was a true friend.

But Siobhan had troubles of her own.

"What is it?" Ella studied the expression on her face as she sat on the bed, while Ella was putting a few things away into her dresser drawers. They were hanging out at the Hurley house, passing time before they headed over to the matinee movie. But Siobhan looked distracted. Had been preoccupied and distant since coming up to her room, fidgeting with various trinkets on the bedside tables while staring into space.

Siobhan lifted her eyes, an element of worry shining through. "Is it that obvious?" Her mouth twisted at the corner, and she sighed. "I suppose I might as well tell you. You'll find out sooner or later anyway."

Ella felt her heart pick up in tempo. Laying aside the article of clothing she had been folding, her head tilted in question. "Find out?"

For a few moments Siobhan just gazed forward, seemingly gathering her thoughts. And then, in slow motion, her hands went to the printed fabric of the dress she was wearing. Resting on the anatomical spot which was the stomach.

That's when Ella knew. "Siobhan," her voice grew soft, enquiring. "Are you—"

Siobhan nodded several times. "I am...and I feel like a real chucklehead." She let out long breath of air. "How could I let something like this happen?"

"Well, I'm pretty sure *this* didn't *happen* on your own. Don't lay the fault on yourself alone. How...how far along do you think you are?"

"Not sure exactly...but obviously sometime before Surf left in May. That means two to three months."

"Have you...told him. Does he know?"

Siobhan's face fell. "Not yet. I will though...soon. I'm just trying to put the words together...so I can send him a letter." Pressing hands to her stomach once more, she looked over at Ella. "A baby though, El," she whispered. "A real live baby of my own. Am I that much older than a baby myself? What am I going to do?"

It was a thought to ponder, alright. Ella didn't have the answers. How did anyone know how to plan anymore? With a world war going on, it was a *take it one day at a time* mentality. The answers to all questions would unfold with the dawning of each new sunrise. One thing that was for sure—regardless of peacetime or state-of-war—Ella would be there to support her friend come what may.

Around town, others felt the same way, waiting for reports of wartime activities in order to plan their next move on the chessboard of life. With thoughts of loved ones across seas, fighting, being heavy on the mind, all attention and focus was on *what was next*. And *what was next* depended on which part the U.S. held in the regime of combat. Many, keeping a particular soldier close to the heart, followed along on sprawling paper maps, piecing together accounts of where they were posted, where they were headed, of where the battles had ensued.

It was late July and all divisions of the United States Military continued to be busy world-wide, creating some firsts for the armed branches. For the first time, American Air Force Pilots took part in fighter sweeps over Northern France, part of the German occupation.

In other places, Americans being part of the Allied aircraft—the Allied Forces; including the three great powers of the United States,

Great Britain, and the Soviet Union—attacked the Japanese—at Gona—who were still attempting a take-over campaign in Papua New Guinea.

At the Hurley home, things continued to spiral downward. Melvin Hurley spending more and more time at Belvidere Ships Tavern, arriving on the home front in a drunken mess. Often to the point of passing out haphazardly in the armchair, not even making it up to his bedroom to sleep off the results of the liquor.

One particularly temperate summer afternoon, Ella was walking home from a trip to the grocery store when she noticed a pile of clothing on the front steps of their house. Experiencing a sense of unease, she kept moving forward until she was yards away from the porch. The closer Ella got, the more she realized it was not articles of clothing at all but a human being, half catawampus, half curled into a ball. At once, she knew who it was.

Rushing forward, she set her purchases down on the sidewalk and bent over for a closer look. Sure enough, it was her father. *Was he dead?* Getting onto her haunches, she leaned in toward his lifeless form, studying the orb of misshapen clothing until she saw his chest move. Seconds later, she began shaking his shoulders.

"Dad...Melvin," she called out in a stiff tone. "Wake up...get up."

But the figure on the porch didn't move.

Ella continued the shaking, getting a little firmer in voice and exertion of strength. Finally, she began to detect movement, if only slightly. But it was not enough. She glanced around, thankful that the neighborhood kids were not outside playing streetball, witnessing the humiliating mess that was her father. "Melvin Hurley," she called out one more time in an exasperated voice, his jawline pinched between her hand. She had a good notion to just leave him there. Cover his body with bags of garbage and miscellaneous, discarded items from the house so that passersby would think it was just a pile of junk. That they were just cleaning house.

And maybe they were.

Instead, she went inside to fetch a large pitcher of water. She could get Chance to help her drag him through the front door but figured there was too much dead weight for just the two of them. And her mother was at work. Tipping the container she'd retrieved from the kitchen, Ella began pouring directly over Melvin's head, aiming right at the face, all the while anger, shame, and embarrassment welled up inside for having to do such a thing to her own parent.

"Damn…wha…ho…dammit," came a sputtering voice, lifting into the air.

Ella took advantage of the moment. "Get up, Father," she spat. "We need to get you inside." For a few moments, Melvin acted like he was going to protest, anger evident in his flailing movements. But finally, he gathered himself together just enough for Ella to help him make it through the door and into his armchair. Albeit haphazardly, stumbling the whole way, almost pulling Ella over on himself in the process.

For several hours Melvin Hurley laid in the living room, passed out, snoring loudly, while the rest of the household went about their business as if nothing was amiss. Except deep inside, Ella was boiling. Maybe it was an accumulation of everything going on in her life, but she'd had enough. When her dad began to show signs of stirring, she was right there waiting in anticipation.

"Time to wake up, Father," she said.

Melvin only twisted around to reposition himself.

Rolling her eyes, Ella waited some more. After two more squirming flops, his lids popped open. Then closed again after seeing Ella's looming figure. A few minutes later, he began running wind-chafed hands over his face.

"Here." Ella stuck out her hand. "Take this coffee and drink it."

This time when Melvin approached wake-mode, the transition appeared to stick. But the coffee wasn't something he was accustomed to. "Get that damn stuff 'way frum me," he said, words gluing to the roof of his mouth.

"Drink it," Ella repeated. "You need it." Hand steady, she didn't budge an iota with the cup. Though on the inside, she was holding back a tremor, knowing full-well the result could be a container of hot liquid being flung everywhere.

For what seemed like minutes, her father stared through squinting eyes. "Who d'you think you are?" The question was intended to intimidate. Fueled by anger, Ella swallowed back the fear that it roused and stayed her ground.

"The daughter who scraped your drunk self off the sidewalk outside the house and brought you inside...that is who. So, drink the coffee."

"I didn't need yer help," Melvin said, taking the cup from her extended hand. Facing away from his daughter, he began taking sips, scrunching up his nose, face contorting, shoulders shuttering with each swallow.

Ella waited awhile while he continued to drink. When enough time had passed, and a fair amount of the coffee had been ingested, she took a seat in the nearest chair. "Do you want to keep wasting your life," she asked, leaning forward, voice steady and quiet.

"What?" Melvin's gaze shot over to his daughter.

Ella glanced around, making sure Chance wasn't in the room. "Wasting your life, I said. Like you are doing. Quitting your job when the household could use every drop of money earned. I don't really care about myself as much...but Mom...having to pick up extra hours just so we can get by. So we don't loose the house, so we can eat. So Chance can eat...and have the things he needs for school. You...spending every last dime on liquor instead. Running up your tab at the Belvidere Ships Tavern. Don't you—" She started, then stopped, uttering a sigh. "Don't you ever get tired?"

Melvin grimaced. "Oh, I get tired alright," he clapped back. "Tired of my daughter getting in my business...treatin me with disrespect."

Ella took a large breath. "No...I mean do you get tired of the blame...of blaming *yourself*. Of wallowing around day after day, year after year in a cavity of darkness? Of existing in a black hole. Of not living. Just wallowing, instead. Of hating everything around you...but most of all yourself? Do you ever just get tired of it all? Do you ever with you wish you could begin again...start fresh?"

Melvin stared straight ahead, jaw set, nostrils flaring. "Doesn't matter what I wish...start fresh or not," he said, shoulders sagging. "Thomas isn't coming back."

"No...he's not." Ella swallowed, hanging her head. "But this isn't what he'd want. Not for you. Not for me. Not for the rest of the family either." *In truth—who was she preaching to really, though,* she wondered inside?

Melvin Hurley spent the rest of the night up in his room in bed. The following week too. If Ella had thought her father been living in a black hole before, it seemed the torrents of his existence had been stepped up tenfold, bouncing between the agony of pelting meteorites and other menacing debris floating dangerously around in space.

Oh, the sounds coming from the upstairs sleeping quarters of her parent's bedroom.

But when asked if help was needed, Grace Hurley only shook her head, judiciously running back and forth between lavatory, kitchen and bedroom, carrying the necessary supplies to sooth her husband's latest temperament.

After it was all over, the Hurley family had a new father. Liquor-less indeed. But also, a shadow of his formal self. When he finally emerged from the bedroom to sit in the lounge chair again, it was like a zombie had taken the place of the person who was formally known as Melvin. No more angry outbursts, no more demands and bossing around of the family unit, no more haranguing on and on about soldiers occupying the town.

No more nothing.

Not even when the wooden radio played from the corner of the room, announcing the latest about the war, did Ella's father react in any sort of way. Choosing instead, to stare for hours into space. Barely eating, scarcely subsisting, just getting by.

It was the end of July when the voice on the receiver spoke of the sinking of the steam passenger ship, SS. Robert E. Lee as it passed through the Gulf of Mexico. Taken down by a U-166, a Nazi U-boat, via torpedo fired from the German submarine, the 407-passenger watercraft was damaged, killing some crew and travelers along with destroying the ship.

"*See Father*," Ella wanted to say. "*They are here…in our America…the Germans. That is why we have the soldiers stationed in town. Why the anti-craft postings. Why we have the torpedo nets strung along the Locks. Because this very sort of thing could happen to one of our ships here. The German U-boats could make it here too…destroying ships and cargo and people's lives and parts of the city too. All-the-while interrupting the transportation of materials needed for the war…like steel. It's a big deal…all the steel need for combat comes directly through the Locks of our St. Mary's.*"

Instead, Ella said nothing, glancing over at the armchair across the living room that held her father's stock-still body and immovable face. Nary a comment from him about the newsworthy narratives being carried across the radio waves. Not an iota of a reaction.

The question then presented itself—*was the new version of Melvin Hurley any better than the old one?*

Radios weren't the only means of transmitting information about the war though. There were the newspapers and the dreaded wiring of telegrams too. Also, the propaganda being played over the big screen of the theatre, prior to the main show. The new Melvin didn't pay any attention to those sources either, of course.

But for Siobhan it was different.

She relied on the local newspaper, The Evening News, for daily updates of the great conflict being carried out throughout all of the world. Or oppositely, checking it regularly for what she hoped was *lack* of information about the status of the war. The absence of a potential name that could be documented in the section that listed losses.

Siobhan would never forget the newspaper that was dated July 30, 1942. It was the same date that the SS. Robert E. Lee had sunk. The same day that WAVES was signed into law. *Women accepted for volunteer emergency service.* The U.S. Navy's corps of female members. A new possibility for women. But it briefly passed through Siobhan's mind as an *impossibility* for her now that she carried another person inside herself—even if she had been considering the idea. (Which really, she hadn't been anyway.)

It was one and the same with the day the dreaded name in bold typescript that she'd been searching for—or not searching for, rather—had forever imprinted itself into her mind.

James Robert O'Malley

Her dearest Surf!

Gone.

Listed among the deceased.

CHAPTER 35

Ella was to meet Siobhan in town. From the message, it had sounded urgent, causing Ella to jump into action. Throwing her hair into a ponytail and smoothing her A-line skirt and floral blouse, she set out on foot, making her way through Maple, toward Ashmun, and on down to Spruce. A familiar route. In some ways it felt like she was headed over to the hospital. Except it was the wrong time of day and of course she was lacking the customary feel of her white nursing pinafore and cap.

The warmth of the sun on her skin had a pleasant touch to it in-spite-of the uneasy feeling that was churning through her stomach. The tone of Siobhan's voice when she had spoken with her was off. Something was wrong. She was almost to Peck Street when Ella saw a familiar figure in the distance. At the same time, it seemed Siobhan saw her too. All-at-once, a change took place in Siobhan's gate, and she began to approach at a faster pace—practically a run. The bad feeling Ella was holding in her chest began to increase ten-fold. As her friend came closer and a puffy, red face was revealed, the bad feeling transformed into all out pandemonium.

"What is it, Sib," she soothed as Siobhan fell into her arms. Sirens of alarm were going off in Ella's brain. Clearly it was *something* bad or she wouldn't be willingly causing a scene right out on the main street of town. *Oh, what a pair they were as of late.* It hadn't been that long ago that Ella had been running into her friend's arms with a tear-stained face, crying over a boy.

A boy.

A soldier.

Ella froze as Siobhan continued to cry. She had yet to answer her query. *Had something happened? Say, to Surf?* "He's gone," Siobhan finally spit out, pulling away, wiping her eyes.

"Gone?" Ella cocked her head. Gone, meaning—a dump job? Or the *other* gone? *Really* gone!

"His name, El." Siobhan could barely speak. Ella's heartrate was escalating. "I found...found his name in the newspaper. He was listed under...gone. Under losses from the war. Categorized under the deceased."

"Oh Siobhan." Ella pulled her close again. She didn't know what to say. "I'm sorry," she whispered. "So, so sorry." *Damn the war.* She hurt so bad for her friend.

Siobhan cried some more, then pulled away for a second time. After wiping her tears once again, she grabbed Ella's hand. "Let's go." Tugging her in the opposite direction, she began directing her back up Ashmun.

"Where are we going?" Ella's voice was cautious, filled with concern.

"This way," Siobhan motioned as they turned onto Dawson. "How could he really be gone, El," she asked as they neared Court Street. "I just can't believe...it just can't be...it can't be so."

Ella squeezed her hand and shook her head. "I know, Sib...I know. I mean I don't know."

They continued walking, until they stopped in front of the Greek Orthodox Church. Siobhan turned toward the expansive, brick building and stared up the wide display of front steps, framed by double turrets, each with a cross soaring high into the air. Ella stared with her, not sure of what exactly was going on. "I'm going in," Siobhan finally said.

Ella nodded. "Okay...yeah, okay. For—" She still wasn't sure of the plan.

"To pray."

Ella continued to nod, though she wasn't too sure what they'd be praying for. Surely not the safety of one James O'Malley. It was too late for him. He was already gone. "What is it that we'll—"

"That we'll be praying for?" Siobhan swallowed hard, reaching for her stomach, touching it lightly. "I'll be praying for my baby. My baby who will never know her father." She paused, once more fighting back tears. And for all the babies who will never have a father...because of this war."

An hour later, Ella left Siobhan still sitting in a pew as she made her way back outside from the dim lighting of the sanctuary into the bright afternoon sunshine. Siobhan had thanked her for being there but wanted some alone time. *She just needed more time.* Ella had reluctantly agreed, giving Siobhan's hand one last squeeze.

When the heavy double doors closed behind Ella, she proceeded down the steps and onto the street. Her mind was abuzz with all that had been going on as of late. Her dad recouping from the bottle at home, Siobhan and her future baby, the continual presence of the war. Added to the list, Siobhan and the loss of her soldier.

And of course, the perpetual assault of Benji's life-long betrayal turned fresh-cut wound.

Ella had just angled onto Spruce Street when, so lost in her own head, she wasn't paying close attention to the feminine sway of the figure approaching from up ahead. Until it was too late. Snapping from the torment of her reverie, with a jolt to the heart, Ella's pulse began tripping at a runaway pace as she recognized who was headed her way. *It was Jane Beckwith.* All-of-a-sudden, the city of Sault Ste. Marie seemed way too small. If only there was a way to find anonymity. To avoid every-last person that belonged to the BJ Marek club.

But of course, there wasn't. Ella had been finding that out in all too real of a way since the United State's entry into the war it seemed. Since her first encounter with a maimed soldier named Benjamin had rolled into War Memorial Hospital by stretcher that cold day in December. Since then, she'd been encountering him or one of his friends everywhere.

Why?

Had she become some sort of celestial target?

Was she meant to live out her life in continuous torture?

At the last second, Ella thought to turn her head away from the exigency of Jane's advancing gate, feigning interest in the side of the brick building she was passing by.

"Well, well if it isn't Miss Eleanor Hurley." The words covered the side of Ella's face like a slap on a wind-burned cheek. With knee-jerk reaction, her neck whipped around. She noticed Jane had stopped walking, blond locks done up in a bouffant hairdo per usual flair. But she, herself, would continue on. *No need to linger.* With every intention of avoiding eye contact, Ella pointed her chin back in a forward direction. But a second too late, Jane caught her passing glance. "Yes...what do you know...Eleanor it is...the bane of BJ Marek's existence."

At the sound of Benji's name, Ella felt her feet freeze in place.

Slowly, she turned back around, a sigh escaping her lips.

"Quite a history you two have."

Do we? Ella felt taken aback. She cleared her throat. *Yes, it seems we do,* she mused. "Do we, really, though?" The repeat question was spoken aloud. *But why do we, exactly?* That was the million-dollar question. Truly—BJ Marek was the bane of *her* existence. *Not*—the other way around.

A smattering of laughter left Jane's mouth. "Surely you've noticed."

"Oh...I've noticed," Ella conceded. *Also noticed that you've been right there at his side for the entire ride, cheering him on. Shall we speak to that?* Sucking in a breath, Ella fought to not roll her eyes, to not speak the whole of her thoughts aloud. "Where is this going, Jane?" She was sick of the decade-long assault coming from the BJ Marek gang. With all that she currently had on her plate, that day was not the occasion to endure some more.

Jane's eyes widened a little. Obviously, she was not expecting any sort of sass coming from Eleanor Hurley. But somewhere along the way, Eleanor Hurley had begun to grow up. No longer was she the cowering waif they had known from back in the day. *Also—obviously—the BJ squad had not grown up in the least over the years.*

"I don't know why I'm telling you this," Jane said. Then half laughed, half frowned. "On second thought. I think I do. BJ has been getting on my nerves lately. Adamik too. All of them, really." Her eyes narrowed as if in thought, an inscrutable memory of sorts. "I no longer care what any of them think."

Ella looked on in perplexity. Things felt like they were getting weird. Experiencing a sensation of antsiness, she glanced at the street ahead. Thoughts of commencing into motion, continuing on in the direction she was headed, crossed through her mind.

"It all started with that little brother of yours."

At Jane's words, a new swirl of confusion fell over Ella. She cocked her head, focusing her attention back on the present conversation. "Chance? Charles, rather," she questioned. "I'm not sure what you mean."

"No...no, not him," Jane interjected. "Whoever that is, really... Chance. I'm talking about your brother from back in grade school. Thomas. His name was Thomas if I remember correctly."

Ella went very still. A false covering for the inside of the body, where her heart had kickstarted in the chest cavity. One thousand beats per minute.

Beloved Thomas.

She took a cleansing breath. What had any of this to do with him? Nothing—not one thing in the least, that's what.

Her eyes shot toward Jane, daring her to be careful with her words. *Sacred ground was being entered.* "I don't know what you are talking about," she said. All the while, thoughts of shame were circulating through her brain. What all did Benji know about her? Did he know the truth? The deception and the lies she lived with on a daily basis.

Did he hate her because of it?

Could that really be the crux of their disheveled relationship all of these years?

"Don't pick her...We don't want that one. She's worthless."

She really *was* worthless. Had he known all along?

In a flash, a feeling of panic shot through Ella's veins, consuming her. The street sign in front of her began to blur, everything turning into a spin. Fighting to regain presence of mind, she pinched her arm—hard.

She had to do it twice before the needed effect took place.

"Of course, you don't know what I'm talking about...obviously." Wrinkling her nose, Jane crossed lightly tanned arms over the front of her floral sundress. "Let's just say BJ is not all he seems. He's worse."

Worse? Not possible, Ella thought. But the way Jane was talking, she failed to see how this involved her brother, Thomas.

"He hasn't been able to stomach you all of these years, couldn't look you in the face, practically hated you...all because of the guilt over what he's done."

Ella felt paralyzed, her mouth dropping into a frozen *O*. "I still don't—"

"No...no, you probably don't." Jane narrowed her eyes, zeroing directly on Ella's countenance, as if wanting to catch her every reaction. "But let me just tell you a dirty little secret about BJ Marek, wounded soldier, you helped nurse back to good health. He lives with a lot of guilt because of what happened with your brother all those years ago. Because he is in fact responsible for his death."

CHAPTER 36

Ella was confused. Over and over, she kept questioning, thinking, wondering—what had Jane been talking about back there on Spruce Street as she dropped the bomb shell about Benji? *About Thomas.* Her mind had been thrown into a tailspin. She wanted to ask questions, but stunned into silence, had just stood there watching Jane walk away afterwards—no explanation, whispers of the wind, sifting through her bouffant hair, a rather triumphant gleam in her eye.

The one thing Ella felt confident of—there was no way Benjamin Marek was involved in her brother, Thomas' death. This information she knew firsthand. *Knew all-too-well.* Lived and breathed it every single day of her life. Was it possible she could have missed something that day—the way it all went down? Just then, the sound of a ship's foghorn and the return salute came drifting up from the Locks, causing a shiver to pass over her skin, interrupting her thoughts. It took everything Ella had to focus.

What to do. Where to go with the newly delivered information. Certainly not back home to Maple Street. She thought about heading down to the water, east of the Locks. The infamous place of heartache—landmark of pain for the Hurley family. Would it trigger more memories if she did? Something that could have possibly been missed, placing Benji into the scenario that dreadful evening? In the end she decided to go right to the source. To Benji himself.

Stepping onto city transit, Ella headed for the Marek home up on Easterday Hill. The bus ride felt long. Though, in some ways too short. Heart thudding in her chest, she knocked on the front door, the lavishness of the house as intimidating as the mission itself. When Benji's mom answered, it was with a confused expression crossing over her countenance. Clearly, she didn't recognize Ella, and wouldn't have, since she was never part of the high school gang. In the same token, Ella only knew her by the look-alike resemblance of Benji's blue eyes.

But Benji wasn't home.

Next, she boarded back up on the bus and tried his presumed place of employment. His father's excavating company. With even more intimidation, Ella gathered some moxie and approached the front shop, keeping her shaking hands and spinning thoughts under some semblance of control.

"Nope, the junior's not in today," she was told. *"Hasn't been for the last few days, matter-a fact."* Frustrated, Ella was about to walk away, when a voice behind her said, *"You might want to try the Savoy Café. Heard the fella's been spending a lot of time there lately. Being a real knucklehead if you ask me."*

Ah—the Savoy Café.

The last place she had run into Benji out on the street in front.

Ella wasn't thrilled with the idea of going back.

Still, this was information that couldn't be put on hold.

This time the bus ride felt even longer. With thoughts in a whirl the entire route, Ella's heart exploded in her chest as she stepped off on the corner of Portage and Ashmun. Making her way to the Savoy Café, she tried to reel herself in. But it was no use. By the time she was reaching for the doorhandle of the restaurant, it felt like dangling on the edge of a cliff. She was this close to coming undone.

The moment Ella heard her name being called from the side of the building; she jumped a mile. She'd know the sound of that voice anywhere. In a moment's time, she felt a sort of calm settle in despite the overall angst surrounding her intellect. "Benji," she breathed, turning away from the door.

Back tracking, Ella turned to face him. Something felt off though. The glaze covering his eyes, the ungainly movements of his steps. It was Benji alright, as the voice had confirmed. But he was drunk. "Whatcha doing here," he asked. His eyes hadn't left hers. Drunk or not, he was very focused. On her.

Ella fought back an unwanted ripple of exhilaration as it shot through her veins. She was there on mission. She needed answers—an entire explanation, really. "Looking for you, actually." But now that she'd found him drunk, was it time for mission abort? What was going to be accomplished with his current state?

Benji looked surprised. "You were? Well, you found me." He lifted his arms to the side, palms up.

Ella stared for a moment. Deer caught in the headlights. Then started taking hesitant steps in his direction. "Yeah...I...well, I ran into Jane Beckwith earlier today." She continued walking forward until she was standing only three feet away. Close enough to tell Benji's clothing was a bit disheveled from being liquored up and not giving a rat's ass about things.

"Well, killer diller. How'd that go?"

"It went...it went about as expected when it comes to her or any of your friends, really." *Except, that really, it hadn't gone as expected at all.*

Benji half chuckled, but it came out as more of a grimace. "Touché."

Yeah—touché alright. Ella took a deep breath. What to say? Was now the time? No—clearly it wasn't. Not with him being all drunk. But there was something bubbling up inside of her. Something with the name Thomas Hurley written all over it. And it couldn't be held down. "Actually...let me rephrase. It didn't quite go as I would have anticipated. Jane said something...told me something I didn't understand. Something about you."

A look of caution covered Benji's face, but he recovered quickly. "Hope she didn't give me some sort of bum rap...that dame." This time his laughter seemed real.

Or did it?

"I'm not sure if it is a bum rap or not. You'll have to tell *me*. Because I failed to understand what she was saying. I didn't know what she was talking about. I was confused, to be honest."

All semblance of congeniality left Benji's face. "Okay...so spill the beans," he said. Something had flipped, every part of his essence conveying discomfort with the situation.

Ella's breath caught in her throat. She wasn't dealing with a sober, rational person. Clearly, he was on a bender. And dealing with Benjamin Marek on a good day was sometimes tricky at best. "Okay then." She looked right at him. "Jane said…what she said was—" Pausing, a wave of emotion flooded over psyche. This was going to be harder than she thought. Looking up to the sky, she swallowed down a waft of air. Then refocused her gaze. "—that you were responsible for the death of my brother, Thomas." There—she'd spit it out.

Benji looked stricken.

Like he was having a hard time catching his breath. The anguish that covered his countenance left Ella all that much more confused. Seconds later, his face turned to stone. Facing away from Ella, he perused the side of the building, staring at seemingly nothing, before turning back. "Okay…so she told you. So now you know."

"What? No—" Ella began shaking her head.

"Oh, but yes," Benji interrupted. "You want to know everything about me…the whole truth? My name is Benjamin Joseph Marek, and I am your worst enemy." The look of fire was in his eyes. A wild person on the loose. "I not only didn't save that boy who was dying from the bombing on the Hawaiian Islands, December seventh, I didn't save your brother, Thomas Hurley, that day all those years ago either. In fact, I killed him."

This time Ella was stunned into silence. She didn't know what to say—couldn't begin to process what she was hearing, being told to her by a drunken man in front of Savoy Café. A person that she thought she knew well—*all too well*. Surely, the whole thing—the entirety of the tale reaching her ears—was surreal. She'd fallen into a dreamlike stupor, and at any moment it would be time to wake up.

Benji fed into the look of shock that was covering her face, talking wilder, slurring his words to get the story out at a quicker rate. He'd told her a portion of the story—now he might as well spit the whole thing out and fast. "Me…some of my buddies…all chasing some kids down by the parked freighter, east of the Locks. You know the one. Young boys…group of them. Younger than us. We were bigger…badder. It was getting dark, and we were scaring them. They were scattering, running like crazy to get away. They were so damn scared…and we knew it. Enjoyed it." Nostrils flaring, Benji paused to swallow, words getting ahead of his lung capacity. Ella stared on, mouth agape. "We weren't going to hurt them if we caught them…exactly. But it was so much fun watching the fear in their eyes…the desperate movements of their bodies…the way they couldn't get away fast enough. But after a while, the rest of my buddies got sick of it, they wanted to move on, find something else to do…enough already, it was getting boring. Not me though…there was one boy I'd been chasing, and I could hear him still on the loose. He hadn't gotten away. So, I kept going…finding ways to sneak up on him, making him run the other way. He kept getting stuck, running into dead ends. It was getting darker and darker outside. Harder to see in all the crevices, nooks and crannies down on the docks. Hard to see around the freighter. I could hear him panting, running, stopping. He was getting tired out. But I didn't let up. *I never let up.* Then, finally, when I lost sight of him, lost sound of him, I heard a loud noise, a yelp, and a splash in the water. A moment of panic set in. It was a long way down from the docks to the waves that night. I began to go in search of the sound. Tried to find the kid…kept calling out. But there was never any answer. Eventually it got late…and whatever had happened, by then I knew it was *too* late. And so, it was. The next day, I read the paper. Heard the news that there was drowning around town… Thomas Hurley had drowned down by the Locks. Time of death, just after dusk. I was responsible for his dying"

It took several moments before Ella could open her lips to speak. The anguish of the story settled over her soul, words coming from Benji's mouth, transporting her back to a place and time that it was so difficult to revisit—this time taking old thoughts and emotions to a new twisted level in her brain.

"How could it be—" she began to say. But the sound of her voice was drowned out the second it hit the air.

"What are you fellas looking at?" Benji called into a group of soldiers as they walked by, turning his attention away from where he and Ella had been talking. "Have you never seen an ace spilling his guts to a dame? Well, you best keep on…or I'm going give you a knuckle sandwich. This is none of your damn business."

The soldiers did not look impressed. "Looks like a pain in the ass to me," one of them spoke out of the corner of his mouth, nudging a fellow-private with an elbow for effect. But in a blink of an eye, something in the air had changed, all four of them suddenly standing a little taller, chests puffed, shoulders thrust backward.

"Listen here, fat head, take that back or you're going to be sorry." Another one of them spoke louder, taking a step toward Benji.

It was fuel to the fire. "Look who just called me fat head. Come closer and say that." Benji challenged in a drunken slur.

In horror, Ella watched as everything imploded around her, all hell breaking loose. In a blink of an eye, the soldiers and Benji left their positions on the sidewalk, lunging instead for one another. It was an all-out brawl, civilians and soldiers coming from out of the wood-work, joining in on the fight. An orb of bodies quickly evolved, with punches, pushes, shoving, and shouting everywhere. Ella couldn't tell what was what—who was who.

It left her head whirling.

What had just happened?

Not only with the abrupt fight, but with the story of her brother's death as well.

It seemed she wasn't to find out. Before long, a squadron of police officers showed up to break up the fracas, dragging Benji away for drunken disorderly conduct. Ella, left behind in a tailspin, walked in circles around town, before heading home, her mind a mess, trying to sort through all she had just been handed.

CHAPTER 37

Easterday Hill seemed steeper than ever as Ella climbed to the top on the way to the Alby house. Unable to make sense of her mind, she hadn't stayed at home long after witnessing the drunken brawl involving Benji. Besides, Siobhan needed her. Sure, Ella had just been handed a lot of information—*but what had she been handed exactly though?* She wasn't at all sure. What she *was* sure of—Siobhan had to be hurting. Alone and pregnant, she had just lost the love of her life. Ella needed to go check on her.

Having last left Siobhan at the Greek Orthodox Church to pray and be alone with her thoughts, Ella wasn't entirely sure that company would be welcomed. Still, she needed to check in. She would never be able to forgive herself if her friend was sitting at home in a miserable heap, wishing she had someone to hold her, someone to listen, someone to sit in silence while she cried or stared into space. Hesitantly, Ella knocked at the Alby door.

Mrs. Alby answered and waved her in. From the look on her face, Ella wasn't able to decipher how much she knew. Next, she knocked on Siobhan's bedroom door. Hearing nothing more than a grunt, she entered and found her friend sitting on the floor, back wedged against the bed. Quietly gazing—at nothing in particular. Or at *everything* in particular—though known only to her own mind. Ella walked over and sat down, parallel in position. "How are you doing," she whispered.

Siobhan shrugged. "Copasetic."

Looking into Siobhan's face, Ella raised her eyebrows.

"Okay…I lie. Not the best…but hanging in there I guess."

Ella draped an arm around her shoulder. "I came to check on you."

Siobhan's eyes began to fill with mist. "You're on the beam, El… but I'll be okay…really. You don't have to—"

"But I want to though," Ella interrupted. "If not for you…for me then." *And maybe in all actuality it was for herself, indeed. Truth was, there was no way she wanted be alone with her mind right then.* "Okay if I stick around?"

That night, Ella didn't sleep a wink. She wasn't sure if Siobhan did either. But each time she peered over at Siobhan's side of the bed, the rise and fall of the chest seemed regular, giving the appearance of slumber.

Not for Ella though. Not in the least! No even rising and falling of the chest where her body laid, head resting on the pillow. Only tossing and turning, with a runaway heartbeat. Her mind was a torrent of questions and replays from the past. Of one night in particular. One particularly miserable night that she didn't like to think about. But was now being forced to. And unbelievably—that despairing evening was now involving Benjamin Marek, somewhere in the mix too.

But how?

As the hours on the clock ticked off, the answer to that question became very clear in her mind.

It simply didn't.

Couldn't!

There was no way it included him in the least.

Upon the rising of the sun, Ella made a decision. She needed to go talk to Benji. Leaving a note with a still sleeping Siobhan, she dressed in the clothes discarded on the floor from the day before, took a big gulp of water from a glass on the dresser, ran a brush through her hair and left the Alby house, knowing she looked a mess.

Crossing Easterday to the wealthier side of the neighborhood, she made her way to the Marek house, hoping like everything that Benji had been let out of jail by then—if that was even where he had ended up after the run-in with the police. And that also enough time had gone by, rendering him sober in order to conduct a real conversation. Gather needed answers and clear the air.

Heart thudding in her chest, Ella knocked on the Marek door. But after several increasingly loud raps, no one answered. Had everyone left for the day? Did his mom even work? True, Mrs. Marek had been there last visit. But maybe with the increased need for workers due to the war, she was putting in her time on a line somewhere. It was possible that his dad had already left for the shop. But what about Benji? Had he already left to go to work at the excavating business too? *Or it was that he was still in the clinker?*

The knocks continued coming from Ella's balled-up fist, turning into several in a row.

Just when she was about to leave, the sound of a jiggling knob reached her ears. Holding her breath, Ella watched in slow motion as the door creeped open. Then inwardly gasped for air as she came face to face with one, Benjamin Joseph Marek—BJ from the old days—Benji from the hospital, soldier extraordinaire. He looked equally surprised to see her as she him. And in similar disarray.

"Ella," he said, furrowing his brow in confusion. A thought hit her then. Maybe he didn't remember their conversation from the day before in the least. Maybe he'd been too drunk.

"I just came by to—" she motioned to the door. Her hand was shaking. "Can you come out…or I in?"

His answer was slow in coming. "You can—"

"I mean—"

They both started talking at once. Then stopped abruptly. *Who would go first?* Ella bit her lip.

"You can come in," Benji clarified. "No one else is home." He looked sheepish, reserved.

"Okay…alright." Ella stepped inside. She glanced around nervously. "So, you made it home alright? Yesterday…Savoy Café." *Did he even remember?*

Did he remember his confession about Thomas?

Benji lifted a hand to his face where Ella noticed bruising for the first time. "Yeah, I made it home," he sighed, gazed averted. He was basically staring at the floor.

So, he did remember. There were tell-tale signs to prove it. But *did* he remember? About Thomas. Ella began shaking her head. She couldn't stand another second of dancing around the subject. "I had to come find you…tell you that you are not responsible for Thomas' death, you know."

What? Benji's eyes shot in Ella's direction.

Ella kept shaking her head. "I don't know or care what you think...I heard your version of the story yesterday...but there's no way—"

"I don't understand." Benji's mouth seemed dry. The look on his face incredulous. He could hardly get the words out. "But I was...he did die that night...right?"

Ella's breaths were coming fast. She could feel the tears lurking, all the emotions welling up, ready to burst. *Oh, Thomas, Thomas.* She hugged trembling arms to her chest.

This was so hard to talk about. So hard to utter the truth aloud after all these years. "Yes," she nodded. "He died that night...but not because of something you did. Because of something I did."

Benji looked stunned. Mouth falling open, he stared in disbelief. "I don't understand... but I told you...at the Savoy Café...I remember telling you how I chased that kid—"

"I know that's what you thought happened. But the thing is, I was there." She began wiping at her wet cheeks. "Just listen...oh God, this is hard." For a moment or two Ella looked down, pressing hands against her thighs. Then swallowing hard, faced toward Benji again. "That night...the evening that Thomas died, he was going fishing with my dad. He *did* go fishing with my dad. I was supposed to go too. My dad is a drinker. Even back then he could drink one too many. My mom knew this. She had to work and had asked me to go with them fishing. She didn't have to say what for. I knew she wanted me to be an extra set of eyes...for safety's sake. Because my dad wouldn't be a reliable adult." Once again, Ella bowed her head.

Benji was frozen in place.

"But I didn't...didn't want to go. I was sick of being my brother's keeper. Of being my father's keeper. So, I stubbornly refused. They went anyway...down to the St. Mary's, just east of the Locks. A couple of blocks from where you were that night, chasing whatever kid that was. But it wasn't Thomas. I know that for sure." Ella paused to catch her breath. "My mom didn't know. She was still at work while it all happened. Sometime while they were gone, I was jarred from my own selfishness by the sound of ships saluting one another as they passed through the channel. I'll never forget that sound. *Ever*. Out of nowhere, a bad feeling came over me, a premonition, and I took off to their fishing spot. When I got there…it was too late. Dad was frantic, pulling a drown Thomas onto the bank. In his excitement over spotting a large fish, he had tripped and fallen in. My dad didn't get to him in time. I didn't either. I've…I've lived with the guilt of that all of these years. I hate myself for not being there for Thomas. I could have saved him, watched him more closely when Melvin Hurley hadn't been. So, you see, Benji…it wasn't your fault at all…couldn't have been. It was my fault…and my dad's. I was the one who killed my little brother. I was selfish…so, so selfish—"

The tears were coming at full speed by then. Ella could no longer speak. Her shoulders were shaking as sobs overtook her body. She didn't see Benji moving in her direction, barely felt the strength of his arms as they encircled her withering form. Drawing her to his chest, he held her tightly against his body. So close, she couldn't move. There she cried and cried into his shoulder.

And he hers.

Many minutes later they eased apart. Ella looked a little shocked as the realization of their proximity set in. It was as if she had entered another time and place. Another dimension entirely. A special place set aside for those who needed to shed tears. Now she was back, and the realization of who held her was becoming evident. In an instant, she felt sheepish. Overcome. She attempted to take a step backward. But Benji wouldn't let her go. With one arm he reached for some tissue on the hallway bureau and handed it over, saving some for himself. "Come with me," he said, leading her to the davenport in the adjacent room.

For what seemed like a long time, they sat there quietly, side by side, legs pressed together, Benji rubbing Ella's arm in a soothing fashion. His own draped across her shoulder. "I don't…I don't know what to say," he finally offered. "I can hardly…my mind can hardly conceive this story. I am so sorry. Sorry for you. Sorry that you lost Thomas this way. Sorry for your hurt." He paused, voice becoming soft. "Sorry for the way I've treated you over the years."

Ella gave a barely-there nod. She felt like an exhausted zombie.

"I still can't believe…it seems nearly impossible. All of these years, I truly believed I was responsible for your brother's death. I hated myself for what I did to your family. For what I did to you. But you…you just said you hate yourself too. Don't."

What? Ella twisted around to peer up at Benji, eyes puffy and red. Surprising to her, was the idea that Benji's looked the same.

"You can't hate yourself, El. You have to stop. From what you've told me, it's possible that he could have fallen in before your very eyes and you wouldn't have been able to save him anyway. Possible that your father wouldn't have been able to prevent it either…stone cold sober. You have to forgive yourself. Thomas would want that for you. I saw the letters you've been writing to him throughout the years last time I was at your house. It was at that point I felt the depth of your connection… and it was at that point I felt the true depths of the pain I had caused having severed that connection. I had to get out of your life that night… for good. But you…you shouldn't feel that pain from guilt. Someone you were that connected to wouldn't want that for you."

Ella felt a little zing of something traveling through her chest. *Of course.* A select part of her mind knew that is why Benji had changed his disposition, leaving prematurely the night of their last date. And yet she hadn't known why.

"Though," Benji started up again. "I admit…I haven't been able to forgive myself all of these years either." His head dropped. "I have so much to apologize to you for…for the way I've treated you all of these years. For the homecoming incident in the gymnasium…there aren't enough words—"

His shoulders dropped, causing the brow of his forehead to fall even lower. A shudder appeared to rip through his body.

At once, a decade's-plus of elongating stripes began to pass before Ella's eyes, streaming through her mind. Lids falling tightly shut, she willed them away. Yet there they were—floating, zipping, whooshing. It was time for a confrontation. For a few minutes, they sat together in silence, Ella untangling long bands of pain, Benji untangling remorse. Finally, Benji looked up.

"I've been falling in love with you," he said. "Believe it or not...I *have* been...throughout all of these years."

Ella sucked in a breath. He had her full attention. Arbitrarily, the stripes began to fade.

Benji ran fingers through his hair in an uncertain manner. "I've been so tied to you since elementary school...but not in the way I should have been. But underneath it all...through the façade of irritation, based on my guilt for what I thought I did to your brother, I knew I was being pulled toward you as well. Couldn't get you out of my sight...out of my mind. I hated myself for that...hated that I didn't deserve you. So, I treated you like I *didn't* deserve you...made sure you *wouldn't* want me. And then...meeting up with you at the hospital after my injuries at Pearl Harbor, when I didn't know who you were...the fall was pure, without anything to distort my feelings." Benji smiled for a moment, half chuckled. "Okay...I'll admit, maybe my falling for your may *not* have been entirely pure...It's possible there was an element of caregiver complex...You were a hell of a nurse. And one hot cookie. But even so—"

Ella couldn't help herself. She began to laugh. It felt good—a little moment of comic relief. It was definitely needed with the conversation they were having.

"But," Benji continued, growing serious, his countenance falling again. "When I realized who you were...I hated myself more than ever. It was part of the battle I was going through. The trauma I was experiencing from not being able to help that boy on the Hawaiian Islands was directly tied to not being able to help your brother when I was a kid. I had caused your brother's death and I felt like I had caused the boy's death on Oahu too. Then there was you...saving my life... and I was falling in love with you...and I didn't deserve you. Not in the least."

Blue eyes glazing over with moisture, he looked right at Ella. "Can you ever forgive me?" The question was spoken with such heart-felt sincerity, Ell never thought it possible coming from the likes of BJ Marek. Tears were streaming down her cheeks by then. In a blink of an eye, her mind took a trip through the convoluted years of the past they shared. Who could have known? How was *any* of this possible? Without giving credence to another thought, Ella began shaking her head. Because—*yes.* She knew deep down, the answer to his question was—*yes, yes it was possible!*

Benji reached for her then. Pulling Ella fiercely toward his chest, he pressed his lips hard against hers, until they both couldn't breathe. Falling together afterward, their bodies crushed against one another. Tightly, they clung. As if never wanting to let go.

"Do you think," he whispered into her hair, "that we could start again…fresh? I know there has been a lot of hurt and pain over the years…but do you think…that through it all we could try again?"

CHAPTER 38

Benji held Ella's hand as they knelt on the grass. After placing a bouquet of wildflowers in a vase, they sat staring at a granite headstone that read—*Thomas Mason Hurley 1922-1929*. They'd been there more than once in the past few weeks, visiting history, doing their best to embrace the future—*their future together, moving forward*. It was going to take some work. Some things weren't so easily erased. But they were nothing if not determined. And it had been settled—they loved each other so much. Having asked for vindication from their past transgressions with each other—*or more like mostly Benji with her*—they felt that it was important to do the same. Ask for forgiveness from Thomas too. After all, he was the one, after a fashion, responsible for bringing them together.

Wiping away a tear with her free hand, Ella squeezed Benji's with the other. So much had happened for them recently. And though with every passing day she was feeling a little freer and happier, she would always miss her little brother.

Beloved Thomas.

A smile came to her face, momentarily wiping away the nostalgia, as she thought of what she'd overheard recently sitting in the Brownlee Ross downtown. It was the mention of BJ Marek's name that had caught her attention. There was a group of young adults sitting together that she recognized from back in school, a couple years her junior. *"That bully,"* she heard one of them say. *"I'll never forget the time he and his pals were chasing me, Billy, and Pete, down by docks. Billy and Pete finally got away, but not me. I was about to go belly up, when at the last second, I decide to jump...my duds on and all. I don't know what he thought. Obviously, he heard the splash. It was getting dark. He spent some time looking for me, but eventually gave up. The reason he couldn't find me though...was because I was holding on to the ladder, tucked underneath the dock. I'd outsmarted the knucklehead."* He pointed to himself, face wide with a grin. *"You're looking at the person who outsmarted BJ Marek,"* he bragged. At that the whole tabled laughed.

It had been the story Benji had told her about the day Thomas had drown. A chill covered Ella's skin as the tale unfolded from the mouth of the true victim concerning the BJ Marek Group antics down on the docks. It felt like a confirmation. Their stories were lining up and coming together. Also though, it was a fresh reminder of the bully Benji had been. *Hopefully he had indeed changed.* All she knew—at that point, her heart was telling her to give him a chance.

Things were changing and moving forward for others close to Ella as well. Siobhan was becoming more emotionally sound with each passing day. Her friend was stronger than she'd given her credit for. It was hard situation, finding out she was expecting a baby and losing the soldier on the battlefield who was the father of her child in such a short timeframe. But Siobhan was going to be okay. And Ella would be right there by her side to help her through each step of the way.

Change was happening at the Hurley house too. After a period of hibernation, tail tucked between his legs, Melvin had asked for his position back at the electricity company on Ashmun. And they had welcomed his return, happy to see him sober after all of these years. In-turn, Grace's spirits were being lifted, seeing her husband finally stepping up to the plate. In domino effect, Chance, paying close attention to his mom's new disposition, began performing antics to the nth degree on the home front trying to draw out more smiles in the process.

Darling Chance.

It seemed more and more he was succeeding.

Around town, efforts for the war continued that summer.

Across the rest of the world, the battles raged on:

In the European theater, the Allies attacked a German-occupied Port of Dieppe in Northern France. A testimony of the UK's committal to re-opening the Western Front.

In the Mediterranean, a British operation—Relief of Malta—carried supplies to the base that implemented attacks on the Axis convoys to Libya. A vital resource, being the fuel carried by the *SS Ohio*, an American tanker manned by British crew.

Meanwhile, the First Battle of El Alamein was taking place in North Africa. The British Army, retreating east into Egypt, took a defensive position where the Axis Forces were unable to breakthrough—ending in an impasse.

In the Pacific Theater's Solomon Islands, the Allied Forces moved on the offensive. After the victory from the Battle of Midway earlier in the summer, they sought to fight the Japanese in the Battle of Guadalcanal, protecting communication to Australia, while apprehending Japan's building of an airfield.

On the Eastern Front, the Battle of Stalingrad began. Looking for a great propaganda victory by hoping to seize control of the city named after the famed Russian leader, Joseph Stalin, the Germans marched in. But Russian forces put up a fight, stopping the assault. Shaping the confrontation into one of the fiercest battles of the war, it marked the pivotal moment for the Allies.

Hitler's most devastating defeat.

The End.